SLIGHTLY SINFUL

"Smart, playful, and deliciously satisfying . . . Balogh once again delivers a clean, sprightly tale rich in both plot and character. . . . With its irrepressible characters and deft plotting, this polished romance is an ideal summer read."
—*Publishers Weekly* (starred review)

SLIGHTLY TEMPTED

"Once again, Balogh has penned an entrancing, unconventional yarn that should expand her following."—*Publishers Weekly*

"Balogh is a gifted writer. . . . *Slightly Tempted* invites reflection, a fine quality in romance, and Morgan and Gervase are memorable characters."
—*Contra Costa Times*

SLIGHTLY SCANDALOUS

"With its impeccable plotting and memorable characters. Balogh's book raises the bar for Regency romances."—*Publishers Weekly* (starred review)

A SUMMER TO REMEMBER

Simply Magic

Mary Balogh

A DELL BOOK

SIMPLY MAGIC
A Dell Book

PUBLISHING HISTORY
Delacorte Press hardcover edition published April 2007
Dell mass market edition / March 2008

Published by
Bantam Dell
A Division of Random House, Inc.
New York, New York

This is a work of fiction. Names, characters, places, and incidents
either are the product of the author's imagination or are used
fictitiously. Any resemblance to actual persons, living or dead,
events, or locales is entirely coincidental.

Library of Congress Catalog Card Number: 2006048480

ISBN: 978-0-440-24198-0

Printed in the United States of America
Published simultaneously in Canada

www.bantamdell.com

OPM 10 9 8 7 6 5 4 3 2 1

Simply Magic

"Hmm." Peter Edgeworth, Viscount Whitleaf, frowned at the letter he had been reading as he folded it and set it down beside his breakfast plate.

John Raycroft, seated at the opposite end of the table, lowered the morning paper from in front of his face and raised his eyebrows.

"Bad news?"

Peter sighed audibly.

"I have been really looking forward to going home," he said, "despite the fact that I have enjoyed the last couple of weeks here with you and your family and hate to drag myself away when the whole neighborhood has been so hospitable. I have been actually eager to go at last, dash it all. But I made the mistake of letting my mother know my intention, and she has planned a grand welcome home. She has invited a houseful of guests to stay for a few weeks, including a Miss Rose Larchwell, whoever the devil she may be. I have never heard of her. Have you? I tell you, Raycroft, this is no laughing matter."

But his protest came too late. John Raycroft was

already chuckling as he set down the paper and gave his full attention to his friend. They had the room to themselves, the rest of the family having breakfasted earlier while the two of them were still out riding.

"Clearly your mother is eager to marry you off," John said. "It is hardly surprising, Whitleaf, when you are her only son and in the wrong half of your twenties."

"I am only twenty-six," Peter protested, frowning again.

"And five years older than you were the last time your mother tried something similar—and failed," Raycroft reminded him, still grinning. "Doubtless she thinks it is high time she tried again. But you can always say no—as you did last time."

"Hmm," Peter said again, not sharing his friend's amusement. That was an episode in his life that had been far from funny. He had outraged the *ton,* which collectively believed that he had come far too close to betrothing himself to Bertha Grantham to withdraw honorably, even though no formal announcement had yet been made. And he had delighted the younger male members of the beau monde, who had thought him one devil of a fine fellow for thumbing his nose at the polite world by crying off from a leg shackle at the last possible moment.

Dash it, it had not been funny at all. He had been at the tender age of twenty-one, innocent as a babe in arms, and cheerfully proceeding along the path through life his family and guardians had mapped out for him. Good God, he had even fallen dutifully in love with Bertha because it was expected of him. He had not even realized he possessed such a thing as a backbone until shock had caused him to flex it and put an end to that almost-engagement in a damnably gauche and public manner. It had been a very raw and painful backbone for a long time after that, though he had flexed it again only an hour or so later by sending his uncles—and former guardians—packing with the declaration that since he had reached his majority he did not need them any longer, thank you very much. Though he was not at all sure he had thanked them.

"The thing is," he said, "that the girl's hopes have possibly been raised, or her mama's anyway—not to mention her father's and her sisters' and brothers' and grandparents' and cousins'. Lord!"

"Perhaps," John Raycroft said, "you will *like* her, Whitleaf. Perhaps she will live up to her name."

Peter grimaced. "I probably will," he agreed. "I like women in general. But that is not the point, is it? I don't intend marrying her—or anyone else not of my own choosing—even if she is as lovely as a thousand roses combined. And so I will be in the impossible situation of having to be courteous and amiable to her without giving the impression that I am courting her. And yet everyone else at this infernal house party will know very well why she has been invited—my mother will see to that. I tell you, Raycroft, you can wipe that grin off your face anytime you like."

John Raycroft laughed again as he tossed his napkin on top of the newspaper.

"My deepest commiserations, old chap," he said. "It is a nasty affliction to be rich and titled and eligible—and to have been known since the tender age of

twenty-one as a breaker of hearts. That fact only adds
to your attractions, of course, at least as far as the gentler sex is concerned. But you are going to have to
marry sooner or later. It is one of the obligations of
your rank. Why not sooner?"

"But why not later?" Peter said hastily, picking up
his knife and fork and tucking into what remained of
his eggs and ham. "I am not like you, Raycroft. I cannot look upon a woman across a crowded ballroom
one evening, recognize her as the one and only love of
my life, court her devotedly to the exclusion of all others for a whole year, and then be content to betroth
myself to her and wait for another year while she gal-
livants off to the ends of Europe."

"To Vienna to be precise," his friend said. "With
her parents, who planned the treat for her aeons ago.
And not for a full year, Whitleaf. They will be back
next spring. We will be married before the summer is
out. And one of these days you will know why I would
wait three times as long if I had to. Your problem is
that you are undiscriminating. You only have to look
at a woman to fall in love with her. You fall in love
with everyone—and therefore with no one."

"There is safety in numbers." Peter grinned reluctantly. "But I say, Raycroft—I do not exactly fall in
love with women, you know. I just *like* them."

He did too—perhaps fortunately. It was only *love*
or any other deep commitment that he had cried off.
But his liking for women—and for all people, come to
that—had saved him from moving from babe in arms
to cynic in the course of one ghastly day.

His friend shook his head.

"What are you going to do, then?" he asked, nodding in the direction of the letter. "Go home and land slap in the middle of your mother's matchmaking party or stay here at Hareford House? Why not change your mind about leaving tomorrow and stay for the full month after all? Write and tell your mama that I was devilish disappointed when I heard you were planning to cut your visit short. Tell her my mother was brokenhearted. Tell her you feel obliged to stay for the village assembly the week after next. None of those facts would be an outright lie. In fact, the neighborhood will probably go into deep mourning if you do not make an appearance at the assembly. It might be canceled for lack of interest. It is a good thing I am betrothed to Alice and secure in her affections. Being with you is enough to plunge any unattached fellow into mortal gloom. No other male exists for the ladies when you are within a ten-mile radius."

Peter laughed—though he was still not really feeling amused.

The thing was that after five years of floundering around with only his own very limited wisdom to guide him, leading meanwhile the empty, aimless existence of a typical young gentleman about town, he had finally made a few firm decisions about his future.

It was time to go home to Sidley Park. For five years he had made only brief visits there before returning to his life in London or Brighton or at one of the spas.

It was time to take charge of his life and his estate and the responsibilities that went with his rank.

It was time, in other words, to grow up and be the

man he had been educated to be—and actually the man he had always dreamed of being, even if the dream had been interrupted for rather too long. He had grown up loving Sidley and the knowledge that it was his and had been since the death of his father when he was three.

Aimless pleasure was not really for him, he had decided during the Season in London this year. Neither were wild oats, though he had sown a few. He had wasted five years of his life. Though they had not been wholly wasted, he supposed. He *had* learned to stand on his own feet even if he was still not as firm on them as he hoped to be. And he had learned to filter through everything he had been taught by a loving mother and five sisters, and by a host of strict guardians, to decide what was important and what was to be permanently rejected.

They had let him down badly five years ago, those guardians—not to mention his mother. But basically, he had come to realize, they had given him a sound upbringing. It was time to stop feeling sorry for himself and punishing himself as well as them—it was time to become the person he wanted to be. No one else could do that but him after all.

It had felt enormously satisfying to put himself finally in charge of his own life.

Of course, he *had* promised to spend a month at Hareford House with Raycroft after the Season was over, and he would honor that promise, he had decided, and go home afterward. But the closeness of the Raycroft family, the warmth of their dealings with one another and with their friends and neighbors, had only strengthened his resolve and his yearning finally to be master of his own home. And so he had decided to cut short his visit and go home to Sidley Park after only two weeks. It was already late August and the harvest would be ready soon. He longed to be home for it this year and to *stay* home.

Now his mother's letter had put a dent in his dreams. It appalled him that she appeared to have been so little affected by the events of five years ago. Or perhaps she was merely trying to make amends in the only way she knew how. It was *her* dream to see him settled in life with a wife and a few children in the nursery.

They were interrupted before he could reply to Raycroft's invitation by the arrival in the breakfast parlor of Miss Rosamond Raycroft, John's young sister, who was looking rosy-cheeked and bright-eyed and remarkably pretty after an hour spent out in the garden gathering flowers with her mama. Peter looked at her with affectionate appreciation as she kissed her brother's cheek and then turned a deliberately pouting face toward him. He stood to draw back a chair for her.

"I am quite out of charity with *you*," she said as she took the seat. "You might have agreed to stay a little longer."

"You break my heart," Peter said, resuming his own place. "But I am not at all out of charity with *you*. I have something to beg of you, in fact, since you are dazzling my eyes with your beauty and would have robbed me of appetite if I had not already eaten. I humbly beg you, Miss Raycroft, to reserve the opening set at the coming assembly for me."

The mock pout disappeared, to be replaced with a

look of youthful eagerness. "You are staying after all?" she asked him. "For the *assembly*?"

"How can I resist?" He set his right hand over his heart and regarded her soulfully. "You ought not to have gone out into the sunshine and fresh air this morning and improved upon your already perfect complexion. You ought to have appeared here pale and wan and dressed in your oldest rags. Ah, but even then I fear I would have found the sight of you irresistible."

She laughed.

"Oh, you *are* staying," she said. "And I *am* dressed in my oldest rags, silly. You are *staying*. Oh, I knew you were just teasing when you insisted that you must leave tomorrow. I shall dance with you—of course I shall. You would not know how very few young gentlemen ever attend the assemblies, Lord Whitleaf. And even many of the ones who *do* attend play cards all evening or merely stand about watching as if it would kill them to dance."

"It probably would, Ros," her brother said. "It is a strenuous thing, dancing."

"The Calverts will positively *expire* of envy when they know that I have already been engaged for the opening set, and by no less a person than *Viscount Whitleaf*," Miss Raycroft continued, clapping her hands together. "I shall tell them this morning. I promised to go over there so that we can all go out walking together. You really ought to ask Gertrude for the opening set, John. You know Mama and Mrs. Calvert will expect it even if you *are* betrothed to Alice Hickmore. And Gertrude will be relieved. If she has promised to dance it with you, she will not be able to dance it with Mr. Finn, who was born with two left feet, both of them overlarge, the poor gentleman."

Peter grinned.

"I'll come with you and ask her now," John said cheerfully. "Finn is a farmer and a dashed good one too, Ros. And he could shoot a wren between the eyes at a hundred paces. One cannot expect him to be an accomplished dancer too."

"Shoot a *wren*?" Miss Raycroft paused with her hand stretched toward the toast rack and looked stricken. "What a horrid idea. I certainly hope he does not ask *me* to dance."

"It was merely a figurative way of speaking," her brother told her. "What would be the use of shooting wrens? Nobody would eat them anyway."

"Nobody would shoot a wren for any reason at all," Peter assured the girl as he got to his feet. "They are gentle, beautiful birds. I shall accompany you on the walk too, if I may, Miss Raycroft. The weather and the countryside alone would tempt me, but even if it were raining and cold and blowing a gale, the company would be quite irresistible."

She acknowledged the blatant flattery with a bright smile and eyes that still twinkled. She was seventeen years old, not yet officially "out," and she knew as well as anyone that he was not seriously smitten with her charms—or with anyone else's of her acquaintance for that matter. He would not have dared flatter and flirt with her if there were any likelihood that she might misunderstand—her brother was his closest friend and he was staying in their parents' home.

"I shall go up and change my clothes and wash my hands and face," she said, getting to her feet again, the toast forgotten. "I shall be ready in fifteen minutes."

"Make it ten, Ros," her brother said with a sigh. "You look perfectly decent to me as you are."

Peter, meeting her pained glance, winked at her.

"Go and improve further upon perfection if it is possible," he said. "We will wait for you even if you take twenty minutes."

It seemed, he thought ruefully, that his decision had been made. He was not going home after all. Not yet, anyway.

An hour later Viscount Whitleaf was reflecting upon the singular handicap of possessing only two arms when three or four would have been far more convenient. He had Miss Raycroft on his right arm and the eldest Miss Calvert on his left, while Miss Jane Calvert and Miss Mary Calvert flittered and twittered about them like dainty, colorful birds, chattering and laughing, and John Raycroft walked nearby, swinging his arms and lifting his face to the sun and the sky when he was not beaming genially about him at the late summer countryside and remarking that the harvest was sure to be an excellent one this year.

Peter certainly hoped it would be good on his own farms at Sidley Park too. Having once thought about it, he ached to be there for the harvest, to be able to tramp the fields in old breeches and top boots, to be with his laborers, to shed his coat and roll up his shirt-sleeves and work alongside them, to feel the sweat of honest labor along his back. To do all those things, in fact, that he had not been allowed to do as a boy and had done only one glorious year when he was twenty and looking forward with such eagerness to reaching his majority.

Dash it all, *why* had he let his mother know that he intended coming this year? Why had he not simply turned up there unannounced?

He sighed, but almost instantly recovered his spirits when he brought his attention back to the present.

Miss Calvert was a handsome young lady even if she did not have the enticing dimples of her younger sister, Miss Jane Calvert, or the very blue eyes of her youngest sister, Miss Mary Calvert. All three sisters were, in fact, renowned in the neighborhood for their beauty. They would turn heads in a place like London too—and would probably make decent matches even without dowries.

"You simply *must* consider staying for two more weeks, Lord Whitleaf," Miss Mary Calvert urged, turning to look at him and taking little backward running steps in order to keep ahead of him and the two ladies on his arms. "There is to be a dance at the assembly rooms—did you know?—and we *so* much want you to be there."

The blue ribbons under her chin and those beneath her bosom—they exactly matched the color of her eyes—fluttered to her movements, and her fair curls bobbed beneath the brim of her bonnet. Trim ankles were visible beneath the swaying hem of her cotton dress. She looked very pretty indeed.

"Must I?" he said with an exaggerated sigh. He

smiled at each of the ladies in turn and thought how very pleasant a morning this was and how fortunate a fellow he was to have such company with which to share it—even if he would have preferred to be getting ready to go home tomorrow. "The temptation is well nigh irresistible, I must say."

But Miss Raycroft was not to be deprived of making the grand announcement herself.

"Viscount Whitleaf decided this very morning that he will stay," she cried. "And he has reserved the first set of dances with me."

"No coercion was necessary, you see," Peter assured them all as the Misses Jane and Mary Calvert clapped their hands and the eldest Miss Calvert's hand tightened about his arm. All three of them beamed happily at him. "How could I possibly *not* stay when there are four such lovely ladies with whom it will be my pleasure to dance—*if*, that is, they can be persuaded to dance with me?"

But though he was flirting—and they all knew it very well—he spoke the truth too. He had seen a great deal of Raycroft's neighbors during the past two weeks, and he genuinely liked them all, especially the young ladies.

A chorus of amused laughter greeted his final words.

"Perhaps Miss Calvert will honor me by reserving the second set for me," he said, "and Miss Jane Calvert the third and Miss Mary Calvert the fourth. If, that is, I am not too late and every set has not already been spoken for by all the gentlemen hereabouts. It would not surprise me in the least if that were the case."

Another burst of merriment greeted his words and then an assurance from all three sisters that the relevant sets would indeed be reserved and not forgotten.

"As if *that* would be possible," Miss Mary Calvert added ingenuously.

"You had better dance the opening set with me, Gertrude," John Raycroft said cheerfully and without any tactful gallantry whatsoever. "I understand that the alternative is Finn, and Ros assures me that that would be a fate akin to death."

The ladies all laughed again.

"That is very obliging of you, John," Miss Calvert said. "Thank you. Mr. Finn is kind and earnest and I like him exceedingly well. But I must confess that he is no dancer."

It had been obvious to Peter that she did indeed like Finn and that Finn had every intention of working up his nerve within the next year or ten to make her an offer.

"I have it on excellent authority," he said, smiling down at her, "that Finn is a good farmer. And I have had more than one conversation with him myself on the subject of crops and livestock and drainage and such and have found him a most knowledgeable fellow."

She beamed happily back at him.

They proceeded on their way between green fields just beginning to turn to gold and thick hedgerows in which wildflowers were entangled, their collective perfumes lying heavy on the air, all the ladies chattering merrily about the coming assembly.

Before the subject had been exhausted they approached a fork in the lane and John interrupted, pointing with his cane to the branch on the right and explaining to Peter that it would take them back to the village by another route whereas the one on the left led to Barclay Court, to which the Earl and Countess of Edgecombe had still not returned. But even as he spoke, Miss Calvert exclaimed with pleased surprise, and her sisters turned their heads to look and then went skipping off to meet two ladies who were proceeding toward them on foot from the latter direction.

"It is the countess," Miss Calvert explained. "They *are* back home, John. How delightful!"

Peter recognized the Countess of Edgecombe—the earl was an acquaintance of his. He had always admired the lady, who was tall and dark and strikingly beautiful—and who had the most lovely soprano voice he had ever heard. She enjoyed considerable fame in the musical world and traveled all over Europe performing before large audiences.

"So it would seem," John Raycroft said cheerfully. "Famous!"

But Peter's eyes had come to rest upon the countess's companion. She was a young woman, small and shapely. Beneath her green bonnet, which was a shade darker than her dress, he could see that her hair was a bright and interesting shade of auburn. She had a smiling, pretty face that did the hair full justice.

She was, in fact, a notable beauty, and he gazed at her with considerable admiration.

But even as he looked a strange thought verbalized itself with crystal clarity in his mind.

There she is, he thought.

What his mind meant by those three innocent-sounding but somehow ominous words he did not pause to ponder. He was always admiring the pretty young ladies he met. He was always eager to make their acquaintance. He was always preparing to be obliging and charming. He was always preparing to flirt. But his heart was well guarded against any deeper feeling—had been for five years.

It was an unguarded thought he had just had, though.

There she is.

As if she were some long-misplaced part of his soul, for God's sake.

He might have felt a little foolish—not to mention uneasy—at the almost theatrical extravagance of his reaction to the unknown beauty had he been at leisure to ponder it.

But he was not.

There was a flurry of exuberant greetings as the two parties came together at the fork in the lane. Everyone, it seemed, had an acquaintance with everyone else except for Peter and the lady whose name, he soon learned, was Miss Osbourne. He waited for someone to make the introductions. She had sea green eyes, he could see now that he stood within a few feet of her. They formed a marvelous combination with her hair. Her clothes had been well chosen to complement her coloring.

Lord, but she was a beauty. Why had he not met her before? Who the devil was she, apart from Miss Osbourne?

"Lord Whitleaf," the countess said, "may I present my friend, Miss Osbourne? She teaches at Miss Martin's School for Girls in Bath, where I was also a teacher before I married Lucius. This is Viscount Whitleaf, Susanna."

Susanna Osbourne. The name suited her. And her eyes were large and long-lashed and surely her finest feature, though in truth he could not discern the smallest imperfection in any of the others.

She curtsied. Unencumbered by Miss Raycroft and Miss Calvert, who had released their hold on his arms while greeting the ladies from Barclay Court, he made her an elegant bow and fixed upon her his warmest, most charming smile.

"Miss Osbourne," he said. "An already glorious summer day suddenly seems even warmer and brighter."

His female entourage laughed with collective merriment at the outrageous compliment. Miss Osbourne did not. And the warm smile she had been wearing since her eyes alighted upon his party cooled considerably as she looked back at him with . . . with *what* in her eyes? Dislike? Contempt? It was one or the other.

"My lord," she murmured in acknowledgment of the introduction before looking away to smile more warmly again at everyone else.

"But how lovely that we have met some of our friends so soon after leaving Barclay Court," the countess said. "Lucius and I arrived home yesterday, bringing Susanna with us from Bath for a couple of weeks before school resumes for the autumn term, and now we are on our way to pay our respects to some of our neighbors. We were going to Hareford House first, in fact. Mr. Raycroft, we were hoping to persuade you to walk back with us to visit Lucius, who is shut up with his estate manager this morning. Are you staying at Hareford House, Lord Whiteleaf? You must come too if you will. Lucius *will* be pleased."

"Lord Whiteleaf is to stay until after the village assembly the week after next," Miss Mary Calvert announced brightly and triumphantly. "He is to dance with each of us, though I am not even *speaking* to Rosamond since she has the advantage over us of living at Hareford House and is thus to dance the opening set with him while I have to wait for the fourth set since Gertrude and Jane are older than I. Yet Rosamond is two weeks *younger*. It is all most provoking, Lady Edgecombe."

But she laughed as she spoke to indicate that she was not seriously chagrined and took advantage of the moment by skipping up to Peter's side and taking his right arm. She smiled up at him while Miss Jane Calvert appropriated his left arm.

"Will you and Lord Edgecombe and Miss Osbourne be there?" Miss Calvert asked the countess.

"At the assembly? This is the first I have heard of it. But we almost certainly will be," the countess assured her. "It will be delightful. Ah, thank you, Mr. Raycroft."

John was offering one arm to the countess and the other to Miss Osbourne, who took it with a warm smile.

Peter proceeded after them down the lane with the four remaining ladies, who were all more animated than ever by the addition to their numbers and called out frequent comments and questions when they were not twittering among themselves or chattering to him.

So Miss Susanna Osbourne was a schoolteacher, was she? In Bath. It was no wonder he had not met her before.

What a sad waste of youth and dazzling beauty.

She was probably intelligent and bookish too.

Certainly she was not susceptible to male charm and flattery—not to his particular brand, anyway. He ought to have taken more notice of the countess's introduction and avoided flatteries altogether. He ought to have chosen instead to dazzle them both with his intelligence and erudition by rattling off the names of all the wildflowers growing in the hedgerows—preferably the *Latin* names.

Perhaps *that* would have impressed her.

Of course, he did not know any Latin flower names.

Miss Martin's School for Girls. He allowed himself a mental grimace even as he laughed at some witticism Miss Jane Calvert had just uttered.

It sounded formidable. And she taught there.

Like the quintessential lady schoolteacher, her character was totally devoid of humor.

But no, that was unfair. What the devil was it he had said to her? Something about the summer day seeming warmer and brighter for her presence in it? He winced inwardly. Good Lord, could he not have done better than that? Had he really expected her to simper all over him with gratitude at being so complimented?

Sometimes he embarrassed himself.

He focused his attention on the two ladies on his arms and the other two in his orbit and flirted good-naturedly with them for the rest of the outing.

Raycroft and the ladies from Barclay Court appeared to be holding a sensible conversation, he noticed, except when interrupted by a comment or question from behind.

Peter felt faintly envious. He almost never held sensible conversations with females. He flirted with them instead, and flirting had become a habit. It had not always been the case, had it? He remembered talking endlessly and earnestly to Bertha about all the subjects that had fascinated him at university and about religion and politics and philosophy—until, that was, he had recognized the glazed look in her eyes as one of unutterable boredom.

2

Susanna Osbourne had thought she was not going to be able to come to Barclay Court and had been dis—appointed, even though she had tried to tell herself that it did not really matter.

She had remained at the school in Bath all summer with Claudia Martin to care for the charity pupils, who had nowhere else to go during the holiday. Anne Jewell, the other resident teacher, had gone to Wales for a month with her son, David, at the invitation of the Marquess of Hallmere, an old acquaintance of hers.

But while Anne was still away, Frances Marshall, Countess of Edgecombe, a former teacher at the school herself, had stopped off in Bath with the earl, her husband, on the way back to their home, Barclay Court in Somerset. They had been away for a few months in Austria and other European countries where Frances had been engaged to sing. They had come to invite Claudia or Anne or Susanna to go home with them for two weeks. The three of them were still Frances's dearest female friends, even though she had been married for two years.

Claudia had urged Susanna to go. She could manage the girls perfectly well alone, she had said, and there were always the nonresident teachers to appeal to if necessary. Besides, Anne would surely be back any day. But Susanna had a loyal heart. Claudia Martin had given her employment five years before when she had still been a charity pupil at the school herself, and she would not easily forget her gratitude or the obligation she felt to set duty before personal inclination.

She had told Frances without any hesitation at all that no, she would not go this time. And of course, Frances had not argued. She had understood. But then, just the day before Frances and the earl were to leave, Anne had come home and there had been no further necessity for Susanna to stay too.

And so here she was in Somerset during a particularly sunny and warm spell in late August. It was not the first time she had been here, but the wonder of such visits would never pall, she had been sure. Barclay Court was stately and spacious and lovely. Frances was as dear as ever, and the earl was exceedingly kind. The neighbors, she remembered, were amiable. She knew that Frances would go out of her way to entertain her royally. Not that any effort was necessary. Just the rare enjoyment of being on holiday was entertainment enough, especially when the setting was so luxurious.

She and Frances were out for a visit to the Raycrofts, whom Susanna had particularly liked when she first met them. They had decided to walk rather than take a carriage since the weather was lovely and they had been traveling all of yesterday. When they were scarcely half a mile on their way, they had heard cheerful, laughing, youthful voices and had seen that the younger Raycrofts and Calverts were out walking too.

Susanna had felt her heart lift with gladness. Life had seemed very good indeed.

Until it no longer did.

Frances and Mr. Raycroft were talking about Vienna. Frances had been there very recently, and Mr. Raycroft's betrothed, Miss Hickmore, had just gone there with her parents to spend the autumn and winter months.

Mr. Raycroft, tall, loose-limbed, sandy-haired, his face good-humored more than it was handsome, had always been particularly amiable. Frances had once suggested, only half in jest, that Susanna set her cap at him. But he had shown no romantic partiality for her—and she had felt none for him. She felt no pang of regret to learn now of his betrothal, only a hope that Miss Hickmore was worthy of him.

He was gentleman enough to draw Susanna into the conversation, explaining that he was as ignorant as she of what such places as Vienna were really like, having never set foot outside the British Isles himself.

"It is undoubtedly a most lovely city," he said, smiling kindly at her, "though I am sure it cannot surpass London in beauty. Are you familiar with London, Miss Osbourne?"

She determinedly tried to concentrate upon the conversation rather than upon the other thoughts that whirled in jumbled disorder through her mind.

"Only very slightly," she said. "I spent a short time

there as a girl but have not been since. I envy Frances's having seen Vienna and Paris and Rome."

"Lady Edgecombe," one of the young ladies called from behind them, "do you suppose there will be any waltzes at the assembly the week after next? I shall simply *die* if there is one and Mama forbids us to dance it as she surely will. Is it really quite shockingly *fast*?"

"I have no idea, Mary," Frances said while Susanna turned her head to see who had spoken. "I did not even know of the assembly, remember, until you mentioned it a few minutes ago. But I hope there will be a waltz. It is a lovely, romantic dance and really not shocking at all. At least, it has never seemed so to me."

And there he was in the middle of them, Susanna saw with a sinking heart, one lady on each arm as he had been when she first set eyes on him, the other two hovering about him as if he were the only man in the world of any significance—an opinion with which he undoubtedly concurred.

She was not inclined to think kindly of him, though she would concede that he could not be blamed for his name.

Viscount Whitleaf.

She turned suddenly cold at the remembered name—as she had done a few minutes ago when Frances introduced her to him.

He was without any doubt the most handsome gentleman she had ever set eyes upon—and she had thought so even before she was close enough to see that he had eyes of an extraordinary shade of violet. He looked as if his valet might well have poured him into his coat of dark blue superfine and his buff pantaloons.

His Hessian boots looked supple and expensive, even with their shine marred by a light coating of dust from the lane, and his shirt was white and of the finest linen. His tall hat sat upon his dark hair at just the right angle to look slightly rakish but not askew. And he had the physique to display such clothes to full advantage. He was tall and slender, though his shoulders and chest were broad and his calves were shapely.

If there were any physical imperfection in his person, she certainly had not detected it.

The very sight of him among the Raycrofts and the Calverts had filled her with awed wonder.

Then Frances had mentioned his name.

And he had bowed with studied elegance—so out of place on a country lane—and smiled with practiced charm and paid her that lavish, ridiculous compliment while looking so deeply into her eyes that she would not have been surprised to discover that the hair on the back of her head was singed. He had white, straight, and even teeth to add to all his other perfections.

There had been delighted laughter from the other young ladies, but Susanna would not have known what to do or how to reply even if she had not still been stunned from hearing his name. Her mind had been paralyzed and it was only by sheer chance that her body had not followed suit.

Even if he could *not* help his name, Susanna thought now, remembering that it was not any *Viscount* Whiteleaf against whom she held a grudge, nevertheless she already disliked him quite heartily. A gentleman ought to set about making a strange lady feel comfortable, not throw her into confusion. She did not know much about men, but she could recognize a vain and shallow one when she met him, one so wrapped up in the splendor of his own person that he expected every woman he encountered to fall prostrate at his feet.

Viscount Whitleaf was such a man. He lived up to his name.

She had accepted Mr. Raycroft's offered arm with gratitude. But with every step she had taken along the lane since, she had felt the presence of Viscount Whitleaf behind her like a hand all along her spine. She resented the feeling and despised herself for allowing it.

Of course the name *Osbourne* would probably mean nothing whatsoever to him. And he could not really be blamed for that either. He had been only a boy . . . But he *ought* to remember. It ought to be a name burned on his brain as his was on hers.

She wished fervently now that Anne had not returned to Bath when she had and that *she* had not come to Barclay Court with Frances and the earl. She wished herself back in the safety of the school—in the dreary, endless safety.

Though why *should* she? And why *should* she allow her holiday to be ruined by a shallow, conceited, careless man who clearly thought he only had to look at a woman with those fine violet eyes for her to fall head over ears in love with him?

Susanna turned to face the lane ahead again, unconsciously squaring her shoulders and lifting her chin as she did so, and asked Mr. Raycroft where he would go if he could choose anywhere in the world. Would he choose Greece, as she would?

"Greece would be well worth a visit, I believe, Miss Osbourne," he replied, "though I have been told that travel there is very uncomfortable indeed. I am a man who enjoys his creature comforts, you see."

"I do not blame you at all," Frances said. "And I can assure you that I have not yet seen a country to rival England in beauty. It feels very good to be home again."

They reached the village soon after that and stopped to speak with Mrs. Calvert, who came outside the house to greet them, though they declined her invitation to step inside. When they continued on their way without the Calvert sisters, Viscount Whitleaf walked ahead with Miss Raycroft on his arm, and the two of them chattered merrily all the way to Hareford House, obviously very pleased with each other's company.

The two visitors drank tea with the Raycrofts and exchanged civilities for half an hour before Frances got to her feet and Susanna followed suit.

"I do not suppose," Frances said, "you would care to go walking again, Mr. Raycroft, after having been out once. Perhaps we may hope for you to call at Barclay Court tomorrow?"

"I seem to recall," Viscount Whitleaf said, "that your original invitation included me too, ma'am. And indeed I *would* care to go walking again today. I look forward to paying my respects to Edgecombe. Raycroft, are you coming too? Or am I to enjoy the pleasure of having two ladies to myself for the walk to Barclay Court?"

Susanna's eyes flew to Mr. Raycroft's face. She was vastly relieved when he expressed himself ready for further exercise.

Her relief was short-lived, however. She desperately hoped to maneuver matters so that she would walk with Frances or Mr. Raycroft, but as fate would have it, he was saying something to Frances as they descended the garden path and it was natural that he should offer her his arm after they had passed out through the gate. That left Susanna to walk behind with Viscount Whitleaf.

She could hardly have imagined a worse fate. She glanced up at him in a sort of sick dismay and clasped her hands firmly behind her back before he should feel obliged to offer his arm.

Whatever were they to talk about?

She was horrified to discover that she could *feel* him down her right side like a fever, even though there was a foot of air between their shoulders. Her stomach muscles were tied in knots—not to mention her tongue.

She despised the fact that she could feel none of the ease that Miss Raycroft and the Calvert sisters had felt with him earlier. He was only a man, after all—and a shallow man at that. He was not anyone she would wish to impress. All she need do was be polite.

Not a single polite topic presented itself to her searching brain.

She was twenty-three years old and as gauche as a girl just stepping out of the schoolroom for the first time. But then she never had stepped outside the schoolroom, had she?

She was twenty-three years old and had never had a beau.

She had never been kissed.

But such sadly pathetic thoughts did nothing to calm her agitation.

She might have spent the past eleven years in a convent, she thought ruefully, for all she knew about how to step into the world of men and feel at ease there.

By the time they were halfway to Barclay Court by Peter's estimation, he had spoken six words and Miss Osbourne had spoken one.

"What a lovely day it is!" he had said as a conversational overture at the outset, smiling genially down at her—or at the brim of her bonnet anyway, which was about on a level with his shoulder.

"Yes."

She walked very straight-backed. She held her hands firmly clasped behind her back, an unmistakable signal that she did not want him to offer his arm. He wondered if she simply had no conversation or if she was still bristling with indignation because he had compared her to a summer's day—though he was in good company there, was he not? Had not Shakespeare once done the same thing? He rather suspected that it was indignation that held her mute, since she had been speaking in more than monosyllables with Mrs. Raycroft less than half an hour ago—though he would swear her eyes had never once strayed his way. He would have known if they had since his eyes had scarcely strayed anywhere else *but* at her.

He had been puzzling—he still was—over that strange thought he had had when his eyes first alighted on her.

There she is.

There *who* was, for the love of God?

It was a novel experience to be in company with a lady who clearly did not want to be in company with him. Of course, he did not usually find himself in company with lady schoolteachers from Bath. They were, perhaps, a different breed from the women with whom he usually consorted. They were quite possibly made of sterner stuff.

"You were quite right," he said at last, merely to see how she would respond. "This summer day was not *really* made warmer and brighter by your presence in it. It was a foolish conceit."

She darted him a look, and in the moment before her bonnet brim hid her face from view again he was dazzled anew by the combination of bright auburn hair and sea green eyes—and by the healthy flush the fresh air had lent her creamy, flawless complexion.

"Yes," she agreed, doubling her contribution to their conversation since leaving Hareford House.

So she was not going to contradict him, was she? He could not resist continuing.

"It was my heart," he said, patting it with his right hand, "that was warmed and brightened."

This time she did not turn her face, but he amused

himself with the fancy that the poke of her bonnet stiffened slightly.

"The heart," she said, "is merely an organ in the bosom."

Ah, a literalist. He smiled.

"With the function of a pump," he agreed. "But how unromantic a view of it. You would put generations of poets out of business with such a pronouncement, Miss Osbourne. Not to mention lovers."

"I am not a romantic," she said.

"Indeed?" he said. "How sad! There are no such things, then, you believe, as tender sensibilities? There is no part of one's anatomy or soul that can be warmed or brightened by the sight of beauty?"

He thought she was not going to answer. They came to the fork in the lane where they had met a couple of hours ago and followed Raycroft and Lady Edgecombe onto the branch that led to Barclay Court.

"You make a mockery of tender sensibilities," Miss Osbourne said so softly that he bent his head toward her in case she had more to say.

She did not.

"Ah," he said, "you think me incapable of feeling the gentler emotions. Is that what you are saying?"

"I would not so presume," she said.

"But you would. You already have so presumed," he said. He was rather enjoying himself, he discovered, with this curiously serious, prim creature who looked so like an angel. "You told me I made a mockery of tender sensibilities."

"I beg your pardon," she said. "I ought not to have said such a thing."

"No, you ought not," he agreed. "You wounded me to the heart—to that chest organ, that mundane pump. How differently we view the world, Miss Osbourne. You listened to me pay you a lavish and foolish compliment and concluded that I know nothing about the finer human emotions. I on the other hand looked at you, serious and disapproving, and felt—ah, as if I had stepped into a moment that was simply magic."

"And now," she said, "you make a mockery of *me*."

She had a low, sweet voice even when she sounded indignant. She was small in stature and very slender, though she was curved in all the right places, by Jove. He wondered how well she controlled a class of girls, most of whom undoubtedly wished themselves anywhere else on earth but at school. Did they give her a rough time? Or was there steel in her character, as there appeared to be in her spine?

He would wager there was steel—and not a great deal of tenderness. Poor girls!

"I fear," he said, "that with a few foolish words I have forever condemned myself in your eyes, Miss Osbourne. Shall we change the subject? What have you been doing with your school holiday up until now?"

"It was not really a holiday," she said. "Almost half of the girls at the school are charity pupils. They remain there all year long and some of us stay too to care for them and to entertain them."

"Us?" he asked.

"There are three resident teachers," she told him. "There used to be four until Frances married the earl two years ago. Now there are Miss Martin, Miss Jewell, and I."

"And you all give up your holidays for the sake of *charity* girls?" he asked.

She turned to look at him again—a level, unsmiling look in which there might have been some reproof.

"I was one of them," she said, "from the age of twelve until Miss Martin made me a junior teacher when I was eighteen."

Ah.

Well.

Extraordinary.

He was walking and talking with an ex–charity schoolgirl turned teacher. It was no wonder they were having a difficult time of it communicating with each other. Two alien worlds had drifted onto the same country lane at the same moment, none too happily for either. Though that was not quite true—he was still enjoying himself.

"There is no question of *giving up* our holidays," she continued. "The school is our home and the girls our family. We welcome a break now and then, of course. Anne—Miss Jewell—has just returned from a month in Wales with her son, and now I am here for two weeks. Occasionally Claudia Martin will spend a few days away from the school too. But in the main I am happy—we are all happy—to be busy. A life of idleness would not suit me."

She was a prim miss right enough. She had nothing whatsoever to say about the weather, and had only brief reproaches to offer when he would have spoken of hearts and sensibilities. But she could wax eloquent about her school and the notion of teachers and charity pupils being a family.

Lord help him.

But she was more gloriously lovely than almost any other woman he had set eyes upon—and the word *almost* might even be withdrawn from that thought without any great exaggeration resulting. He had often thought fate was something of a joker, and now he was convinced of it. But the apparently huge contrast between her looks and her character and circumstances had him more fascinated than he could remember being with any other woman for a long time—perhaps ever.

"The implication being that idleness suits *me* very well indeed?" He laughed. "Miss Osbourne, you speak softly but with a barbed tongue. I daresay your pupils fear it."

She was not entirely wrong, though, was she? His life *was* idle—or had been for all of five years anyway. It was true that he intended to reform his ways and put idleness behind him in the very near future, but he had not really done so yet, had he? Thinking and planning were one thing; doing was another.

Yes, as he was now, today, Miss Osbourne was quite right about him. He had no defense to offer.

He wondered what it must be like to *have* to work for a living.

"I spoke of myself, sir— my lord," she said, "in answer to your question. I made no implication about you."

She had small, dainty feet, he could see—which was just as well considering her small stature. He had noticed during tea that her hands were small and delicate.

Miss Susanna Osbourne disapproved of him—probably disliked him too. In her world people worked. What had it been like, he wondered, to be a charity girl at the school where she now taught?

"Do you *like* teaching?" he asked.

"Very much," she said. "It is what I would choose to do with my life even if I had myriad choices."

"Indeed?" He wondered if she spoke the truth or only said what she had convinced herself was the truth. "You would choose teaching even above marriage and motherhood?"

There was a rather lengthy silence before she replied, and he regretted the question. It was unmannerly and might have touched her on the raw. But there was no recalling it.

"I suppose that even if I could imagine myriad choices," she said, "they would still have to be within the realm of the realistic."

Good Lord!

"And marriage would not fit within such a realm?" he asked, surprised.

He did not realize until he found himself gazing at the tender flesh at the arch of her neck that she had dipped her head so far downward that she must have been able to see nothing more than her own feet. He *had* embarrassed her, dash it all. He was not usually so insensitive.

"No," she said. "It would not."

And of course he might have known it if he had stopped to consider. How often did one hear of a governess marrying? Yet a schoolteacher must have even fewer opportunities to meet eligible men. He wondered suddenly how the countess had met Edgecombe. He had not even known before today that she had been a schoolteacher at the time. There must be an interesting story behind that courtship.

In his world women had nothing to hope for or think about *but* marriage. His sisters had not considered their lives complete until they had all followed one another to the altar with eligible mates in order from the eldest to the youngest, at gratifyingly young ages—gratifying to them and even more so to his mother.

"Well," he said, "one never knows what the future holds, does one? But you must tell me sometime what it is about teaching that you enjoy so much. Not today, though—I see we are approaching Barclay Court. We will talk more when we meet again during the next two weeks."

She stole another quick glance at him and he laughed.

"I can see the wheels of your mind turning upon the hope that such a fate can be avoided," he said. "I assure you it cannot. Neighbors in the country invariably live in one another's pockets. How else are they to avoid expiring of boredom? And I am to be at Hareford House for the next two weeks just as you are to be at Barclay Court. I am glad now that I decided not to return to my own home tomorrow as I had originally planned."

He spoke the truth and was surprised by it. Why on earth would he wish to extend an acquaintance with a woman from an alien world who disliked and disapproved of him? Just because she was dazzlingly beautiful? Or because he could not resist the unusual challenge of coaxing a smile and a kind word from her? Or because with her there might be a chance of actually conversing sensibly—about her life as a teacher? His conversation—and his life—had been far too trivial for far too long.

"I daresay," she said, "you will be busy with Miss Raycroft and the Misses Calvert."

"But of course." He chuckled. "They are delightful young ladies, and who can resist cultivating delight?"

"I do not believe," she said, "you expect me to answer that."

"Indeed not," he agreed. "It was a rhetorical question. But I will not be busy with them *all* the time, Miss Osbourne. Someone might misconstrue my interest in them if I were. Besides, with them I have felt no moment of magic."

He smiled down at her bonnet.

"I would ask you," she said as their feet crunched over the gravel of the terrace before the house, her voice as cold as the Arctic ice, "not to speak to me with such levity, my lord. I do not know how to respond. And moreover I do not *wish* to respond. I do not wish to have you single me out on any future occasion. I wish you would not."

Dash it all. Had he offended her more than he realized?

"Am I to look your way whenever we are in company together during the coming weeks, then, and pretend that I see only empty air?" he asked her. "I

fear Edgecombe and his lady would consider me un-
pardonably ill-mannered. I shall bow to you each time
instead and remark upon the fineness or inclemency of
the weather—without drawing any comparisons with
your person. Shall I? Will you tolerate that much attention from me?"

She hesitated.

"Yes," she said, ending their conversation as
monosyllabically as she had begun it.

Edgecombe must have observed their approach
and was coming out through the front doors and
down the horseshoe steps to greet them, a smile of
welcome on his face.

"You *did* persuade him to come, then, Frances," he
said, setting one hand at the small of the countess's
back and smiling briefly and warmly down at her.
"Raycroft—good to see you again. And Whitleaf is
staying with you? This *is* a pleasure. Do come inside.
Did you enjoy the walk, Susanna? And did you find
Mrs. and Miss Raycroft at home?"

He smiled kindly at the schoolteacher and offered
her his arm, which she took without hesitation.

"We met Miss Raycroft at the fork in the road,"
she said. "She was out walking with her brother and
the Calvert sisters. We walked back to the village together and then on to Hareford House, where we took
tea with Mrs. Raycroft. It was indeed a pleasant outing. There can be nowhere lovelier than the Somerset
countryside."

Her voice was light and happy. Peter smiled ruefully to himself as he followed them up the steps and

into the house, the countess between him and Raycroft.

By the time he stepped over the threshold, Miss Osbourne was already moving off in the direction of the staircase without a backward glance.

"You will wish to entertain Mr. Raycroft and Lord Whitleaf in the library, Lucius," the countess said. "We will not disturb you."

"Thank you," he said, setting a hand at her back again. "The vicar called. I daresay by now you know all about the village assembly the week after next?"

"Of course," she said.

"I said we would attend," he told her, "on condition that there be at least one waltz. The vicar has promised to see to it."

He grinned at her and she smiled back, her face alight with amusement, before turning to follow Miss Osbourne up the stairs.

"Right." Edgecombe turned his attention back to his visitors, rubbing his hands together as he did so. "Shall we step into the library? We will have some refreshments, and you can both tell me everything I missed in London during the Season. I *have* heard that you are finally betrothed to Miss Hickmore, Raycroft. My felicitations. A fine choice, if you were to ask me."

3

"I disliked him intensely," Susanna replied bluntly when Frances asked her what she thought of Viscount Whitleaf.

"Did you?" Frances looked surprised. "But he is rather good-looking, is he not? And very charming, I have always thought."

Susanna did not comment on his looks, though it seemed to her that he was considerably more than just "rather good-looking."

"*Calculatedly* charming," she said as she removed her bonnet and fluffed up her curls with the visual aid of the mirror in her bedchamber while Frances stood in the doorway, twirling her own bonnet by its ribbons. "He does not utter a sincere word. I doubt he has a sincere thought."

"Oh, dear." Frances laughed. "He *did* make a poor impression on you. I suppose he tried to flirt with you?"

"You heard what he said when we first met," Susanna said, turning from the mirror and gesturing to the chair beside the dressing table.

Frances stepped into the room though she did not sit down.

"I thought his words rather amusing," she admitted. "He did not mean to offend, you know. I daresay most ladies enjoy such flatteries from him."

"He is shallow and vain," Susanna said.

Frances set her head to one side and regarded her friend more closely.

"It might be a mistake to jump too hastily to that conclusion," she said. "I have never heard of any vice in him. I have never heard him called a rake or a gambler or a ne'er-do-well or any other of the unsavory things one half expects to hear of a young, unattached gentleman about town. Lucius likes him. And so do I, I must confess, though I have never been an object of his gallantry, it is true."

"I do not understand," Susanna said, "how those girls can be so taken in by him."

"Miss Raycroft and the Calverts?" Frances said. "Oh, but they are not really, you know. He is *Viscount Whitleaf,* high-born, enormously wealthy, and quite out of their orbit. They understand that very well. But they enjoy his attentions—and who can blame them? Life in the country can be exceedingly dull, especially when one rarely travels farther from home than five miles in any direction. And he is very skilled at flirting without ever favoring one particular lady above all others and therefore inspiring hope in her that can only lead to disappointment. Women understand him very well, I daresay, and look for husbands elsewhere. Society often works in such ways."

"I am very glad, then," Susanna said tartly, "that

I do not belong to society. It all sounds very artificial to me."

But as she caught her friend's eye, she first smiled and then dissolved into unexpected laughter.

"And just *listen* to me," she said when she caught her breath, "sounding like a dried-up prune of a spinster schoolteacher."

"And looking like anything but," Frances said, joining in the laughter. "I suppose he flirted on the way back to Barclay Court too, the rogue, and you responded with a sober face and a severe tongue? The poor man! He must have been utterly confounded. I wish I could have listened."

They laughed together again. Perhaps she *had* overreacted, Susanna thought. Perhaps she would not have judged him quite so severely if he had been introduced to her as Viscount Jones or Viscount Smith or anything but Viscount *Whitleaf*.

"Anyway," she said, "I have always said that I will hold out for a duke or nobody. I believe a mere viscount must count as nobody."

They both chuckled at the absurdity of her words. A *mere* viscount, indeed!

"Come along to my sitting room with me," Frances said, "and we will order up some tea and have a comfortable coze until the visitors have gone away. It was rather a long walk on such a warm day, was it not? I am thirsty again. But it felt *so* good to stretch my legs. I have done enough sitting in a carriage during the last few months to last me for the next year at the very least."

Susanna followed her to the small sitting room of

the private apartments she shared with the earl and sank into a comfortable brocaded easy chair while Frances pulled on the bell rope to summon a servant.

But Frances had not finished with the topic of the viscount.

"Of course," she said, "you are quite right to be wary of Viscount Whitleaf, who is well known for having an eye for beauty but who may not have realized at first that you are far too intelligent to respond gladly to empty flirtation and dalliance. You are certainly wise not to be dazzled by him. But, Susanna, there has to be someone out there who is just perfect for you. I firmly believe it. And I *so* want to see you contentedly settled in life. Mr. Birney, our vicar, was new here just before we left for Europe and so I do not know him well. But he is pleasing to look at and has refined manners and is unattached—at least he was six months ago. And he cannot be a day over thirty, if he is that. Then there is Mr. Finn, a gentleman farmer, Lucius's tenant. He is earnest and thrifty and worthy and quite personable in appearance. But I believe you met him last time you were here."

"I did," Susanna said, her eyes twinkling. "I believe he is sweet on the eldest Miss Calvert."

"You may be right," Frances admitted. "But I am not yet convinced she is sweet on him. Well, let us dismiss him just in case she is—or just in case he is not heart-free. There is also Mr. Dannen. He owns his own property and is in possession of a modest fortune, I believe. Certainly he appears to be comfortably well off. You have not met him. He was away the last time you were here—in Scotland, I believe. He is short in stature—but then so are you. Otherwise he is well enough favored. Of course, he is—"

"Frances!" Susanna interrupted her, laughing. "You do not have to matchmake for me."

"Oh, but I do." Frances sat on a love seat facing her friend's chair after giving her order to the housekeeper, and gazed earnestly at her. "You and Claudia and Anne are still my dearest female friends, Susanna, and I fervently wish for you all to be as well settled and contented as I am. Surely there must be enough unattached gentlemen in this neighborhood for all of you."

Susanna laughed again, even more merrily, and after a moment Frances joined in.

"Well, for *one* of you anyway," she said. "I cannot seriously imagine Claudia ever marrying, can you? And Anne is so attached to David that I daresay she would be unwilling to risk subjecting him to a stepfather who might mistreat him."

David Jewell was an illegitimate child, Anne never having been married.

"So I am the one?" Susanna said.

"And so you are the one," Frances said, reaching for both her hands and squeezing them tightly. "You are so *very* pretty, Susanna, and so sweet-natured. It seems unfair that fate landed you in a girls' school at the age of twelve and has kept you there ever since, far from the world of men and potential courtships."

"It is *not* unfair," Susanna said firmly, pulling her hands free. "Except perhaps to the hundreds and thousands of other girls who were not so privileged. And you know how much I love the school and all the girls and Claudia and Anne and even Mr. Keeble and the other teachers."

Mr. Keeble was the elderly school porter.

"I do know it," Frances said with a sigh. "Just as I loved teaching until Lucius forced me to admit how much more I wanted to sing—and how very much more I wanted him. Well, I will say nothing else on the subject. And here comes the tea."

They were quiet while the tray was brought in and set down and while Frances poured the tea and handed Susanna her cup.

"And so there is to be an assembly in the village the week after next," Frances said. "We arrived home at the perfect time."

"An assembly will be wonderfully exciting," Susanna said. "Even a little frightening. I have never been to any such thing."

"Oh." Frances looked at her with sudden realization. "Of course you have not. But you have danced at the school forever, Susanna, demonstrating steps for the girls. Now at last you will be able to put your skills to work at a real dance. And you need not be afraid that you will make a cake of yourself and everyone will notice. This is a country assembly with country people who will go to enjoy themselves, not to observe one another critically. And if that suddenly wary look has anything to do with the fact that Viscount Whitleaf will be there too, you silly goose, I will be wishing that he were to take himself off back home to Sidley Park before the fateful night. You must not allow yourself to be intimidated by him."

Sidley Park. Susanna's heart sank again at the

name. *Why* did Viscount Whitleaf have to be a friend of Mr. Raycroft? And *why* did he have to be staying with him at Hareford House now of all times? For so many years—eleven, in fact—there had been no real reminders of her childhood and its abrupt, ghastly ending. She had been able to convince herself that she had forgotten.

"Oh," Frances continued, "and Lucius has bullied the vicar into seeing to it that there will be at least one waltz at the assembly. Have I ever told you about our first waltz together—in a dusty assembly room above a deserted inn with no one else present, no heat though it was the dead of winter, and no music?"

"No music?" Susanna laughed.

"I hummed it," Frances said. "It was the most glorious waltz ever waltzed, Susanna. Believe me it was."

They lapsed into a companionable silence while Frances's dreamy expression and slightly flushed cheeks indicated that she was reliving that waltz and Susanna wondered if anyone would dance with her at the assembly. Oh, how she *hoped* so! She would not even think about the waltz. Just one set—*any* set.

She knew the steps of the waltz, though. It was a dance Mr. Huckerby, the dancing master, always taught the girls at school. He was not, however, allowed to dance it with any of them, but only with any teacher who was willing to oblige for demonstration purposes. That had used to be Frances. Now Susanna and Anne and sometimes Mademoiselle Étienne, the French teacher, took turns.

Susanna loved the waltz more than any other dance. Not that there was anything even faintly romantic about performing the steps with Mr. Huckerby, it was true, especially when an audience of girls, many of them stifling giggles, looked on. But she had always dreamed of waltzing in a glittering, candlelit ballroom in the arms of a tall, handsome gentleman who smiled down into her eyes as if no one else existed in the world but the two of them.

I am not a romantic, she had said earlier to Viscount Whitleaf. What an absolute bouncer of a fib! She lived a busy, disciplined life as a schoolteacher, and she did indeed love her job—she had spoken the truth about that. But her dreams were rich with romance—with love and marriage and motherhood.

All those things she would never experience in the real world.

As if I had stepped into a moment that was simply magic.

She had wanted to weep when he spoke those words, so meaningless to him, so achingly evocative to her. How she longed for the magic of someone to love more than anyone or anything else in life. Of someone to love her in the same way.

For an unguarded moment she pictured herself waltzing with Viscount Whitleaf, those laughing violet eyes softened by tenderness as they gazed into her own.

But she shuddered slightly as she shook off the image and reached for a ginger biscuit. She must certainly not begin sullying the splendor of her dreams by imposing *his* image on them.

And then she thought of something else he had said.

You wounded me to the heart—to that chest organ, that mundane pump.

She almost ruined her aversion to him by chuckling aloud with amusement.

Frances would think she had taken leave of her senses.

And then she thought again of Sidley Park. She had lived until the age of twelve only a few miles away from it, though she had never actually been there. She had known it as the home of *Viscountess Whitleaf,* though she had always known too that the young viscount lived there as well as his five sisters, who bore the name of Edgeworth. She recalled that when she had first heard Frances speak of the Earl of Edgecombe she had had a nasty turn, wondering if he was of the same family—until she had realized that the names were not identical.

But apart from that, she had done a good job of holding the memories at bay. They were just too excruciatingly painful. She had heard that some people blocked painful memories so effectively that they completely forgot them. She sometimes wished that could have happened to her.

A specific memory came back to her then. She must have been five or six years old at the time and was playing close to the lake with Edith Markham when they had been joined by a young boy a few years older than they. He had asked them with great good humor and open interest what they were doing and had squatted next to Susanna on the bank to see if there was a fish on the end of her makeshift fishing line.

"Oh, hard luck!" he had said when he had seen

that there was not. "I daresay the fish are not biting today. Sometimes they do not—or so I have heard. My mama will not let me go fishing. She is afraid I will fall in or catch a chill—instead of a fish, ha-ha. Did you get it? Catching a chill instead of a fish? Does your mama fuss you all the time? Oh, I say! You have the greenest eyes, don't you? I have never seen eyes of just that color before. They are very fine, and they look very well with your red hair. I daresay you will be pretty when you grow up. Not that you are not pretty now. I do beg your pardon—I forgot my manners for a moment. A gentleman *never* lets a lady believe that perhaps she is not pretty. May I hold the rod? Perhaps I will have better luck than you though I daresay you have had more practice."

But no sooner had he seated himself on the bank and taken the rod from her, looking bright and happy and friendly, than an older girl had appeared and told him in a hushed, rather shocked voice that he ought not to be playing with *that* little girl, and then another girl, even older, had come rushing up to catch him by the hand and pull him firmly away from the bank and tell him that he must never, *never* go so close to the water again. He would fall in and die, she had said, and *then* what would they all do to console themselves?

Edith had gone off with them, and later Susanna had learned that they had come from Sidley Park on an afternoon visit—Viscountess Whitleaf with the young viscount, her son, and her daughters.

Susanna had not thought of that incident for years and years. She was surprised she remembered it at all.

Were that friendly, talkative, overprotected little boy and the viscount she had met this afternoon one and the same, then? But they must be. She had liked him then and wanted him for a friend. She had hoped he would visit again, but though she believed he had, she had never seen him again.

Even then they had been worlds apart.

"We have been invited to spend the evening with Mr. Dannen and his mother tomorrow," Frances said. "It will be something for you to look forward to. And you will have a chance to take a look at him and find out if you like what you see."

She chuckled at the look on Susanna's face, and then they both laughed together.

Peter had spoken quite truthfully about neighbors in the country frequently coming together, either for impromptu walks and rides and drives and daytime calls at one another's homes or for more formal entertainments like dinners and carriage excursions and garden parties.

The evening of the day after he first met Susanna Osbourne offered one such formal gathering.

Dannen's mother had recently come from Scotland, where she lived with a widowed brother, to spend a few weeks with her son. And so he had invited his neighbors to meet her at an evening of cards and music followed by supper.

The Raycrofts were among the first to arrive, but by the time Peter looked up to observe the arrival in the drawing room of the Earl and Countess of Edgecombe with Miss Osbourne, Miss Krebbs was seated beside him on a sofa, the Misses Jane and Mary Calvert were sitting close by, one on a chair, the other on an ottoman, and Miss Raycroft was leaning on the back of the sofa, having declined his offer to allow her to sit.

They were talking—almost inevitably—about the assembly. Miss Krebbs had asked him about the waltz and whether it was embarrassing to dance a whole set face-to-face with one partner and actually *touching* that partner all the time.

There had been a flurry of self-conscious giggles from the other ladies at the question, and then they had all fallen silent in order to hear his answer.

"Embarrassing?" he had said, looking from one to the other of them in mock amazement. "To be able to look into a lovely face while my one hand is at the lady's waist and the other in hers? I cannot think of any more congenial way to spend half an hour. Can you?"

"Oh," Mary Calvert said with a deep sigh. "But Mama *will* insist that it is too fast a dance for any of us to perform—and I am not talking about tempo."

"The beauty of the waltz, though," Peter said, "is that it is danced in public with every mama able to keep an eye upon her daughter—and upon her daughter's partner. No man with a grain of sense would attempt anything remotely indiscreet under such circumstances, would he—despite what he may *wish* to attempt."

They were all in the middle of a burst of merry and slightly risqué laughter when Peter looked up and his eyes met Susanna Osbourne's across the room.

Ah.

Well.

If someone had told him that a lightning bolt had penetrated the roof and the ceiling and the top of his head to emerge through the soles of his feet on its way through the floor, he would not have contradicted that person.

Which was the strangest thing really when one came to think of it, considering the fact that in the brief moment before she looked away he saw neither stars in her eyes nor adoration in the rest of her face. Quite the contrary, indeed. Her look made him uncomfortably aware of how he must appear sitting here, surrounded by young beauties and laughing his head off with them.

Vain, shallow popinjay.

He did not catch her eye again for all of the next couple of hours or so while he conversed with almost everyone else, played a few hands of cards, and then turned pages of music at the pianoforte while several of the young ladies displayed their talent at the instrument or twittered merrily about it. All the other men, he noticed, went to extraordinary lengths to avoid such a chore, though they did applaud politely at the end of each piece.

It seemed unsporting of them to keep their distance even though they were probably having interesting conversations about farming and hunting and horses and such things—as he had done yesterday with Edgecombe and Raycroft in the library at Barclay Court. When one was at a mixed entertainment, though, one ought to make oneself available to the ladies.

Miss Osbourne, he was interested to observe, did

not sit in a corner looking severely and disapprovingly about her at all the frivolity and vice—money was actually changing hands at the card tables, though in infinitesimal amounts, it was true. Rather, she moved about among several groups with the countess until Dannen himself appropriated her and engaged her in conversation while the countess moved on. He was doing most of the talking, Peter noticed. He had observed on other occasions that Dannen liked nothing better than a captive audience for his monologues.

She looked even lovelier tonight than she had yesterday, if that was possible. She was not wearing a bonnet tonight, of course, and he could see that her hair was cut short. It hugged her head in bright, soft curls that were less fiery than red, warmer than gold, but with elements of both. She wore a cream-colored gown that showed off her hair color to full advantage.

He deliberately stayed away from her—she had made her wishes quite clear yesterday. Perhaps he would not have spoken to her at all if he had not sat down beside Miss Honeydew after supper because he saw that she was all alone. Miss Honeydew was the elderly sister of a former vicar, now deceased. She had, he suspected, never been a beauty, since her top teeth protruded beyond her upper lip, and they and her long nose and face gave her a distinctly horsey appearance. Her hair always managed somehow to escape in untidy gray wisps from beneath the voluminous caps she wore, she squinted myopically at the world through large eyeglasses that were forever slipping down her nose and listing to the left, her head seemed to be in a constant nodding motion, whether from habit or infirmity it was not clear, and there was an air of general, smiling vagueness about her.

The neighbors, Peter had noticed during the past two weeks, were invariably kind to her and she had been included in various groups earlier in the evening. But he guessed that she lived a lonely existence with no children or grandchildren or even nieces and nephews to claim her or fuss over her.

And so he went to sit beside her and engage her in conversation.

She was asking him if he had heard of the upcoming assembly when Miss Osbourne walked by. Miss Honeydew grasped her by the wrist, shook her arm back and forth, and beamed up at her.

"Miss Osbourne," she said, "there you are. I am delighted that you are staying at Barclay Court again. This is the first chance I have had all evening to speak with you."

She had been talking with—or listening to—Dannen when the countess had spent some time with Miss Honeydew earlier.

Miss Osbourne smiled kindly down at Miss Honeydew without looking at Peter.

"How are you, ma'am?" she asked. "It is a pleasure to see you again."

"This young lady," Miss Honeydew said, looking at Peter while her hand still held Miss Osbourne's wrist, "was remarkably kind to me the last time she was here. She came to visit me one afternoon when I had hurt my foot and could not get about, and she read to me for longer than an hour. I have eyeglasses, but I still find it difficult to read. Print in books is so small these days, do you not find? Sit down, child, and talk to me. Have you met Viscount Whitleaf?"

She had no choice then but to look at him, though it was a brief glance as she sat on a stool close to Miss Honeydew's chair.

"Yes," she said, "I have had the pleasure, ma'am."

"Miss Osbourne," he said, "what a pleasant day it has been. I looked up several times during the course of it, but not once did I observe a single cloud in the sky. And the evening is almost as balmy as the day, or was when I left Hareford House."

She looked at him again, her green eyes grave. He smiled at her. He had promised to make nothing but bland conversation about the weather when they were forced into company with each other. He saw a sudden gleam of understanding in her eyes. She came very close to smiling.

"I believe," she said, "I saw one fluffy cloud at noon, my lord, when I was returning from a drive with Frances. But it was a very little one, and I daresay it soon floated out of sight."

He was utterly charmed as his eyes laughed back into hers. She *was* capable of humor, even wit, after all. But she colored suddenly and looked back at Miss Honeydew.

"I will walk over to your cottage and read to you again one day, ma'am, if you wish," she said. "I will enjoy it."

"I should like it of all things," Miss Honeydew cried, nodding her head more forcefully than usual. "But you cannot walk all that way, child. It must be all of three miles from Barclay Court."

"Then I shall ask—" Miss Osbourne began.

But Peter, totally forgetting his resolve to stay away from her and talk only about the weather when they *did* come face-to-face, yielded to a more impulsive instinct.

"For your pleasure, ma'am," he said to Miss Honeydew, "I would be prepared to go to considerable lengths. It is your pleasure to have Miss Osbourne come to your cottage to read to you, and you will not be disappointed. You will allow me, if you please, to bring her there myself in my curricle."

As if it were Miss Honeydew's permission that was needed.

"Oh—" Miss Osbourne said, perhaps indignantly.

"Oh," Miss Honeydew said, enraptured, her thin, arthritic hands clasped to her bosom. "How exceedingly kind you are to an old lady, my lord."

"Old lady?" He looked about the room in some surprise. "*Is* there an old lady present? Point her out to me, if you would be so good, ma'am, and I shall go and be kind to her."

She laughed heartily at his sorry joke, drawing several glances their way. Peter guessed that she did not often laugh with genuine amusement.

"How you tease!" she said. "You are a rogue, my lord, I do declare. But it is exceedingly kind of you to offer to bring Miss Osbourne to me. You will both stay to tea when you come? I shall have my housekeeper make some of her special cakes."

"Your company and a cup of tea will be quite sufficient to reward me, ma'am," he said. "Ah, and Miss Osbourne's company too."

As if that were an afterthought.

Miss Honeydew beamed happily at him.

"It is settled, then." He looked at the younger woman. "Which afternoon shall we decide upon, Miss Osbourne?"

She was looking back at him, the color high in her cheeks, an expression in her eyes he could not interpret—or perhaps he simply did not want to. And her eyes were not actually looking directly into his own, he noticed, but somewhere on a level with his chin.

It struck him then that, even apart from the fact that she did not like him, she might also be a little intimidated by him—or at least by his title. Perhaps the way he had greeted her when they were introduced was so far beyond her experience that he had made her uncomfortable. Worse, perhaps he had humiliated her. What was it she had said before they parted—*I would ask you not to speak to me with such levity, my lord. I do not know how to respond.*

It was a disturbing thought that perhaps he had been less than the gentleman with her.

"*Will* you allow me to drive you to Miss Honeydew's in my curricle?" he asked. "It will give me great pleasure."

"Thank you, then," she said.

"Tomorrow?" Miss Honeydew asked eagerly.

Miss Osbourne looked at her, and her expression softened. She even smiled.

"If that will suit Lord Whitleaf, ma'am," she said.

"It will," he said. "Ah, I see that Miss Moss must have found the music she was looking for earlier. She is beckoning me to come and turn the pages for her. You will excuse me?"

Miss Honeydew assured him that she would. Miss Osbourne said nothing.

"You looked," Miss Moss said, giggling with a group of other young ladies as he came up to the pianoforte, "as if you needed rescuing."

"Actually," he said, "I was enjoying a comfortable coze with Miss Honeydew. But how could I resist the chance of being surrounded by music again—and by beauty?"

"Miss Osbourne will keep her company," Miss Krebbs said. "She does not need you too, Lord Whitleaf."

He humored the young ladies and flirted good-naturedly with them for the rest of the evening while wondering if Miss Osbourne would find some excuse not to ride in his curricle with him tomorrow.

Somehow, he realized, he had been aware of her all evening—even, oddly enough, when they were in different rooms or when both his eyes had been focused upon the sheets of music so that he could turn a page at the right moment.

He had not been similarly aware of any other woman.

Dash it all, one day of the fourteen they would both spend in this neighborhood had already passed. Was he going to be content to allow the remaining thirteen to slip by too without at least making an effort to overcome her aversion to him and make a friend of her?

A friend?

Now that was a strange notion. Women and

friendship—deep friendship, anyway—did not usually go together in his thoughts. He had come to think of them as mutually exclusive interests.

What exactly *was* his motive, then? But did there have to be one? She was an extraordinarily pretty woman and he was a red-blooded male. Was that not motive enough? He was not usually so self-conscious about his approaches to women. But then he had never before known a lady schoolteacher from Bath—except, without realizing it, the Countess of Edgecombe.

Anyway, he would have to see what tomorrow brought. At least they would be alone together for the three-mile drive to Miss Honeydew's and back again—if Miss Osbourne did not find some way out of accepting his escort, that was.

And if it did not rain.

Frances's matchmaking schemes were going to be doomed to disappointment, Susanna thought as she tied the ribbons of her straw bonnet beneath her chin the following afternoon. They were green to match her favorite day dress—not that she had many others to compete with it.

The Reverend Birney, good-looking in a fresh-faced, boyish sort of way, had been polite to her last evening. He had even conversed with her for a short while at the supper table, expressing an interest in a school that took in almost as many charity girls as paying pupils. But there had been nothing approaching ardor in his manner toward her.

Mr. Dannen, short—as Frances had warned—and slightly balding at the crown of his head, but not by any means unpleasing of countenance, had engaged her in conversation for almost an hour before supper even though he was the host and ought to have circulated more among all his guests. But she had asked him about Scotland, his mother's country of birth, and he had proved to be the sort of man who needed very little prompting to talk at great length on a subject of personal interest to him. His descriptions had been interesting and she had not minded at all having to listen to them. But she had felt not the smallest spark of romantic interest in him. Or he in her, she guessed.

Miss Calvert was indeed interested in Mr. Finn—and he in her.

"Ah, you are ready," Frances said from the open doorway of Susanna's room. "Viscount Whitleaf is here. He is downstairs, talking with Lucius."

Susanna grimaced and reached for her gloves. Her stomach felt suddenly queasy and her knees less than steady.

"I wish I were going to *walk* to Miss Honeydew's cottage," she said.

"You know we would have called out a carriage for you before we allowed that to happen," Frances said.

"But he was there when I offered to go read to Miss Honeydew," Susanna explained, "and he felt obliged to offer to take me in his own conveyance. Poor man! I was horribly embarrassed."

Frances laughed and moved aside to allow Susanna to step out of her room.

"I do not suppose he minded in the least," she said. "He is nothing if not gallant to ladies. It is very sweet of you, Susanna, to be willing to give up an afternoon for Miss Honeydew. I try to call on her a few times whenever we are at home. It has never occurred to me, though, to offer to read to her, despite the fact that I remember you did it the last time you were here too."

By that time they were downstairs and approaching

the front doors. They were open, and Susanna could see the Earl of Edgecombe and Viscount Whitleaf standing just outside them at the top of the horseshoe steps. They turned at the approach of the ladies, and the viscount swept off his hat and bowed.

"It is a glorious day again," he said, his eyes laughing at Susanna. "Today there are definitely a few clouds in the sky—I counted twelve on my way over here—but they are small and white and harmless and actually add to the beauty of the sky."

Susanna might have laughed out loud or at least smiled if she had not just stepped outside and seen the vehicle in which she was to ride—Frances and the earl must wonder why he was making such an issue of what ought to have been a passing mention of the weather. But she *had* seen the vehicle. He had said last night that he would escort her in his curricle, but she had been too caught up in the knowledge that *he* was going to drive her to reflect upon the fact that she had never ridden in one before. And this was no ordinary curricle. It was, she guessed, a gentleman's racing curricle, light and flimsy, its wheels large, its seat looking small and fragile and very far up off the ground.

"And the occasional shade is welcome," Frances said. "It is very warm today."

"Miss Honeydew seems determined to ply us with tea and cakes after Miss Osbourne has read to her," the viscount said. "We may be gone for quite a while, but you may rest assured that I will return Miss Osbourne safe and sound."

"Whitleaf is a notable whip, Susanna," the earl

said with a laugh as they all descended the steps to the terrace. "You need not fear for your safety."

"I am not afraid," she said. "It is just that I have never ridden in a curricle before."

And the seat looked even higher and the whole thing flimsier from down here—and marvelously elegant. The horses, which were being held by one of the grooms from the stable, looked alarmingly frisky. But even before she need start worrying about the journey itself . . . how on earth was she going to get *up* there?

Fortunately it proved easier than it looked. She climbed up to the seat with no dreadful loss of dignity, though she clung to the viscount's hand as she did so. She moved over on the seat as far as she could go, but even so . . .

But even so, when he joined her there and gathered the ribbons into his hands, his outer thigh and hip were touching hers—and there was nothing she could do about it. And she had thought two days ago when they were walking back to Barclay Court from Hareford House that she had never felt more uncomfortable in her life! She had known nothing then about discomfort.

He gave the horses the signal to start, the curricle swung into motion, and her hand took a death grip on the rail beside it. For a few moments she could think of nothing but her own safety—or lack thereof.

"I will not let you fall," he said as they moved from the terrace onto the lane. "And I will not spring the horses—unless you ask me to do so, that is."

Ask him to . . .

She laughed and turned her head toward him. He

looked back, and she felt all the shock of discovering that their faces were only inches apart.

"Laughter, Miss Osbourne?" he said, raising his eyebrows. "You are not *enjoying* the ride by any chance, are you?"

She was *terrified*. Her toes were curled up inside her shoes, her hand was still gripping the rail hard enough—or so it seemed—to put five dents in the metal, and every muscle in her body was clenched. The hedgerows rushed past them somewhere below her line of vision, the little clouds dashed by overhead, the horses trotted eagerly down the lane, their chestnut coats gleaming in the sunshine, the seat swung effortlessly on its springs. She was . . .

She laughed again.

"This is *wonderful*!" she cried.

Then, of course, she felt terribly foolish. How gauche of her! She was behaving like a child being given a rare treat. And yet she did not *feel* like a child as she became aware again of his thigh and shoulder brushing against hers.

His laughter mingled with her own.

He had caused her a largely sleepless night, she recalled. She had dreaded this afternoon and the thought of being alone with him again. What would she talk about? She had no wish to talk with Viscount Whitleaf of all people. Even apart from the name he bore she had decided on her first acquaintance with him—on her first *sight* of him—that he was shallow and frivolous. And yet she had not been able to forget that he had been sitting with Miss Honeydew when most of the other young people had avoided her all evening whenever they could do so without appearing ill-mannered. And that he had made her laugh with that foolish but surely kindly-meant flattery about an old lady. And he had voluntarily doomed himself to the tedium of an afternoon at Miss Honeydew's cottage. He had not—as Susanna had led Frances to believe—been trapped into offering her a ride in his curricle. He might easily have avoided doing so.

"You certainly enjoyed yourself with all the young ladies last evening," she said. "They would have been perfectly happy if there had been no other gentlemen present."

"I did," he admitted, turning the curricle onto the fork of the lane that led directly to the village with hands that looked very skilled indeed on the ribbons. "Enjoy myself, that is. It is a pleasure, you know, to listen to young ladies chatter and to turn the pages of their music when one knows that doing so makes them happy. But your barbed tongue was at work again, was it not? *Would* they have been happy with only me? I doubt it. Miss Calvert would not have been happy if Finn had not been there. Perhaps you did not notice that she spent some time in his company? And Miss Krebbs was very happy indeed when Moss asked her to reserve a set for him at the assembly—so happy that she allowed him to fill a plate for her at supper and sit beside her. Miss Jane Calvert would have spent a less enjoyable evening if she had not had the Reverend Birney in her sights for most of the time. And you would have sat all alone for an hour if Dannen had not been there."

"Mr. Dannen was the *host*," she protested. "Besides, I was not talking of myself."

"And as a final word in my defense," he said, "it might be pointed out that all the gentlemen had an equal opportunity to gather at the pianoforte and turn pages of music."

She could not think of an answer to that one.

"Is this a *racing* curricle?" she asked.

"The thing is, you see," he said, "that no self-respecting gentleman below the age of thirty would want to purchase for himself a curricle that could *not* race."

"And I suppose," she said, "you *do* race in it?"

"Now what would be the point," he asked her, "in owning a racing curricle if all one did with it was crawl about country lanes as I am doing now?"

"Is this *crawling*?" she asked. She had been finding the speed exhilarating and had been feeling very daring indeed.

"My poor chestnuts," he said, "will never forgive me for the indignity of this journey."

She laughed.

He turned his head again to smile down at her.

"What?" he said. "I am not about to find myself at the receiving end of a lecture about the danger of risking my neck and those of my horses by dashing fruitlessly along the king's highway merely for the sake of winning a race? The last one, by the way, was from London to Brighton, and honesty forces me to confess that I lost it by a longish nose."

"Why should it concern me," she asked him, "if you risk your neck?"

"Now that, Miss Osbourne," he said, "was unkind."

"I suppose," she said wistfully, "it is the most glorious feeling in the world to fly along as fast as your horses can gallop."

Or simply to fly. She had a recurring dream in which she was a bird, free to soar into the blue and ride the wind.

"I have a curious suspicion," he said, "that my first impressions of you were quite, quite inaccurate, Miss Osbourne."

His words jolted her into a realization that she had actually been *talking* with him—and even rather enjoying herself. And already they were passing through the village. They were halfway to Miss Honeydew's cottage.

"Your silence speaks loudly and accusingly," he said as he touched his whip to the brim of his hat and she raised her free hand to wave to Mr. Calvert, who was walking along the village street in the direction of his home. "Obviously you believe that your first impressions of me *were* accurate."

Did she? He enjoyed spending his time flirting with young ladies. He owned a racing curricle and had raced it all the way from London to Brighton. She had seen nothing that suggested there was any substance to his character—though he *had* sat with Miss Honeydew last evening and been kind to her.

"You still dislike me," he said with a sigh, though it seemed to her that he was amused rather than upset in any way.

"I do not—" she began.

"Ah, but I believe you do," he said. "Do you not teach your pupils that it is wicked to lie? Is it something about my looks?"

"You know very well," she said sharply, "that your looks are perfect."

It was only after the words were out that she wished, wished, *wished* that she could recall them. Goodness, she must sound like a besotted schoolgirl.

"Oh, I say," he said, laughing, "is that true? My eye color is not effeminate?"

"You know very well it is not," she said indignantly. How had the conversation suddenly taken this uncomfortably personal turn?

"I have a cousin," he told her, "who has the same color eyes. I have always thought they look so much more appropriate on her."

"I would not know," she said, "since I do not know the lady."

"It is not my looks, then," he said, "unless you happen to have a bias against perfection. There would be little logic in that, though. It must be my character, then."

"I do not dislike you," she protested. "There is nothing I find objectionable about your character— except that you do not take anything seriously."

"That," he said, "is very akin to those annoying pronouncements with which certain people preface nasty remarks: 'I do not wish to be critical, old chap, but . . .' Ah, the condemnation in that *but*. And in your *except that*. You think me a shallow man, then."

The words had not been phrased as a question, but he was waiting for an answer. Well, she was not going to deny it merely because good manners suggested that she ought. He *had* asked.

"Yes, my lord," she said, gazing along the road and wondering when Miss Honeydew's cottage would come into view. "I do."

"I suppose," he said, "you would not believe me if I told you I sometimes entertain a serious thought or two and that I am not entirely shallow?"

She hesitated.

"It would be presumptuous of me to call you a liar," she said.

"Why?" He had dipped his head even closer to hers so that for a moment before he returned his attention to the road she could feel his breath on her cheek.

"Because I do not know you," she said.

"Ah," he said. "What would you say, Miss Osbourne, if I told you that despite my admission of a moment ago, I still think you beautiful beyond belief but also harsh in your judgments and without feelings, incapable of deep affection or love?"

She bristled.

"I would say that you know *nothing* about me or my life," she said, trying in vain to move farther to her side of the seat.

"Precisely," he said, a note of satisfaction in his voice. "We do not know each other at all, do we? How do you know that I am not worth knowing? How do I know that you *are*?"

She gripped the rail beside her more tightly.

"But surely," she said, "we have no wish to know each other anyway. And so the answers to your questions do not matter."

"But they do to me," he said. "I certainly wish to know who Miss Susanna Osbourne is. I very much wish it, especially after discovering the surprising fact that she would love to race to Brighton in a curricle. *That* I would not have guessed about you in a thousand years."

"I would not—" she began.

"Too late," he said. "You have already admitted it in so many words. I have a strong suspicion that you might be interesting to know. And I feel the need to be known, to justify my existence to someone who believes me to be worthless."

"That is not what I said!" she cried. "I would never say such a thing to anyone. But do you feel such a need with all the ladies you meet? Do you feel the need to know and make yourself known to the Misses Calvert and Miss Krebbs and Miss Raycroft?"

"Good Lord, no," he said, and laughed.

"Why me, then?" she asked, turning her head to frown at him. "Only because I do not respond to your flatteries as other women do?"

"That is a possibility, I suppose," he admitted. "But I hope there is another. There is a gravity about you when you are not laughing at the danger and exhilaration of riding in a curricle. I suspect that— horror of horrors—it stems from superior intelligence. *Are* you an intelligent woman, Miss Osbourne?"

"How am I to answer that?" she asked him in further exasperation.

"It is one of the things I need to discover about you," he said. "The Countess of Edgecombe has invited you here out of friendship, not obligation—or so

I have been led to believe. The countess is a woman of intelligence. I would imagine that her friends must be intelligent too. And of course you are a teacher and must have an impressive store of knowledge rattling around in your brain. But I need to discover for myself if I am right."

She was speechless. And the reality of the situation suddenly hit her. It must *be* reality—none of her muddled and troubled dreams last night had conjured quite this scenario. Here she was talking quite freely with *Viscount Whitleaf* of all people and actually rather enjoying herself.

"Do you think, Miss Osbourne," he asked her, "we could be friends if we tried very hard? *Shall* we try?"

She stared at his face in profile. But she could see no mockery there.

"It is not possible, even if you are serious," she said. "We are from different worlds—almost from different universes. Besides, men and women do not become friends with each other even if they are of the same world."

"You had better not tell Edgecombe or the countess that," he said, raising his eyebrows. "Nevertheless, I might have agreed with you until yesterday. I am not in the habit of making friends of any of the women I have known. But you refuse to allow me to flirt with you, you see, and so you leave me with no alternative but to befriend you."

"Or to ignore me," she said sharply.

"That is not an option," he told her, and he grinned.

"This is absurd," she said. "Utterly absurd."

"Then humor me," he said. "Will you? Will you allow me to try to be your friend even if you will not be mine? I really do not think I can wax eloquent about the weather alone for twelve more days."

She laughed unexpectedly. At the same moment she was aware that the curricle had slowed and looked up in some surprise to see that they had arrived at Miss Honeydew's cottage.

"Ah." He turned his head to look intently at her. "This is better. You are laughing again. I have been leading up—again—to asking you what it is about teaching that you so love. But—yet again—our arrival at a destination has thwarted me. You will give me the answer, if you please, during the return journey."

"Lord Whitleaf," she said as he jumped down from his seat and looped the ribbons over the top bar of a painted white fence that surrounded the garden, "you can have no possible interest in my teaching career."

He raised both arms and lifted her to the ground before she could think of looking for safe foot- and handholds. He made her feel as if she weighed no more than a feather. He also made her feel as if she were running a slight fever.

"And you, Miss Osbourne," he said, keeping his hands on either side of her waist, "can have no idea what would interest me. Can you?"

He waited for her answer.

"No," she admitted.

He grinned at her and released her.

They both turned to greet Miss Honeydew, who

had come to the front door to hail them. She was dressed in what was very obviously her Sunday best, and she was glowing with happiness.

Susanna was terribly afraid that Frances might be wrong after all. She was terribly afraid that Viscount Whitleaf might be very dangerous indeed.

5

After the first flurry of greetings was over—they must have lasted a good fifteen minutes, by Peter's estimation—he went back outside to tend his curricle and his horses. Then, having discovered several loose boards in the fence but no handyman on the premises, he went in search of a hammer and nails, found them in the stable that doubled as a garden shed, left his coat there, and made the repairs himself despite the fact that the housekeeper gawked at him as if he were the unfortunate possessor of two heads when she came to the door to see what was creating the noise.

And then, because a scruffy little terrier dog had barked incessantly at him since his arrival and danced about him and even attempted to nip his wrists and ankles until informed that it would do so at its own peril, he decided that the animal needed more exercise than a prowl about the garden provided. He found an old leather leash in the shed, brushed it free of cobwebs, attached it to the dog, and took it for a brisk walk along some narrow country lanes until, on the way back to the cottage, he removed the leash so that it could dash about in all directions, beside itself with exuberant glee at discovering such wide open spaces and the freedom to explore them.

The stable, which had been built to accommodate three horses and a small carriage, would only just take his two horses. The curricle had to remain outside. Peter set about tidying the area and creating more space. And then, because the new space looked as if it had not seen either a broom or a pail of water in some time, he gave it both before spreading some fresh, clean-smelling straw, which he had found piled up behind the building.

By the time he entered the house by the kitchen door, he was feeling grubby and sweaty and really rather pleased with life. This was turning into the most pleasant afternoon he had spent since coming to Hareford House.

He washed his hands and his arms up to the elbows in water the flustered housekeeper poured for him, rolled down his shirtsleeves, and shrugged back into his coat—not an easy task without the assistance of his valet—and stepped into the sitting room, where Miss Osbourne was reading aloud but quietly while Miss Honeydew sat in a chair nearby, her head resting against the cushioned back, her eyes closed, her cap askew, her mouth wide open, snoring softly.

His eyes met Miss Osbourne's.

He stepped back out into the corridor, cleared his throat, scuffed his boots on the wood floor, called out a second, more effusive thank-you to the housekeeper for the water, and reappeared in the doorway.

Miss Osbourne was closing the book and Miss

Honeydew was sitting erect and wide awake. She was straightening her cap and beaming with happiness.

"What a wonderful reading voice you have for sure, Miss Osbourne," she said. "I could listen to you all day long. And how splendid to have *two* young persons come to tea. I do hope the afternoon has not been a tedious one for you, Lord Whitleaf, though I daresay it has. I cannot tell you how much your kindness and Miss Osbourne's has meant to me. You must both be ready for your tea."

"It has not been a tedious afternoon by any means, ma'am," he said, seating himself. "I was thinking to myself only a few moments ago that I have enjoyed this afternoon more than any other since I came into Somerset."

"Oh, what a rascal you are!" Miss Honeydew clapped her hands with glee and laughed heartily.

Susanna Osbourne looked back at him reproachfully.

"You will surely fry for your sins," she told him an hour later after they had waved good-bye to Miss Honeydew in the doorway of her cottage and were on their way back to Barclay Court. "The most enjoyable afternoon of your stay here indeed! I *heard* you hammering at the fence, and the housekeeper came and whispered to me that you were cleaning out the stable and wanted to know what she ought to do about it."

"I took the mutt for a run too," he said with a chuckle. "I thought its yapping might well drive you insane."

"Why did you *do* it all?" she asked, sounding rather cross.

"Because I cannot stand being idle?" he said. "But no, you would not believe that, would you? You believe me to be nothing *but* idle. Perhaps I wished to impress you."

"And you flattered Miss Honeydew without ceasing for almost an hour," she said. "She was delighted even though she did not believe a word you said. She will doubtless live on the memory for days or weeks to come."

"Is there anything wrong with that?" he asked her. "She is lonely, is she not?"

"There is *nothing* wrong with it," she said, still sounding cross. "You are kind. You are *very* kind."

Ah, she was cross because she had been proved at least partly wrong about him, was she?

"But frivolous and idle too," he said, realizing suddenly that the elusive perfume he had tried to identify all the way to the cottage was not perfume at all but soap. It was very enticing nevertheless. So were the soft warmth of her thigh and her arm.

She did not reply and he chuckled.

"It is quite unsporting of you not to contradict me, Miss Osbourne," he said. "Shall we use the return journey to discover if there is anything about each other that might make it possible for us to be friends?"

"Or impossible," she said.

"I perceive," he said, "that you are of the half-empty-glass school of thought, Miss Osbourne, while I am of the half-full school."

"Then we are quite incompatible," she said.

"Not necessarily so," he said. "Some differences of opinion will provide us with topics upon which to hold a lively debate. There is nothing more dull than two people who are so totally in agreement with each other upon every subject under the sun that there really is nothing left worth saying."

But why the devil it had popped into his head earlier and even last evening that he wanted her as a *friend*, he had no idea. Except that he knew he could not make her into a flirt, perhaps. She would not allow it—and neither would he. He would flirt with his social equals, with those who knew the rules of the game. He would not flirt with an indigent schoolteacher—she had been a charity pupil at the school where she now taught, for the love of God—whom he might inadvertently hurt.

But he could not simply ignore her. Good Lord, what was it he had thought two days ago when he first set eyes on her?

There she is.

The words still puzzled him and made him strangely uneasy.

It would be a novel challenge to try again to make a friend of a young woman—one who did not particularly like him and one who claimed that they were closer to being universes apart than worlds.

Well, challenges were meant to brighten the dull routine of life.

Not that routine was always dull. Sometimes he longed for it. It was what he had grown up with and expected of the rest of his life—a quiet routine, a fulfillment of duty that was self-imposed rather than enforced from above as it had been all through his boyhood. He had expected very little of his life really—only a sort of heaven of home and hearth and domestic contentment. Most of his current friends would cringe if they knew that of him. Even Raycroft, his closest friend, would be astonished.

"Tell me what you like so much about teaching," he said.

He felt rather than saw her smile.

"It is something I am capable of doing well," she said, "and something I can constantly work upon to improve. It is something useful and worthwhile."

"Educating girls is worthwhile?" he asked only because he guessed the question would provoke her into saying more.

"Girls have minds just as boys do," she said firmly, "and are just as hungry for knowledge and just as capable of learning and understanding. It is true that most of them grow up to lives in which they do not need to know very much at all, but then I suspect that holds true of most men too."

"Like me?" he asked.

"I believe there is a saying," she said tartly, "that if the shoe fits one ought to wear it."

He chuckled softly.

"But most men would argue," he said, "that educating girls gives them brain fever at worst and makes them unattractive at best. Or perhaps I have got the worst and the best mixed up."

"I daresay," she said, "those men are insecure in their masculinity and fear that women may outshine them. How mortifying it would be if they had to ask a woman for the square root of eighty-one."

She was a delight. He had already seen several different facets of her character, but he could always rely upon the prim schoolteacher to keep making an appearance. The square root of eighty-one, indeed!

"Ouch!" he said, wincing noticeably. "But would there ever be such an occasion? I cannot for the life of me think of one. What *is* the square root of eighty-one anyway?"

"Nine," they said in unison.

He laughed, and after a brief moment so did she.

He wondered if she realized what a dazzling combination laughter was with her looks. He wondered too how often she laughed. Perhaps it was more often than he had suspected the day before yesterday. Perhaps she brought light and joy to that school in Bath.

"But that is *not* your cue," he said, deliberately sobering, "to fire all sorts of obscure and tricky questions at me. My masculinity is a fragile enough commodity without being put to that sort of test."

"I doubt that," she said fervently, and then laughed again when he looked at her sidelong and pulled an abject face.

He chuckled once more before turning into the lane from the village that would eventually bring them to the fork into Barclay Court. "And in case you are neglecting to ask for fear of the answer, Miss Osbourne, I detect no signs of brain fever in you, and you are certainly not unattractive. Quite the contrary, in fact."

"I would rather," she said after a brief silence, "that you not try to flatter and flirt with me. You must speak sensibly with me if we are to be friends."

"We *are* to be friends, then?" he asked her. "Very well. Let me be honest. You are quite devoid of any discernible attraction. A small, slender stature combined with shining auburn curls and sea green eyes and regular features is all quite unappealing, as I am sure you must be aware."

When he turned his head to snatch a look at her, she was smiling broadly and looking straight ahead.

"Friends need not be unaware of each other's attractions," he said. "Tell me how you occupy your time when you are not teaching."

"You do not know much about the world of employment, do you, Lord Whitleaf?" she asked. "There is not much time that is *not* taken up with work. When I am not in the classroom I am supervising games in the meadow beyond the school or organizing dramatic presentations or watching over the girls during study sessions or marking papers or examinations or . . . Well, there is almost always something to do. But when there *is* some leisure time, usually late in the evening, I spend it with my friends, the other resident teachers. We usually gather in Claudia Martin's sitting room. Or sometimes if it is daytime and there is the rare luxury of a spare hour I go out walking. Bath is a lovely city. There is much to see there."

Ah, yes, they were from different universes. But he admired her sense of purpose.

"Now it is your turn," she said. "You must tell me something of yourself."

"Are you sure you really wish to know about my idle, empty life?" he asked her, his eyes twinkling.

"You were the one who thought there could be a friendship between us," she reminded him. "There can be no friendship if only one party gets to ask the questions. Tell me about your childhood."

"Hmm." He gave the matter some thought. "It was filled with women—a familiar pattern with me, Miss Osbourne. My father died when I was three years old. I have no memory of him, alas. I do think it unsporting of him not to have waited at least another two or three years. I was left with my mother and five elder sisters. I daresay my parents had despaired of producing an heir and were jubilant when I finally put in an appearance. By that time my sisters too must have been aware that a family without an heir was a family headed for certain disaster. And indeed I came along only just in time to avert it. I was the apple of every female eye as I grew up. I could do no wrong in their sight. I was petted and cosseted and adored. No boy was ever more fortunate than I."

She had turned her head and was looking steadily at him.

"There was no man in your life, then?" she asked.

"Oh, several," he said. "There were official guardians and self-appointed guardians, all of whom ruled my estate and my fortune and me and arranged everything from my education to the reading and answering of my mail. It was all done for my benefit, of course. I was very fortunate."

"I suppose," she said, "they did no more than your father would have done if he had lived."

"Except that then there would have been a relationship," he said. "Perhaps there would have been some sharing. Some love."

He was turning at the fork in the lane as he spoke. Perhaps he would not have spoken so unguardedly if he had not been thus occupied. Good Lord, he did not usually even *think* such abject thoughts. He felt quite embarrassed.

"You missed your father," she said softly.

He glanced down at her. "You cannot miss what you never had, Miss Osbourne," he said. "I do not even remember him."

"I missed my mother," she told him. "Yet she died giving birth to me."

Ah.

"It is odd, is it not," he said, "to miss people one never knew—or knew so far back that there is no conscious memory left. I was inundated with love from my mother and sisters, and yet perversely I wanted a father's love. Did your father love you?"

"Oh, yes," she said, "but I ached for my mother. I used to weave dreams about her. I could always picture her arms reaching out to me, and I could always hear her voice and smell roses when she was near. But I never could see her face. Is that not strange? Sometimes even the imagination lets one down. How foolish!"

She looked away and fell silent, and it seemed to him that she was suddenly as embarrassed as he had been a couple of minutes ago at making such an admission about the child she had been.

Neither of them said any more on the subject— they were approaching Barclay Court, and Edgecombe and the countess were walking across the lawn before the house to meet them.

But something subtle had changed between them, he sensed.

Perhaps everything.

They had shared something of themselves with

each other and he would never be able to return to a relationship of simple banter with her. They had, in other words, taken a step toward friendship with each other—as he had wanted. And yet the realization was slightly unsettling. Banter was safer. So was flirtation.

"Miss Osbourne," he said as he drew the curricle to a halt just before the others came up to them, "*is* it possible for us to be friends, do you think?"

"But we are to be here for only twelve more days," she said.

"You brought her back in one piece, I see, Whitleaf," Edgecombe said, striding up to the vehicle and reaching up a hand to help her down. "Congratulations. Frances would have been upset with you if you had not."

"And you are not looking nearly as frightened as you were when you left here, Susanna," the countess said. "Did you enjoy the ride? And your visit?"

Peter declined their invitation to go inside the house for refreshments. He would be expected back at Hareford House, he told them, and left after bidding them all a collective farewell.

This time, he noticed, Susanna Osbourne did not hurry into the house without a backward glance. She stood with the other two to watch him on his way.

He had also noticed she had not said that it was impossible for them to be friends.

Or that it would be possible either.

It struck him as he drove away that perhaps it would be better if she *had* protested. He was not at all sure that friendship was safe.

• • •

It was a surprise to Susanna to discover that she had actually enjoyed the afternoon—not just the part of it she had spent with Miss Honeydew, but all of it.

She was even more surprised to discover that she actually rather liked Viscount Whitleaf. He might be a basically shallow man who liked nothing better than to flirt with every woman he set eyes upon, but he also had a good sense of humor. More important, he was definitely a kind man—and not totally indolent either. He had actually mended Miss Honeydew's fence and cleaned out her old stable. He had taken her bad-tempered little dog for a walk. He had been careful not to embarrass her when he had discovered her asleep in her chair while Susanna was still reading to her. And then, at her urging, he had eaten three of the cakes she called her housekeeper's specialty even though it must have been clear to him after the first bite that they were undercooked and doughy at the center.

She had discovered when she had found herself quite unable to resist asking him about his childhood, just as if she knew nothing at all about it, that indeed he had been cosseted by his mother and all his sisters and ruled by his male guardians. He could not be blamed in any way, then, for what had happened to her father. And she could not blame him simply for having the name *Whitleaf*.

But despite the softening of her attitude toward him, Susanna could not see any possibility of their becoming friends. It was an absurd idea. They had nothing whatsoever in common.

And yet the idea had a certain appeal. She had never had a male friend. Mr. Huckerby and Mr. Upton, the art master, were not quite friends, though they were colleagues with whom she shared a mutual respect. And Mr. Keeble was just a friendly acquaintance, a sort of father figure as he guarded the door of the school from every imaginable or imaginary wolf.

In the coming days she saw further evidence of Lord Whitleaf's kindness. After dinner at the Raycrofts' one evening, he offered to take the one empty place at a card table that no one else seemed eager to fill even though he knew that his partner was to be old Mrs. Moss, who was deaf and indecisive and invariably played the wrong card when she *did* make a decision. And though the two of them lost all five of the hands they played, he succeeded in keeping everyone at the table amused and in convincing Mrs. Moss that it was his clumsy play that had ensured their defeat.

And when, after church on Sunday, Susanna overheard the vicar greet Miss Honeydew and tell her how gratifying it was to see her at church despite the rain that had been falling earlier, she also heard Miss Honeydew tell him that Viscount Whitleaf had brought a closed carriage to her cottage early enough that she had had time to get ready to come.

The Earl of Edgecombe told Frances and Susanna after he had taken Mr. Raycroft and the viscount on a tour of the home farm one morning that when they had passed the laborers' cottages and he had stopped to call upon one of his men who had cut his hand rather badly the week before, the viscount had wandered off to talk with some of the wives who were outside their homes pegging out their washing, it being Monday and therefore laundry day. He had been discovered half an hour later, without his coat or hat, perched on a ladder held by one woman and two children and making an adjustment to a line that dragged too close to the ground when weighed down by wet clothes. All the neighborhood women and children had been gathered around, calling up advice.

"And of course," the earl added, chuckling, "they were all gazing worshipfully up at him too—when he did not have them all doubled up with laughter, that was."

And he did not forget that he wanted to be Susanna's friend.

She saw him every day. They never spent longer than half an hour alone together at a time—he was too discreet for that, and if he had not been, she would. She certainly did not want to arouse any gossip in the neighborhood. Nor did she want to make Frances uneasy. But almost always when they met he contrived to exchange a few private words with her or to take her apart from the company for a short while.

She came to look forward to those brief interludes as the highlight of her days.

After playing cards with Mrs. Moss at the Raycrofts' dinner, for example, he approached Susanna, asked if he could fetch her a cup of tea, and when she said yes, told her that perhaps she ought to come with him if Dannen would excuse her so that he would be sure to add just the right amount of milk and sugar.

She had been seated beside Mr. Dannen for all of

an hour, listening to stories about his Scottish ancestors, some of which she had heard before.

"You were beginning to look cross-eyed with boredom," Viscount Whitleaf told her.

"Oh, I was not!" she protested indignantly. "I
would not be so ill-mannered."

"But it is interesting to note," he said, "that you do
not deny that you *were* bored. Anyway, I have rescued
you. What are friends for?"

She laughed, and they stood talking to each other
for a while beside the tea tray until Mr. Crossley and
Miss Krebbs joined them.

One afternoon he rode over to Barclay Court with
Miss Raycroft and her brother, and the three of them
stayed for tea. But when Mr. Raycroft rose to leave,
his sister protested that she wanted to see some water-
colors of Vienna the countess had brought back from
Europe and promised to show her since Vienna was
where Alice Hickmore was spending the winter. Mr.
Raycroft sat down again to continue his conversation
with the earl, Frances took Miss Raycroft up to her
room, and Viscount Whitleaf invited Susanna to stroll
out on the terrace with him until his companions were
ready to leave. He told her—at her prompting—about
his years at Oxford, where he had studied the classics.
It seemed from what he said that he actually *had* studied, not merely used the years away from home to kick
up his heels and enjoy life.

Her opinion of him took another turn for the
better.

The next day was chilly and blustery, but Susanna
and Frances decided to walk into the village anyway

for fresh air and exercise and for Frances to deliver a basket of food to a former housekeeper at Barclay Court who had celebrated her eightieth birthday the month before when Frances and the earl were still away. Susanna wanted to buy some new ribbon to trim the old gown she would wear to the assembly.

She explained that to Viscount Whitleaf, whom they met as he was striding along the village street after escorting two of the Calvert sisters home from Hareford House, and at his suggestion Frances proceeded on her way to deliver her basket while he escorted Susanna to the village shop, where she made her purchase before being taken to the village inn to be treated to a glass of lemonade and a pastry.

And then he offered to escort them both back to Barclay Court, insisting when Frances protested that he could never deny himself the pleasure of having a lady for each arm as he walked—and that he hoped *she* would not deny him that pleasure.

"Far be it from me to cause you any such misery," Frances said with a laugh, taking one of his arms while Susanna took the other. "And thank you."

He talked about music with Frances, skillfully drawing Susanna in too. He had, she realized, considerable conversational skills when he chose to use them. And considerable knowledge too.

If Susanna felt some small disappointment in the friendship, it was in the fact that Viscount Whitleaf had not solicited her hand for any of the sets at the assembly, which was fast approaching. He was, of course, engaged to dance at least the first four sets—

she remembered that from the day they had met. Perhaps he had promised all the others too.

Or perhaps friends did not feel the need to dance with each other.

No one had yet reserved any sets with her. She was almost sure, of course, that the earl would dance with her, and probably Mr. Raycroft too. Perhaps even Mr. Dannen. But how lovely it would be—what a crowning delight—to dance with Viscount Whitleaf. It would be something to tell her friends about, something to relive in memory all the rest of her life. And if it happened also to be the waltz . . .

But she would not dwell upon that slight disappointment. Already this was turning into a holiday that would buoy her spirits all through the autumn term at school. She must not be greedy.

Perhaps he would ask her when the evening came.

Or perhaps, if he had no free sets, he would at least find some time to come and talk with her so that she would feel less of a wallflower.

It did not matter. She had a *gentleman friend*. What startling stories she would have to share with Claudia and Anne when she returned to Bath.

In the meantime, the holiday was still not at an end.

6

*The whole neighborhood had been invited to an af-*ternoon picnic at Barclay Court, and fortunately the good weather had returned for the occasion after a few days of clouds and winds and chill.

Peter was greatly enjoying himself despite memories of an affectionate, subtly reproachful letter that morning from his mother, whose house party was proceeding without him. If he were there at Sidley Park now, he thought, he would very possibly be attending just exactly the same type of event as he was here. Except that there he would know that one in particular of the young ladies present had been selected as a potential bride for him—Miss Rose Larchwell. And he would know that his mother's fond, anxious eyes were following him wherever he went. There he would feel all the burden of being loved dearly by someone he had forgiven, though he had not forgotten.

Perhaps it would have been better *not* to have forgiven, or at least to have forgiven conditionally. Perhaps he ought to have made it crystal clear to her that he would not accept any further interference in his life, especially as a matchmaker. Perhaps he ought to have told her that Sidley could no longer be her home. But she had been so brokenhearted—for him as well as for herself. And he had been only twenty-one. Besides all of which, he had *loved* her and still did. She was his mother.

And so she seemed to feel it was her mission in life to atone, to find him a bride in place of the one she had lost for him.

He shook off the thought of what might be proceeding at Sidley and concentrated on what was happening at Barclay Court. Here he could relax and enjoy himself with whomever he chose—or with whoever chose him.

The picnic site was a wide, grassy bank close to the narrower end of a large lake, at some remove from the house. There was a picturesque three-arched stone bridge spanning its banks nearby. The waters from a river flowed rather swiftly beneath it into the lake. From the center of the bridge, where he stood for a while early in the afternoon with Miss Raycroft, Miss Mary Calvert, and Miss Krebbs, he could see that the swiftness of the water was caused by a waterfall farther back along the river among the trees. He gazed appreciatively at the scene while they chattered about the upcoming assembly.

Partway along the bank on the far side of the lake there was a pretty octagonal wooden pavilion. He walked there a little later with Finn, Miss Calvert, Miss Jane Calvert, and Miss Moss and her brother. They sat inside the structure for a while admiring the view, talking merrily, and laughing a great deal.

Most of the conversation there too concerned the assembly, to which they were all looking forward with eager anticipation. It was the first, apparently, since last Christmas.

After they had returned to the picnic site, Peter sat for a while on one of the blankets that had been spread for the convenience of the guests, conversing with the Countess of Edgecombe and a few of her older neighbors. In answer to their questions she told them something of her recent singing tour of Europe.

The sky was blue and cloudless, the sun warm without being oppressively hot. There was a very light breeze. It was a perfect summer day.

The boats were proving popular. There were four of them, each designed for no more than two persons, one rower and one passenger, though Peter found himself with two ladies squeezed onto the seat facing him every time he was at the oars. He made no complaint. Why should he when there was a pair of ladies to admire each time instead of one? In their flimsy summer finery and bonnets, they all looked good enough to eat. And they were all clearly enjoying the rare treat of a lovely summer day coinciding for once with an outdoor social event.

"The last time we were invited to a picnic," Miss Mary Calvert said, trailing one hand in the water, "it rained cats and dogs all day and all night. Do you remember, Rosamond? It was for the retirement of the old vicar and we all had to be crammed into the vicarage and pretend that we were not hugely disappointed."

Peter did not speak with Susanna Osbourne for all

of the first hour or so. Each day since their visit to Miss Honeydew's he had found himself looking forward to spending some time with her, but each day he had felt the necessity of having to keep their encounters short since he could not simply include her in the crowd of young ladies who often hung about him for long spells at a time—she would not have appreciated the frivolity of the group conversation. Having an actual lady *friend* was a novel venture for him, but he was very aware that his interest in her might be misconstrued by others if he was not careful. And so he *was* careful never to single her out immediately at any entertainment, and even when he did, to spend no more than half an hour with her.

Earlier in the afternoon he had bowed to her on the terrace when he arrived, made some deliberately bland observation about the weather just to see the light of amusement in her eyes, and turned his attention elsewhere. And then he had proceeded to enjoy himself—as had she.

The Reverend Birney, the fair-haired, fresh-faced young vicar, took her for a row on the lake and engaged her in earnest conversation the whole time—Peter watched them.

Dannen, that prize bore, took her walking along the near bank with Raycroft and the countess. And then he kept her standing close to the water for all of fifteen minutes after the other two had returned to the picnic site. Peter knew because he timed what was obviously a monologue.

Crossley, a widower in his forties, fetched her a glass of lemonade on her return and sat with her for a while, pointing out features of the view with wide arm gestures. Peter knew because he watched.

It struck him suddenly that her own assessment of her marriage prospects was quite possibly overpessimistic. Poor and dowerless as she must be, she had not failed to catch the eye of almost every eligible bachelor in the neighborhood. But she was surely far too sensible to marry Dannen and too lively to consider Birney. And Crossley was too old for her—he could be her father, for God's sake.

In fact, the very thought of her marrying any of the present prospects made Peter quite unreasonably irritable. And he *was* being unreasonable. Surely any half-decent marriage was preferable to life as a spinster schoolteacher. At least, that was what he knew any of his sisters would tell him.

But even as he was wool-gathering with such thoughts and neglecting the ladies who chattered about him, someone suggested a game before tea, and a chorus of enthusiastic voices was raised with a dizzying variety of suggestions, which ranged from cricket to hide-and-seek. Cricket could not be played, however, unless someone dashed back to the house for all the necessary—and bulky—equipment. Besides, Miss Moss complained with the obvious support of most of the other ladies, cricket was really a man's game. And hide-and-seek was not practical, as the trees did not grow thickly on this side of the lake and there were very few other hiding places. All of the other suggestions were rejected too for one reason or another.

It seemed they were to proceed gameless to tea after all—until Miss Osbourne spoke up.

"How about boat races?" she suggested.

There was a swell of excited approval—and then the inevitable dissenting voice.

"But there are too few gentlemen to row all of us," Miss Jane Calvert pointed out. "Some of us would have to stand and watch."

The other ladies looked at her in dismay, all of them, it seemed, with mental visions of being among the excluded.

"But who is to say," Miss Osbourne asked, "that the men have to have all the fun? I was thinking of races in which *all* of us would row and none of us would be passengers."

"Oh, I say," Moss said, and laughed.

"That is the best idea I have heard yet, Susanna," the countess said.

Peter folded his arms and pursed his lips.

"But I have never rowed a boat," Miss Raycroft protested.

"Neither have I," Miss Krebs wailed. "I could not possibly . . ."

"We must think of something else, then," Miss Mary Calvert said.

But Miss Osbourne raised her voice again, more firmly than before.

"What?" She looked about at the circle of those who had gathered to choose a game, and it was immediately apparent to Peter's amused eye that she had forgotten herself and had slipped into an accustomed role of teacher rallying unenthusiastic pupils. "We are going to miss the chance of taking the oars ourselves and demonstrating that we are not just decorative ornaments who must always be passengers? We are not going to strive to beat the men?"

"Oh, I say," Moss said again, while Peter grinned and caught an identical expression on Edgecombe's face.

"*Beat* the *men*?" Miss Krebbs half shrieked again. She looked as if she were close to swooning.

A few of the other young ladies were giggling, but they looked definitely interested.

"There are only four boats," Miss Osbourne pointed out. "We will have to have elimination heats—across the lake to the pavilion and back again ought to be far enough. The ladies will compete against one another and the men against one another. At the end there will be a race between the winning man and the winning woman. *Then* we will see what sort of competition the lady will offer the gentleman."

She was flushed and bright-eyed and full of energy and enthusiasm—a born leader, Peter guessed, gazing at her, intrigued and not a little dazzled. And she was going to get her way too, by Jove. Despite the misgivings with which almost all the young ladies had greeted the initial suggestion—especially when they had known that they were not to be mere passengers in the boats—they were now fairly bouncing with eagerness to get the races under way.

"This is going to be the best picnic ever," Miss Mary Calvert declared with youthful hyperbole as she flashed Peter a bright smile.

Had Miss Osbourne told him she was the games teacher at school? He seemed to recall her saying something to that effect though he had not taken much notice at the time. A *games* teacher? *Was* there such a thing as a games teacher at a girls' school?

For the next hour there was far more bouncing up and down and cheering and squealing and laughing—and some good-natured derision—on the bank than there was great expertise shown in the water. A few of the races were close—Miss Calvert narrowly beat the countess, though Miss Moss and Miss Mary Calvert were left far behind, an outcome brought about by the twin facts that each of them moved in circles as much as they moved in a straight line and that neither of them could stop giggling. Raycroft beat Dannen by a nose, a come-from-behind victory that resulted from a final, impressive burst of speed while Finn and Moss were only a boat length or so back. A few of the races were runaways by the winner—Miss Osbourne in her heat, for example, Peter in his. She beat Miss Calvert in the runoff ladies' heat too, and he beat Edgecombe in the men's, though only by half a boat length.

And so everything came down to the final race and everyone without exception gathered on the bank even though the countess laughingly protested that they must all be half starved and would flatly refuse any further invitation to one of her entertainments. They would have tea, she promised, the moment a winner was determined.

"I daresay it will not be Miss Osbourne," Raycroft remarked cheerfully, but with a lamentable lack of either tact or gallantry.

Miss Raycroft punched him on the arm and the other ladies' voices were raised in collective indignation. Both Peter and Susanna Osbourne laughed. He grinned at her, and she looked back, bright-eyed and determined.

She looked absurdly small and fragile to be taking on such a challenge. And quite irresistibly attractive too, by Jove. There *was* something attractive about an athletic woman, he thought in some surprise.

The young ladies seemed uncertain whom they should champion. They solved the problem by clapping and jumping up and down and calling their encouragement indiscriminately to both contestants. Most of the older people were intent upon offering advice to Miss Osbourne, who was climbing into one of the boats with Edgecombe's assistance. Most of the other men were unashamedly partial.

"I say," Moss called, "you had better win, Whitleaf. It would be a ghastly humiliation to us all if you did not."

"You have the honor of our sex on your shoulders, Whitleaf," Crossley agreed.

"I think you had better not win, my lord," the Reverend Birney advised. "Gentlemanly gallantry and all that."

But his suggestion was met by a burst of derision from the men and a chorus of indignant protest from the ladies.

Susanna Osbourne took the oars and flexed her fingers about them.

Everyone stood back, Edgecombe told them to take their marks, there were some urgent shushing noises, and then they were off.

Peter grinned across at the other boat as soon as they had cleared the shore, but Miss Osbourne was concentrating upon setting her stroke. She had learned much during the past hour, he noticed. She had learned not to dip her oars too deeply into the water and thus impede her progress rather than help it. Now she was skimming along quite neatly with the minimum of effort. It was actually amazing what strength was in those small, fair-skinned arms. The brim of her straw bonnet fluttered in the breeze.

He had not told anyone—and Raycroft had not divulged his secret—that he had been a member of the rowing team at Oxford. Even against the men he had not put out his finest effort. Now he kept his boat just ahead of Miss Osbourne's as they approached the pavilion, the halfway mark. She maneuvered with only slight clumsiness as she turned her boat.

There was a great deal of noise proceeding from the opposite bank, he could hear.

Susanna Osbourne was laughing. She glanced across at him as she straightened out her boat for the return journey and he grinned back at her, pausing for a moment.

"If you dare to patronize me," she called to him, "by allowing me to win, I shall never forgive you."

"Allow you to win?" He raised his eyebrows and waggled them at her. "How would I ever live with the shame of losing to a woman?"

He settled in to rowing just ahead of her again while the screams from the bank became fevered. He turned his head to grin at her again when the race was almost over, intending to put on a spurt and leave her at least a boat length behind. But he turned at just the wrong moment. A sudden gust of a breeze caught his hat and tipped it crazily over one eye. He lifted a hand hastily to save it from the ignominious fate of being blown into the water and lost his oar instead.

Oh, it did not exactly slip all the way into the lake, but it did get caught at an awkward angle in the rowlock and had to be wrestled into place again. In the meanwhile his boat had veered slightly off course.

Susanna Osbourne had also planned a final burst of speed, he soon discovered, and they were close enough to the bank that he had insufficient time to catch up.

She won by a hair's breadth.

They were both laughing helplessly as she turned to look at him in triumph—and she looked so dazzlingly vital that he would have conceded a thousand victories to her if she had asked it of him. Though he had not actually conceded that one, had he? It had been an honest win, though he might have made it impossible, of course, by doing less dawdling and grinning along the way.

The female vote, he discovered, had deserted him utterly in favor of their own champion. The ladies bore her off in triumph to the blankets, where the picnic baskets awaited them.

"Shall I die of mortification now?" Peter asked, grinning at Edgecombe, who held the boat while he stepped out. "Or shall I eat first?"

"I think you had better die now, Whitleaf," Raycroft said. "Our sex will never live down the disgrace in this neighborhood, old chap. I would not be surprised if it makes the London papers and you will never be able to show your face there again."

"But you have made the ladies happy," Edgecombe said, slapping him on the shoulder, "and that is the best any man can ever hope for in this life. You had better come and eat or Frances will be offended."

"I must say," Crossley said, "that for such a small lady Miss Osbourne put on a jolly good show at the oars."

The young ladies had taken pity on Peter by the time he sat down for tea. A group of them sat with him and assured him that he would certainly have won the race if his hat had not almost blown off. But the mention of that inglorious moment sent them off into peals of merry laughter as they all tried to outdo one another in a description of just how he had looked when it happened.

He laughed with them.

Susanna Osbourne was seated on one of the other blankets. He could not hear her talking, but he was aware of her at every moment. And finally he could wait no longer. The boat race did not count as time alone together. And soon after tea the guests might begin to take their leave. He would be quite out of sorts if he missed his chance and had to go a whole day without a private conversation with her.

He got to his feet and smiled down at the young ladies before any of them could get up too.

"I had better go and eat humble pie before Miss Osbourne," he said.

She looked up as he approached her group, and smiled.

"Miss Osbourne," he said, "you must come and

walk with me, if you will, and allow me to congratulate you on your victory. I was soundly defeated."

He held out a hand for hers and helped her up.

"Thank you," she said, brushing the creases from her dress. "Yes, indeed you were."

She laughed as she took his offered arm.

And suddenly, it seemed to him, the pleasure of the afternoon was complete. The sky seemed bluer, the sun brighter, the air warmer.

It was too bad—it really was—that a friendship between a man and a woman could not be conducted at long distance. They would not be able to correspond with each other after they both left here—it would not be at all the thing. And there were only five days of the two weeks left. It was very unlikely they would ever see each other again after that.

Dash it, but he would be sorry to say good-bye to her.

However, five days were still five days and not four—had he not described himself to her as a man with a half-full-glass attitude to life? And there was the rest of this afternoon too. He did not believe anyone would remark too pointedly upon his spending half an hour alone with the woman who had beaten him at the boat race.

Yes, he would allow himself the luxury of half an hour today.

He led her off in the direction of the bridge.

Susanna had thoroughly enjoyed the picnic, espe-
cially the final boat race. She realized, of course, that
Viscount Whitleaf could have reached the finish line
long before she had even turned at the pavilion if he
had chosen, though she knew too that he had had no
intention of allowing her to win. The satisfaction of
actually doing so had been immense.

She had enjoyed every moment of the afternoon,
but, oh, she had to admit as she walked in the direction of the bridge, her hand drawn through the viscount's arm, that now her pleasure was complete.
Finally she was to spend a short while alone with her
new friend.

And she did indeed like him. There was always
laughter and gaiety wherever he happened to be. And
yet when he and she were together there was almost
always more than *just* laughter and gaiety. She felt
that she was getting to know him as a person and discovering that he was not nearly as shallow or self-
centered as she had thought at first. And she felt that

he was interested in *her* as a person and not just as another woman with a reasonably passable face.

There was magic, she thought, in discovering a new friendship in an utterly unexpected place.

"I suppose," she said, "this afternoon was not the first time you have rowed a boat."

"It was not," he admitted.

"Though I do not suppose," she said, "you were allowed to do it as a boy."

"How did you guess?" He grinned down at her. "Not when I was at home, at least. I did all sorts of things at school and university that had never been allowed at home, on the theory that what my mother and sisters did not see would not cause them grief."

She remembered how one of his sisters had pulled him away from the bank of the lake where he had been trying to fish with her line, horrified that he might fall in and die. An eager, active little boy had not even been allowed to sit at the water's edge with a fishing line in his hand.

"I cannot remember the last time I was vanquished in a boat race," he said as they stepped onto the bridge. "Accept my most heartfelt congratulations!"

She laughed. "Someone has to keep you humble."

"Unkind," he said. "I *did* admit to having lost a curricle race, if you will remember."

"By a long nose," she said. "I wonder how long. An elephant's trunk stretched on the rack, perhaps?"

"Sometimes," he said, "I believe that your tongue must be sharp enough to slice through a slab of tough beef."

She laughed again.

"And had *you* rowed before this afternoon?" he asked her. "Please say yes. My humiliation will be complete if the answer is no."

"A few times long ago, when I was a child," she said. "But I have not tried it since."

"And where was that?" he asked.

"Oh, where I grew up," she said vaguely.

They stopped by unspoken consent when they reached the middle of the bridge. She had crossed it before, on her last visit to Barclay Court, but there had been no opportunity this afternoon until now. The sun beamed down upon them from a cloudless blue sky. A slight breeze cooled her face. She could hear the river rushing beneath the bridge. If she turned her head she would see the sunlight sparkling on the lake water behind them.

All her senses were sharpened. She could feel his body heat. She could smell his cologne. It was an intensely pleasurable feeling. She felt awash in contentment.

"I noticed," he said, "when I sat inside the pavilion earlier that the reflection of the house is perfectly framed in the lake water. That particular spot was obviously chosen with great care by the landscape artist. He must have been a master of his art."

"Oh, yes," she agreed. "I am sure he was."

"Do you suppose that waterfall has been as artfully positioned as the pavilion?" he asked. "Is it there in that exact spot for maximum visual effect from here?"

"Perhaps it was the bridge that was deliberately placed," she suggested.

"Or both," he said. "My money is upon its being both."

"But can nature be so ordered?" she asked him.

"Assuredly so," he told her. "Do we not often plant flowers and vegetables in ruthlessly regimented rows and beds for our own convenience and pleasure? And can we not create a waterfall if we wish? We manipulate nature all the time. In fact, we often make the mistake of believing that we are its masters. And then a storm blows in from nowhere and lifts the roofs off our houses and floods them and reminds us of how little control we have and how helpless we are in reality. Have you noticed that once-mighty structures that have been abandoned are soon taken over by nature again? Wildflowers grow in the crevices of once-impregnable castle walls, and grass grows on palace floors where kings once entertained the elite of an empire."

"I find that thought reassuring more than frightening," she said. "I have heard of how ugly some parts of the country are becoming with the slag heaps from coal mines and other waste products of industry. I do not suppose those activities will end anytime soon. But when they do end—if they ever do—perhaps nature will reclaim the land and erase the man-made ugliness and create beauty again."

"I have an uneasy feeling," he said, "that if we continue to stand here, someone or other is going to feel invited to join us. I do not wish to be joined, do you?"

"No." She looked up at him, her cheeks warming at the admission.

"And if we walk toward the pavilion, the same

thing might happen," he said. "I can see that there is a path beside the river on the other side of the lake. My guess is that it goes as far as the waterfall."

"It does. And beyond," she told him. "It is part of the wilderness walk that begins close to the house and extends all about the lake. I have walked along parts of it with Frances, but I have never been to the waterfall. The path is rather rugged in that area and there had been a lot of rain just before I came here last time. The earl thought it might be unsafe."

He looked down at her thin shoes.

"Is it *too* rugged," he asked, "for someone who just won three separate boat races, including, to my eternal shame, the final one?"

"I have always thought," she said, "that the walk must be at its wildest and loveliest by the waterfall."

"We will walk there and back, then," he said, "and hope that no one else is adventurous enough to follow us."

She took his arm again, and they proceeded on their way.

Susanna wished as they walked that she could seal up every minute in a jar and take them all with her into the future. She did not believe she had ever been as happy as she was when they turned onto the river path and she could feel confident that they would be alone together for at least half an hour.

She could not think of anyone with whom she would rather share such beauty and solitude.

"Ah, magnificent!" Viscount Whitleaf said, stopping on the path when they were in the shade of a forest of tall trees and looking back to where the waters of the river bubbled and foamed beneath the bridge to join the calmer lake water, which was indeed sparkling in the sunshine.

He was genuinely admiring the scenery. It was something that just a week ago she would not have expected of him. She had judged him to be a man who could be happy only when surrounded by adoring females.

"I think Barclay Court must be one of the loveliest estates in England," she said. "Not that I have seen many others."

"Or any?" He turned his head and his eyes smiled at her.

"One other," she said, stung. "The place where I grew up."

He raised his eyebrows. "And where was that? You have never spoken of your childhood, have you—except that you missed your mother?"

"It does not matter," she said.

She wondered what he would say if she told him and he realized that they had once been neighbors of sorts. She wondered if he would have any memory at all of that day by the lake when he had visited with his mother and sisters and they had met briefly. And she wondered if he would remember everything that had happened later.

But a painful churning in her stomach warned her not to say any more—or *think* any more—about that.

"Now, Miss Osbourne," he said with mock severity, "one of the cardinal rules of friendship is that one withhold nothing from the friend."

"But that is not so," she told him. "Even friends

need private spaces, if only within the depths of their own soul, where no one else is allowed to intrude."

He was looking fully at her, obviously pondering the truth of what she said.

"There are deep, dark secrets from your past that you would rather keep, then, are there?" he said, waggling his eyebrows. "Very well, then. But you grew up on an estate, did you? As a daughter of the house?"

"As daughter of a . . . a servant of sorts," she said. "He was a gentleman, but he was without property or fortune and so had no choice but to work for a living. And so I suppose I am a lady by birth even if only just. Are you satisfied?"

He smiled slowly, and it struck her that the creases at the corners of his eyes would be permanently etched there when he was older. They would be an attractive feature.

"That I have not made a friend of a chimney sweep's offspring?" he asked her. "That would have been enough to send me off into a fit of the vapors, would it not? The path slopes upward rather sharply from here, I see, though there are several large, flat stones to act as steps. Are you sure you are up to the climb?"

"Are you?" She laughed at him.

"Earlier on," he said, "I thought I heard the echo of something you told me several days ago, though it might have been my imagination. You are not a *games* teacher, by any chance, are you, Miss Osbourne? In a *girls'* school?"

"I am," she said. "I teach games, and sometimes I cannot stop myself from participating in them. I was always good at them when I was a pupil myself. Yes, there *are* girls' schools that teach more than embroidery and deportment."

"Heaven help us," he said, wincing. "I was about to play the gallant and offer my hand for the climb instead of my arm. I will still do so, in fact. If I do not need to haul you up the path, *you* can haul *me*."

He took her hand in a firm clasp and she thought for one absurd moment that she might well weep. It seemed to her that no one had ever held her hand before, though surely her father must have done so when she was a child. There was such intimacy in the gesture, such an implied bond of trust.

His hand was slender and long-fingered. It was also strong and warm and somehow very masculine. Something tightened in her breasts, and her inner thighs suddenly ached though they had not even begun the climb yet. Something fluttered low in her abdomen.

She had, she admitted, grown very fond of him very fast. Belatedly it occurred to her that perhaps it had not been a good idea after all to agree to be his friend. Next week, when she was back in Bath, she was going to miss him, and she knew that the missing him would bring considerable pain, even grief.

But there was no point in thinking of that now. It was too late to make a different decision and keep her distance from him. And she was not sure she would have decided differently even if she had known then what she knew now. Her life had been so very sheltered. She must not regret walking out into the sunshine, even if only for a brief while.

And he *was* someone about whom the sun seemed to shine.

Hand in hand they clambered up the steep path even though it was not in any way treacherous and she did not really need his support—or he hers. They stood hand in hand and breathless when they stopped halfway up to look down over the steep bank to the fast-flowing water below. The dappled surface of the river and the lights and shades cast on the greenery by the sun shining through tree branches created a stark contrast with the bright, open, calm lake still fully visible off to their left.

The magic of it all assaulted her anew—the beauties of nature at their finest *and* a new friend.

They did not exchange a word. They did not need to. Their thoughts were in perfect harmony—she could sense that. After a few minutes they resumed the climb while the rushing sound of the waterfall drowned out all other sounds—except, she noticed, the shrill song of an invisible bird.

They scrambled the last few feet to the crest of the rise, on a level with the top of the waterfall. The view was breathtaking. Susanna could feel droplets of water cool on her face. Although the lake was still in view—as well as the other picnickers—there was an air of wild seclusion here. Perhaps it had something to do with the sound of the water.

They stood hand in hand gazing at the waterfall until Viscount Whitleaf looked behind him.

"Ah," he said, "a grotto built artfully into the hillside to look like a natural cave. I almost expected to see it there. And of course it is facing in just the right direction. Capability Brown and his ilk could always be relied upon to provide such conveniences on wilderness walks. Shall we sit for a while?"

"It ought to be cool in there," she said hopefully. Climbing had been a warm business even though the trees had protected them from the direct sunlight for much of the way.

The grotto was provided with a wooden bench that circled the inner wall. It was the perfect shelter from sun or wind or rain or simple weariness, a place to sit and feast the senses on the beauties provided by nature—even if man had lent a helping hand. The opening to the outside world was framed on three sides with lush green ferns.

The waterfall was centered in their line of vision, just as the reflection of the house was from the pavilion on the lake. Ferns grew thick on the steep banks on either side and trees stretched above. There were the smells of water and greenery and earth. And of course there was the sound of rushing water—and of the song of the lone bird.

"I like friendship," he said softly, after they had sat in silence for several minutes. "It enables one *not* to talk." He chuckled. "Does that make sense?"

"Yes," she said. "Silence is an uncomfortable thing between casual acquaintances or strangers."

"Like you and me the day we met," he said. "*Were* you uncomfortable?"

"Very," she admitted.

"Why?"

She had taken her hand from his when they sat down in order to settle her skirts about her. Now she realized her hand was in his again, though she did not know how it had got there. Their clasped hands were lying on her skirt on the bench between them.

"You were *Viscount* Whitleaf," she said, "handsome, fashionable, obviously wealthy, sure of yourself, a man of the world."

"Shallow," he added, "conceited, flirtatious."

"I judged too hastily," she said.

She was aware for several silent moments that he was looking at her.

"And there was another reason," she said hastily. "You were Viscount *Whitleaf*. I grew up not far from Sidley Park."

"Good Lord," he said after a moment or two of silence. "*Osbourne*. He was Sir Charles Markham's secretary for years when Markham was a government minister. I thought of him when you were introduced to me, but Osbourne is not an entirely uncommon name. I did not dream . . . When I come to think of it, though, I recall that he *did* have a daughter. You?"

"Yes," she said, considerably shaken. She had really not intended telling him who she was.

"Did we ever meet?" he asked.

"Once," she said. "You came down to the lake, where I was playing with Edith, but two of your sisters came and took you away. One of them did not like the fact that you were playing with me, and the other was afraid you would fall in and drown."

"I don't remember," he said. "But wait. Was there something with a fishing line?"

"Yes," she said. "You wanted to try mine. You thought you might have better luck than I had had, but actually I do not believe there were any fish in that lake. I never heard of anyone catching any there."

"That was you," he said. "I *do* remember. Vaguely, anyway."

And it would be as well, she thought, if the memories were left there, vague and unspecific.

"Your father died," he said.

She turned her head and looked sharply at him.

"Yes."

"I am so sorry," he said, "though it seems a little late to commiserate with you. It was sudden, was it not? A heart attack?"

Ah, he really did not know, then. He really had been sheltered by all his various guardians.

"Yes," she said. "His heart stopped."

Which was certainly not a lie.

"I am sorry," he said again. "But tell me how you ended up as a charity pupil at Miss Martin's school in Bath."

She had never spoken about her past. Deep as was her trust in her three closest friends, she had never entrusted them with the whole of her story—just as they had never revealed everything of their past to her. Friends really did need secret places inside themselves. But he already knew more than they ever had.

She closed her eyes for a few moments.

"I do beg your pardon," he said, squeezing her hand more tightly. "Please forgive me for arousing what are obviously painful memories."

She had learned to cope with her essential aloneness, not even to dwell upon it. And she did have her employment now and friends who were almost as good as family. But there had been a time when she had felt like a helpless babe all alone and abandoned in a vast and hostile universe. She doubted there was any worse feeling. Even her very survival had been in question.

"Mr. Hatchard sent me to the school," she said. "He is Claudia Martin's solicitor and agent in London. He sought me out when I was seeking a position through an employment agency. At first, when he asked me if I had ever been to Bath, I thought he had some employment to offer me there. But then he explained that there was a place at a school there for me if I wanted it—as a pupil. He told me that someone he represented was willing to pay my fees, that in fact I would be one of several charity pupils."

She could clearly remember the mingled relief and humiliation with which she had listened to his wholly unexpected offer.

"And you accepted," Viscount Whitleaf said.

"I really had no choice," she told him. "I was staring starvation in the face. I had had only one promising interview—for a position as a lady's maid. I had said at the agency that I was fifteen though I was only twelve. But the lady who interviewed me did not believe me and dismissed me out of hand. She was not the housekeeper, as I had expected, but my prospective employer herself. She told me that since she was going to have to put up with the maid who was hired, she was going to have the choosing of her. I was terrified of her, even though she was very young herself. And yet I have always had the strange conviction that she must have had something to do with Mr. Hatchard's finding me."

"Really?" he said.

"How else would he have found me and why else would he have singled me out?" she asked. "London is teeming with destitute girls. And her name keeps popping up in connection with the school in the most puzzling way. Claudia Martin was once her governess but left in outrage at her unruly behavior and haughty manners. Then she turned up unexpectedly at the school one day after I was there and asked Claudia if she needed anything. Poor Claudia was outraged. But the school has a secret benefactor, you see. It seems never to have occurred to Claudia that perhaps it is Lady Hallmere herself, but I wonder if perhaps it is."

"Lady Hallmere?" he said.

"She was Lady Freyja Bedwyn before her marriage," she explained. "Sister of the Duke of Bewcastle. And then she married the Marquess of Hallmere, who just happens to have his home and estate in Cornwall, in the exact place where Anne Jewell lived before she was recommended to the school as a teacher."

"I know the Bedwyn family," he said. "Bewcastle is a close neighbor of my cousin Lauren, Viscountess Ravensberg." He grinned. "I do not imagine that being Lady Hallmere's governess would have been a comfortable thing. And I would guess that you had a fortunate escape in not being taken on as her maid. She is a formidable lady. But you think it was she who sent you to Bath? Interesting!"

"I may be wrong," she said.

And if she had needed any further reminder that he

was of a different world from her own, here it was. He actually knew Lady Hallmere and the Bedwyn family. His cousin was a viscountess.

But such knowledge was no longer a cause for intimidation. She and Viscount Whitleaf were indeed friends, she believed, though only for a short while. Soon they would return to their separate worlds.

She withdrew her hand from his, smoothed out her skirt without looking at him, and got up to step outside the grotto and stand on the path looking out on the waterfall. He followed her out.

"I have been very fortunate in my life," she said. "Once I had settled at the school I was very happy there. And since becoming a teacher I have been happier."

"In some ways," he said, "I envy you."

She looked up sharply into his face to see if he joked. What a very strange thing to say! But he was squinting off toward the waterfall and seemed to be talking to himself rather than to her. He had certainly not been joking. When he looked back at her, he was smiling again.

"Are you preparing to dance the night away at the assembly tomorrow?" he asked her.

"It is a country entertainment, Lord Whitleaf," she said. "I daresay it will be over well before midnight."

"One of the first things I noticed about you," he said, "was that you are literal-minded—hearts as organs in the chest, for example. My poet's soul still winces over that one. Let me rephrase my question, then. Are you preparing to dance the *evening* away?"

"I am preparing to *enjoy* myself," she said. "I have never been to a ball or even a country assembly."

"Never?" He looked arrested. "You do not know how to dance, then?"

"Learning to dance is a necessary part of any lady's education," she said, "even if she is only a charity pupil. We have a dancing master at the school—Mr. Huckerby. I learned from him. And now I often demonstrate the dances with him while the girls look on."

"But you have never danced at a ball," he said quietly.

She felt horribly embarrassed then. That was one pathetic piece of information she ought to have kept to herself.

"We should go back," she said. "It must be getting late. Everyone will be thinking of going home, and our long absence will be remarked upon."

"Miss Osbourne," he said abruptly, "will you dance the first waltz with me at the assembly?"

Oh!

She stared at him, filled with such longing that for a moment she could not even speak.

"Oh," she said then, "there is no need to ask such a thing just because I told you it will be my first assembly and I am in a sense your friend."

He seized her hand again then, but not just to hold. He raised it to his lips and held it there for a few moments while he looked intently into her eyes over the top of it.

"What does this *in a sense* mean?" he asked. "How can two people be friends *in a sense*? Either we are or we are not. I have asked you to waltz with me because I wish to waltz with you and no one else. Sometimes motives are as simple as that."

She had watched her hand held against his lips, and she had *felt* it there—not just with the hand itself but with every cell in her body. No man had ever made her such a courtly gesture before. Ah, no one had. And it felt very good indeed. It felt *more* than just good.

And then his face blurred before her vision and she realized in some horror that her eyes had filled with tears.

She tried to pull her hand away, but he held on to it, his grasp tightening.

"Susanna," he said, "have I upset you? I do beg your pardon. Do you not wish—"

"Yes," she said shakily, dashing her free hand across her eyes. "I do. I will. I mean, it would give me the greatest pleasure to waltz with you, my lord. Thank you."

But her stomach felt as if it had performed a somersault inside her. He had called her *Susanna*. How foolish to be so affected by that slight breach of good manners—by that wonderful sign of friendship.

He bowed elegantly over her hand and grinned at her.

"The evening preceding that waltz will be dull indeed," he told her, his free hand over his heart.

Ah, he had seen that she was upset and otherwise discomposed, she realized. And so he was deliberately lightening the atmosphere by teasing her, even flirting with her. Oh, he *was* a kind man.

"Nonsense, Lord Whitleaf," she said with a laugh that came out on a strange gurgle. "I have not forgotten that you are engaged to dance at least the first four sets of the evening with other partners. You cannot pretend that the prospect of so much female company is dull."

He chuckled.

"But I had engaged to dance with them," he said, "before I even met you. Once I did, I became impervious to all other female charms."

"Flatterer!" She clucked her tongue and laughed again, with genuine amusement this time, and withdrew her hand from his.

"I *am* speaking the truth, you know," he added. "I have found that friendship is far more stimulating than flirtation."

"The female population of England would go into a collective decline if they heard you say such a thing," she said. "We must go back."

"Must we?" he said. "Or shall we run away and stay away forever and ever? Do you ever wish you could do that?"

"No." But she gazed wistfully at him. Sometimes she did wish it. She *had* run away once. But in her dreams she could sometimes fly . . .

"You once told me you were not a romantic," he said. "Are you not an adventurer either?"

"No," she said. "My feet are firmly planted on the ground."

"And your heart firmly pumping away in your chest," he said, reaching out one hand to brush his knuckles lightly beneath her chin. "I am not quite sure I believe you, Miss Osbourne—on either count. But you are right, I suppose. If we are not to run away together, we had better return."

He fell into step beside her and they proceeded on their way in a silence that soon became companionable again.

But a nameless yearning grew in her as they descended the path—a yearning perhaps to throw caution to the winds and step out of herself entirely into an unknown . . .

An unknown what?

Adventure?

Romance?

Neither was being offered her with any seriousness, and she would refuse even if they were. Dreams were all very well as long as one never confused them with reality.

The reality was that she was walking beside Viscount Whitleaf along the wilderness walk at Barclay Court during a lovely summer afternoon. The reality was that she was going to waltz with him tomorrow evening at her first-ever assembly. Even after that there would still be three days of her holiday left.

There was nothing whatsoever wrong with reality. Reality was very close to being perfect.

And even after those three days were over there would be Anne and Claudia waiting for her in Bath and the security of her teaching position. There would be the other teachers and the girls, including several new ones. There would be all the challenge of a new school year to prepare for. And pleasant memories of her holiday.

"A penny for your thoughts," he said after they were down the steep part of the path and were drawing closer to the lake.

"I was realizing how many blessings I have to count," she said.

"Were you?" He looked more closely at her. "In my experience people count blessings only when they are feeling sad. *Are* you sad?"

"No," she said. "How could I be?"

He heaved a deep sigh, which he did not immediately explain.

"It beats me," he said after a short silence. "But I feel melancholy too."

Mr. Dannen and Mr. Raycroft were coming across the bridge to meet them with Miss Moss, Miss Krebbs, and Miss Jane Calvert. Soon the two groups came together, and a great deal of chatter and laughter ensued.

By the time they reached the picnic side of the bridge, Mr. Dannen had taken Susanna on his arm, and Viscount Whitleaf had offered one of his to Miss Krebbs and the other to Miss Jane Calvert. Mr. Raycroft was walking beside them.

The viscount was telling them that he had thought it was the late afternoon sunlight that was dazzling his eyes at the center of the bridge until he realized that it was their presence there that had been doing it.

The rogue!

But of course they were not taken in by such flatteries for a single moment. The tone of their laughter told Susanna that.

He was being kind to them, bringing happiness and gaiety to their day.

He had also donned a mask of frivolity. Or maybe it was not a mask at all. Maybe he had a gift for spreading joy. And yet he had said just moments ago that he felt melancholy. Could he feel both?

Yes, perhaps so. *She* was feeling both. She was living through one of the most joyful afternoons of her entire life. And yet . . .

And yet soon they would go separately back into their own very separate universes.

8

The mood of slight melancholy that had oppressed Susanna after the picnic had disappeared without a trace by the time she arrived with Frances and the Earl of Edgecombe at the assembly rooms above the village inn the following evening.

She doubted she had ever been more excited in her life, though she tried very hard not to show it— without a great deal of success, it seemed.

"Well, Susanna," the earl said as he handed her down from the carriage, "you are fairly sparkling, I must say. Jewels would be superfluous."

She was wearing none, of course. But then neither was Frances. Susanna suspected that despite the fact that her friend wore a gorgeous royal-blue satin gown, which was clearly expensive and made by the most skilled of seamstresses, Frances was actually making a deliberate effort not to outshine either Susanna or her less affluent neighbors.

Frances linked her arm through Susanna's as they stepped inside the inn, leaving the earl to follow them in.

"I know just how you must be feeling," she said. "I remember how *I* felt that night in Bath when Lucius's grandfather and sister had invited me to a ball in the Upper Assembly Rooms. I was half frightened to death and half *elated* to death. Do you remember?"

"Claudia, Anne, and I noticed at the last moment that part of your hem was down," Susanna said, "and we were all involved in stitching it up again with you inside it—in the school hallway of all places—when Mr. Keeble let the Earl of Edgecombe in, or Viscount Sinclair, as he was then."

They both laughed at the memory and there was a low chuckle from behind them to indicate that the earl appreciated the joke too.

The room where the dancing was to take place would probably appear small and plainly decorated in comparison with any London ballroom, Susanna guessed when they entered it. It was certainly smaller and plainer than the Upper Assembly Rooms in Bath, to which she had taken a party of girls from the school on a sightseeing walk one afternoon. But these rooms were full of people she knew and felt comfortable with, and everyone was dressed smartly for the evening. The noise level was high with the excited voices of ladies and young girls and the hearty, booming voices of men trying to talk above them. There was a great deal of laughter everywhere. And the orchestra members were making their own contribution to the noise as they tuned their instruments on a small dais at one end of the room.

It all appeared splendidly dazzling to Susanna.

She was at her first ball—in her mind she called it

that even if strictly speaking it was but an assembly. And she was going to *dance*.

The earl had asked her to reserve at least one set for him, though he had not spoken for any one in particular. Mr. Dannen, at the end of yesterday's picnic, had solicited her hand for the all-important opening set.

And Viscount Whitleaf had asked her for the first waltz.

She could hardly *wait* for that particular set—there was to be only one. And yet even as the impatient thought entered her mind she chastised herself. This was sure to be the most exciting evening of her life. She would not wish the first half of it away. She wanted to live every moment of it, from first to last.

Mrs. Raycroft and her daughter came to meet them as soon as they appeared in the doorway, and Miss Raycroft exclaimed with awe over Frances's gown and admired Susanna's hair, which Frances had insisted her own maid dress for the evening.

"And is that the ribbon you bought in the village shop?" she asked, surveying the hem of Susanna's pale green gown, about which the darker green ribbon had been sewn in two rows. "It gleams in the candlelight, does it not? It looks very smart. Viscount Whitleaf told us you had purchased it."

"My gown needed to be made more festive for the occasion," Susanna explained. "I have never worn it to a ball before."

After that all was a whirlwind of activity and excitement as neighbors greeted neighbors and gentlemen searched out their partners for the opening set.

Susanna had been forced to admit in the privacy of her own heart that she found Mr. Dannen something of a bore. They had spent several hours in each other's company during the past two weeks, but she doubted he knew anything about her except that she was a schoolteacher from Bath. She, on the other hand, knew surely all there was to know about his Scottish ancestors and heritage.

But her lack of romantic interest in him really did not matter at all as he led her out onto the floor and placed her in the line of ladies while he took his place opposite her among the gentlemen for the opening set of country dances. There had surely never been a happier moment. The eldest Miss Calvert stood to her left, opposite Mr. Raycroft, and Rosamond Raycroft stood next to Miss Calvert. Viscount Whitleaf, across from her, smiled indulgently and said something that had her laughing merrily. Briefly he caught Susanna's eye, but he was too polite to withdraw his attention from his partner for longer than a moment or two.

Just feeling him close filled Susanna with an even warmer glow of happiness.

But soon she had thoughts for nothing except the dance as the orchestra struck up with the music and the line of gentlemen bowed while the line of ladies curtsied.

Music filled her ears as the floor vibrated to the rhythmic thumping of many feet and dancers twirled and promenaded and circled about one another. The air grew warmer and heavier with the mingled scents of perfumes and colognes and flowers. The very candles in the candelabrum and wall sconces seemed to move with a lilting rhythm in time to the music.

And she was a part of it all.

Ah, she was a *part* of it all.

She would perhaps have felt some disappointment when the set came to an end except that Mr. Raycroft had already asked her before it began if she would dance the second with him. And the earl claimed the third set.

By the end of that she was feeling flushed and warm and breathless—and wanted the evening never to end. Mr. Finn approached and asked for the fourth set, but when he came she was seated beside Miss Honeydew, who was fanning herself and looking rather faint and admitted when Susanna asked that she had not eaten anything since luncheon. Susanna thanked Mr. Finn and asked if he would excuse her and then took Miss Honeydew into the refreshment room, fetched her a cup of tea and a plate of food, and sat with her while she ate, her foot tapping out the rhythm of the dance music coming from the other room.

But she did not mind missing the dance. Mr. Crossley had already asked for the next, and the one after that was to be the waltz.

Viscount Whitleaf was looking extremely handsome tonight in a brown tailed evening coat with ivory satin breeches, a dull gold embroidered waistcoat, and white, crisp linen. He was also, Susanna had noticed, a graceful dancer and one who looked as if he were enjoying himself. Whenever she glanced at him, he was smiling, his eyes on his partner. His partners, of course, were ecstatic.

Mr. Crossley led Susanna toward Mrs. Raycroft at the end of the next set and stood conversing with them there while Viscount Whitleaf and Frances, who had been dancing together, approached across the floor. Susanna fanned her hot cheeks and watched him come. How very *much* she liked him.

"Goodness," Frances said, "that was a vigorous dance. I am quite robbed of breath. Thank you, Lord Whitleaf."

"Ma'am?" He bowed. "It was entirely my pleasure."

"But I simply must recover my breath quickly," she said. "The waltz is next and I have been looking forward to it for longer than a week. So has Lucius."

The Earl of Edgecombe was striding across the floor toward them, his eyes on Frances.

Viscount Whitleaf made Susanna a slight bow.

"This is my dance, Miss Osbourne, I believe," he said.

"It is, my lord." She curtsied and discovered that the evening really *could* turn brighter and even more exciting.

"*Do* you waltz, Miss Osbourne?" Mr. Crossley asked her, sounding surprised and even perhaps a little disapproving.

"I know the steps, sir," she said. "I learned them at school—from a dancing master who is a stickler for doing all things correctly."

"He is indeed," Frances agreed.

"I have even given permission for Rosamond to waltz with Mr. Moss," Mrs. Raycroft said, "since both my son and Viscount Whitleaf have assured me that it is danced at Almack's. And if *you* are to waltz, Lady Edgecombe, then it must be unexceptionable."

"We fell in love with the waltz the first time we danced it together," the Earl of Edgecombe said. "It was in an assembly room not unlike this, was it not, Frances?"

Mr. Crossley was silenced.

Viscount Whitleaf held out a hand and Susanna placed her own on top of it. He led her out onto the empty dance floor. They were the first there. They could probably have waited five minutes longer, but, oh, she was glad he had not waited. This was the moment she had anticipated eagerly ever since he had asked her yesterday. She was going to *waltz*. With *him*. The happiness of it all was almost too much to bear.

"Well?" he said when they were alone together— though they were, of course, surrounded by their fellow guests. "What is your verdict on your first assembly? Not that I really need to ask, I believe."

"It is that obvious?" She pulled a face. "But I really do think it is splendid, and I do not care how gauche I sound to you. This is my very first ball—at the age of twenty-three—and I am not even going to pretend to be indifferent to it all."

"Ah, but it *is* splendid," he said, holding her eyes with his own—as he had done with each of his partners. "Far more splendid, in fact, than any other ball or assembly I have ever attended in my twenty-six years."

Which was a Banbury tale if ever she had heard one. She laughed again.

"Oh, but I believe you did not complete that thought," she said. "Were you not supposed to add that it is more wonderful because *I* am here?"

"I *was* going to say that," he told her, "but I thought you would accuse me of flattery and flirtation."

"Indeed I would," she said. "But really, *are* you enjoying yourself? I know that all the other young ladies are thrilled that you are here."

"The *other* young ladies," he said, setting one hand over his heart. "Not you too?"

But she laughed and fanned her face. Talking nonsense, even mildly flirting, could be enjoyable after all, she thought, when both parties were well aware that it *was* nonsense they spoke.

"I will remember this," she said, "all my life."

"This assembly?" he asked her. "Or this waltz?"

The smile was arrested on her face for a moment.

"Both, I hope," she said. "Unless I fall all over your feet during the waltz. But then I suppose I would remember all the more."

Other couples were gathering around them. The orchestra members were tuning their instruments again.

"If you fall over my feet," he said, "it will be because of my unpardonable clumsiness and I shall atone by going home and burning my dancing shoes. No, correction. I shall atone by burning my dancing shoes and *then* walking home."

She laughed once more.

And then stopped laughing.

He had set his right hand behind her waist and

taken her right hand in his left. She lifted her left hand to set on his shoulder. She could smell his cologne. She could feel his body heat. She could hear her heartbeat throbbing in her ears.

His violet eyes gazed very directly into her own—they smiled slightly.

Ah, she thought, the magic of it.

The sheer wonderful magic.

Then the music began.

It occurred to her afterward that a number of other couples had taken to the floor with them. She even had one fleeting memory of seeing the Earl of Edgecombe twirling Frances about one corner of the room, holding her rather closer than Mr. Huckerby would approve of. She could recall the swirling colors of the ladies' gowns, the warm glow of the candles, the sounds of voices and laughter, the sight of a number of people gathered at the sidelines, watching.

But at the time she was oblivious to it all. She was aware only of the music and the dance and the man who held her. She performed the steps faultlessly if a little woodenly for the first couple of minutes, and she held her body stiff and as far distant from his as the positioning of their arms allowed. But then came the moment when she raised her eyes from his intricately tied neckcloth to look into his own eyes—and he smiled at her and she relaxed.

"Oh," she said a little breathlessly, "I *do* remember how."

"And so," he said, "do I. I hope I live up to the exacting standards of your Mr. Huckerby."

She laughed. "Yes, I would have to say you do."

They did not speak after that, but it seemed to her afterward that they gazed into each other's eyes the whole time they danced. It ought to have caused intense discomfort. Gazing into another person's eyes from such a short distance even when conversing always gave her the urge to take a step back or to glance away from time to time. But she felt no such urge with Viscount Whitleaf. They danced, it seemed to her, as if they were one harmonious unit.

She remembered the quickly suppressed mental image she had had almost two weeks ago of waltzing in his arms. That dream had come true after all.

And, ah, it was exhilarating beyond words.

But it could not last forever, of course. Eventually she could sense that the music was coming to an end.

"Oh," she said, "it is over."

She had been quite unaware of the passing of time.

"But it was lovely," she added after the music had stopped altogether. "Thank you, my lord. Will you take me to Frances?"

She must not be greedy, she told herself. She might well have been doomed to watch everyone else waltz while she pretended to be enjoying herself as an onlooker. She would always have this memory of her first—and probably her last—waltz.

"It is customary, you know," he said, leaning his head a little closer to hers, "for a man to lead his partner at the supper dance into the refreshment room. Will you take supper with me?"

"Is it suppertime already?" she asked as she looked about to see that yes, indeed, the room was fast emptying. "Oh, I am so glad. Yes, I will. Thank you."

And so, she thought happily as he led her off to the refreshment room, her half hour with him was to be extended, even if they were to sit with other people.

What a very precious evening this was. With only three days left of her stay at Barclay Court, it had become a fitting finale for a memorable holiday.

Though there *were* still three days left.

9

Peter found them two seats wedged between the teapot and the window before going to the food table. One thing a person could always count upon at a country assembly, he thought appreciatively as he filled plates for them both, was plenty of good food.

"Where will you go when you leave here?" Miss Osbourne asked him after he had set down their plates and fetched some tea and seated himself opposite her at their small table. "Will you go home?"

"To Sidley Park?" he said. "Not immediately. I do not wish to intrude upon the end of my mother's latest house party there."

"There is a house party at your own home, yet you are not there to host it?" She raised her eyebrows as she selected a small cucumber sandwich and bit into it.

"The thing is," he said, "that my mother is desperately trying to marry me off. There is someone there whom she wishes me to court—and all the other guests would have been well aware of the fact if I had gone there."

"You do not wish to marry?" she asked him.

"I most certainly do not," he assured her. "Or at least, I do not wish to be *trapped* into a marriage not entirely of my own choosing."

Her eyes laughed into his.

"I absolutely do not want my mother choosing my bride," he said.

"I daresay," she said, "she loves you."

"She does," he agreed. "But love can sometimes be a burden, you know. She first tried to marry me off when I was twenty-one years old and still wet behind the ears."

"You did not love the girl?" she asked.

"I *did*." He grimaced. "I was head-over-ears in love with her—because I was expected to be, of course. I was a cocky boy, Miss Osbourne, and was thoroughly convinced that I was my own man. But in reality I did everything I was expected to do. I *thought* I loved her."

"But you did not really?" She set one elbow on the table against all the rules of etiquette and rested her chin in her hand. She gazed steadily at him. "What happened?"

Oh, good Lord, he was not prepared to go *there* with her. He smiled, though the expression felt somewhat crooked.

"One could say that I had an awakening," he said. "It was really quite spectacular. I woke up one morning an innocent, cheerful babe, my head in the clouds, stars in my eyes, and I went to bed that same night a cynical old man, with my eyes opened to all the ugly realities of life. My almost-engagement was the biggest casualty. The woman I had loved so devotedly but no longer loved at all left the next morning with her family and I never saw any of them again. Fortunately, they live far to the north of England and seem never to come near London. Though I did hear that she married less than six months later."

The loss of Bertha was not the biggest casualty, though, was it? His relationship with his mother was that. He had never been what can only be described as a mother's boy, but he *had* loved her totally. She had been perfect in his eyes. When all was said and done, though, all he had really discovered about her on that day was that she was human.

And dash it all, had he actually been talking about that event, no matter how vaguely, to Susanna Osbourne? He *never* spoke about that episode. He rarely even thought about it. He grinned sheepishly at her.

"I was left with a rather rakish reputation as a breaker of female hearts," he said. "Entirely undeserved. She did not have a heart."

She continued to gaze at him.

"And so my mother's ongoing . . . concern over my marital state—or my *un*marital state—is a continual burden," he said, "though she means well."

"One's family *can* be a burden," she said softly, "even if one's mother died at one's birth and one's father died when one was twelve."

His eyes sharpened on hers, but she was gazing through him rather than at him, he thought.

"Was there no other family for you," he asked her, "on either side?"

It had seemed strange to him, when he thought about it after the picnic, that the Markhams had not found anyone of her own to take her in—or, failing that, that they had not done something themselves to make provision for her. She had been only twelve years old, for the love of God. And he had never thought of the Markhams as heartless people. What the devil had she been doing alone in London, looking for employment at the age of twelve?

"I do not really know," she said, her eyes focusing on him again. "My father had . . . quarreled with his family and would never even talk about them whenever I asked. He would never talk about my mother or her family either. Perhaps, like me, he did not enjoy memories of the past."

Who did when those memories were painful? And yet it seemed odd, even cruel, that Osbourne had not told his daughter anything about her heritage. Perhaps he had not expected to die young. No one did really, did they? Perhaps he had had no warning of his impending heart seizure. And so Susanna Osbourne had no one. Her mother had died at her birth, and Osbourne had told her nothing that would in any way have brought her mother alive for her. In her childhood dreams she had never been able to put a face on her mother—even an imaginary one.

He must remember Susanna Osbourne the next time he thought to complain about the number of sisters' and nieces' and nephews' birthdays he was expected to remember.

"Will you go home after the house party is over, then?" she asked.

"I planned to go home the very day after I met you," he said. "Finally, after five years of being away from it as much as I could, I was going back. But a couple of hours before you and I met I had my mother's letter telling me of the house party she had planned in my honor—complete with eligible marriage prospect."

"And so you are not going after all?" she asked.

He shrugged. *Was* he going to go? He was no longer sure. Sidley was his mother's home as well as his, as it had been since her marriage to his father. And she ruled it with firm efficiency as she always had done. He was not sure they could both live there now—he was no longer her biddable little boy. He was even less sure, though, that he was prepared to ask her to leave or even insist that she make her home in the dower house at Sidley.

She was his *mother*. And cruelty had never come easily to him.

"Your finest asset and your greatest problem," Susanna Osbourne said, "is that you are very kind."

He realized, startled, that he had spoken his thoughts out loud.

"That sounds very like weakness," he said, embarrassed, as he tackled the food on his plate.

"Kindness is *not* weakness," she said firmly.

"It was kind to stay away from her party?" he asked.

She gazed at him, her chin in her hand again. The food on her plate had hardly been touched, he noticed. She sighed.

"What you need," she said, "is a dragon to slay."

He chuckled. "And a helpless maiden to rescue?"

"Tell me your dreams," she said.

"Those bizarre wisps of things that flit through my head when I am asleep?" he asked, grinning at her.

But she did not smile back. She would not allow him to make light of the question.

"Your *dreams*," she said.

He pushed his plate away from him and thought for a few moments.

"They are not grand things at all," he said. "I dream of tramping about my own land with a stout staff in my hand and dogs panting at my heels. I dream of knowing the land from the inside out, working it, knowing the feel of its soil between my fingers, the thrill of seeing crops I have helped plant poke green and fragile above the earth. I dream of knowing my workers and their families, of knowing *their* dreams and working with them to bring harmony to all our lives and aspirations. I dream of being master of my own home and my own life at last. I dream of knowing my neighbors in such a way that I can drop in on them at any time of the day or evening or they can feel free to drop in on me without any discomfort. I dream of a time when being *Viscount Whitleaf* does not set me apart from most other mortals who live in the vicinity of my home. There—is that enough?"

"Yes," she said, smiling. "I am glad you convinced me that we could be friends. I am glad to have known you. I like you."

He felt strangely touched by her words.

"Well, now." He laughed softly. "That is praise indeed. Miss Susanna Osbourne *likes* me."

She sat back in her chair and lowered her hands to her lap.

"I was *not* being sarcastic," he told her. "I have always assumed that most people of my acquaintance like me—I do not believe I am a difficult fellow to get along with. But I do not recall anyone's actually saying so. The words coming from you warm my heart—that pumping organ in my chest."

Her smile held genuine amusement this time.

"Tell me *your* dreams," he said.

She looked instantly wistful.

"Oh," she said, "I have no dreams, really. I am contented with what I have."

"If that is true," he told her, "it is the saddest thing I have heard in a long while. We all need dreams. But I do not believe that you have none. I can see from your eyes that you have plenty."

"From my eyes?" She looked suddenly wary. "Eyes cannot speak."

"There you are wrong, Miss Literalist," he said. "Eyes can be very eloquent indeed, yours more than most. Tell me your dreams. I have told you mine, and we are friends, are we not? I am not likely to shout with derision or stand on my chair to announce your secret dreams to the whole company."

"They are as humble as yours," she said, smiling again. "A home of my own. I lived in someone else's house for my first twelve years and since then I have lived at the school in Bath. I dream of a home of my own in a place like this, where there are neighbors and friends. It does not have to be large. A cottage would suffice. And a small garden where I could grow flowers and vegetables and create beauty and plenty around me. And . . . Oh, and my ultimate dream."

She stopped and bit her lower lip. But she continued when he said nothing.

"A husband and a few children, a family of my own to cherish and be loved by," she said. "I do not dream of wealth or grandeur—only of love. There, you *did* insist. Those are my dreams."

And they were indeed humble ones. No woman, he thought, should be denied her own home and family if she wished for them, and yet she believed they were impossible dreams for her. *Were* they? She was beautiful beyond belief and sweet-natured. And yet where, apart from here, would she ever go to meet eligible men? Perhaps he could . . .

But no. He could not. He certainly could not. There was no point in beginning to plot or scheme. Besides . . . Well, besides nothing.

Both their cups of tea, he noticed suddenly, had a grayish film of coldness covering the surface. Both their plates were still almost full of food.

"Let me get you a fresh cup of tea," he suggested.

But her face showed surprise when she looked beyond him and, glancing over his shoulder, he could see that they were alone. Sounds of music and merriment were coming from the main room. The final set of the evening was already in progress.

"Good Lord!" he exclaimed. "Are you engaged to dance this set?"

"No," she said.

"Neither am I," he said in some relief. "It is exceedingly warm in here, is it not?"

"Yes," she said.

"Shall we stroll outside," he suggested, "until everyone else is ready to leave?"

She hesitated for only a moment.

"That *would* be pleasant," she said.

And so five minutes later they were strolling along the village street, past the crush of carriages and servants waiting to pick up their respective passengers, past the shop, the churchyard, and the vicarage, and the church itself. She had taken his arm, and after a few minutes he clasped her hand in his, lacing their fingers and pressing her arm to his side.

"Being here for these last two weeks has reminded me of how very much more I enjoy the country than London or Brighton or any other large center," he said. "I think I really must go home as soon as my mother's house party has ended. Perhaps I will not have missed the whole of the harvest. And perhaps . . . Well, never mind."

"Perhaps," she said, "your dream really will come true one day soon. I hope so. You belong with people like these."

"I would not have enjoyed these two weeks half as much, though, if I had not met you," he told her, and was surprised by the sincerity of his words. They were the sort of empty, meaningless words he usually spoke when flirting

"The two weeks are not quite at an end," she said. "There are still three days left. Oh, dear, *only* three days."

Her tone was wistful. After those three days for her, of course, there was only a return to school and work to look forward to—though he knew from what she had said on other occasions that she genuinely enjoyed teaching. He knew too—she had just admitted it—that the idea of teaching for the rest of her life fell far short of her dreams.

They had stopped outside the church, in the shadow of an elm tree.

"Do you wish you could stay longer, then?" he asked.

"Oh, no," she said. "All good things must come to an end, and it is time to go back. It is just that this has been the loveliest holiday I have ever spent, and there is a certain sadness in knowing that it is all but over."

"Has it been made lovelier by the fact that I have been here?" he asked her.

Again it was the sort of question he would ask when flirting with a woman—and he would smile and *she* would smile, and they would both know he meant nothing by it. But Susanna Osbourne was giving serious consideration to the question, and he waited for her answer as if it were somehow important to him.

"Yes," she said softly. "I have valued our friendship."

She was, he noticed, already referring to it almost in the past tense. Soon it would be fully in the past—it was very unlikely that they would meet again after they left here. He never went to Bath, and she almost never left it.

"*Friendship,*" he repeated softly, bending his head closer to hers. "It does not seem a strong enough word, does it? Are we not a little more than just friends?"

And what the devil did he mean by that? But unfortunately it was only later that he thought to ask himself the question. At present he was caught up in an uncharacteristic moment of seriousness and sincerity.

"Oh, don't say so," she cried, and he could hear distress in her voice. "Please don't say so. Don't spoil what we have shared. Don't flirt with me."

Oh, good Lord!

"Flirtation is the farthest thing from my mind," he assured her.

Yet if it was not flirtation, what *was* it exactly? He had the dizzying feeling that he had inadvertently steered his boat into uncharted waters.

And then, because he had tipped his head downward and she had not moved, their foreheads touched. He closed his eyes and did not move. Neither did she.

He felt a sudden, deep melancholy again, even worse than he had felt yesterday after their walk to the waterfall.

He opened his eyes, moved his head slightly, and brushed his lips over hers.

But only for a brief, mad moment before lifting his head and gazing off toward the church. Their hands were still clasped tightly, he realized.

He was aware of her ragged breathing for a few moments and had a ghastly thought. That was probably—no, undoubtedly—her first kiss. And yet it hardly qualified for the name. But he could not now make the occasion more memorable for her by returning his lips to hers and doing the deed more thoroughly and more expertly.

It would be the very worst thing he could do.

He ought not to have kissed her at all.

He just did not go about toying with the sensibilities

of innocent young schoolteachers. Or with his own for that matter.

Good Lord, they were just friends. *Just friends!*

"I think," she said softly, "we ought to go back to the inn, Lord Whitleaf. I see that people are coming out, and I cannot hear music any longer."

He ought to apologize, dash it all. But that would draw attention to what had not really been a kiss at all.

He could still feel the shock of her warm, soft mouth against his.

Dash it all, why had he not listened to her when she told him over a week ago that a friendship was impossible between a man and a woman? He had used the example of Edgecombe and the countess to prove her wrong. But he had failed to consider the fact that they were lovers as well as friends.

A single man and a single woman could not be both.

Nor could they be just friends, it seemed. The devil of it was that he wanted her—sexually. And it simply would not do.

"I will escort you," he said, vastly relieved that the assembly had ended in time to avert further indiscretions.

Edgecombe and the countess were waiting outside their carriage. Other people and carriages and horses milled about them in high-spirited disorder as everyone called good night to everyone else.

Peter smiled and looked cheerfully about him.

"Miss Osbourne and I have been wiser than all of you," he called as they approached the crowd. "We have been strolling quietly out here and enjoying the cool air."

She too, he saw when he glanced down at her, was smiling brightly.

"Frances," she said, "this has been a lovely evening, has it not? Thank you so much for bringing me."

Edgecombe smiled kindly down at her while offering his hand to help her into their carriage, the countess bade Peter a good night before climbing in after her, Edgecombe vaulted in behind, and within moments their coachman was maneuvering the carriage out of the crowd.

Peter heaved a silent sigh of relief as he lifted a hand in farewell and then gave his attention to Miss Raycroft, who had grasped his arm and was prattling excitedly to him about the delights of the evening.

But he was only half listening to her.

What you need is a dragon to slay, she had said while they were still inside the refreshment room.

What you need is a dragon to slay.

When Frances tapped on the door of Susanna's bedchamber, Susanna mumbled something that was certainly not *come in,* but she must not have spoken clearly enough. Frances turned the knob, opened the door a crack, and peered around it.

"Oh, you *are* still up," she said, opening it wider when she saw in the light of a single candle burning on the dressing table that Susanna was standing by the window. "I thought you might welcome someone with whom to mull over your first-ever ball. You were very quiet on the way home after saying it was a lovely evening. A *lovely evening,* Susanna? Is that all? Lucius said you were probably too shy with him to talk volumes. But now I have left him in our bedchamber, and it is just you and I."

She stepped into the room and closed the door behind her.

"Oh," Susanna said brightly as she busied herself with closing the curtains and realized even as she did so that now she would have no excuse not to turn around, "it was all very pleasant, was it not?"

"Now it is only *pleasant*? And *lovely* too? Is that not damning the evening with faint praise?" Frances laughed softly. And then she fell silent as her friend fussed with the fall of the curtains. "Susanna? You are not *crying,* are you?"

"No, of course I am not," Susanna protested. But her brief words ended on an ignominious squeak.

"You *are*. Oh, you poor dear!" Frances exclaimed, hurrying across the room toward her. "Whatever *happened*?"

Susanna laughed shakily and fumbled in the pocket of her night robe for her handkerchief as she turned. Frances too, she saw, had undressed, ready for bed. She was wearing a long, flowing dark blue dressing gown, and her dark hair lay loose down her back.

"I feel very foolish at getting caught being a watering pot," Susanna said after blowing her nose, "especially on such an inappropriate occasion. They are not tears of grief, I do assure you. Quite the contrary. It really was a wonderful, *wonderful* evening, was it not? I'll remember it all my life. I danced every set but two.

It was all quite beyond my wildest dreams. And even one of those two I could have danced. Mr. Finn offered to lead me out, but Miss Honeydew was feeling a little faint and I took her to the refreshment room instead. And during the last set Viscount Whitleaf and I strolled outside where it was cool rather than dance."

She went and sat on the bed and, when Frances took the chair beside the dressing table, she drew up her legs so that she could hug her knees, and tucked the folds of her robe about her feet.

"Ah, this feels just like old times," Frances said with a smile. "I still miss you and the others, you know, and life at school and those times when two or more of us would sit up talking far too late into the night. Which is not to say I would give up my present life to return there, but . . . Well, even happy choices involve some sacrifice. And most of us, I suppose, would like to both have our cake and eat it if only it were possible."

"Did *you* enjoy the evening?" Susanna asked.

"Of course I did," Frances said. "I always enjoy a local assembly better than any grand ball. And this one was made special by the fact that you were there and that you had a number of agreeable partners. And that there was a waltz and I was able to dance it with Lucius and see that you were dancing it too. Yes, it was all quite nearly perfect."

"I will have a great deal to tell when I return to Bath," Susanna said. "Among a dizzying number of other things, I will be able to tell Claudia and Anne—and Mr. Huckerby—that I actually waltzed at a real ball—or at a real assembly anyway—and with no less a personage than a *viscount*. Not quite a duke, perhaps, but close enough."

She had always made a joke with her friends of her determination to snare a duke one day. She smiled and then rested her forehead on her up-drawn knees.

"It *is* lovelier than any other dance," Frances said with a sigh. "It is so . . . oh, *romantic*."

"Yes." Susanna closed her eyes and remembered the glorious wonder of it. It had seemed to her that she had almost floated over the boards beneath her feet without actually touching them. It had seemed as if waltzing and her dream of flying free had become one and the same. Except that waltzing had not been done alone, but with a man who had held her in the circle of his arms and smelled of musk cologne and masculinity. For the space of that one set of dances dream and reality had touched and merged and she had known complete happiness—one of those rare interludes in any life.

It had been sheer magic.

She would *always* remember—half with wonder, half with a sort of pain. For a while, she feared, the pain might outweigh the wonder.

And then, quite unexpectedly and ignominiously, the tears were back and soaking into her robe and she uttered a quite audible hiccough as she tried to control them.

"Oh, goodness," she said, fumbling in her pocket for her handkerchief and managing to produce a shaky laugh, "what an idiot you will think me."

There was a brief but disconcerting silence.

"Susanna," Frances said then, "you have not fallen in love with Viscount Whitleaf, have you?"

Susanna jerked her head upward and gazed horrified at her friend, wet, reddened eyes and all.

"No!" she exclaimed. "Oh, no, Frances, of course I have not. Whatever put such a silly notion into your head?"

But the trouble was that her tears seemed to be beyond her control tonight. Her eyes filled again, and she felt two tears spill over onto her cheeks. She mopped at them hastily with her handkerchief and held it to her eyes.

"Ah, my poor dear," Frances said softly.

"But you are quite wide of the mark. Oh, this is very silly of me," Susanna wailed. "I am not in *love* with him, Frances. Truly I am not. But I do *like* him exceedingly well, you see. We have even become friends during these two weeks. And tonight I *waltzed* with him. But now that the assembly is all over, I cannot help remembering that the holiday is almost over, that within a few days I will be returning to Bath. Don't mistake me—I look forward to going back. It is my home and my other friends are there. And the prospect of a new teaching year with some new girls and the return of the old is always exhilarating. But just at the moment I am contemplating the sadness of saying good-bye to you and Lord Edgecombe and everyone else here."

"Including Viscount Whitleaf," Frances said softly.

"Yes." Susanna smiled wanly as she put her handkerchief away again. "Including him."

"But he *is* just a friend?" Frances asked, frowning, her eyes looking troubled even in the candlelight.

"Yes," Susanna assured her, making her smile brighter. "Of course that is all he is, you silly goose."

Friends do not kiss.

He had kissed her under the elm outside the church. Or was it pathetic to call that brief brushing of lips a kiss? She knew, though, that she would remember it for the rest of her life as a kiss—her first and doubtless her last.

Friends do not kiss.

But they *were* friends.

There was nothing else between them but friendship, in fact.

She did not want there to be anything else.

There *could be* nothing else.

She rested her forehead on her knees again.

"Susanna." Frances had got up from her chair and come to sit on the side of the bed. She set a hand between her friend's shoulder blades and patted her back gently. "I am so sorry. I am *so* sorry."

Susanna concentrated upon taking deep, steadying breaths and holding the tears at bay. She had never been a weeper. Tonight's tears were quite uncharacteristic of her.

"He *is* just a friend," she said when she could be sure her voice would be reasonably steady. "But friends can become very dear, Frances. My heart would break if I had to say good-bye to you or Anne or Claudia and knew it would be forever."

"Your heart is breaking, then?" Frances asked.

"No. Oh, no, of course not," Susanna said. "It is just a figure of speech. I will be *sad* when this fortnight is over. Very sad. And also grateful for the many happy memories. But it is not even quite over, is it? There are three more days to enjoy."

"I feel so very helpless," Frances said after a minute or two of silence. "I feel absolutely wretched for you, Susanna. But I do not know what to say or what comfort to offer."

It was obvious that Frances did not believe any of her protestations concerning Viscount Whitleaf. And because Susanna did indeed feel miserable about having to say good-bye to him—though truly they were only friends—she bowed her head and said nothing for a minute or two longer.

"You have been a comfort to me just by being here," she said firmly at last, getting off the bed to stand beside it. "By being a friend. It *was* a lovely evening, Frances— the most wonderful of my life, and it has been a lovely holiday. You must forgive me, please, for shedding a few sentimental tears because it is almost all over. Now, do go back to Lord Edgecombe. I need my beauty sleep even if you do not."

Frances took her hands and squeezed them, kissing her on the cheek as she did so.

"That's my girl," she said. "That's my brave Susanna. Good night, then. I do hope you will sleep well."

Susanna folded back the bedcovers as soon as she was alone, snuffed the candle, and climbed into bed. She pulled the sheet up to her chin and closed her eyes.

And was again waltzing with him.

And sharing dreams with him in the refreshment room and strolling with him in the fresh air outside, her arm linked through his, their hands clasped, their fingers laced together.

And again she was reliving that brief kiss.

In three days' time she was going to be saying good-bye to him.

Her dear, dear friend.

Which was really a very foolish way of thinking about him when she had known him for less than two weeks and had not spent much longer than half an hour with him during any of those days. And when he was Viscount *Whitleaf* of all people.

Friendship. It does not seem a strong enough word, does it? Are we not a little more than just friends?

She could hear him speak those words—just before he touched his forehead to hers and then kissed her.

But she did not want to remember those words— or that kiss. She did not want to believe that they were anything more than friends. There would be just too much pain to bear if . . .

She turned over onto her side and slid one hand beneath the pillow. She drew up her knees and tucked the sheet beneath her chin.

Once more she was twirling about the dance floor, enclosed in his arms and music and magic.

Once more she was feeling his lips touch hers.

10

Peter could not think back upon the last hour or so of the assembly with any great pleasure.

He remembered it with considerable discomfort, in fact.

He had broken several of his own strict self-imposed rules.

He had waltzed with Susanna Osbourne and then had supper with her—tête-à-tête when he might have joined other people at one of the larger tables—and then gone walking outside with her, also tête-à-tête. He had spent at least an hour exclusively with her—more than twice as long as he ever allowed himself to spend alone with any lady who was not his sister.

He had not even been content to draw her arm through his as they walked. He had also held her hand—and actually laced his fingers with hers. It had bordered very closely on impropriety. No, actually it had slipped beyond the border. Well beyond.

And then—the pièce de résistance of atypical behavior for him—he had kissed her. Honesty compelled him to admit that that brief meeting of lips could be called nothing less than a kiss.

It was all enough to make him break out in a cold sweat—because of course he could not simply obliterate the memories. On the contrary. They kept poking accusing fingers into his conscious thoughts.

He had trifled with her feelings. It was all very well to try telling himself that it was of no real significance, that he would forget within a week. Perhaps he would. But he also knew very well—good Lord, he had *five* sisters—that women remembered such things far longer than men did and set far more store by them.

He had always been aware of that, and he had always respected feminine sensibilities—except perhaps on one memorable occasion. And except on the evening of the assembly.

He had the uneasy feeling that Susanna Osbourne might just possibly be more hurt when they said the inevitable good-bye than she would otherwise have been.

Which was perhaps a conceited thought, he was willing to admit, but even so, she was the last person he would ever want to hurt.

And the worst of it—surely the *very* worst of it—was that that wretched apology for a kiss had surely been her first.

Dash it all, he was *not* proud of himself. He was downright ashamed if the truth were told.

And of course he could not court her even if he wanted to, which he did not—he *liked* her, that was all. There was an insurmountable gap between them socially.

Such differences ought not to matter, but of course they did. He lived in a society in which titled gentlemen were expected to choose brides from their own select upper circles. And there were sensible reasons for such exclusivity beyond simple snobbery. The wives of titled men had duties to perform for which their upbringing must have prepared them, and they had social obligations in the fulfillment of which they must be adept and comfortable.

It all sounded like weak enough reasoning when verbalized in his mind, but really it was not. It was all part of the fabric of society with which he had grown up and in which he had lived since his majority.

There was only one thing for it, he decided during the largely sleepless night that followed the assembly. He must keep his distance from Miss Susanna Osbourne for the three days that remained of her stay in Somerset—he was to leave the day after her. He must prevent himself from saying or doing anything that he might regret. Or anything *else,* anyway.

It was an eminently sensible resolve, and he kept it for two days. On the first, he was invited with the Raycrofts and a number of other neighbors to dine at Barclay Court and play charades and cards afterward. He did not ignore Susanna Osbourne—how could he? She was on the opposing team to his at charades, and she threw herself into the game with much the same energy and enthusiasm she had demonstrated at the boat races. She fairly sparkled with exuberant high spirits and made him believe—to his relief—that he must not have seriously upset her on the night of the assembly after all. He certainly did not ignore her or avoid her. He spoke with her and laughed with her and competed against her. But they did it all in the setting of the larger group and spent not even a minute alone together.

The following day, as the result of a suggestion made by Miss Moss at the Barclay Court dinner, a large party of young people drove into Taunton in four carriages for a look around the shops and a picnic on the banks of the River Thone. Peter deliberately did not ride in the same carriage as Susanna Osbourne, and though they were often close enough during the few hours in Taunton to exchange a few remarks and smiles, they were never alone together.

And then on the third day he awoke with a start at least an hour earlier than usual to the almost panicked realization that this was her last day at Barclay Court, and that they had wasted two whole days when with a little ingenuity they might have contrived to spend some time enjoying each other's exclusive company.

Dash it, he *wished* he had not kissed her. Or walked along the village street with her, their hands clasped, their fingers laced together.

It would be altogether wiser, he decided as he made his way down to breakfast some time later, to avoid being alone with her for one more day. Tomorrow she would be gone, and he would be getting ready to leave.

Raycroft and his sister, he discovered at breakfast, were going to walk over to Barclay Court during the morning to bid farewell to Miss Osbourne. They were to call for the Calvert sisters on their way.

"You simply must come with us, Lord Whitleaf," Miss Raycroft said. "Is it not sad that Miss Osbourne will be leaving so soon?"

Going with them would present him with the perfect opportunity to do the polite thing—take his own leave of her—but to do it from within the safety of a largish group. Yes, it would be eminently sensible. And he would have the congenial company of four young ladies for the walk to Barclay Court and back again.

But when he opened his mouth to reply, the words he spoke were not the ones he had intended to say.

"I have promised to call upon Miss Honeydew this morning," he said—though in fact he had done no such thing. "It is almost my last day here too, you know, and I have grown fond of the lady. I will try to call at Barclay Court sometime this afternoon."

Miss Raycroft pulled a face, but she did not suggest—as he thought she might—that the planned walk to Barclay Court be postponed until the afternoon so that they might all go together after all.

And so she and Raycroft set off without him, and he spent the morning chopping wood for Miss Honeydew, despite her vociferous protests, a task for which he was rewarded with effusive thanks, a few tears, and an insistence that he eat half a dozen of her housekeeper's special cakes, which this time were suspiciously black at the bottom and nearly rock-hard in the center. He took the dog for a run before driving his curricle back to Hareford House.

The morning had been cloudy—one of those days that could not make up its mind whether to dissolve into rain or open out into sunshine. If it had rained, he might have persuaded himself to remain at the house to play chess with Raycroft's father, who was always eager for a game with someone who could at least come close to beating him.

But the sky cleared off instead and the sun shone. The outdoors beckoned.

Peter rode over to Barclay Court. He left his horse in a groom's care at the stable and strode across the terrace and up one branch of the horseshoe steps. The butler was already in the open doorway and informed him that his lordship and the ladies had just finished luncheon and would surely be delighted to receive him in the drawing room.

He would, Peter decided as he followed the butler up the stairs, stay for fifteen or twenty minutes and then leave. He would wish Susanna Osbourne a pleasant journey and a happy autumn term at school. Perhaps he would kiss the back of her hand—or perhaps he would merely bow over it.

Good Lord, such self-conscious planning was quite uncharacteristic of him, he thought ruefully. The appropriate good manners normally came so naturally to him that he did not have to think them out in advance.

The butler opened the double doors of the drawing room with a flourish, as if he were about to announce the Prince of Wales himself—and then paused.

Susanna Osbourne was rising from a window seat. The large room was otherwise empty.

"Oh, Mr. Smothers," she said, "the earl and countess went downstairs to the library. Did you not see them?"

The butler turned an almost comically mortified face to the guest, but Peter spoke up before him.

"But it was Miss Osbourne I came particularly to see, Smothers," he said. "If she will receive me, that is."

The butler looked back to the lone occupant of the room.

"But of course," she said, walking halfway across the room before stopping. "It is quite all right, Mr. Smothers. How do you do, my lord?"

He was not doing very well at all actually. He had been assaulted again by the rather foolish panic he had felt when he awoke. This was the last time he would see her. Tomorrow morning she would be gone. The day after so would he. It was no comfort at the moment to try telling himself that by this time next week he would probably have forgotten her.

He smiled and advanced into the room, and the butler closed the door behind him.

"Frances received an invitation this morning to sing at a series of concerts in London later in the autumn," she explained. "She and the earl have gone down to the library to check on dates and make some plans. But they will not be long."

They would not be long. Suddenly their absence seemed to him like a gift he had avoided but longed for.

She was looking rather pale, he thought, until he looked more closely and realized that actually her face was slightly bronzed from exposure to the sun. But there was something . . . It was in her eyes even though they smiled. No, the rest of her face smiled. Her eyes surely did not. Like him, he thought, she was not unaware that this was the last time they would be alone together, the last time they would see each other.

Of course she was not unaware of it. Over the course of ten days or so they had developed a friendship that was rare in its warmth. How foolish of him to have deprived them both of two days.

"I came to say good-bye," he said.

"Yes." She spoke softly.

"It has been a pleasure knowing you," he said, though it struck him that there was so much knowing yet to do—if only they had more time.

"Yes," she said. "It has. Been a pleasure."

"Yesterday's excursion was enjoyable," he said.

"Yes," she agreed. "I have never been to Taunton before."

"Nor I," he said.

He saw her swallow, and she turned her head away for a moment before looking back at him.

"I hope you have a pleasant journey the day after tomorrow," she said.

"Yes. Thank you." He clasped his hands at his back.

"Shall I—"

"Will you—"

They spoke together and stopped together, and she gestured for him to proceed.

"Will you come out for a stroll with me?" he asked her, abandoning without a thought his careful plan for a fifteen-minute formal call. "It has turned into a beautiful day out there."

"I will fetch my bonnet," she said.

She left him on the landing while she ran up to the next floor, and panic returned. What if they could not get out of the house and out of sight before Edgecombe and his lady emerged from the library? There was this *one* afternoon left. This was it—his last chance. This time tomorrow . . .

His last chance for *what*, for God's sake?

As they stepped through the stairway arch into the hall, Edgecombe and the countess were coming out of the library, all hospitable smiles when they saw him.

"Ah, there you are, Whitleaf," Edgecombe said. "Smothers came and told us you were here—sorry about the misunderstanding, old chap. We were on our way up to join you. You are not leaving already, are you?"

"Please do not," the countess said.

"Miss Osbourne and I are going to take a stroll outside," Peter explained. "This sunshine is too lovely to miss."

"You should go and see this end of the wilderness walk," Edgecombe suggested. "It is all very picturesque—deliberately so, of course. In fact, we will come with you, will we not, Frances?"

Her hand came to rest on his sleeve.

"You were concerned yesterday," she said, "that I had had too much exposure to the sun during the picnic. Remember?"

"Eh?" He looked down at her with a frown.

"I think I had better do the wise thing and stay indoors today," she said.

Peter saw comprehension dawn in Edgecombe's eyes at the same time as it dawned in his own mind.

"Oh, absolutely, my love," Edgecombe said. "I'll stay here with you. Will you mind, Susanna?"

"No, of course not," she said.

"Sunstroke can be a dangerous thing," Peter added.

And so they stepped out of the house alone together, he and Susanna Osbourne—with the blessing of the Countess of Edgecombe, it would seem.

But blessing for what?

She had not misunderstood, had she? She did not expect? . . .

But he would not torture his mind further or waste another moment of this suddenly precious chance to be alone one more time with Susanna Osbourne—his friend.

He offered her his arm without a word, and without looking up into his face she took it.

There was suddenly a strange—and potentially disturbing—sense of completion.

11

Susanna's bags were almost completely packed. She had done the job herself after breakfast, though Frances had told her not to bother, that she would have a maid sent up later to do it for her. But she had come and watched anyway—and admitted while they chatted that she would still rather do many things for herself than rely upon servants to wait upon her hand and foot.

Susanna had been feeling almost cheerful. She was genuinely looking forward to returning home—and that was what the school was to her. It was home. And the ladies and girls waiting there for her were her family.

She had determinedly thrown off the depression that had weighed her down the night after the assembly. She had spent a wonderful two weeks of relaxation in lovely, luxurious surroundings and in company with one of her dearest friends and a whole host of other amiable acquaintances. And if that were not enough, she had had her first ride in a gentleman's curricle, she had engaged in—and won—a boat race, she had attended her very first ball—the assembly *did* qualify for that name, she had decided—and she had danced all but two sets there, each with a different partner. She had even waltzed, and she had been kissed for the first time—that brief meeting of lips *did* qualify. She had decided that too. Friends of opposite gender could occasionally kiss even if the sentiment behind the gesture was affection rather than romance.

She had decided—very sensibly—that she would remember everything about these two weeks down to the last little detail, and that she would enjoy the memories rather than allow them to oppress her.

It had helped that Viscount Whitleaf had not singled her out for any particular attention during the past two days. They had been able to smile amicably at each other and even speak with each other, but as part of a group of acquaintances.

It had helped too that he had not come this morning with Mr. Raycroft and his sister and the Calverts. All four of the young ladies had hugged her when they were leaving, and Miss Raycroft and Miss Mary Calvert had actually shed a few tears. Mr. Raycroft had taken her hand in both of his and patted it kindly as he wished her a safe journey and a pleasant autumn term at school.

Ah, yes, it had helped that *he* had not come too, that he had avoided actually saying good-bye to her.

And yet it had been very hard at luncheon to maintain a cheerful flow of conversation with Frances and the earl.

It had been hard to swallow her food past the lump in her throat.

It had been hard to avoid admitting to herself that

she was hurt—both by his absence this morning and by the care with which he had avoided being alone with her yesterday and the day before. She knew it had been deliberate.

It was as if that kiss, which had perhaps not been a real kiss at all, had destroyed their friendship.

But now he had come after all.

Alone.

And he had found her alone. Yet when the earl had suggested that he and Frances join them on their walk outside, Viscount Whitleaf had conspicuously not grasped at the chance of having company. He had said nothing. And Frances seemed to have believed that Susanna *wanted* to spend a few minutes of this last afternoon alone with him.

Did she?

She and Frances had intended spending the afternoon walking all about the lake. Just the two of them. The earl had said at luncheon that he would leave them to enjoy each other's company since they were soon going to be separated for a while again.

Viscount Whitleaf's arm, Susanna noticed, was not quite relaxed beneath her hand. There was a certain tension in the muscles there. He did not speak for a while as she directed them across the terrace and diagonally across the lawn toward the woods, where the wilderness walk began.

She could not help remembering the silence in which they had walked more than halfway from Hareford House to Barclay Court the day they met—not quite two weeks ago.

But there was a different quality to this silence.

It was almost impossible to believe that just two weeks ago she had not even met him—except once, briefly, when they were both children.

"There it is," she said, breaking the silence at last as she pointed ahead to where a clearly defined path disappeared among the trees. "The wilderness walk. It winds its way through the woods and over the hill to a small bridge across the river, and then it follows the river past the waterfall to the lake and continues all around it to approach the house from the other side."

"A long hike," he said.

"Yes."

"Are you up to it?" he asked her.

"I have always loved walking," she told him.

"I have too," he said. "I have been on walking tours of the Scottish Highlands and the Lake District. I intend to try North Wales one of these days."

"Mount Snowdon is said to be quite breathtaking," she said, "and the whole country rugged and beautiful."

"Yes," he said, "so I have heard."

The path was well kept and allowed them to walk comfortably two abreast. There was an instant feeling of seclusion as tree branches offered shade overhead and tree trunks closed in around them like pillars in a cathedral. A number of birds were trilling out a summer song from their perches above.

"I would be interested to hear about your walking tours," she said.

He did not answer for a while, and she was aware that his head was turned toward her. She kept looking ahead.

"We can do it this way if you wish," he said softly at last. "We can find topics upon which one or both of us is able to converse eloquently and at some length. And when we have reached the end of the walk and arrived back at the house we can each congratulate ourselves on the fact that we allowed not a moment's silence to descend between us after the first few awkward minutes. We can take a cheerful farewell of each other and that will be it. The end of the story."

She did not know what she was supposed to say. He had asked no question.

"Yes," she said.

"It *is* what you wish?" He bent his head closer to hers, and she risked turning her own to look into his eyes, darker than usual in the shade of the trees, only a few inches from her own.

It was her undoing.

"No," she said, not knowing exactly what she meant but quite certain that she did not want to chatter politely with him about inconsequential matters when this was their last time alone together.

Ever.

"No," she said again, more firmly, and she smiled fleetingly and turned her head to look ahead along the path once more. "But in what way *are* we to do it, then?"

"Let us simply *enjoy* the afternoon and each other's company. Let us laugh a little," he said. "But real enjoyment and real laughter. Let's be friends. Shall we?"

It *was* foolish to feel tragic. This time next week, next year, she would look back and wonder why she had not taken full advantage of every moment instead of living with the emptiness of what the future would hold. How did she *know* the future would be empty? How did she know there would even be a future?

"What a good idea," she said—and laughed.

"I think it quite brilliant."

He laughed too, but though their laughter was about nothing at all—her comment and his retort could hardly be called witty—it felt very good. And suddenly she felt happy. She would *not* peer into the future.

"Have you noticed," she asked him, "how we live much of our lives in the past and most of the rest of it in the future? Have you noticed how often the present moment slips by quite unnoticed?"

"Until it becomes the past?" he said. "*Then* it gets our attention. Yes, you are perfectly right. How many present moments will there be before we arrive back at the house, do you suppose? How long *is* a present moment, anyway? One could argue, perhaps, that it is endless, eternal."

"Or more fleeting than a fraction of a second," she said.

"I believe," he said, "we are dealing with the half-empty-glass attitude versus the half-full-glass attitude again. Are we by any chance talking *philosophy*? It is an alarming possibility. If we are not careful we will be trying to decide next how many angels can dance on the head of a pin."

"None at all or an infinite number," she said. "I have never been sure which. If there *is* a correct answer."

"Well," he said, chuckling, "shall we agree to live

this particular endless moment strictly in the present tense? Or this myriad succession of present moments?"

"Yes, we will so agree," she said, laughing with him again.

And as they strolled onward, Susanna lifted her face to the changing patterns of light and shade, warmth and coolness, and was aware of the sounds of birdsong and insect whirrings and the scurrying of unseen wildlife and the smells of earth and greenery and a masculine cologne. She felt every irregularity, every small stone on the path beneath her feet, the firm but relaxed muscles of his arm beneath her hand, warm through the sleeve of his coat.

She turned her head again to smile at him and found that he was smiling back—a lazy, genuine, happy smile.

"I see a seat up ahead," he said. "It is my guess that it looks out on a pleasing prospect."

"It does," she said. "This path was *very* carefully constructed for the pleasure of the walker, as you observed yourself when we walked to the waterfall."

They stood behind the seat for a while, looking through what appeared to be a natural opening between trees across wide lawns to the house and stables in the distance. An old oak tree in the middle of the lawn was perfectly framed in the view.

And she was *here now* looking at the view, Susanna thought, deliberately feeling the soft fabric of his coat sleeve without actually moving her hand.

"The path moves up into that hill," she said, pointing ahead. "There are some lovely views from up there. The best, though, I think, is the one down onto the river and the little bridge."

They stopped a number of times before they came there, gazing alternately out onto the cultivated beauty of the park and over the rural peace and plenty of the surrounding farmland.

"I wish you could see Sidley," he said, squinting off into the distance when they were looking across a patchwork of fields, separated by low hedgerows. "You *did* say you had never been there, did you not? It always seems to me that there is nowhere to compare with it in beauty. I suppose I am partial. *Undoubtedly* I am partial, in fact. It smites me *here*." He tapped his heart and then turned to her suddenly and smiled roguishly. "It smites this chest organ, this pump."

"The heart, the center of our most tender sensibilities," she conceded, "even if only because we feel they must be centered somewhere. It must indeed be wonderful to have a home of your very own. I can well imagine that you would come to see it more with the emotions than with the eye or the intellect."

"I hope you will have a home of your own one day," he said, tapping her hand as it rested on his arm.

They strolled onward, following the path down through the lower, wooded slopes of the hill until it climbed again into the open and they could see down to the river, narrower here than it was closer to the lake. And there was the little wooden footbridge that spanned it, so highly arched that the path across it formed actual steps up to the middle and down the other side. The water flowing beneath it was dark green from the reflections of trees growing thickly up the slopes from its banks.

"Ah, yes," he said as they stopped walking, "you were quite right. This is the best view of all. Even better than the view from the waterfall. That is spectacular, but like most of the views here it encompasses both the wilderness and the outside world. This is nothing but wilderness."

Susanna let go of his arm and turned all about. The hill rose behind them to meet the sky. On the other three sides there was nothing to see but trees. Below were more trees and undergrowth and ferns and the river and bridge.

"I had not really noticed that before," she said. "But it is true. That must be why I love being just here so much. It offers total . . ."

"Escape?"

But she frowned and shook her head.

"*Retreat,*" she said. "It is a better word, I think."

"Shall we sit down for a while?" he suggested. "There is no seat just here, but I don't suppose the ground is damp. There has been no rain for several days, has there?"

He stooped down on his haunches and rubbed his hand hard across the grass. He held the hand up, palm out, to show her that it was dry.

She sat down, drawing her knees up before her and clasping her arms about them. He stretched out on his side beside her, lifting himself onto one elbow and propping his head on one hand while the other rubbed lightly over the grass.

The sun beamed down warm on their heads.

"Oh, listen," she said after a few moments.

His hand fell still.

"The waterfall?"

"Yes."

They both listened for a while before he lifted his hand from the grass and set it lightly over one of hers about her knees.

"Susanna," he said, "I *am* going to miss you."

"We are not supposed to be thinking about the future," she said, but she had to draw a slow, steadying breath before she spoke.

"No," he agreed. His hand slid from hers and he tossed his hat aside and lay back on the grass, one leg bent at the knee with his booted foot flat on the ground, the back of one hand over his eyes to shield them from the sun.

There was the rawness of threatened pain at the back of her throat. It was no easy thing to hold the future at bay. She concentrated her mind again upon the distant sound of the waterfall.

"Do you ever wish," he asked after a couple of minutes, "that you were totally free?"

"I dream of it all the time," she said.

"So do I."

Two weeks ago—less—she would have assumed that such a man had all the freedom he could possibly want or need. Indeed, it had seemed to her that most men were essentially free.

"What ungrateful wretches we are," he said with a low chuckle.

"But it is not freedom from school or from relative poverty or from anything else in my circumstances that I yearn for," she said. "It is . . . Oh, I once heard it described as the yearning for God, though that is not quite it either. It is just—mmm . . ."

"The longing for something beyond yourself, beyond anything you have ever known or dreamed of?" he suggested.

"Yes," she said with a sigh.

"Are we talking philosophy again?" he asked, and he removed his hand from his eyes, turned his head, and grinned up at her. "Twice in one afternoon? I think I must be sickening for something."

She laughed and looked back at him.

And something happened.

Suddenly the moment was very present indeed, as if past and future had faded to nothingness or else collapsed into the present. And the moment was simply magic.

And unbearably tense.

Their eyes held, and neither spoke as their smiles faded—until he lifted his hand and set the knuckles lightly against her cheek.

"Susanna," he said softly.

She could have said or done any number of things to cause time to tick back into motion. But she did none of them—did not even consider any of them, in fact. She was suspended in the wonder of the moment.

She turned her head so that her lips were against his knuckles. And she gazed down into his eyes, violet and smoky and as deep as the ocean.

He slid the hand down and pulled loose the ribbons of her bonnet. He brushed it backward and it fell to the grass behind her. She felt the air warm against her face and cool in her slightly damp hair. He cupped her face in both hands and drew it downward. She released her tight hold on her legs and turned so that she was kneeling beside him.

And then their lips met—again.

It was a kiss as brief—and as earth-shattering—as the last one. He lifted her face away from his and gazed up into her eyes, his thumbs circling her cheeks.

"Let me kiss you," he said.

It was something of an absurd request, perhaps, in light of the fact that he had just done exactly that without asking permission. But despite her almost total lack of experience with kisses, she possessed enough woman's intuition to know exactly what he meant.

"Yes," she whispered.

She continued to kneel over him, one hand spread over his chest, the other bracing herself on the grass on the far side of him, while he kissed her again.

But this time the kiss did not end after a brief moment. It did not end at all for a long, long time. And this time it was not a mere touching or brushing of lips.

This time his lips were parted and warm and moist, and he nibbled at her lower lip with his teeth and touched both her lips with his tongue and with its tip traced the seam between them from one corner to the other and back again but pressing a little more firmly this time until it curled up behind her top lip to caress the soft, sensitive flesh inside. And then he feathered little kisses across her mouth and down to her chin before kissing her fully again, his mouth pressed harder, more urgently to hers. His tongue pushed past her lips, past her teeth deep into her mouth. And then finally the kiss softened, and he lifted her head away from his again.

His eyes were heavy-lidded as they gazed into hers.

"Lie down beside me," he suggested. "You look uncomfortable."

She was still crouched over him, her hands clutching one lapel of his coat and a clump of coarse grass.

She stretched out beside him, lying on her side, his arm beneath her head. She rested her hand over his heart and closed her eyes. She did not want him to speak. She did not want to think. She was too busy *feeling*.

Did people—men and women—really kiss like that? She had had *no* idea. She had imagined being kissed, and in her imagination she had been swept away by the sheer romance of the meeting of lips. In her naïveté she had not considered the possibility that a kiss, as a prelude to sexual activity, might have powerful effects on parts of her body other than just her lips. *All* parts of her body, in fact, even parts she had been only half aware of possessing. She ached and throbbed in all sorts of unfamiliar places.

Neither had it ever occurred to her that a kiss might involve the mouth as well as just the lips.

She could feel his heart beating heavily beneath her hand.

And then, before she had even begun to recover her wits, he turned onto his side to face her, and his free hand touched her cheek again and his fingers feathered through her hair, moving it away from her face.

She both saw and heard him swallow.

"The trouble with kisses," he said softly, "is that inevitably they make one want more."

"Yes."

More?

Kisses as a prelude to . . .

He kissed her again, softly and lazily, and they lay with their arms about each other while she responded with moves of her own. She moved her lips over his, touched them with her tongue, stroked his tongue with her own when it came into her mouth again, sucked on it. When he made a low sound in his throat, she spread her hand over the back of his head, twining her fingers in his sun-warm hair.

That was when he brought the rest of her body against his and she felt all the unfamiliar thrill of being flush against the hard-muscled body of a man from the lips to the toes. One of his Hessian boots hooked about her legs to hug her closer.

"Susanna," he whispered into her mouth.

"Yes."

"Say my name," he murmured.

"Peter."

It was so much more personal, so much more intimate, than his title. She had never even *thought* of him as Peter before now. But it was his name, his most personal possession. It was how she would remember him.

The ache of—of *wanting* became almost unbearable.

His hand was at her breast, exploring it lightly, caressing it, his palm lifting it, his thumb rubbing over her nipple, which was taut and tender. He hooked the same thumb beneath the fabric of her dress at the shoulder and eased it down her arm until her breast was exposed. His hand covered it again, warm and dark-skinned against its paleness. And then he lowered his head and, before she could guess his intent, took her nipple into his mouth and suckled her.

Sensation stabbed like a knife up into her throat and behind her nose, down through her womb and along her inner thighs.

It was the moment at which she abandoned self-deception.

This was no ordinary, innocent friendship.

It never had been.

She could not bear the thought of tomorrow. But it was not just because she would be losing a friend. She would also be leaving behind the man with whom she had tumbled headlong and hopelessly in love.

Hopelessly being a key word.

Hopelessly. Without all hope. Without any future. There was only now.

He lifted his head and brought his mouth close to hers again. But instead of kissing her, he gazed deep into her eyes, his own heavy with a desire that clearly matched her own. It was not hard to interpret that look even though she had not seen it on a man's face before.

"Stop me now," he murmured, "or heaven help us both."

Stop?

No! Oh, no. If there was no future, if there was

only now, she would not have it snatched away from her—forever. She would have the whole of it.

It was not rational thought, of course, with which she considered his words. She was past rational thought—but had no experience with anything else. Her mind did not even touch upon virtue or morality. Even less did it touch upon consequences or the very real dangers inherent in *not* stopping him.

There was only now.

Now he was here with her.

Tomorrow she would be gone, and the day after so would he.

"Susanna?" he whispered again.

"Don't stop," she said. "Please don't stop."

He did not stop. He turned her onto her back, kissing her, baring her other breast and fondling her with expert hands and lips while she lay beneath him, bewilderment and desire and sheer physical sensation tumbling together through every vein and bone and nerve ending in her body.

And then he lifted the hem of her dress, drawing it all the way up to her hips and disposing of undergarments until she could feel the grass against her bare flesh. He fumbled with the waist flap of his pantaloons and brought himself over between her legs, which he parted with his own before sliding his hands firmly beneath her to cushion her against the hardness of the ground.

She knew what happened. With her intellect, she knew the process—or some of it anyway. She knew about penetration and the spilling of the seed. It had always seemed to her that it must be both painful and embarrassing, though she had always wanted to experience it anyway.

There *was* pain. He came into her slowly but firmly, pressing past the barrier of her virginity until he was deeply embedded in her.

There was no embarrassment.

She had not known how large he would feel, how hard, how deep.

And she had known nothing of what happened between penetration and the spilling of the seed.

What happened was pain and pleasure and shock and satisfaction all rolled into one. Pain as he withdrew and thrust over and over again past the soreness of her newly opened womanhood. Pleasure because it was more wonderful, more exhilarating, than any other sensation she had ever experienced. Shock because she had not expected such a deep and vigorous and prolonged invasion of her body. Satisfaction because now, before it was too late, he was her lover. Because she would always be able to remember him as her lover.

Despite the pain and the shock, she wanted it never to end. She braced her feet on the ground, feeling the supple leather of his boots along the insides of her legs as she did so, wrapped her arms about him, closed her eyes, and allowed herself to feel every painful, powerful, wonderful stroke of his body into hers, to hear every labored breath they both drew, to smell his cologne and the very essence of his maleness, to understand that at last, for once in her life, she was celebrating her sexuality—with a man she loved.

She would not be sorry afterward.

Surely she would not.

She would not even think of afterward.

But it came anyway.

His rhythm quickened and his strokes deepened until he held still in her, every muscle tense, and then sighed and relaxed even as she felt the gush of a greater heat deep inside.

She swallowed against a moment's disappointment that now it was over.

Forever.

It did not matter. It *would* not matter. She would always remember.

He drew free of her and rolled off her, careful to lower her skirt over her legs and lift her bodice over her breasts as he did so. He lay on his back beside her after setting his own clothing to rights, one arm flung over his eyes, the other hand palm-down over the back of hers as it lay on the grass between them.

It seemed to her that he slept for a few minutes.

How could anyone possibly *sleep* after that? But he had, of course, expended a great deal of energy.

Deep inside her she harbored his seed.

The beginnings of rational thought niggled at the edges of her mind.

"Susanna," he said sleepily, while she lay with closed eyes, reliving every moment of what had just happened.

She turned her head to look at him. He was tousled, slightly flushed, impossibly handsome.

"Come away with me," he said.

"What?" An irrational hope blossomed for a moment.

"Let's go away," he said. "Why say good-bye when neither of us wants it to happen? Let's go to North Wales. Let's see Mount Snowdon together and go walking over the hills and along the beaches. Let's do it. Let's run free."

And the horrible thing was, she thought as she stared at him, that he meant it. And that for two pins she would have cast caution and good sense to the winds and agreed to go with him.

"And afterward?" she said.

"Afterward?" He laughed softly. "To the devil with afterward. We will think of that when the time comes. I won't ever leave you destitute, though, I promise. Come with me. Let's do it."

Rational thought came crashing back from wherever it had been hiding and took up residence in her conscious mind again.

She would be his mistress.

They would have a wild, doubtless glorious fling together, and then he would pay her off. Because he was a basically decent and kind man, he would see to it that she did not starve after he discarded her.

She could be his mistress.

His whore.

"I like my life as it is," she said. "I love the school and my work there and my pupils and my fellow teachers. I have to go back tomorrow."

"You do not *have* to do anything," he said.

"You are right." She sat up and straightened her dress as best she could with slightly shaking hands. "I do not. I do not have to go away with you."

He sat up too.

"I cannot bear to let you go," he said as she reached for her bonnet and pulled it on over her disheveled curls. "Can you bear to let *me* go?"

"No," she admitted, pausing as she tied the ribbons beneath her chin. "But there are no alternatives that I can bear even as well as saying good-bye to you."

"Susanna—" he began.

But she had got to her feet and stood looking down at him. She had even dredged up a half-cheerful smile from somewhere.

"I will treasure the memory of this fortnight," she said. "Even the memory of *this*. But this is the end. It must be. Anything else would be sordid."

"*Sordid.*" He frowned up at her and then reached for his hat and got slowly to his feet to stand beside her. "Would it?"

"Yes," she said. "I am a teacher, not a courtesan. I will remain a teacher."

He looked at her for a long moment, his eyes unfathomable, and then he nodded.

"I beg your pardon," he said. "I do beg your forgiveness for the insult."

"It was not insulting," she said softly, "to let me know that you would prolong your acquaintance with me if you could. Shall we go back instead of walking farther? We must have been gone for some time, and Frances will wonder what—"

"We have been up to?" he suggested.

Slowly and ruefully they smiled at each other.

When he offered his arm, she took it, and they resumed their walk, albeit in the opposite direction. She felt all the unreality of the past half hour or so.

Except that it was not unreal.

Between her thighs she could feel the trembling aftermath of what they had done together.

Inside, she felt an unmistakable soreness.

Deep inside she harbored his seed.

Too late she thought of consequences.

12

*Peter returned home to Sidley Park in September af-*ter he could be sure that all his mother's houseguests had left. He wondered a little uneasily as his carriage approached the house if he was going to find it easy—or even possible—to share his home with his mother now that he had made a decision to settle here. He loved her dearly, but she *had* always ruled Sidley as though it were her own domain and everyone in it as though she were a supreme deity who knew what was best for them. It was a good thing she had ruled her children with a loving as well as a firm hand—though that very fact, of course, would make it harder to exert his will against her now.

But why anticipate problems when they did not even exist yet?

When his carriage drew to a halt before the house and the coachman opened the door, Peter did not even wait for the steps to be set down but vaulted out onto the cobbled terrace like an eager boy home from a dreary term at school.

It did not take him long to discover that problems did indeed exist.

His mother had been alleviating the tedium of her days since the departure of the houseguests by having the drawing room refurbished with a preponderance of pink colorings and frills. Most notably there were frilly pink cushions everywhere, though even they were preferable to the pink curtains, which were pleated and ruched and frilled and scalloped in ways that made him feel slightly bilious.

"This has always seemed such a plain, dark, gloomy room," she explained, her arm linked through her son's as she took him to inspect what had been done. "Now already it looks light and cheerful, would you not agree, my love? It will look even better when the portraits have been replaced with some pretty landscapes."

"Where are the portraits going?" he asked her, masking the dismay he felt with a tone of polite interest. They were portraits of some of his ancestors, and he had always been proud of them, fascinated by them, and altogether rather fond of them. They were a link to his father, whom he could not remember, and to his heritage on his father's side, in which no one else but he had ever seemed interested.

"To the attic," she said. "I have always hated them. One does not need such gloomy reminders of the past, would you not agree, my love?"

He grunted noncommittally.

The drawing room, he thought—though he did not say so aloud—looked like an oversize lady's boudoir. It would look even more so with different pictures.

"Well, what do you think?" she asked, beaming up at him.

It was time, perhaps, to play ruthless lord and master. But she looked so very happy and so very sure that he would be pleased too. And it was a mere room when all was said and done. He could live with a pink room—provided it was not the library or his bedchamber.

"It is very . . . *you*, Mama," he said. It really was a room suited to her. She had always been pretty—she still was—and delicate and very feminine. Pink had always been her favorite color.

"I *knew* you would adore it," she said, squeezing his arm. "It is *so* good to have you home again. But, my love, it was most provoking of the Raycrofts to insist that you remain in Somerset when they knew you wished to be here. Our guests were very disappointed, especially Lady Larchwell, who was hoping, I daresay, that her daughter would take your eye. Miss Larchwell is a pretty young lady and modest too, considering the fact that her maternal great-grandfather was a duke. You would like her. You really ought to have asserted yourself with the Raycrofts, you know. You are just too kindhearted for your own good."

"I must confess, Mama," he said, "that I enjoyed my stay at Hareford House very much indeed."

"Well, of course you did," she said, seating herself on a chair and almost sinking out of sight amid a pile of cushions. "Though I daresay the company was not very distinguished. It is not so here either now that all the houseguests are gone. I will be glad of your company, my love."

"Well, there are the Markhams," he said. "I will certainly be happy to see Theo again. And there are the Harrises and the Mummerts and the Poles."

But his mother pulled a face and made no reply.

She had always behaved graciously enough toward their neighbors, but she had always treated them too with a condescension that spoke of the social distance she felt existed between them. The Markhams were a distinguished enough family, it was true, and had always been prominent in political circles—Theo's father had actually been a minister in the government for a number of years. But though there had been a time when his mother visited often at Fincham Manor and occasionally took him and his sisters with her, the relationship had cooled long ago. It was a pity. Theo's mother still lived at Fincham during the winter months, and she was much of an age with his mother. They might have been friends.

"And speaking of the Markhams," he said, suddenly thinking of something, "do you remember Mr. Osbourne?"

Her fingers stopped playing with the lace frill of one of the cushions, and she stared blankly at him.

"I cannot say I do," she said.

"He was the late Sir Charles Markham's secretary for a number of years," he explained.

"Was he?" She gave the matter some thought, but then shrugged and shook her head. "Then I would not have known him, would I?"

"You scolded me once," he said, "when he was teaching Theo and me to write in some fancy script in his study. You came dashing in and then were very upset because you had thought we were up in Theo's room when instead we were breathing in ink fumes and probably giving ourselves a headache."

"You had very delicate health, my love," she said. "I always feared for you, especially if I could not find you where I expected you to be. But I do not remember that particular incident."

"And then there was the time," he said, "when I was home from school for a week and went over to Fincham with you—without the girls—only to discover that Theo did *not* have a school holiday and Edith was away at a birthday party somewhere. I went riding off on one of the horses from the stable to run an errand with Mr. Osbourne—I daresay I told him I had your permission or else he thought that at my age I did not need it. You were so upset by the time we came back that I believe you were actually ill after we came home. It was the last time I saw him."

"Oh?" she said. "Was he dismissed? I daresay he ought to have been."

"He died," he said. "Suddenly. Of a heart attack."

"Oh?" she said. "That was unfortunate. But what can have put a mere secretary into your mind years after his death? *Do* be a love and ring for the tea tray."

He did so without answering her question. It made perfect sense, of course, that she would not remember a man who had really been no more than a glorified servant. It was even less likely that she would remember Susanna Osbourne—not that he had been about to mention *her* name to his mother.

He was trying hard to forget it himself—or at least the guilt with which he remembered it.

He called upon all his neighbors in the coming weeks. The Harrises told him about their recent stay at Tunbridge Wells, the Mummerts wanted to know about all the latest fashions in London, since they were planning to spend a few weeks there in the spring, and the Poles regaled him with stories of the exploits of their numerous grandchildren. They were all perfectly amiable, but none of them issued any invitations to him to dine or play cards or join them at any other entertainment. It had never been done—he was *Viscount Whitleaf* and as far above them in station as the stars. Everything in their manner during his visits demonstrated an almost awed respect. All of them assured him that they were deeply honored that he had called. But *he* issued no invitations either—his mother would be uncomfortable, even upset, about having her house invaded by inferior company.

Her house!

It was *his*!

Dash it all, it was harder than he thought to change his way of thinking. Sidley had been his mother's domain since her marriage. And though it had been his property for twenty-three years, for eighteen of those he had been a minor and it was only natural that his mother remain in charge.

Why the devil had he not told his uncles and his mother when he turned twenty-one that he was far too young to think of marriage but that he was at exactly the right age to take over the running of his own life and home and estate? It would have been easy then. It would have been the natural thing to do. It was what everyone had surely been prepared for.

Or why, when he had decided *not* to marry, had he not told his mother quite firmly that she was going to have to find somewhere else to live than the main house at Sidley?

But of course he had been too young for all of it. His life had been effectively lived for him for twenty-one years. How could he have developed the wisdom overnight to act as he ought?

He called one day at Fincham and was delighted to find Theo at home. Edith was no longer there, of course. She had married Lawrence Morley two years ago and now lived in Gloucestershire with her husband. Lady Markham was currently there with her, lending her support after the recent birth of Edith's first child.

Peter called several times after that first visit and sometimes went riding with his longtime friend. On one of those occasions he asked the same question he had raised with his mother.

"Do you remember Osbourne?" he asked.

"*William* Osbourne?" Theo asked. "My father's secretary, do you mean?"

"I rather liked him," Peter said. "He always had time for us, if you remember. It was a pity about his death."

Theo leaned forward out of his saddle to open a gate into a field so that they could ride across country instead of having to keep to the dusty lane.

"It was a tragedy," he agreed. "Avoidable too, as such deaths always are. Though I do not suppose he saw it that way, poor fellow."

"He *could* have avoided it?" Peter asked.

"Easily," Theo said dryly, as he shut the gate behind them. "By not putting that bullet through his brain."

"He *killed* himself?" Peter's hands tightened so suddenly upon the reins that his horse reared up and he had to struggle to keep his seat and bring it back under control.

"You did not *know*?" Theo was frowning when Peter finally looked back at him. "No one *told* you?"

"Only that he had died," Peter said.

"Hmm." Theo continued on his way across the field. "That makes sense, I suppose. You were always sheltered from any unpleasantness, weren't you? What put you in mind of him now, anyway?"

"I ran into his daughter this summer," Peter said.

"*Susanna?*" Theo said. "I was under the impression she had fallen off the ends of the earth, poor girl—though I suppose she is a woman now. Edith was inconsolable, apparently, when she ran off, and my mother was frantic. Fortunately I was away at school and missed all the drama. I was sorry about Osbourne, though. He was a decent fellow."

"*Why* did he kill himself?" Peter asked.

"All sorts of unlikely possibilities were suggested to me when I asked the same question at the time," Theo said. "Either no one knew the real reason or else everyone was being very cagey about it. He had to be buried in unconsecrated ground—which probably did not matter much to him but would have been hard on Susanna if she had stayed for the funeral. Apparently she did not. Anyway, should we change the subject?"

They did not refer to it again either on that afternoon or on any subsequent occasion. But Peter was left wondering what the devil could have been so dire in Osbourne's life that he had put an end to it despite the fact that he had a daughter to support. Her running away was a little more understandable now, though. Her father had committed suicide—a nasty sin according to Church doctrine. Poor child—running off to London and trying to find employment there. If Lady Hallmere was indeed responsible for sending her to Miss Martin's school in Bath, then he would forever feel kindly toward her.

But he still tried hard not even to think of Susanna Osbourne—or of what he had done to her the day before she left Barclay Court.

He spent some time out on the home farm, though not as much as he would have liked. The harvest was almost all in and it would have seemed mildly ridiculous to jump in to help now, all energy and enthusiasm, when there was very little left to do.

He spent some time with his steward and went over all the books with him, despite the fact that he carefully examined each monthly report that was sent him. But Millingsworth had been appointed by Peter's guardians when he was a very young child. The man was organized, efficient, knowledgeable, and experienced and looked upon Peter—or so it seemed—as if he were still a boy whose presence in his domain was a slight nuisance that had to be endured only because he was the official employer.

When he was in the house, his mother hovered over him, worried that he was not eating properly or dressing in a manner appropriate to the weather or giving serious enough thought to his future—to marrying well and setting up his nursery, that was. She was careful to see to it that the servants answered his every summons promptly, that his every whim was catered to, that he was served the very best of everything at mealtimes even if the portion in question had already been set on her plate. She came close to tears if he ever decided to set foot outdoors when it was raining or damp or when the wind was blowing at any force above the merest breeze. She even appeared in the library doorway one night well after midnight when he was reading to ask him if he did not think it was time he went to bed as he knew how easily he got a headache the next day if he stayed up too late at night.

It was all horribly irksome. Perhaps he would have faced it all and dealt with it all if he had not been so mortally depressed. But despite the enthusiasm with which he had jumped from his carriage on his arrival, he could not shake off the gloom he had carried with him from Hareford House.

Everything seemed somehow ruined.

Finally, after a few weeks, he thought to himself— and his reasoning seemed quite sound—that he might as well leave until the new year when he could be present for all the upcoming spring planning. A new year would be a better time—the perfect time—for starting the new life he had promised himself. He might even go back for Christmas. Some of his sisters were sure to be there, and he was fond of them—and of his numerous nieces and nephews.

And so he drifted off back to London, using as an excuse the fact that he needed to visit his tailor and his bootmaker. There he lived a life of increasingly busy idleness as he searched out one diversion after another. It was surprising how many could be found even during such an unseasonable month as October.

There was a comfortable familiarity about such a life.

Except that diversions did not always divert.

Activities that had always amused him well enough before suddenly seemed to have lost their power to distract his mind from his overall dissatisfaction with the way his life was proceeding.

His mother's letters informed him that the new paintings had arrived for the drawing room, which was now looking so much lovelier than any other room in the house that she was considering making changes to the dining room next.

Good Lord, he was going to have to do something to stop her.

Barbara, his eldest sister, who happened to spend a few days in London with her husband during the autumn, mentioned Christmas.

"You will be at Sidley, I hope," she said. "Clarence and I will be there with the children, and it will be too, too dreary if you are not also there, Peter. Besides, Mama is inviting other guests, and it is only right that you be there as host."

"Other guests?" He grimaced. "Who is she this time?"

Barbara clucked her tongue while Clarence waggled his eyebrows at his brother-in-law and held his peace.

"I have no idea," she said. "But there will be *some-*

one, of course. Mama is *concerned* about you, Peter. She wants to see you well settled. It is foolish of you to be stubborn merely because you did not like Bertha Grantham five years ago and did not admit it until the last possible moment."

None of his sisters had any idea what had happened on that occasion, and he had no wish to enlighten any of them.

Peter met his brother-in-law's eyes again and watched one of them depress in a slow wink.

"I'll choose my own bride in my own good time, Barb," he said. "I'll think about Christmas."

But thinking about brides made him feel more wretched than ever. In the almost two months since he had left Somerset, he had still not recovered from his terrible sense of guilt.

Good Lord, he had debauched an innocent!

There were no excuses. None.

He felt sick whenever he thought of that afternoon on the wilderness walk. And it was almost impossible not to think of it at least a dozen times every day.

It seemed somehow worse to have learned that her father had killed himself. Not that that sad event was in any way his fault or linked to the events of the summer, but even so . . . He had *liked* Osbourne. He liked the daughter.

Whenever such thoughts threatened to cause his head to explode, he went out again in search of another entertainment to take his mind off things.

Finally, at the end of October, he decided that a change of scenery might cheer him up and headed off to spend a week or two with his cousin Lauren,

Viscountess Ravensberg, at Alvesley Park in Wiltshire, where she lived with Kit, her husband, and their children, and with Kit's parents, the Earl and Countess of Redfield. He had a standing invitation to go there and always enjoyed himself when he did.

They were fond of each other, he and Lauren, perhaps because they had been kept apart until he reached adulthood and discovered an invitation to her wedding among his pile of mail one day after he returned from one of his walking tours. His mail had never come directly to him until he turned twenty-one, and he had never met Lauren—had hardly even heard of her, in fact, except as the possibly illegitimate daughter of a mother of loose morals: widow of his father's elder brother, a former Viscount Whitleaf. He had gone to the wedding, though he had arrived only just in time, and discovered that Lauren was lovely and charming and most definitely not illegitimate— her eyes were the exact same unusual color and shade as his own.

He went to Alvesley now to stay and did indeed enjoy himself there—spending hours in company with Lauren and the Countess of Redfield, playing with the three children, riding and discussing farming business and politics with Kit and the earl, visiting neighbors, including the Duke and Duchess of Bewcastle, playing with *their* baby, much to the amusement of the duchess and her sister, Miss Thompson, who remarked with a laugh that the babe was habitually too cross to be anyone's favorite except his mama and papa's. And his grandmama's, Mrs. Thompson added reproachfully.

Though *enjoyment,* of course, seemed to be a relative term these days. He still could not shrug off his underlying feeling of restlessness and dissatisfaction with himself.

And then fate took a startlingly strange hand in his destiny.

Perhaps it ought not to have startled him quite as much as it did. Already, soon after his arrival, he had discovered the almost incredibly coincidental fact that he had just missed seeing Sydnam Butler, Lauren's brother-in-law, who had been home for a week with his new bride, the former Miss Anne Jewell, a teacher at Miss Martin's School for Girls in Bath—and one of Susanna's particular friends, Peter remembered. And already, on visiting Bewcastle, he had remembered the connection Susanna had felt existed between the school and Lady Hallmere, Bewcastle's sister.

But then, almost a week into his stay, he learned that Lauren and the duchess between them had just finalized plans for a surprise wedding breakfast in honor of the newlyweds, who had married quietly and by special license in Bath. Lauren was involved because Sydnam was her brother-in-law, the duchess because he was the steward at Bewcastle's Welsh estate.

Their plan was to gather as many relatives and friends in Bath as they could muster on short notice, lure the bride and groom there on some pretext, and then surprise them with a grand celebration of their marriage at the Upper Assembly Rooms.

"We are all going from here," Lauren explained one day during tea. "We would love for you to come with us, Peter, would we not, Kit? But I understand that a journey to Bath and a wedding breakfast may hold out no great allure for you. Perhaps you would prefer to go home, though if you do go, I will feel that I have driven you away." She laughed. "Oh, *will* you come? To please me?"

She would never know the turmoil her words had set up within him.

He was actually being invited—even urged—to go to Bath. But not just that. It seemed altogether probable that he would see Susanna there if he went. Surely as a friend and former colleague of the bride she would be invited to this wedding breakfast.

He could see her again.

She surely would not wish to see *him*, though, he reminded himself. By now she probably hated him as some sort of archvillain, and how could he blame her if she did? Dash it all, first he had debauched her, then he had made her a most improper offer, and then he had escorted her back to Barclay Court, bidden her a cheerful farewell in company with the Edgecombes, and gone riding off without a backward glance.

At the time he had convinced himself that it was because she had said it must be that way.

But he had guessed something about the newlyweds, though neither Lauren nor the duchess was indiscreet enough actually to put it into words. The new Mrs. Butler was probably with child—a fact that would explain both the haste and the secrecy of the nuptials. She had spent a month of the summer in Wales, he could recall Susanna's saying—doubtless on the very estate where Sydnam was steward. She had gone there with the Hallmeres, had she not?

And his suspicions led him suddenly to wonder if perhaps Susanna too . . .

The very thought was enough to cause his stomach to lurch into a somersault and leave him feeling decidedly queasy.

But surely if it were so she would have let him know. She would have written to him.

Would she?

He knew very well she would not.

Good Lord! Damn it to hell! He should have thought of it sooner and made an effort to discover the truth for himself. That would have been the gentlemanly thing to do—if there *were* a gentlemanly way to handle such a situation. Or *had* he thought of it and suppressed the ghastly possibility? He was not a total ignoramus after all, was he? He knew what frequently resulted when men slept with women.

Perhaps he had assumed that if he suppressed the thought, the whole ghastly possibility would just go away.

All these jumbled thoughts and counterthoughts flashed through his head in a mere second or two while he smiled cheerfully back at Lauren.

"I have nothing better to do with myself," he said, "and I would like to see Sydnam again and wish him happy. Yes, I would be delighted to go with you."

He had thought he would never see Susanna Osbourne again.

He had even thought that within a week or two he might forget how badly he had treated her. Perhaps it was to his credit that he had not done so, though he certainly did not congratulate himself too highly on that score.

But now he was going to Bath. And he almost certainly *was* going to see her once more.

It was necessary that he do so, he told himself. He would far rather go somewhere else. But he did need to discover if he had done her any lasting harm, and it really was too bad of him that he had left it so long.

Oh, dash it all! What if? . . .

Yes, indeed.

What if?

13

Susanna returned to Bath in the Earl of Edgecombe's well-sprung traveling carriage. By the time it rocked to a halt outside the school on Daniel Street, she had tucked away all her raw, bruised emotions deep inside herself and was able to smile as the door opened and Mr. Keeble peered out. Almost immediately Claudia and then Anne came hurrying past him out onto the pavement, both beaming happily as they waited to hug her.

All her emotions were generally happy ones for the next little while as she assured her friends and then the girls, whom she joined in the middle of their tea, that she was *very* delighted to be back even though she had had an absolutely *marvelous* time in Somerset. And they all looked delighted to see *her*. She felt enveloped in familiarity and love.

She was home.

And from this moment on she would have plenty with which to occupy her mind. There was a whole busy school term to plan for and look forward to.

The journey, comfortable as the earl's carriage undoubtedly was, had been dreadful. With only herself for company, she had been unable to stop the memories of the past two weeks from churning around and around in her head—particularly, of course, the memory of that last afternoon. She could still scarcely believe that it had actually happened—that she had *allowed* it to happen. But it had—and she had. She had been aware with every turn of the carriage wheels that she was moving farther and farther from *him*— which was a foolish thought indeed when they had always been universes apart.

Even when they were children his sister had been horrified to see them playing together and had dragged him away.

She had had her great adventure, her grand romance of a lifetime, Susanna decided with great good sense once she was back home, and now it was time to get back to reality.

And yet her determination to be cheerful was tested the very evening of her return. Claudia had gone out to dine with the parents of one of the new pupils, and Anne had invited Susanna to come and sit in her room for a while after all the girls had gone to their dormitory.

Susanna sat on the bed, always her favorite perch, her arms clasped about her raised knees, while Anne sat on the chair beside her desk. They talked about Frances for a while until Anne broke a short, not uncomfortable silence with a question.

"And what of you?" she asked. "Did you really have a lovely time? Did you meet anyone interesting?"

For one moment Susanna considered pouring out the whole sorry story to her friend. But it was just too intensely personal—especially its ending. Maybe later, when the memories were not quite so raw, she would confide in Anne, but not now. Not yet.

"Like a duke to sweep me off my feet and bear me off to his castle as his bride?" She laughed at the old joke. "No, not quite, alas. But Frances and Lord Edgecombe were very obliging, Anne, and made sure that there was some entertainment for me to attend almost every day, even though I am sure they would have been just as happy to relax and be quiet together after being away for so long. I met some amiable and interesting people, most of whom I knew from before, of course."

"But no one special?" Anne asked.

Susanna's heart felt like a leaden weight in her chest.

"No," she said. "Not really."

Anne raised her eyebrows.

"Only one gentleman," Susanna said reluctantly, "who made his intentions very clear, and they were not honorable ones. It was the old story, Anne. Yet he was very handsome and very amiable. Never mind. And you? You told us a great deal about your Welsh holiday the evening before I left, but nothing that was very personal. Did *you* meet anyone interesting?"

Anne and her son, David, had gone to Wales to spend a month with the Bedwyn family on the Duke of Bewcastle's estate.

"The Bedwyns," Anne said, smiling, "are all quite fascinating, Susanna—and that is actually an understatement. The Duke of Bewcastle is every bit as formidable as he is reputed to be. He has cold silver eyes and long fingers that are forever curling about the handle of his quizzing glass. He is quite terrifying. And yet he was unfailingly courteous to me. The duchess is a delight and not at all high in the instep, and it is quite clear that he adores her though he is never ever demonstrative in public. He also adores their son, who is a cross, demanding little baby—except when his father is holding him. And he holds him rather often. He is a strange, mysterious, fascinating man."

Susanna rested her chin on her knees. She was thinking of how words could be true and yet a massive lie at the same time. *It was the old story, Anne. Yet he was very handsome and very amiable. Never mind.* Just as if the whole relationship with Viscount Whitleaf had been that trivial, that unimportant.

"All this talk of married dukes is depressing me," she said, smiling as if her heart were not breaking. "Was there no one who was *unmarried?*"

"No dukes." Anne smiled too.

Something in her tone alerted Susanna.

"Oh, Anne," she said. "*Who?*"

"No one really," Anne said quickly, shifting position on the chair. "Oh, what a dreadful thing to say of another human being. He very definitely is *someone.* He is the duke's steward at Glandwr. He was alone and I was alone, and so it was natural enough that occasionally we walk out together or sit together on evenings when he was invited to dine. That is all."

"All," Susanna repeated. "And was he tall, dark, and handsome, Anne?"

"Yes," Anne said. "All three."

Susanna continued to gaze at her.

"We were merely friends," Anne said.

"Were you?" Susanna spoke softly.

"We were. We were . . . very dear friends," Anne said.

But Susanna knew something as clearly as if they had both poured out their hearts to each other. They had both met someone very special indeed during their holidays. And they had both returned with bruised, perhaps even broken, hearts.

"But he did not make an offer," she said. "Anne, I am so sorry."

There was a lengthy silence, during which Anne did not contradict her.

"Do you think," Susanna asked at last, "life would be easier, Anne, if one had parents and family to take one about, to make sure one met suitable people, to arrange for one to meet eligible suitors? Would it be easier than living at a girls' school as one of the teachers?"

It seemed absurd, she thought, to miss her mother so very much even now when she was twenty-three— her mother, whom she had never known.

"I am not sure," Anne said, closing the curtains again, "that life is ever easy. Very often girls and women make disastrous marriages even while surrounded by family to help guide their choice or make it for them. I think given the choice between a bad marriage and life here, I would choose being here every time. In fact, I am certain I would."

"It was *so* ungrateful of me," Susanna said, "even to ask that question. Good fortune was smiling on me when I was sent here to school, and I was blessed beyond belief when Claudia offered me a position on the staff. And I have such very good friends here. What more could I ask of life?"

"Ah, but we are women as well as teachers, Susanna," Anne said as she resumed her seat. "We have needs that nature has given us for the very preservation of our species."

Ah, and that was the trouble. That was the whole trouble. Without those needs, Susanna thought, she might have escaped unscathed from her summer holiday. She might have gone through the rest of her life convincing herself that Viscount Whitleaf had been just a temporary though dear friend whom she missed.

"And sometimes," she said, "they are very hard to ignore. I was *very* tempted this summer, Anne. To be a man's mistress. Part of me is still not convinced that I made the right choice. And will I be able to make the same choice next time? And the next?"

As if there ever would or *could* be a next time.

And she had been tempted in more than one way, hadn't she? And had certainly not resisted one of those temptations.

"I don't know," Anne said.

"What poor, sad spinsters we are," Susanna said, laughing and getting up from her perch on the bed. "I am for my lonely bed. The journey has tired me out. Good night, Anne."

Three days later all the boarders returned to school and with them several new girls, including two charity pupils who needed a great deal of care and attention. And the day after that the day girls returned and classes started.

It was a relief to be busy again.

It was even more of a relief—and that was a massive understatement—to discover two weeks later that she was not with child, that her great indiscretion had had no lasting consequences. None that would be observable to anyone else, anyway.

And yet, perversely, the discovery left her feeling freshly bereft.

Now it was all definitely and finally over.

Her heart, her very life, had never felt more frighteningly empty.

It was not finally over for Anne.

One Saturday morning late in September a sudden deluge of rain sent Susanna and a class of girls under her supervision dashing back inside the school from the open meadows beyond Daniel Street, where they always went for their games lessons. Susanna sent the girls up to their dormitories to dry off and would have taken her own wet cloak and bonnet up to her room before meeting them in the grand hall for indoor games, but Mr. Keeble informed her that she was wanted in the office, that he had already asked Miss Walton to supervise the hall.

She found Claudia and Anne waiting for her and smiled when she saw a nice warm fire crackling in the grate. It was a chilly day outside.

"We are to lose Anne, Susanna," Claudia said sternly and without preamble. "She is to marry Mr. Sydnam Butler, son of the Earl of Redfield and steward at the Welsh estate of *the Duke of Bewcastle.*"

Poor Claudia could never utter that last name without some venom in her voice. Her final position as a governess, which had been with Lady Freyja Bedwyn as her pupil and the Duke of Bewcastle as her employer, had left her with a lasting antipathy toward both. She heartily despised them though she did concede that without that more-than-unpleasant experience she might never have summoned the courage to open her own school.

But Susanna did not spare much thought for Claudia. She had looked into Anne's ashen face, and she instantly *knew*.

"Oh, Anne," she said, closing the distance between them and hugging her friend tightly.

"I have told her that she need not do it," Claudia said. "I have told her we will find some alternative. But she insists."

"Of course I do." Anne stepped back from Susanna's arms and smiled with ghastly cheerfulness at both of them. "I *want* to marry Mr. Butler. I am *fond* of him. I am not marrying him just because I am with child. I *am* with child, Susanna."

"We are all going to have a nice cup of tea," Claudia said with iron calm. "And we are all going to sit down. Not necessarily in that order."

Susanna was glad of the chair. She could guess exactly the way it was. Anne was more than fond of Mr. Butler, but Mr. Butler was the son of an earl. He had allowed Anne to return to Bath without offering her marriage. Yet now he was doing the honorable thing and marrying her after all—but only because he must.

Poor Anne! What a dreadful thing it was for her to

be facing a marriage in which her feelings were engaged when she would always know that his were not.

And it could so easily have happened to her too, Susanna thought, a chill about her heart even while the fire warmed her toes and her face.

Except that she would never have let Viscount Whitleaf know if she had shared Anne's fate. And she doubted he would have offered marriage even if she had.

Oh, but she did not know, did she, what she would have done if it really had happened. Or what he might have done if he had found out. Her knees turned weak at the thought of how close she had come to disaster.

Anne had not had her fortunate escape.

Susanna did not meet Mr. Butler until the day, two weeks later, when the wedding took place by special license in Claudia's private sitting room. He had been badly maimed as a soldier during the Peninsular Wars—he had lost an arm and an eye and was badly burned all down the right side of his face. He was also, as Anne had told Susanna on the evening after her return from Somerset, tall, dark, and handsome. Susanna told him so with a twinkle in her eye after the brief service, when Anne was already his wife—but she said it only because it seemed to her that he was a good-humored man and she thought it altogether possible that he did care for Anne.

She hoped so. Oh, she *hoped* so.

And she tried very hard not to be envious—but how very foolish to even *think* of being envious when she had been pitying Anne so deeply for the past fortnight. Sometimes human emotions made no sense at all.

She did dare to hope, though, that Anne had found

her happily-ever-after despite everything. It appeared that Mr. Butler was even going to be kind to David, though it was not equally obvious that David was going to take kindly to the existence in his life of a new stepfather.

Susanna and Claudia stood on the pavement outside the school after the small reception they had given for the newlyweds, waving the three of them on their way back to Wales.

"Susanna," Claudia said as the carriage turned the corner onto Sutton Street and moved out of sight, "I expected that my heart would break today. But maybe it does not have to after all. What do you think?"

"I believe," Susanna said, "there is fondness on one side and honor on the other—and even that would offer promise for the future. But I think there is also a little bit of love on both sides."

"Ah," Claudia said with a sigh, "it is my thought too. Let us hope we are right and not just a couple of hopeless romantics. Ah, Anne! I suppose we will not see her again for a long time. I *do* object to losing my friends, not to mention my teachers. I will have to look about for her replacement, though Lila is coming along quite nicely, would you not agree?"

Lila Walton was a junior teacher, promoted at the end of the summer term from the ranks of the senior girls. Like Susanna before her, she had been a charity girl.

"She shows great promise, as I knew she would," Susanna agreed as Claudia linked an arm through hers and they stepped back inside the school.

But they were to see Anne again far sooner than

Claudia had expected. She and Mr. Butler did not go directly home to Wales, as it turned out, but instead went first to Alvesley Park in Wiltshire, family home of Mr. Butler, and then to Gloucestershire to visit Anne's estranged family. The day after a letter arrived at the school from Anne at her father's home, another letter came from Viscountess Ravensberg at Alvesley Park. Claudia held it open in one hand when Susanna answered a summons to her study at the end of a composition class—a subject she had taken over from Frances two years before.

"There is to be a surprise wedding breakfast for Anne and Mr. Butler at the Upper Assembly Rooms next week," Claudia said. "The Viscountess Ravensberg and the Duchess of Bewcastle have arranged it and have devised some sort of devious plot for luring the couple back here. We are invited, as well as Mr. Huckerby and Mr. Upton."

They stared at each other. The strange coincidence of Mr. Butler's being a brother-in-law of Viscountess Ravensberg, cousin to Viscount Whitleaf, had not escaped Susanna's notice at the time of Anne's wedding. Now she would have an unexpected opportunity to meet the lady—the very cousin, she believed, who had the same color eyes as he.

Certain wounds, healed over nicely but still tender to the touch, were going to be in danger of being ripped open again, she thought. She would just have to make very certain they were not.

Claudia was tight-lipped.

"You know what this means, Susanna, do you not?" she said, folding the letter and tapping it against her leg. "If the Duchess of Bewcastle has had a hand in organizing this breakfast, then undoubtedly the *duke* will be in attendance. And since Lady Potford on Great Pulteney Street is a friend of Anne's and grandmother to the Marquess of Hallmere, it is altogether possible that the marquess and *that woman* will come to Bath and be there too. I would rather have every fingernail on both my hands pulled out than be in company with those two people. But some things cannot be avoided. This is for *Anne*. I will go. You will come too?"

She stood ramrod straight and spoke as if she were inviting Susanna to accompany her to a funeral.

"I will come and hold your hand," Susanna promised.

Claudia snorted and then laughed.

"I do not suppose," she said, "that either one of them will even recognize me or care if they *do*. Though Lady Hallmere did come here a few years ago to look down her nose at me *and* my school and ask if there was anything I needed. The nerve of the woman! But, Susanna, we will see our beloved Anne again after all—and our dear David. I miss them both very much indeed."

"Yes." Susanna smiled. "We will see them again."

And Viscountess Ravensberg.

How absurd to think that seeing her would somehow bring Viscount Whitleaf closer. Or that it would be a desirable thing even if it did.

Yes, that healed wound was *very* tender to the touch.

The Duchess of Bewcastle had reserved the ballroom as well as the tearoom at the Upper Assembly Rooms in Bath in order to give the children somewhere to run and be noisy while the adults conversed in civilized fashion over tea and listened to a few speeches. But she had engaged the services of an orchestra too, Peter discovered when he arrived early on the appointed afternoon with Lauren and Kit. After all, she explained with a laugh while the duke looked on with a supercilious air and incongruously fond silver eyes resting upon his lady, it would be a tragic thing indeed if the presence of the ballroom aroused in anyone a desire to dance but there was no music to make dancing possible.

"What you mean, Christine," Bewcastle said, his long fingers curling about the handle of his quizzing glass and raising it halfway to his eye, "is that you are quite determined to dance if only Sydnam and Mrs. Butler can be persuaded to lead the way."

"You know me all too well, Wulfric," the duchess said with a laugh.

Peter was looking forward to the social gathering with uncharacteristic unease. He probably ought not to have come. If he suddenly, after several months of inaction, felt it necessary to check on Susanna's health—marvelous euphemism—then he ought to have done it by writing to her or calling at the school. He ought at the very least to have somehow let her know that he was going to be here today. He was almost certain that she *was*. Lauren had told him that four teachers were coming from the school as well as the former teacher who was now married to the Earl of Edgecombe.

And yet it struck Peter even as he entertained these troubled thoughts that the chance to meet Susanna again this afternoon *ought* to have been a cause of pleasure to both of them. They really had been friends—until the very end. How he kicked himself now for not having stayed in the drawing room with her that last afternoon—or for not taking Edgecombe up on his suggestion that he and the countess accompany them on their walk. Then they would have been meeting today with shared pleasure as friends who had not expected to see each other again so soon.

Other guests began to arrive. Peter was introduced to Mrs. Butler's parents and siblings and their spouses from Gloucestershire and to Lord and Lady Aidan Bedwyn, whom he had not met before. He hailed Lord and Lady Alleyne Bedwyn and a number of Kit and Sydnam's cousins, whom he had met on various occasions at Alvesley.

Normally he would have been in his element.

But his uneasiness was growing by the minute, and

he found himself glancing at the door every few seconds instead of concentrating upon making himself agreeable to those with whom he conversed. A dozen or more times he thought about making his escape before it was too late, but escape might well be impossible, he realized as time went on. Even if he dashed out *now,* he had a long hall to traverse and a largish courtyard outside to cross before he could hope to slink out of sight of someone who would surely be arriving at any moment.

He wandered in the direction of the ballroom and forgot his woes for a while after Andrew and Sophia, two of Lauren's children, grabbed a hand each, dragged him triumphantly inside the large room, and demanded that he play with them. A whole host of other children gathered hopefully about him, and he proceeded to play Blind Man's Buff with them with a great deal of noise and energy and good humor.

It was only when he heard a loud burst of applause and even cheering coming from the tearoom that he realized the guests of honor must have arrived and that therefore all the other guests must now be gathered there too.

Even then he was tempted to slip out and hope no one would notice his absence.

But he would not add arrant cowardice to his other shortcomings, which were legion. He extricated himself from the children's game and went to stand in the shadowed half of the doorway into the tearoom so that he could peer cautiously about him.

Like a thief in the night, he thought with some disgust.

Sydnam Butler and a lady dressed in rose pink, who was presumably his bride, stood in a pool of red rose petals inside the door at the far side of the room, looking startled and bewildered. The Duchess of Bewcastle was clapping her hands for silence.

"Well, Mr. and Mrs. Butler," she said, her voice warm and cheerful, "you may have thought yourselves very clever indeed when you married in great secrecy a few weeks ago. But your relatives and friends have caught up with you after all. Welcome to your wedding breakfast."

The children, without the distraction of an adult to play with them in the ballroom, had left it and were streaming past Peter to see what all the fuss was about. They were soon adding to the cheerful mayhem that ensued for a few minutes while everyone attempted to get close to the bride and groom and pump the hand of the one and kiss the cheek of the other.

But Peter, still and silent in the doorway, took no part in the collective merriment.

He had seen her.

She was dressed neatly in pale blue, her short curls vibrantly auburn in contrast. She was bending down to hug a little boy who, he guessed, must be Mrs. Butler's son, and then she was reaching for Mrs. Butler herself and holding her in a close embrace for several seconds. She was laughing and tearful and bright-eyed and dazzling.

For several moments he simply gazed at her, his reluctance to see her again vanished without a trace. By Jove, he *had* missed her. He drank in the sight of her, more lovely and more vibrant than any other lady he had ever met.

She stepped aside so that the ladies with her—the Countess of Edgecombe and a brown-haired, severe-looking though not unhandsome woman who was probably Miss Martin—could take their turns greeting the bride. Susanna was waiting to pay her respects to Butler and was looking around at the other guests as she did so with bright, happy eyes.

And then those same eyes met his across the room—and her smile froze and then died altogether.

Peter was instantly conscious of himself again—and of the dashed uncomfortable fact that he had ruined her, made her a dishonorable offer, and left her without a backward glance, all within the space of one afternoon. And that now he was reappearing in her life without any warning and at just the time when she was celebrating the marriage of her friend.

He *really* ought not to have come, he thought again.

But dash it all, it was too late now to go away.

He strode purposefully across the room, intending to speak with her. But Lauren, flushed and animated, caught his arm as he approached, linking her own through it, led him up to the newlyweds, and proceeded to introduce him to Mrs. Butler, who was, he discovered, very lovely indeed. He bowed over her hand and raised it to his lips. He shook Sydnam's left hand with his left and wished him well. Then he shook the boy's hand—he was David Jewell—and winked and grinned at him.

"If you want to make your escape anytime soon,"

he said, "you will doubtless find hordes of other young people in the ballroom—once they have found their way back there."

The boy smiled back.

"Do come and sit at our table, Peter," Lauren said as order began to replace the cheerful chaos of the past several minutes and the children made their way back to the ballroom rather than be caught up in the tedium of an adult tea party.

"I will, thank you, Lauren," he said, "but there is someone to whom I must pay my respects first."

Before he could delay too long and set up a greater awkwardness than he already felt, he strode over to the table where Susanna sat with Edgecombe and the countess, Lord and Lady Aidan Bedwyn, the un-known severe-looking lady, and the duchess's sister, Miss Thompson.

"Whitleaf," Edgecombe said, standing to shake hands with him. "Good to see you again."

"But of course," the countess said, smiling at him, "you are related to Lady Ravensberg, are you not? It is a pleasure to see you again, Lord Whitleaf."

And yet there was a hint of something in her tone that suggested she was not entirely pleased. Or perhaps his conscience was just playing tricks on him.

He bowed to her and to Miss Thompson, who must have arrived with her mother after he went into the ballroom, and turned his eyes on Susanna.

"Miss Osbourne?" he said. "I trust you are well?"

"Yes, thank you," she said with perfect composure and a polite smile on her face—as if they had never lain together on a secluded hill above the river at Barclay Court. "And you, my lord?"

"Quite well," he said, "thank you."

Good Lord, where was his arsenal of small talk when he most needed it? But perhaps it was as well it had deserted him utterly, or he might have found himself saying something totally asinine like great beauty having to be a prerequisite for a teaching position at Miss Martin's School for Girls. He had the feeling that present company would not be at all amused by such a compliment.

"My lord," Susanna said before he could make his escape to his own table, "may I present Miss Martin, owner of the school where I teach? This is Viscount Whitleaf, Claudia. He was staying not far from Barclay Court while I was a guest there."

The severe-looking stranger whose identity he had guessed earlier inclined her head while he bowed and favored her with his most charming smile.

"Ma'am," he said. "This is a pleasure I have long desired."

They were only mildly extravagant words, but looking into her unsmiling gray eyes, he felt suddenly stripped naked. Not in any physical way, it was true, but he felt as if every layer of artifice were being stripped away and she was recognizing him for the shallow fribble that he was. He wondered if Susanna had told her anything about him.

"How do you do, Lord Whitleaf," she said.

He retreated in reasonably good order after that and sat with his back to their table while he took tea and conversed with all around him and listened to the few speeches and toasts that followed it. He would have enjoyed the afternoon, he knew, if there had not been those few minutes of uncharacteristic gaucherie to bother him. And if he could have convinced himself that he had any business being here.

He *knew* she was not pleased to see him.

"You may all expect," Sydnam Butler was saying to the whole gathering after commenting on the surprise of finding so many guests awaiting them here, "that Anne and I will put our heads together over the winter when there is nothing else to do and devise a suitable revenge."

Peter joined in the general laughter.

And then, soon after the speeches and toasts were at an end, his ears sharpened to something Hallmere was saying at the next table.

"It was just here that we waltzed for the first time, Freyja," he said. "Do you remember?"

Peter had been wondering how Susanna felt to be in the same room with Lady Hallmere, who had once refused to give her employment as her maid and who had perhaps been responsible for sending her to Bath as a charity pupil in Miss Martin's school. And he had been wondering if Lady Hallmere remembered her.

But the lady was speaking.

"How could I forget?" she said. "It was while we waltzed that you begged me to enter into a fake betrothal with you, and before we knew it we were in a marriage together—but not a fake one at all."

They both laughed—as did everyone else at their table and a few at Peter's.

Kit had certainly heard the exchange.

"It would be a shame," he said, raising his voice and getting to his feet at the same time, "to have an orchestra and the use of one of the most famous ballrooms in the country and not dance. I shall instruct the orchestra to play a waltz. But we must remember that this is a wedding celebration. The bride must dance first. Will you waltz with me, Anne?"

Sydnam stood up too.

"Thank you, Kit," he said firmly, "but if it is not the custom for the bridegroom to be first to dance with his bride, then it ought to be. Anne, will you waltz with me?"

It was a courageous offer, Peter thought amid the general buzz of excitement as chairs scraped back and guests got to their feet to remove to the ballroom, from which music had been wafting all during tea. How did one waltz when one was missing a right arm—as well as an eye?

"Yes, I will," Mrs. Butler said—and it struck Peter at that very moment that theirs was a love match.

He watched them waltz alone together a few minutes later, a little awkwardly at first, then more smoothly and confidently. And then Hallmere led the marchioness onto the floor to join them, and Kit and Lauren, Edgecombe and the countess, Bewcastle and the duchess, followed after them. Other gentlemen were taking their partners.

It was a *waltz*.

Peter never missed an opportunity to dance it at any of the balls he attended. But he was actually remembering the last time he had waltzed. He had enjoyed it enormously even though it had been at a small, unsophisticated country assembly. It had also been a prelude to all his woes, though—well, to the worst of them anyway. Without that waltz, there would probably have not been that kiss. And without that kiss, there probably would not have been . . .

Well.

Greeting her at the tea table had simply not been enough, had it? That atoned for absolutely nothing. Having made the decision to come, he must now make the further effort to find out what he had come to learn. And what better time than now?

He strode over to where she stood watching the dancers, between Miss Martin and Miss Thompson, who in his fancy resembled two stern avenging angels, except that Miss Martin had tears in her eyes as she watched the bridal couple dance and Miss Thompson looked amused.

He bowed in front of them and donned his most disarming smile.

"Miss Osbourne," he said, "would you do me the honor of waltzing with me?"

He was aware of the eyes of the headmistress suddenly turned on him, sharp despite her tears though he looked only at Susanna, whose green eyes were fathomless as she gazed back at him.

He thought she was going to refuse him. Dash it, what an unexpected humiliation that would be—but one he doubtless thoroughly deserved.

"Yes," she said then and licked her lips. "Yes, thank you, my lord."

He held out his hand, palm-up, and she placed her own on it.

And he was immediately assaulted by familiar words speaking loudly and distinctly in his head—though one word was different from usual.

Here she is, the voice said.

And it was quite indisputable, was it not? Here she was indeed, her hand on his, about to waltz with him.

Susanna had been trying to convince herself for the past two and a half months that she was not nursing a broken heart.

Now, finally, she had succeeded.

Viscount Whitleaf was in no way worthy of the tears she had shed over him, the painful dreams she had woven about him, the guilty memories of him in which she had sometimes indulged.

He ought not to have come without any warning like this. He must have *known* that she would be here. What interest could he possibly have in Anne? Or in Anne's husband either, even if Mr. Butler *was* Viscountess Ravensberg's brother-in-law?

When she had looked around the tearoom after hugging Anne, feeling completely happy for once because it had been instantly apparent to her that Mr. Butler did indeed care for Anne and that Anne was happy and that even *David* was happy—when she had looked around and seen Viscount Whitleaf standing in the shadow of the doorway at the far side of the room, she had . . .

Ah, but it was impossible to put into words what had been a purely physical reaction. Her knees had turned weak, her heart had hammered at her throat and in her ears, her hands had become clammy, her breath had seemed suspended. It had taken her brain a second or so longer to catch up.

And then he had stridden confidently into the room, and he had been *smiling,* as if he did not have a care in the world—as doubtless he did not. He had approached with his cousin on his arm and turned his smiles on Anne and Mr. Butler. He had even paid attention to David, lest one person in the tearoom not become his adoring admirer. When he had come to speak to *her* and spend a few brief, polite moments standing by her table, he had turned on the full force of his charm, especially upon Claudia—and had then gone away to sit with his back to them all through tea.

A man without a care in the world, indeed. He probably scarcely remembered her.

Claudia had not been taken in by his charm.

"There is a gentleman who thinks a lot of himself," she had said as he walked away from the table.

"Ah, but I believe he is genuinely amiable," the Earl of Edgecombe had said.

"I have always found him unfailingly cheerful and courteous," Miss Eleanor Thompson, the duchess's sister, had added.

Susanna had said nothing—though she had been feeling inexplicably grateful to the earl and Miss Thompson.

Neither had Frances.

The whole tea, to which Susanna had looked forward so eagerly for a whole week, had been ruined for her. She had been quite unable to swallow more than a few mouthfuls of food or to relax into the pleasure of being in a room with her three closest friends again, Frances and Claudia at the same table with her, Anne not far away with her new husband, looking flushed and very happy. She had not been able to marvel in peace that she was in the same room and at the same entertainment as the Marchioness of Hallmere, whom she had recognized instantly as that long-ago prospective employer.

It was simply not fair.

And now—ah, *now* he had asked her to waltz with him and she had said yes.

She had come into the ballroom with Claudia and Miss Thompson, smiling brightly and knowing that she was going to have to stand and watch Anne waltz with Mr. Butler and Frances with the earl. She had been feeling more wretchedly bleak than she had felt since the end of August, especially knowing that *he* was in the ballroom too and would probably dance with one of the other ladies.

And now?

Now, as she turned to face Lord Whitleaf on the dance floor and fixed her eyes on a level with his chin, a smile on her lips, she felt nothing at all—except happy to know that her heart was not broken after all.

His hand came behind her waist, and she lifted her hand to his shoulder. His other hand clasped hers.

He still wore the same cologne, she noticed.

The waltz was already in progress. They moved into it without further delay.

The memory of that other waltz was still precious to her despite everything. She did not want it to be

overlaid with *this* memory. But now it forever would
be, she supposed.

It was not *fair*. He ought not to have come. And
now she would remember him harshly because he *had*
come, without any regard to her feelings—probably
not even remembering that there was anything about
which she might have feelings.

And yet, she thought, if that last afternoon at
Barclay Court had proceeded differently—if Frances
and the earl had come with them, if they had kept
walking across the bridge and down to the waterfall
instead of sitting on the hill, if she had said *stop* instead of *don't stop*—if any of those things had happened, she would have been very happy to see him this
afternoon. She would not have blamed him at all for
coming. He would have been no more than her dear
friend.

She lifted her eyes to his as he twirled her about
one corner of the ballroom and found that he was
looking back, a smile on his own face too. But how
could they *not* smile? They were surrounded by wedding guests.

"Susanna," he said softly, "you look as lovely as
ever."

"Is the day warmer and brighter for my presence in
it?" she asked him, unable to keep the bitterness out
of her voice.

He tipped his head slightly to one side as he gazed
back into her eyes.

"You are not happy to see me," he said.

"Ought I to be?" she asked him.

"I thought perhaps you would not be," he admitted. "But it was a wedding celebration, you see, and involved a number of people whom I know and like. How could I have resisted coming?"

And that was the trouble with him, she thought. He could not resist being blown along by any wind that happened in his direction. She had once told him that he was a kind man. But was it kind of him to come here today only because there was to be a party and congenial company?

"You knew I would be here, then?" she asked him as they twirled about another corner.

"Yes," he said. "It is why I came."

And now he was contradicting himself. Was there any firmness of character in him at all?

"Susanna," he asked even more softly than before, "are you with child?"

If she had been, the child would surely have turned over in her womb. Every other part of her insides seemed to somersault as she drew breath sharply and stumbled slightly. He drew her closer until she had regained her balance and fitted her steps to his again.

"No," she said.

His eyes found hers and searched them. His smile had slipped, she noticed. So had hers. She donned it once more.

"I am glad," he said.

"No doubt."

She lowered her eyes and tried to recapture some of the magic she had felt the last time they waltzed. She deliberately let her attention move to their fellow dancers and could see Anne and Mr. Butler dancing with surprising grace despite the fact that his right arm was missing. Anne was looking a little less slender than usual, especially below the high waistline of her dress. The duchess was laughing up into the austere face of the duke, whom Claudia detested so fiercely. His pale silver eyes looked back at her with a total absorption that spoke of emotions burning just behind the autocratic façade. Frances twirled in the earl's arms, and it was obvious that they had eyes for no one but each other.

The world was filled with happy couples, it seemed—and her very lone self.

Ridiculous, self-pitying thought!

"You are bitter," Viscount Whitleaf said.

Was she? She had no reason to be, had she? He had not seduced her. He had given her the opportunity to stop him. He had asked her afterward to go away with him and had promised that he would look after her even when all was over between them. She had said no. They had parted as friends. Ah, that parting—that memory of him riding away across the terrace and down the lane until he was out of sight. It was a memory that had always gone deeper than pain because she had thought she would never see him again.

Now she was waltzing with him once more in the Upper Assembly Rooms in Bath. The reality of it, she felt, had still not quite hit her.

"Silence is my answer," he said. "And I cannot blame you. It would be trite of me to say I am sorry. But I do not know what else *to* say."

"You need not say anything." She looked back into his eyes. "And you need not feel sorry—any more

than I do. It happened. Our friendship had to end anyway. Why not that way?"

"*Did* it end?" he asked her.

She gazed back at him and then nodded. Of course
it had ended. How could they even pretend to be
friends now?

"Then I really *am* sorry," he said. "I liked you,
Susanna—I *like* you. And I thought you had come to
like me."

She swallowed.

"I did."

"Past tense?" he said, and after a short silence between them, "Ah, yes, past tense."

They stopped dancing for a few moments while the
orchestra ended one waltz tune and prepared to play
the next one in the set.

Did she not even like him now, then? Because he
had come here today to disturb her peace again? He
had come because she was to be here. He had come to
ask her if she was with child.

What would he have done if the answer had been
yes? Would he have gone away again faster than he
had come? She knew he would not have.

She looked up at him again as they resumed their
dance.

"I do not dislike you," she said.

"Do you not?"

He was smiling—no doubt for the benefit of those
around them. She smiled too. And then, because they
were still looking at each other, both their smiles became more rueful—and then more genuine.

"I have told myself," he said, "that it would have

been far better for me—and considerably better for you—if I had left Hareford House two days after your arrival at Barclay Court, as I had originally planned. I would have remembered you, if at all, as a rather straitlaced, disapproving, humorless schoolteacher."

"Is that how I appeared to you?" she asked him.

"And as someone who made an already glorious summer day seem warmer and brighter." He whirled her twice about a corner, startling a laugh out of her. "But then another part of myself answers with the assertion that I would hate never to have got to know you better."

She looked about with leftover laughter on her face. Mr. Huckerby, she could see, was watching her feet—to see if she remembered the steps correctly, no doubt. She caught Claudia's eye as she danced past and smiled at her.

"Do *you* wish," Lord Whitleaf asked her, "that I had left when I intended to do so?"

Did she? She would have been saved from a great deal of heartache—and from a great deal of vividly happy living.

"No," she said.

"Why not?" He bent his head a little closer.

"You once told me," she said, "that in your childhood you were surrounded by women. It is what has happened to me since I was twelve. I have had almost no social contact with men. I have been shy with men, unsure how to talk or behave with them. I was terrified when I first met you because you were handsome and self-assured and titled. And then I learned that you were amiable and kind and really rather easy to talk with. And then I came to genuinely like you and look forward to seeing you each day and spending a short while in conversation with you. Knowing you brightened my life for a time and provided me with memories that will give me pleasure in future years—riding in a curricle with you, racing a boat against you, climbing to the waterfall with you, waltzing with you."

Kissing you.

Making love with you.

"I am not sorry you stayed," she said.

"Are we friends again, then?" he asked her.

She smiled back at him and then laughed softly.

"Oh, yes, I suppose so," she said, "for what remains of this afternoon, anyway."

Though it struck her that the celebration would probably not go on much longer and that then she would go back to school and he would go away somewhere with the Ravensbergs and that that would be the end of it—the real end this time.

And there would be pain all over again.

But pain was something that life inevitably brought with it. If there was no pain, there was no real living and therefore no possibility of happiness. She had been happy—truly, exhilaratingly happy—on a few occasions in her life, almost all of them with Viscount Whitleaf. She must remember that. She *must*. There were two particularly perfect incidents that had drawn her so completely into happiness that no *un*happiness had been able to intrude. One had occurred at the assembly rooms when she had waltzed with him. The other had occurred on the hill above the river and the little bridge when they had made love.

It was so easy to remember that lovemaking as the worst thing that had ever happened to her—because it had brought her a far deeper unhappiness than she would have felt otherwise in saying good-bye to him. But actually it was the most wonderful thing that had ever happened too.

It was. That had been easily the happiest half hour or so of her life.

Now she was waltzing again—with the man who had waltzed with her then, and with the man who had been her lover on that hill. And if she was not perfectly happy now, the reason was that she was allowing past pain and future unhappiness to encroach upon the magic of the moment.

It *was* magical.

"Let's just waltz," she said to him.

The smile deepened in his eyes.

"Yes," he said. "Let's."

And for what remained of the set they did not speak at all but just danced and smiled into each other's eyes.

She was glad he had come, Susanna thought. Ah, she *was* glad. There was surely something healing in his being here—he had not just carelessly dismissed both her and their lovemaking from his mind. She thought she would be less unhappy after today. Or perhaps she was just fooling herself. Tomorrow her life would be without him again.

But she *would not* think of tomorrow.

She danced, aware of their splendid surroundings and of the company and the music, all her senses sharpened. And she was aware too that the man in whose arms she danced was the man who had kissed her and caressed her and been deep inside her body.

She could never *ever* regret that she had had that experience once in her life.

Once was enough.

It would have to be.

He laughed aloud as he took her into a swooping turn before the orchestra dais, and she laughed back at him.

"And so that is that," Claudia said with a sigh as she stepped inside the school with Susanna and the door closed behind them. "Too many good-byes. It does nothing to buoy the spirits, does it?"

They had just said good-bye to Frances and the Earl of Edgecombe, who had insisted upon giving them a ride back from the Upper Rooms in their own carriage despite Claudia's protestation that she and Susanna were perfectly capable of walking. The Edgecombes were leaving Bath for London early in the morning. And before they all left the Upper Rooms, they had said good-bye to Anne and David, who were also setting out in the morning with Mr. Butler for their new home in Wales.

"But it was *very* good," Susanna said, "to see Anne so happy—and David too. Mr. Butler must have been kind to him."

"Well, now it is back to business," Claudia said briskly, taking off her cloak and looping it over her arm. "We have a school to run, Susanna. I happened to mention to Miss Thompson after tea that I was looking for another teacher and was quite taken aback when she expressed an interest in the position for herself."

"Did she really?" Susanna asked.

"The duchess has persuaded Mrs. Thompson to take up residence in a cottage close to Lindsey Hall," Claudia said. "Miss Thompson is expected to move there with her, of course, but she says she feels she will be losing some independence when she leaves their own cottage and village behind. She will feel like a poor relation of the Duke of Bewcastle, she says. I can well understand that *that* would be a ghastly fate indeed. But it is interesting, Susanna, that she may prefer to teach here. I have asked her to drop by tomorrow or the next day. I really took to her. She has interesting conversation and has read widely. She also has good sense and a dry wit."

"Has she taught before?" Susanna asked, looking back as she proceeded up the stairs on the way to her room.

But Claudia was prevented from replying by Mr. Keeble, who was clearing his throat in such a pronounced manner that it was obvious he had something of import to say to them.

Agnes Ryde, one of the new charity girls, had had an almighty tantrum, it seemed, and reduced Lila Walton to tears and consequently aroused the wrath of Matron, who had sent the girl to bed in the middle of the afternoon and promised dire consequences as soon as Miss Martin returned.

Claudia sighed.

"Thank you, Mr. Keeble," she said. "This *is* returning

to reality with a crash, is it not? Where is Anne when I most need her? She did have a special gift with difficult girls."

"She did," Susanna agreed as she removed her bonnet. "But I have an understanding of what it feels like to be a charity girl here, Claudia. I have seen something of my old self in poor Agnes, I must confess. Let me go up and talk to her."

"Poor Agnes indeed!" Claudia said, tossing her glance at the ceiling. "But go if you wish, Susanna. Matron does seem to have tied my hands. If *I* go up, I shall be obliged to do something horribly dire like confining the girl to her bed and to dry bread and water for at least the next week."

Susanna chuckled at the unlikely image, squared her shoulders, and continued on her way upstairs, prepared to do battle. Lila, as junior teacher, had the unenviable task, once Susanna's own, of teaching elocution to those girls who needed it. And Agnes Ryde needed it more than anyone else. She had arrived at the school at the end of August with such a thick Cockney accent that no one understood a good half of what she said. And since she was resistant to changing her accent in order to talk as if she had two plums in her cheeks like a real nob—her words—Lila was not exactly her favorite teacher.

Susanna did not find the minor crisis at the school unwelcome. It pushed everything else from her mind for the next hour, while she sat in one of the dormitories beside Agnes's bed, at first talking to an uncommunicative ball of hostile girlhood turned toward the wall and then gradually moving into something resembling a conversation after Agnes had rolled over to face her and eye her with open suspicion.

"*You* was a charity girl, miss?" she asked.

"I was indeed," Susanna said, wisely ignoring the girl's grammar. "So was Miss Walton, as she would be very ready to admit. We have both been where you are now. It is not the most comfortable place to be, is it? I can remember believing at one point that I must have been brought here only so that everyone else could laugh at me."

"Everybody *does* laugh at *me*," Agnes said fiercely. "Next time I'll pop 'em a good one, I will . . . miss."

"Everybody?" Susanna raised her eyebrows. "Are you quite sure it is *everybody*? It is not just two or three girls who do not know any better than to want to bring misery upon a fellow pupil? I remember Miss Martin once giving me a piece of advice. The next time one of the paying pupils taunted me by telling me it must be *nice* to have my fees paid for me by strangers, I should smile back as if I had not noticed the sarcasm and agree warmly that yes, it was *very* nice indeed. Where would they take the taunting from there? she asked me. And she was perfectly right. It worked like a charm. Much better than hitting out would have done. That was what they *expected* me to do. That was what they *hoped* I would do so that they could run crying to one of the teachers and get me into trouble."

By the time she went back downstairs Susanna was feeling exhausted but satisfied that yet another problem had been sorted out. But then she had to assure a tearful Lila Walton in Claudia's private sitting room that of *course* she was not a failure, that teaching was always three parts instruction and one part dealing with the various crises that inevitably arose when so many diverse humans lived in close proximity to one another. And of course a teacher could not *always* be popular.

"It is just what I have been telling her," Claudia said. "Now, we will have a cup of tea together and you can have an early night, Lila. And I will take your study hall for you tomorrow evening so that you may have some relaxation time. I daresay I ought to have brought Cecile Pierre in to give you a hand today even though I had declared it a holiday from classes, since Susanna and I were both going to the reception and Mr. Huckerby and Mr. Upton were to attend too. Call it learning to swim by being tossed into the deep part of a lake, if you will. You did remarkably well aside from the unfortunate incident with Agnes. The school is still standing, is it not? It is not burned down to the ground or reduced to rubble by cannon shot. All the girls are still living and breathing—at least, I have not heard anything to the contrary."

Lila laughed and took a cup of tea from Claudia. Fifteen minutes later she was on the way up to her own room, clearly relieved that the day was finally over.

"Academically Lila does very well indeed," Claudia said after she had left. "In other areas she is still fragile. She may discover that teaching really does not suit her at all, though I still have hopes that she will settle. I have *high* hopes that Miss Thompson will come here. She is older and more mature. Did you like her, Susanna?"

"Yes," Susanna said, getting to her feet to pour

them each another cup of tea. "Though I did not talk a great deal with her. She has a twinkling eye, though. I always trust people with twinkling eyes."

Claudia laughed.

"Her sense of humor will be put to the test if she comes here," she said, "though it would be a decided asset. Would it be possible to teach successfully if one did *not* have a healthy sense of the ridiculous? I very much doubt it."

They sipped their tea and lapsed into silence—and Susanna's thoughts inevitably drifted to the afternoon and to Viscount Whitleaf and the waltz they had danced together. And to the cheerful way in which they had taken their leave of each other afterward. She had refused to feel tragic at the time, and she refused to feel it now.

It had after all been good to see him again and to know that it was concern for her—and his possible responsibility toward her—that had brought him.

But now there was an inevitable ache of emptiness inside that was very difficult to ignore.

"I am very sensitive to undercurrents," Claudia said. "It is another asset for a teacher, I firmly believe. I can sometimes sense things that are brewing long before they bubble to the surface and cause trouble or even disaster."

Susanna sipped her tea. She did not know quite where this observation was leading.

"You met Viscount Whitleaf when you were staying at Barclay Court this summer," Claudia said.

"Yes," Susanna said warily. "He was staying at

Hareford House. The younger Mr. Raycroft is his friend. You have met him and his family, I believe."

Claudia nodded. She had spent a few days at Barclay Court earlier in the year, before Frances left for Europe.

"My first impression of the viscount," Claudia said, "was that he was conceited—as well as wondrously handsome, of course. Both the Earl of Edgecombe and Miss Thompson assured me that I was mistaken. Neither you nor Frances expressed any opinion, however. And then you proceeded to eat half a cucumber sandwich and perhaps a third of a currant cake and maintain an uncharacteristic near-silence throughout tea. And Frances did not do much better. She was watching you almost the whole time, a look of troubled concern in her eyes. Indeed, I am not even sure it was undercurrents I felt. It was something altogether more overt than that."

It would be pointless, Susanna decided, to pretend she did not know what Claudia was talking about. They had known each other a long time. They had been friends for a number of years since she grew up. They had been even closer since Anne left.

"It is not quite what you think," she said.

"And what is it that I think?" Claudia asked, her look keen.

"Viscount Whitleaf and I became friends," Susanna explained. "I had no illusions that we were more than that, and absolutely no wish that we *be* more. He *is* amiable, Claudia, and very kind—he showed his kindness in all sorts of ways. It was sad to have to say goodbye to him at the end of the holiday. Frances feared I had fallen in love with him. Perhaps she still fears it. But she is wrong. It was lovely to see him again today and dance with him again, but . . . Well, but nothing. I will never see him again, and I am content that it be so. I will not lose any sleep over him."

She smiled—and sloshed her tea into her saucer. She set the cup down in haste until such time as her hands had stopped shaking.

Good heavens! Oh, gracious heavens. She would be weeping next—as she had the night after the assembly when Frances came to her room. How utterly mortifying.

"Is it not a shame," Claudia said with a sigh after a short silence, "that we cannot just turn off our woman's need to love and nurture and be loved in return, or at least draw enough satisfaction from lavishing those instincts upon our pupils and fellow teachers and women friends? One ought not to have to feel the need for a man and all he can offer by way of physical as well as emotional satisfaction when the chances of finding a suitable mate and making a satisfactory marriage are slim to none."

Susanna had never before heard Claudia talk about her need for a man—her *physical* need. It was all too easy to assume that she did not feel such needs. She was over thirty years old. She had been an adult when Susanna first came to the school. And all that time she had been without a man.

"I was able to offer you the relative security of a teaching position when you grew up," Claudia said. "I was not, alas, able to find you a husband despite your beauty and vitality and intelligence."

"Oh, Claudia," Susanna said, setting her cup and saucer down on the table beside her, "you have done so very much for me. And I am *not* in love with Viscount Whitleaf—or anyone else."

Claudia sighed again.

"Of course you are not," she said briskly. "Come, it is time we went to bed even though it is still not very late, is it? It has been a long and busy and emotional day, though, and I feel like a limp rag. And I have promised to take study hall tomorrow evening on top of everything else."

"I will be conducting a rehearsal for the Christmas play," Susanna said, "or I would do it for you."

Life would go on, she told herself a few minutes later as she shut her bedroom door behind her. She had survived the end of August. She would survive today.

At least there would be much to occupy her mind tomorrow and in the coming days.

And at least there were pleasant memories of today to add to the ones from the summer. She was glad he had come to ask her if she was with child. He would not have abandoned her to her fate if she had been. She *knew* that as clearly as if he had said so.

He was still a man she could like and even . . .

Well, yes, of course she still loved him too.

It would be foolish to deny it.

She would survive the admission. She had survived it in August, and she would survive it now. But she did wonder wistfully when an unfed love died. It did not last forever, surely? She fervently hoped not.

She looked forward to the day when she could

bring out the memories and derive only a sort of nostalgic pleasure from them.

That day had not yet come.

Not by a long way.

Peter did not go with Lauren and Kit when they left for Alvesley Park the following morning even though both of them assured him that he would be very welcome and their children begged him to come. He was going to set out for London a little later in the day, he told them—he had some business to attend to there. The business consisted of keeping his eye out for a new team of horses to buy, though, truth to tell, there was nothing wrong with his chestnuts. He also needed to visit his clubs, notably White's, to discover who was still in town and who was new in town and what the latest news and gossip might be—though those particular pursuits could hardly be described as *business*.

Really, of course, he had no pressing reason for going anywhere in the world, except home. But there was still a while before Christmas, and he had decided not to go before then.

His mother was going to transform his dining room into a lavender monstrosity—she had mentioned the color in her last letter—as a complement to the drawing room. But she was going to leave it until after Christmas since they were expecting guests—she had used the plural pronoun. Christmas would be soon enough, then, to stop such a disaster from happening. A lavender dining room, for God's sake!

Would she start on the library next?

She had invited the Flynn-Posys for Christmas, Lady Flynn-Posy being one of her dearest friends from their come-out year. Peter might recall the name, she had written. He did not. They were going to bring with them their son, a delightful young man who was up at Oxford, and—inevitably—their daughter, an accomplished young lady of considerable beauty, who was to make her official come-out in the spring.

Miss Flynn-Posy and her arsenal would have to be faced, he had decided. He would hide from his mother's loving interference in his life no longer.

He would not go home yet, though.

But what was he to do with himself in the meanwhile? He waved Lauren and Kit and the children on their way from the Royal York Hotel and then, ten minutes later, the Earl and Countess of Redfield and returned aimlessly to his room to stare gloomily at his bags, all neatly packed by his valet.

An hour after that he wandered downstairs and was in time to wave the Duke and Duchess of Bewcastle and Mrs. Thompson, the duchess's mother, on *their* way home. Miss Thompson was to remain in Bath for a few days, but not at the hotel, it seemed.

"My mother thought it really not quite the thing even though I bade farewell to my twenties a few years ago," she explained to Peter as they both looked toward the corner around which the carriage had just disappeared. "And Christine agreed with her. So did the duke, though he did not say a word. He did not have to. I have never known anyone whose silence is so eloquent. He is a formidable brother-in-law, Lord Whiteleaf." Her eyes twinkled with merriment.

"And so you are to stay with Lady Potford?" Peter asked.

"Yes," she said. "I must still be hedged about by chaperones, it seems. It is most provoking."

"May I convey you and your baggage to her house?" Peter asked.

"Oh, that is remarkably good of you," she said, "but my bags have already gone. The duke arranged to have them sent over. He would have sent me with them, I daresay, if I had not told Christine quite firmly that I intend to walk."

"She lives not far away?" he asked.

"On Great Pulteney Street," she said. "It is a fair distance, but I shall enjoy stretching my legs, especially in this lovely sunshine. The house is quite close to Miss Martin's school on Daniel Street. I promised to call there today or tomorrow. Miss Martin needs a new teacher, and I am thinking of applying for the position."

"Indeed?" Peter said. "May I escort you to Great Pulteney Street, ma'am?"

"And delay your own departure?" she said. "You are too kind, Lord Whiteleaf. I really do not need an escort or a chaperone on the streets of Bath."

"But perhaps," he said, bowing to her and grinning, "I would be delighted to postpone my departure until tomorrow, ma'am, rather than forgo the pleasure of your company and Lady Potford's. And I would like to see the school where Miss Osbourne teaches— we struck up an acquaintance during the summer when we were staying with friends in the same neighborhood."

"Ah, Miss Osbourne, yes," she said, laughing. "I did not fail to notice how remarkably lovely she is. Very well, then, Lord Whitleaf. Since you feel such a burning desire for my company, I shall not deprive you of it. Shall we meet downstairs here in half an hour's time?"

"We shall," he said, bowing to her.

And so, instead of setting out for London within the hour, as he had intended, Peter found himself walking through Bath with Miss Thompson on his arm. They walked past the Pump Room and Bath Abbey and along by the river in the direction of the Pulteney Bridge. They crossed the bridge and made their way past Laura Place and along Great Pulteney Street until they came to Lady Potford's. They conversed every step of the way, and Peter found himself genuinely enjoying her company and laughing with her over several absurdities she pointed out.

At the same time he wondered about the wisdom of what he was doing—or rather, the wisdom of what he planned to do after calling at Lady Potford's. Was he really going to accompany Miss Thompson to the school? For what purpose, pray? He had learned what he needed to know from Susanna yesterday. He had enjoyed a pleasant half hour dancing and talking with her, and they had said good-bye.

There was really nothing whatsoever left to say, was there?

But dash it all, he still *liked* her. He still wanted a friendship with her. And, if the bald truth were told, he probably felt a little more than just liking for her. Which uncomfortable—and only barely admitted—fact was all the more reason for bowing to Miss Thompson at the doorway of the house on Great Pulteney Street, returning to his hotel with alacrity, and putting as much distance between himself and Miss Martin's School for Girls in Bath as daylight and the speed of his traveling carriage would allow.

But when Lady Potford's butler opened the door to their knock, he found himself stepping over the threshold.

And a little more than half an hour later, after taking coffee in the drawing room and making himself agreeable to Lady Potford, who was feeling rather down after having waved her houseguests on their way earlier, he found himself escorting Miss Thompson again on the short walk to the end of the street and around the corner onto Sydney Place and almost immediately around onto Sutton Street. The turn onto Daniel Street was not far away.

And so here he was, he thought as he stepped up to the school and rapped the knocker against the door, unable even to change his mind at the last moment and hurry away. Miss Thompson was standing solidly just behind him and would think it odd in the extreme if he suddenly bolted.

What the devil was she going to *think*? *She* being Susanna Osbourne, of course.

An elderly, pinch-faced porter opened the door and glared at Peter with unconcealed suspicion. His black coat, shiny with age, looked almost as elderly as he.

The dragon guarding the maidens, perhaps?

"Miss Thompson and Viscount Whitleaf to call upon Miss Martin," he said.

The man looked beyond Peter's shoulder, and his demeanor grew marginally less hostile.

"Miss Martin is expecting you, ma'am," he said, ignoring Peter, "though she is in the middle of a class at the moment."

"Do not disturb her, then," Miss Thompson said. "I shall wait until she is free."

Ah, reprieve! Peter thought. He had the perfect excuse for bowing her over the threshold and going on his way—*I shall wait*, she had said. Not *we*.

Instead, he stood back to allow her to precede him inside and then stepped in after her.

If ever he came fully to understand himself, he thought ruefully, the world would surely stop spinning on its axis and then they would *all* be in trouble.

He was standing in a dark, narrow hallway. Instantly he could hear the distant hum of girls' voices chanting something in unison. He had stepped into the world of Susanna Osbourne, he realized, breathing in the mingled odors of furniture polish and ink and cabbage and an indefinable something that would have told him he was in a school even if he had not already known it.

16

Susanna was in the dining hall eating luncheon.
The seat beside her at the head table—the teachers'
table—was empty. Claudia was probably eating in her
office with Miss Thompson, who had apparently arrived to look over the school with a view to teaching
here.

It would be good to have another resident teacher,
Susanna thought, and one whom Claudia had instinctively liked at their first meeting.

Where was he now, she wondered, as she had wondered at frequent intervals all morning while she was
teaching. How many miles from Bath? How many
miles from wherever he was going?

She made an attempt to bring her attention back to
the conversation of the other teachers.

But Mr. Keeble, whose boots were squeaking as
they always seemed to have done ever since Susanna
had known him as if he must have them specially
made with just that quality, had entered the room and
was making his way toward the head table. Susanna
looked inquiringly at him.

"Miss Martin wishes to see you in her office as soon as you have finished eating, Miss Osbourne," he said.

The dessert had not yet been served. But she did not need dessert. She did not seem to have much appetite today. She excused herself, got to her feet, and made her way to the office. Was Miss Thompson still here? she wondered.

Miss Thompson was. So—inexplicably—was Viscount Whitleaf. He was getting to his feet as Susanna opened the door, and he bowed to her as she stepped inside.

She felt suddenly robbed of breath—just as she had been yesterday when the sight of him in the Upper Assembly Rooms had been equally unexpected. But at least then she had had a few minutes in which to recover herself without having to feel that everyone's eyes were upon her. Today all three occupants of the room were looking at her.

"Miss Thompson?" She smiled. "Viscount Whitleaf?"

What on *earth* was he doing here? He was supposed to be miles away.

"Miss Osbourne," Miss Thompson said, her eyes twinkling. "I might have guessed that a plain gray work dress would only make your hair appear even more vibrantly auburn. If I were ten years younger I would be mortally jealous of you."

"Miss Thompson will be staying for the afternoon," Claudia said. "Viscount Whitleaf is about to take his leave, but he wishes to call in on Lady Potford with a message. She has sent an invitation for me to join her and Miss Thompson at a concert in Bath Abbey tomorrow evening. I will be unable to attend, having promised to give three of the senior girls extra coaching for their history examination next week. However, Miss Thompson has suggested that perhaps you would like to go instead of me, Susanna."

"I should be delighted if you will agree, Miss Osbourne," Miss Thompson assured her. "And I am sure Lady Potford will be too."

It was hard for Susanna to think straight with Viscount Whitleaf standing silently not six feet away. But the chance to attend an evening concert was certainly enticing. She very rarely attended any entertainment that was not directly related to the school. And the Abbey was such a beautiful church.

"Your drama practice is tonight," Claudia said, "and there is no study hall tomorrow, it being Friday. I see nothing to stop you from going, Susanna, except inclination."

"Oh, inclination would certainly take me there," Susanna assured her.

"Splendid!" Miss Thompson exclaimed. "Then it is settled."

"I shall inform Lady Potford of the slight change in plans," Viscount Whitleaf said. "And I shall take my leave, ma'am." He bowed to Claudia. "Perhaps Miss Osbourne would see me on my way?"

On his way? He should be well on his way beyond Bath by now, shouldn't he?

"Why are you still in Bath?" she asked him after they had stepped out into the hallway and he had closed the study door behind him. For once there was no sign of Mr. Keeble. "I thought all the wedding guests were leaving early this morning."

"I waved everyone else on the way," he said, "and then discovered two things. First that Miss Thompson had no escort to Lady Potford's on Great Pulteney Street or here to the school, and second that really I had nowhere of pressing importance to go myself."

"Have you been home to Sidley Park yet?" she asked.

It felt somehow surreal to see him here inside the school, which was such a very feminine domain. He was wearing a long, multicaped greatcoat, which somehow made him seem larger and more broad-shouldered and more *masculine* than ever. Susanna felt half suffocated by his presence.

"Since August?" he said. "Oh, yes, indeed. I went after my mother's houseguests had left. But the drawing room had turned pink and lacy in my absence—it is horribly hideous. And the dining room is to turn lavender after Christmas, which I am expected to spend at Sidley in company with a certain Miss Flynn-Posy and her mama and papa among other people. I shall have to go if only to save my dining room from such a ghastly fate."

He looked so comically forlorn that she could not stop her lips from twitching with amusement.

"I daresay you are too kind to speak your objections openly to your mother," she said.

"Not at all," he said.

"You were actually *playing* with all the children in the ballroom yesterday when I arrived, were you not?" she said. "I overheard Miss Thompson telling Claudia so after our waltz."

"I was early, you see," he said, "and playing with them seemed as good a way as any of passing the time, especially when they had more or less kidnapped me."

"But no other adult thought to play with them," she said, "and apparently it did not occur to them to kidnap any other adult—only you, because you wished to amuse them and they recognized in you someone who would pay attention to them and make the afternoon fun for them. But you are not at all kind, of course."

He grinned a little sheepishly and she knew that now, within moments he was going to open the door and step outside and she was going to close it after him and be alone again.

"I will bring my carriage to fetch you tomorrow evening," he said. "Will half past six suit you?"

She stared at him, uncomprehending.

"I am staying for a couple of days longer," he explained. "I have offered to escort Lady Potford and Miss Thompson to the concert."

"And maneuvered matters so that *I* would be invited too?" she asked, her eyes widening.

"Not at all," he said. "That was sheer good fortune. I was trying to devise a way of doing it, but it was done for me when Miss Martin said she could not go and Miss Thompson suggested you in her stead."

She stared at him, speechless.

"Tell me you are glad." His smile looked a little crooked to her, even perhaps a little wistful—which was surely nonsense.

"I will be *very* glad to attend the concert," she said. "Bath Abbey is often used for organ recitals. I love nothing more than to listen to the great pipe organ being played though I have not heard it often. Perhaps there will be some organ pieces tomorrow."

"You will be glad to attend the *concert*," he said softly. "Well, I must be content with that. I shall come at half past six?"

"Thank you," she said.

And then he did indeed open the door and step outside, and she did indeed close the door after him and find herself alone again. She closed her eyes briefly and drew a few steadying breaths. Not only was she to attend a concert at the Abbey tomorrow evening as a guest of Lady Potford, but she was also to have Viscount Whitleaf as an escort. It was almost too much to bear. The excitement of anticipation might well kill her.

And she had classes to teach this afternoon—in penmanship and writing. The first class was to begin within the next five or ten minutes, in fact.

Susanna turned away from the door and tried to pretend that this was no different from any other afternoon at school.

This was the damnedest thing, Peter thought as he rapped on the door of Miss Martin's school again the following evening. He liked music. He often attended concerts and even the opera in London, depending upon which artists were to sing. But a concert in Bath Abbey? He had actually postponed his departure from

Bath just because of it—when he had still thought the ladies he was to escort there were to be Lady Potford, Miss Thompson, and Miss Martin?

It really was just good fortune that had replaced the last-named lady with Susanna Osbourne. His mind had been working furiously over various schemes for including her in the party, but he had known perfectly well that it was unlikely that both resident teachers would leave the school together for a whole evening—especially so soon after the wedding breakfast.

It really was the damnedest thing, then, but here he was anyway. And there she was—he saw her as soon as the school porter, looking more sour-faced than ever, opened the door to admit him. She was wearing a plain gray cloak—but Miss Thompson had been quite right yesterday about the effect of such a drab color on her hair. Miss Martin, who was with her, was handing her a paisley shawl, which she would doubtless need inside the Abbey. Churches were notoriously chilly places.

There she was—the phrase repeated itself inside his mind as if there were an echo in there.

"Good evening, Miss Martin, Miss Osbourne." He bowed to them.

She looked wide-eyed and slightly flushed in the light of a table lamp—Susanna, that was—and he realized with a pang of tenderness that this must be a grand occasion for her, just as the assembly in Somerset had been.

"I am ready," she said, her voice slightly breathless.

"I trust," Miss Martin said, "that Lady Potford

and Miss Thompson are awaiting you in your carriage, Lord Whitleaf?"

"They are awaiting me at Lady Potford's house, ma'am," he assured her. "A mere five-minute drive from here."

She inclined her head and turned her attention to her fellow teacher.

"Do have a lovely time, Susanna," she said, her voice softening, "and give my regards to the other ladies."

"I will," Susanna said and stepped forward so that he could cup her elbow in his palm and escort her out onto the pavement.

He took her hand in his to help her up the steps into his carriage. She sat with her back to the horses, he noticed, in order to leave the better seat for the other ladies. He vaulted in after her and sat beside her.

It was only after his coachman had shut the door, climbed up to the box, and set the carriage in motion that the door of the school closed.

"Miss Martin cares about you," he said. "So does the male dragon."

"Mr. Keeble?" She laughed. "He cares about us all, girls and teachers alike. He would guard us all from the wicked world beyond the school doors if he could."

"And I am the big, bad wolf?" he asked as the carriage turned onto Sutton Street.

"You are a *man*," she said, and laughed, "which in his eyes is probably far worse. I may be only a schoolteacher, Lord Whitleaf, but to Claudia and to Mr.

Keeble I am also a lady and must be protected from any possibility of harm."

"You are first and foremost a lady," he said as the carriage made its big turn onto Great Pulteney Street, "who happens also to be a schoolteacher."

She turned her head and their eyes met in the dim light cast by the carriage lamps that burned outside.

And we both know what sort of harm can come to a lady who is not properly protected.

He did not say the words aloud. He did not need to.

He was not in the habit of recalling sexual experiences from the past. They were something for present enjoyment and future anticipation. He rarely even thought of former mistresses. Yet he had a sudden, vivid memory of lying with Susanna Osbourne on the hill above the river at Barclay Court. He could remember the feel of her warm woman's body beneath his, of . . .

Well.

Why did one always remember the very things one would prefer to forget?

"Has Miss Thompson decided to take a teaching position at the school?" he asked.

"She spent all of yesterday afternoon with us," she said, "and seemed to enjoy herself. I believe she very well may decide to stay. I hope so. We all like her exceedingly well. Claudia believes it is simply her misfortune to be a sister-in-law of the Duke of Bewcastle and does not hold it against her. Claudia is *not* kindly disposed to any of the Bedwyns, particularly Lady Hallmere and the duke."

They both laughed. But there was no time for further conversation. The carriage stopped outside Lady Potford's house and he descended in order to rap on the door and then hand in the ladies for the drive to the Abbey at the other side of the river.

Bath Abbey was an impressive building, as most great Gothic churches were. This one was more lovely than most, with its pointed arched windows so large that one wondered how there could be enough solid wall left to support the great height and weight of the building. Tall pillars along the nave stretched upward until they spread into a fan-vaulted ceiling far overhead, drawing the eyes and the mind and the spirit heavenward. It was a magnificent setting for a concert, Peter thought as he escorted the ladies inside. As soon as they stepped through the door, Lady Potford moved ahead with Miss Thompson while Peter took Susanna on his arm and followed them.

"Oh," she said, "I have brought classes here on sightseeing walks. I have even attended church here a few times. I have always been in awe of its splendor. But I have never before seen it lit up at night. It is absolutely . . . magical."

"Magical." He smiled down at her. "You had better not let any clergyman hear you describe it with that word."

She laughed softly.

"Mystical, then," she said. "Oh, look, there must be a thousand candles burning, and the light is shivering in the drafts of air. Have you ever seen anything more . . ."

"Magical?" he said. "No, never."

He loved her innocent enthusiasm, something the typical young lady of the *ton* soon learned to disguise beneath a fashionable veneer of ennui. And yet there was nothing childlike about Susanna Osbourne. She was all vivid womanhood.

Her attention soon moved, though, from their surroundings to the people who occupied it, and she looked immediately apprehensive.

The audience was impressively large. Its nature was much as Peter had expected, though. Most people were elderly or at least past the first blush of youth. Except for Susanna and Miss Thompson, there was no one here he had known longer than a couple of days. It was the wrong time of year for there to be many visitors. These people would be almost exclusively residents of Bath.

He had met a number of them at the Pump Room this morning during the daily promenade, which he had joined for lack of anything else to do—and because he genuinely liked people no matter what their age or social status. He had aroused a great deal of interest, partly because he was a stranger and partly, he suspected, because he was below the age of forty.

Several of those people greeted him now as he moved along the central aisle closer to the front of the church with his party. Several others looked at him and Miss Osbourne with interest. Others greeted Lady Potford, and she stopped a few times to exchange greetings with acquaintances.

"Oh, there is Mr. Blake," Susanna said, and smiled more broadly as she raised a hand in greeting, "and Mr. and Mrs. Reynolds."

"Do you wish to speak with them?" he asked.

"Maybe later," she said. "Mr. Blake is the physician who attends the school when anyone is ill. Betsy Reynolds is a day pupil at the school."

She was holding firmly to his arm, but he suspected that she was enjoying herself.

She *was* a lady, he thought. Her father had been William Osbourne. A mere nobody did not generally rise to the exalted position of secretary to a government minister or take up residence in that minister's country home.

But William Osbourne, for some unknown reason, had put a bullet through his brain.

Peter took a seat next to the aisle. Susanna sat beside him with Miss Thompson beyond her and then Lady Potford. It was a little chilly, but even so he helped Susanna off with her cloak, which he draped over the back of her chair while she arranged her paisley shawl about her shoulders. She was wearing the same green gown she had worn to the assembly, he could see. It was trimmed with the ribbon she had bought at the village shop to which he had escorted her.

For a few moments he was assaulted by nostalgic memories of that fortnight, during which she had so unexpectedly become his friend—before he had spoiled it all by becoming her lover. He could vividly remember her laughing in his curricle and thus revealing the fact that as well as being terrified she was also exhilarated.

She had been so full of surprises during those two weeks. He had come very close to falling in love with her in earnest—something he had not admitted to himself until very recently.

Perhaps fortunately for his peace of mind, the concert began soon after they had seated themselves. There was a full orchestra. More important, there was the great pipe organ, which played several solos and inundated every light-filled space and every shadowed alcove of the Abbey with the music of Handel and Bach.

"You were quite right about the organ," he said, moving his head closer to Susanna's at the end of one of the pieces.

Her eyes were glowing with happiness.

"This is like a little piece of heaven," she said.

This. What did she include in the word? he wondered. But she was quite right. This was easily the best evening he had spent since . . . Well, since he did not know when. His mind scanned all the evenings he had spent in London before going to Alvesley Park and then slipped back beyond them to a certain evening in Somerset when he had waltzed at a mere country assembly and then taken a stroll along the village street.

Perhaps he really *had* fallen a little in love with her. He hoped not. But he did not know quite how else to describe his relationship with Susanna Osbourne or his feelings for her. It was not just friendship, was it? It was a little deeper than that. And it was not quite being in love either. It was less frivolous than that.

He realized that the orchestra was in the middle of Handel's *Water Music,* but he had no recollection at all of the first half of the performance. He focused his mind on the rest of it.

There were several small interludes during the course of the evening, when the audience could relax for a minute or two and exchange comments on the program. At the end, Peter knew, everyone would be reluctant to go home. Everyone would stand about in groups, talking, for perhaps half an hour before drifting off home. He looked forward to that half hour or so even though he would not wish away the rest of the evening.

But as it happened he was almost the first to leave.

Susanna had turned her head several times during the evening and had sometimes tipped it back to look upward. She was unabashedly admiring her surroundings and looking at her fellow audience members, Peter knew. He supposed that she was storing memories to take back to school with her. She turned her head away from him just before the final organ piece and looked back over her shoulder. It seemed to him that she turned to face the front again in great haste, and he noticed that she gripped the edges of her shawl very tightly with both hands.

He looked back himself, but a large, broad man two rows back was just straightening up after talking with someone next but one to him, and he effectively blocked the view of most of the audience farther back.

Peter turned his attention to a triumphant organ rendition of Bach's *Jesu, Joy of Man's Desiring*.

He turned, smiling, to Susanna after the last notes had echoed through the high vaults. She was shivering.

"Are you cold?" he asked, setting a hand over one of her clenched ones—and it was indeed like ice.

"I must leave now," she said, her teeth chattering. "The concert has gone on longer than I expected. Claudia will be wondering . . ." She turned her head, and Peter could hear her speaking to Lady Potford above the hubbub of voices that followed the ending of the recital. "I must leave now, ma'am. I am expected back at school. I do thank you for inviting me—and you for suggesting me, Miss Thompson."

"Oh, but you must not rush away, my dear," Lady Potford said. "Miss Martin will certainly understand, and I daresay there are no classes tomorrow. I was hoping you and Viscount Whitleaf would come back for some tea."

But Susanna did not even wait for her to finish speaking. She was drawing her cloak about her and getting to her feet, though her shoulders were hunched over as she did so. She stepped past Peter and hurried along the aisle, her head down.

"Oh, dear," Miss Thompson said, "whatever has happened to upset her? She appeared to be enj—"

"Pardon me, ma'am," Peter said, getting to his feet. "I will follow and make sure she gets home safely. Lady Potford, please do take my carriage and instruct my coachman not to wait for me."

He did not hear her reply. Susanna was already almost out of the Abbey. He hurried after her.

He caught up with her at the outer doors and took her by the elbow.

"Something has happened to upset you," he said.

"No." She lifted a smiling face to his. "But I am always anxious when I have been away from the school for any length of time. It does not seem fair. Do not let

me take you away early, Lord Whitleaf. I shall walk
back alone. I am used to doing so."

"At night? You most certainly will not walk alone
on *this* night," he said. "Will you not wait for my carriage? It should be here soon."

She shook her head.

"I must go back," she said.

"Then I will escort you." He drew her arm firmly
through his.

"Thank you."

It was all she said for a few minutes as they
walked. Actually, he discovered, it was not a cold
night, and what little wind there was was behind
them.

He wondered what had happened to rob her of her
joy in the evening's entertainment. Perhaps, he
thought as he walked beside her and looked down at
her bowed head, she had started remembering—as he
had earlier. For him the memories were uncomfortable
and touched upon his honor. For her they must be far
worse even than that.

He set one gloved hand over hers on his arm.

"Susanna," he said, "I must ask you, much as it
might be better to let sleeping dogs lie. Did I . . . *hurt*
you in any way at Barclay Court? Not just physically,
I mean, though that too, I suppose. Did I?"

Foolish question. Could the answer be anything
but *yes*? And could he expect her to say anything
but *no*?

"No," she said. "No, you did not."

"I have felt dashed guilty," he told her. "I have
never done anything to compare with it in infamy ei-

ther before or since, I swear. I am not a seducer—or *was* not."

"You did not seduce me," she said firmly as they turned to walk across the Pulteney Bridge. "What happened was by mutual consent."

They were reassuring words, and of course he knew there was truth in them. But they were essentially meaningless words, nonetheless. What else *could* she say? He sighed aloud.

"But it is not good enough," he said. "Dash it all, it just is not. Will you marry me, Susanna? Will you do me the great honor of marrying me?"

The words seemed to come out of their own volition. And yet he felt an enormous relief that he had spoken them. They should have been spoken up on that hill. They should have been spoken the next day—he should have hurried over to Barclay Court before she left. He should have followed her to Bath instead of going first to London and then home and then to Alvesley. He should have spoken the words the day before yesterday in the Upper Assembly Rooms.

Will you marry me?

He knew suddenly that he had done the right thing at last, that he had *wanted* to say those words for a long time. He knew that finally he had done the honorable thing, and the thing he wished to do—he *wished* to protect this woman, who had somehow become his very dear friend, perhaps his dearest friend. The fact that she was not with child did not lessen his obligation to her.

She continued walking at his side, their footsteps echoing along the deserted Great Pulteney Street. He began to think she would not answer at all. He even began to wonder if he had asked the question out loud or only in his thoughts.

"No," she said at last. "No, of course I will not."

"Why not?" he asked after another short silence while they continued on past Lady Potford's house.

"A better question might be *why*," she said. "You cannot marry someone simply because you feel guilty."

Was that his reason? If he had not dishonored her at Barclay Court, would the idea of marrying her ever have crossed his mind? It was a foolish question, of course. The point was that he *had* dishonored her. And it was surely more than guilt that had impelled him to ask the question.

As they turned into Sutton Street, she laughed softly.

"When you say your prayers tonight, Lord Whiteleaf," she said, "you must give special thanks for the narrow escape you have just had."

"You still believe, then," he said, curling his fingers around hers, "that I am incapable of any deep emotion?"

"I know you are *not*," she said. "But I know that kindness is one of your most dominant attributes— that and gallantry to ladies. You cannot—or ought not to—contract a marriage on such things alone. You need to look deeper into your own heart. You need to learn to like yourself too."

Her words smote him deeply. Despite her denials she had looked at him and seen a man incapable of any deeper feeling than kindness. She did not believe that the offer of his heart was a significant enough gift. But did he believe it? He had not offered his heart, had he?

He had lost all confidence in love several years ago. He had given all the love of his eager young heart to Bertha Grantham and had made a prize idiot of himself as a result.

Was the real problem that he had lost confidence in himself? In his ability to love or be loved? Had he stopped liking himself? He *had* felt like an idiot—a gullible, naïve fool. But did that mean he had stopped *liking* himself?

It was such a novel—and disturbing—thought that he said nothing as they approached the school and their footsteps slowed.

"You must not think you owe me marriage," she said, her voice gentle now, as if *he* were the one who needed consolation, "just because you believe I was hurt in the summer and imagine that I am lonely and unhappy with my life as it is. Even if all those things were true—which they are not—they are no reason for a marriage. Not on either side. You owe me nothing."

"I see," he said as they stopped walking. His mind was paralyzed. He could think of nothing else to say to her. It was actually a relief when the door opened even before he could knock upon it, and the ever-present porter peered out at them.

But he could not let her go this way. He could not say good-bye like this.

"Tomorrow is Saturday," he said. "There are no classes, are there?"

"Except the usual games class in the morning," she

said. "I always supervise it out in the meadows unless it is raining."

"May I see you tomorrow afternoon, then?" he asked her. "We can go walking—perhaps in Sydney Gardens if the weather permits. And perhaps we can go somewhere for tea afterward—somewhere public, of course, so that the proprieties may be observed."

It would be altogether better, he thought—for both of them—if she said no. But he willed her not to refuse him. He did not want this to be good-bye. He wanted the chance to laugh with her once again before they went their separate ways forever.

She had drawn her hand free of his arm. She took him completely by surprise now when she drew off one of her gloves and set her fingertips gently against his cheek.

"Yes," she said. "I would like that."

He swallowed and turned his head to brush his lips against her palm. But only for a moment. That porter had not moved back out of sight. Peter half expected that he would growl at any moment—or open his mouth and spew out a stream of fire.

"I shall see you tomorrow, then," he said, stepping back. "Good night."

"Good night. And thank you for walking back with me," she said, before turning and hurrying inside.

The door closed with a click behind her.

. . . you must give special thanks for the narrow escape you have just had.

He ought to agree with her. He tried to imagine his mother's reaction and his sisters' if he had proceeded to present Susanna Osbourne to them as his chosen bride. They would *not* be happy.

But dash it all, he could *not* agree.

And devil take it, if this was what being in love felt like, he had been wise to guard his heart for the past several years.

With a deep sigh he turned to begin the long walk back to his hotel.

17

"*I am glad you are not too late home,*" Mr. Keeble said, just as if he were her father. "I worry when one of you ladies is out after dark. Miss Martin wants you to join her in her sitting room."

"Thank you," Susanna said as he passed her in the hallway in order to lead the way upstairs.

She would give anything in the world, she thought as she followed him up, to be able to go straight to her room, to dive beneath the covers of her bed, to hide from the world and herself there forever and ever. And yet contrarily she could not wait to reach the calming comfort of Claudia's presence.

Oh, how she missed her mother! Ridiculous thought, but really, *how* she missed her.

"Miss Osbourne, ma'am," Mr. Keeble said after knocking at the door of Claudia's sitting room and then opening it, announcing Susanna formally as he always did when given the chance.

It was an enormous relief as she entered the room to see that Lila was not there, fond as she was of her fellow teacher. Claudia was sitting beside a cozy fire, a book in her lap, looking rather weary. But she looked sharply enough at her friend and cast the book aside in order to get to her feet as Mr. Keeble shut the door.

And then quite inexplicably Susanna was in her arms, her head on Claudia's shoulder. Nothing like it had ever happened before. She relaxed into the sheer comfort of the embrace for several silent moments before stepping back, biting her lip, embarrassed.

"I am so sorry," she said.

"Sit down," Claudia said, drawing the other armchair a little closer to the fire, "and I will pour you a cup of tea. It is fresh."

It had always been Susanna's self-appointed job to pour the tea, but on this occasion she did not argue. She sank into the offered chair after setting aside her cloak and gloves with the shawl laid carefully on top of them. She welcomed the warmth of the fire against her chilled body.

"Now," Claudia said after Susanna had taken her first sip of the blessedly hot tea, "what do you wish to tell me, if anything?"

They had never intruded into each other's lives. It was remarkable that they had been such good friends for years without knowing very much about each other's past—though, of course, Susanna had been only twelve when she came to the school.

"I saw someone in the Abbey," she said. "Two people, actually, though I was not sure of the identity of the other person."

"Two people you knew?" Claudia asked.

"A long time ago." Susanna took a long drink from her cup and then set it in the saucer and put both on the table beside her. "I grew up in their home until the age of twelve, until my father died. He was secretary there."

Claudia said nothing.

"He took his own life," Susanna blurted. "He killed himself, Claudia. He shot himself in the head."

"Ah, you poor dear," Claudia said softly. "I did not know that."

"I suppose my existence was not enough to make him want to live," Susanna said. "He did not even make any provision for me."

She was grateful that Claudia said nothing for a while. She had not even fully realized how much she had pitied herself all these years, how much she had resented the fact that her father had chosen death rather than her, even though she thought she understood at least part of his reason for doing what he had done. He had always been an affectionate father, though he had been content to let her grow up in the nursery with Edith and not see her for more than a few minutes in a day and sometimes not at all.

"And the person you saw this evening, the owner of the house, would make no provision for you either?" Claudia asked at last. "That is why you ran away, Susanna?"

"Lady Markham," Susanna said, spreading her hands in her lap and looking down at them. "And I believe it was Edith with her. I shared a childhood with her though she was more than a year younger than I and the daughter of the house. We were very close even though I was really only a servant's daughter. But my father *was* a gentleman."

She had become defensive on that issue lately.

"Of course he was," Claudia said. "I knew from the moment of your arrival in Bath that you were a lady, Susanna. You needed no elocution or deportment lessons, and you could already read. I have always thought that was why Mr. Hatchard noticed you and wrote to ask if I would take you here."

"I was on my way from my bedchamber to the nursery," Susanna said, pressing her palms harder into her lap and stiffening her fingers as she recounted the memories that had rushed at her earlier in the Abbey. "I was desperately seeking for some comfort, I suppose, even though there is no real comfort to be found when one's papa has just blown his head off and one has not been allowed to see him despite one's tears and screams. I wanted Edith. But I never got inside the nursery. I could hear Lady Markham speaking in there, though I have never known whom she was addressing. It could not have been Edith, who was barely eleven."

She paused and drew a deep breath, which she expelled on a sigh.

"I believe I can still remember her exact words," she said. "They are burned into my memory. *The church has washed its hands of him, of course,* she said. *He committed a mortal sin when he took his own life. He will have to be buried in unconsecrated ground. And whatever are we to do with Susanna? This is such a burden for us to bear. She can hardly remain here.*"

She had fled—from the nursery and from the house.

"My father was not buried in the churchyard," she said, "and I did not even stay to see what they actually did with him. I left him as he had left me and somehow found my way to London."

"And now Lady Markham is in Bath," Claudia said.

"Yes." Susanna curled her fingers into her palms and lifted her head to stare into the fire. "And I am almost sure the young lady beside her was Edith. It is foolish to have been so discomposed. I was just looking around between pieces close to the end of the program, as I had been doing all evening. A large man a few rows behind me had moved out of my line of vision, and there they were. I suppose they had been there all the time. But I am fine now." She smiled. "How was your evening with the senior girls?"

But Claudia ignored her question. She also was gazing into the fire.

"There is nothing worse, is there," she said, "than a past that has never been fully dealt with. One can convince oneself that it is all safely in the past and forgotten about, but the very fact that we can tell ourselves that it is forgotten proves that it is not."

Susanna swallowed. "But remembering is pointless," she said, "when nothing can be done to change the past. I am fine, Claudia. Tomorrow I shall be my usual cheerful self, I promise."

But she did wonder about Claudia. Was there something unresolved in *her* past? Was there something unresolved in everyone's past? Was memory always as much of a burden as it could sometimes be a blessing?

Claudia looked up and smiled.

"When I saw your face as you stepped into the room," she said, "I was convinced that Viscount Whitleaf must have put that look there. I was quite prepared to march down to the kitchen, avail myself of Cook's rolling pin, and stride off in pursuit of him."

"Oh, Claudia," Susanna said before she could stop herself, "he asked me to *marry* him."

Claudia went very still.

"And? . . ." she said.

"I said no, of course," Susanna said.

"Did you?" Claudia asked. "Why?"

"He is the sort of man . . . oh, I do not know quite how to describe him," Susanna said. "He often takes gallantry to an extreme. He wants to shoulder the burdens of all women of his acquaintance. He wants to make them comfortable. He wants to make them feel good about themselves. He will go to great lengths not to hurt them or deprive them of what seems important to them. And even that description does not quite express what I am trying to say. He is kind and open and . . . And he is quite muddleheaded. He could see that I was upset when he walked home with me, and he wanted to comfort me. And he thought perhaps that he had raised expectations in me during the summer and so felt that he owed me an offer of marriage. I suppose that he believes being a spinster school-teacher is an undesirable fate for any woman."

"And did he?" Claudia asked, looking at her with disconcertingly keen eyes. "Raise expectations in you?"

"No," Susanna said. "No, he did not."

"Do you love him?" Claudia asked.

Susanna opened her mouth to say no but shut it again. She drew a deep breath and released it slowly.

"Love has nothing to do with anything," she said. "I said no and I meant no. It would not have been a happy marriage, Claudia, for either of us. Love on one side would only have made it worse—for me and perhaps for him too."

"I know you are feeling weak and vulnerable tonight," Claudia said after a few silent moments, "but in reality you are a very strong person, Susanna. And you were a strong girl. I always knew, of course, that your father had died and left you all alone in the world—you told me so when you came here. But I had no idea of the terrible truth until tonight. You were always the sunniest-natured of girls nevertheless—even if you *were* rather wild and rebellious for the first few months. And you are the sunniest-natured of my teachers and very much loved by all the girls—almost without exception, I believe. I will not question your decision to reject Viscount Whitleaf's offer. Such a match would have offered you security and wealth and comfort for the rest of your life, of course, but you know that without my having to tell you so. I am very glad that you had the strength to put happiness and integrity before material security. And of course I am selfishly glad for myself."

Susanna smiled rather wanly.

"He is coming here tomorrow afternoon," she said. "He wants me to go walking with him. Perhaps I ought to have said no to that invitation too after being away from school this evening."

"Ah, Susanna," Claudia said, "we must live too

when given the chance. Teaching is a *job*, my dear, not a life."

Susanna looked at her in some surprise. She would have expected Claudia to be disapproving of the continued relationship.

"It will be the last time," she promised, getting to her feet. "He will be leaving Bath soon."

"Good night, Susanna," Claudia said. "But I have not even asked you about the concert."

"It was wonderful beyond words," Susanna told her.

A few moments later she was on her way up to her room, feeling considerably calmer than she had felt when she first arrived home. But there was still a heavy ache of grief somewhere low in her abdomen.

He had asked her to marry him.

And she had said no.

Ah, she had said no.

And then she had set about comforting him because she knew she had made him unhappy.

But still she had said no. She could not marry him just because he felt guilty about having lain with her.

He did not love her.

As if *that* were a good reason for rejecting a dazzlingly eligible marriage offer.

But she *did* love him, and that made all the difference.

As she let herself into her bedchamber and closed the door behind her, she wished she felt even half as strong as Claudia had assured her she was.

• • •

Bath had long ceased to be a fashionable watering spot. It had become a retirement center for the elderly and the infirm and the shabby genteel and the upwardly mobile middle classes. But it still had its charm, and it had its rituals, one of the most enduring of which was the early morning promenade in the Pump Room to the accompaniment of the soft music provided by the chamber orchestra in the alcove at one end of the room.

Some people went to drink the waters in the hope of improving their health. A few went for the exercise or told themselves that they did. Most went in order to watch for new faces and listen to new gossip and pass on any news they thought someone else might not yet have heard.

Peter put in an appearance there the morning after the concert just as he had the day before. He had always enjoyed mingling with other people even when, as now, there was almost no one of his own age group and no one he knew apart from the acquaintances he had made the day before. That last fact was soon to change, though.

He was conversing with a group of ladies that included Lady Holt-Barron, who, upon hearing that he had attended the wedding breakfast at the Upper Rooms a few days earlier, informed him that she had an acquaintance with the Bedwyns, that the Duke of Bewcastle had actually called at her house on the Circus one afternoon when the present Marchioness of Hallmere had been staying with her daughter—the marchioness had still been Lady Freyja Bedwyn at the time though she had become betrothed to the marquess before leaving Bath. Peter was listening to the lady's convoluted story with smiling indulgence when he spotted two very familiar faces across the room.

Lady Markham and Edith.

He excused himself as soon as he could politely do so and went to meet them, a delighted smile on his face. They watched him come with answering smiles.

"This *is* a surprise," he said after greeting them and bowing to them both, "though I suppose it ought not to be since I discovered from Theo quite recently that Edith lives not far away and that you were spending some time with her, Lady Markham."

"But it is not a surprise to us, Whitleaf, beyond the fact that you are here in Bath at all," Lady Markham said. "We saw you last evening in Bath Abbey and fully intended to speak with you after the concert. But you vanished and left us wondering whether you had been simply a mirage."

"Ah, yes," he said. "One of the ladies in my party was unable to stay longer and so I left as soon as the concert had finished to escort her home."

He remembered even as he spoke that Susanna had spent her childhood at Fincham Manor. He would not mention her name to them, though. It was altogether possible that she would not wish it.

Actually, he had been trying ever since he woke up from a broken, troubled sleep not to think too much of Susanna at all. Good Lord, he had offered her marriage last night—*and she had refused him.*

You need to look deeper into your own heart. You need to learn to like yourself too.

Ah, yes, and then there was that. Best not to think of it.

"I understand that congratulations are in order," he said to Edith. "I trust you have recovered your health after your confinement? And that the child is well?"

"Both," she said, smiling. "But Lawrence thought a change of air would do us good, and so he has taken lodgings on Laura Place for a month. It *is* good to see you again, Peter, and looking surely more handsome than ever. All the ladies here look as if they would gobble you up if given half a chance."

Her eyes twinkled into his, and they all laughed.

"I came to attend a wedding breakfast a few days ago," he explained, "and stayed on for a few days before returning to London."

They chattered amiably for a few minutes before Edith set a hand on his sleeve.

"Peter," she said, "I *must* ask, though it does seem impertinent. The lady you were escorting last evening— she was not . . . Could she possibly have been Susanna Osbourne, by any chance?"

It was impossible to avoid answering such a direct question.

"Yes," he said. "I ran into her this summer and again at the wedding breakfast. The bride is a friend of hers while the groom is my cousin's brother-in-law."

Edith's hand tightened on his arm.

"Oh, she *is* alive, then," she said. "I have always wondered."

"She disappeared," Lady Markham explained, "after her father died. None of our efforts to find her was successful, though we were quite frantic. We never heard of or from her again. It was all very distressing on top of everything else, as perhaps you remember, Whitleaf. Or perhaps not. You were away at school at the time, I believe. Susanna was only twelve years old, far too young to be out in the world on her own. But what could we do? We had no idea where to start looking, though we *did* look for a long time."

"Well," Peter said, smiling, "now after all this time you may take comfort from the knowledge that she did survive."

"Where is she living or staying, Peter?" Edith asked eagerly. "I would love to call on her, to speak with her. We were the dearest of friends. We were almost like sisters. It broke my heart when she disappeared."

"Perhaps," he said warily, looking apologetically from one to the other of them, "she ran away and stayed away because she felt a need to break the connection with her father's employers. Perhaps the memory of anything or anyone to do with him is still just too painful. Perhaps she felt she had good—"

"And perhaps," Edith said, smiling ruefully, "you are too much the gentleman to betray her trust, Peter. We understand, do we not, Mama?"

"You see," he said, "it took her a while during the summer to tell me who she was even though she had recognized me, or at least my name, immediately. And even then she would tell me only that her father had died at Fincham—of a heart attack, she led me to believe. It was Theo who told me the truth about his suicide after I went home. I suppose it is understandable that Miss Osbourne may not want any reminders of that time."

And a distinct possibility had struck him. Had she seen Lady Markham and Edith last evening and recognized them? Was that why she had been in such a hurry to leave the Abbey as soon as the concert ended, even though she had appeared to be enjoying the evening immensely until then?

"But we never understood her leaving," Lady Markham said with a sigh. "She was only a child and her father had just died. We had always treated her well, almost as if she were one of our own, and Edith positively adored her. One would have expected her to turn to us for comfort."

"If you see her again, Peter," Edith said, "will you ask her if I may call on her? Or if she will call on me if she wishes to remain secretive about her exact whereabouts?"

"I will ask," he promised. But he could not resist asking another question of his own.

"*Why* did Osbourne kill himself?" He addressed himself to Lady Markham. "Did you ever find out?"

She hesitated noticeably.

"I am surprised," she said, "that you did not even know of the suicide until Theo told you recently. You were fond of Mr. Osbourne, as I recall, and he of you. However, I suppose it was to be expected that Lady Whitleaf would want to protect you from such a harsh truth, and she would have sworn your sisters to secrecy. As for William Osbourne's reason for doing what he did, that died with him, the poor man."

"He did not leave a note for Lord Markham?" Peter asked.

She hesitated again.

"He did," she said. But she did not elaborate, and he disliked intruding any further into a subject on which she was clearly reluctant to talk. It must, of course, have been a remarkably distressing episode in her life. He did, however, ask one more question.

"Did he also leave a note for Sus— For Miss Osbourne?" he asked.

"Yes, he did," she said.

"Did she read it?"

"Both notes were folded neatly inside the final up-dated page of a ledger inside the drawer of his desk," she told him, "and were understandably not discovered until after his burial. By then Susanna was gone without a trace. It would be as well to leave it at that now, Whitleaf. It is an old, unhappy story and best forgotten. But it does have a happy ending of sorts after all. Susanna is alive and apparently well. Is she? Well? And happy?"

"Both, I believe," he said.

He knew that he had made her very unhappy during the summer. Even now he liked to believe that the prospect of saying good-bye to him again saddened her. But honesty forced him to admit that she lived a life that brought her security and friendship and satisfaction and perhaps even happiness. He was not necessary to her life. She could live very well without him. He had not lied to Lady Markham.

It was a humbling thought—that Susanna did not need him, that last evening she had actually refused his marriage offer, which from any material point of view must be seen as extremely advantageous to her. She had told him he needed to learn to like himself. Before saying good night to him, she had removed her glove and touched his cheek with gentle fingertips—as if *he* were the one who needed tenderness and comfort.

As if *she* were the strong, secure one.

He took his leave of Lady Markham and Edith after promising to call upon them in Laura Place before he left Bath. A few minutes later he left the Pump Room and walked back to his hotel for breakfast.

18

Some days in November could still retain traces of the glory of autumn and even a hint of a lost summer, though the trees were bare of leaves and the plants of flowers. But usually such days came at a time when duty forced one to remain busy indoors, enjoying the weather only in the occasional glance through a window.

This particular Saturday was such a day. But this time Susanna was able to enjoy it to the full. It was games day, and the whole morning was spent outdoors in the meadows beyond the school with those girls who chose air and vigorous exercise over embroidery and tatting and crochet. As often happened, Susanna gave in to the urgings of the girls and her own inclination and joined in the games herself with the result that her cheeks were glowing with color by the time she led the two orderly lines back to school for luncheon. And though she was breathless, her body hummed with energy.

And the morning exercise was not all. The afternoon offered a rare treat—a walk, perhaps in Sydney

Gardens, which were close by but rarely visited because of the admission fee—and with a gentleman, no less.

She would not be quite human, Susanna supposed as she changed into her Sunday-best wool dress after luncheon and brushed her hair, if she were not bubbling over with excitement and exhilaration at the prospect. The first blush of youth had passed her by with very little in the way of entertainments and nothing in the way of beaux.

Her exuberance was not even much diminished by the memory of the night before. Viscount Whitleaf had offered her marriage last evening and she had refused. In all probability she would never see him again after today. But it was by her own choice, was it not? She had refused to go away with him during the summer. Last evening she had refused to marry him. And she would say no again, to both offers, if they were repeated. And so she had no cause to complain or mope or weep—she had done altogether too much of all three. In fact, she had every reason to be proud of herself. She loved him, but she had refused to allow that fact to tempt her to cling, to hold on to him at all costs.

He did not love her, but that did not matter. He *liked* her. That was enough.

He had not mentioned a specific time for coming this afternoon. Susanna went downstairs when she was ready and into the art room, where Mr. Upton was working with some of the girls to design sets for the Christmas play and concert. Miss Thompson was in there with them, her dress protected by a large white apron as if she were about to paint the sets right there and then.

"I have been informed," she told Susanna, detaching herself from the huddled group, "that teaching at Miss Martin's school involves more than just imparting knowledge to a quiet, receptive class of girls. And so here I am, discovering whether I have the talent and the stamina to offer more. And to think that I could be at Lindsey Hall now, peacefully reading a book!"

She looked as if she were enjoying herself enormously. Her eyes were twinkling—a characteristic expression with her.

Susanna laughed.

"But the preparations for the Christmas concert are always a great deal of fun," she said. "*And* hard work."

"How will this suit you, Miss Osbourne?" Mr. Upton called, beckoning her over to a table covered with sketches. He did not usually come in to school on a Saturday, but he probably would do so every week between now and the end of term.

But Susanna had time only to glance at the sketches for her play sets and comment upon what she liked and make a few suggestions for improvement before a chorus of girls' voices called her attention to Mr. Keeble standing in the doorway, looking her way.

Viscount Whitleaf must have come.

Indeed he had. He was awaiting her in the hallway when she arrived there wearing her warm gray winter cloak and tying the ribbons of her green bonnet beneath her chin. He was wearing his caped greatcoat again and looking very solidly male.

"Miss Osbourne." He bowed to her, but though all his usual jaunty charm was in the gesture and in his smile, it seemed to Susanna that there was a certain wariness in his eyes too.

"Lord Whitleaf." She approached him along the hall with an answering wariness.

Last evening stretched between them like a long shadow.

The weather had not changed in the hour or so she had been indoors, Susanna discovered when they stepped out onto the pavement, unless perhaps the air had grown a little warmer. The sun shone down on them from a cloudless sky. There was no discernible wind. She could not have asked more of their last afternoon together.

"Shall we go into Sydney Gardens?" he asked her, offering his arm. "I daresay the park is not at its best in November, but it will be quiet and rural."

And despite the loveliness of the day, they would probably have it almost to themselves, she thought.

"That would be pleasant," she said as they headed toward Sydney Place and across the road to the Gardens.

They talked about the summer and their mutual friends and acquaintances in Somerset. They talked about the school and the busy preparations for the Christmas concert, which was always well attended by the parents and other relatives and friends of the girls and teachers and by various dignitaries of Bath. They talked about his sisters and their husbands and children. They talked about the park surrounding them, barren now in the late autumn but still picturesque and peaceful. And they did indeed have it almost to themselves. They passed one rather noisy party of eight, but it was close to the gates, and those people were on their way out.

This was the way a friendship should end, Susanna thought, if it must end at all. They were placid and cheerful and in perfect accord with each other. Gone were the inappropriate and unexpected passion of their last afternoon at Barclay Court and the embarrassment of his attempt at atonement last evening. Today they talked and laughed, enjoying each other's company and the rare gift of a perfect November day.

And this was how she would remember their relationship, she resolved. There would be no more tears, only pleasant memories. For this was how they had been together during the summer with the exception of the first and last days.

"Ah, the maze," he said as they climbed a steep path toward a straight, high hedge to one side of it. "I knew there was one in here somewhere. Shall we see if we can lose ourselves in it?"

"Perhaps forever?" she said. "What if we can find our way neither to the center nor back out, but are doomed to wander in aimless circles for the rest of our days?"

"It sounds rather like real life, does it not?" he said.

They both laughed.

"But at least," he added, "we will be lost together."

"A definite consolation," she agreed, and they laughed again.

But it was, of course, impossible to remain determinedly cheerful for a whole afternoon. There was a pang of something in the thought that they would not in reality remain lost together within the maze forever. They would find their way in and their way out and complete their walk.

And then the end would come.

He took her hand in his when they entered the maze. Though they both wore gloves, she could feel the heat and the strength of his fingers and remembered how he had laced them with hers while they walked along the village street during the assembly.

They took numerous wrong turns and had to retrace their steps in order to try a different direction. But eventually, after a great deal of conflicting opinions and laughter, they found their way to the center of the maze, where a couple of wooden seats awaited them and offered repose.

"I suppose," he said after she had seated herself and he took his place beside her, "we ought to have come armed with a mountain of handkerchiefs to drop at strategic intervals along the way. Do you know the way out?"

"No." She laughed.

"We must be thankful, I suppose," he said, taking her hand in his again, "that there is no seven-headed monster or its like awaiting us here."

In the silence at the middle of the maze with Sydney Gardens stretching beyond it, it was very easy to forget the world outside, the inevitable passing of time, the ephemeral nature of the friendship between a man and a woman. It was very easy to believe in the perfection of the moment.

They must have sat for all of five minutes—perhaps ten—without speaking. But sometimes, as they had discovered during the summer, conversation was unnecessary. Communication was made at an altogether deeper level.

Her shoulder, Susanna realized after a while, was leaning against his. Their outer thighs were lightly touching. And somehow—she could not remember its happening—her right glove lay in her lap and his left glove in his, and their bare hands were clasped warmly together.

She heard him draw a deep breath at last and release it slowly.

"I wish I had insisted upon being less protected when I was a boy," he said. "*Could* I have insisted, I wonder? Did I have that power? I wish I had at least tried to know you better. I knew your father but not you. If I *had* known you, if I *had* insisted upon knowing what was going on in my home and neighborhood even while I was away at school, perhaps I could have been there for you when your father died. Though I do not suppose I could have offered much by way of comfort."

No, *especially* not him.

"All people must suffer bereavements," she said, "even children. I managed."

"Susanna." He pulled off his other glove with his teeth, transferred her hand from his left hand to his right, and set his left arm about her shoulders. "I spoke with Theo Markham while I was at home. I know about your father."

She almost broke free of him and jumped to her feet. She remained very still instead. What else had Theodore Markham told him?

"I do not believe it was a mortal sin," she said quickly. "I do not care what the church has to say on the question or how much it forbids Christian burial to those who take their own life. It would be a very unfair and uncompassionate God who would condemn forever a man who was driven to ending his own life by people who can live on and repent and redeem themselves. If that were what God is like, I would be a determined atheist."

"You believe that someone else drove him into doing it, then?" he asked.

She waited for him to say more, but he did not.

"Who knows?" she said. "He kept his secrets both before and after his death. It does not matter any longer, does it? He has found his peace. At least, I *hope* he has."

Though there were times even now she was an adult when she knew she had still not forgiven him for choosing peace over her.

"I am so terribly sorry," he said. "I liked him. He used to do things with me and Theo. I cannot even imagine how you must have suffered at his loss."

He could not know, of course, the pang his words had caused her. She had always believed that her father would have preferred a son to a daughter. He had never been actively unkind to her. Indeed, he had always shown her unfailing affection whenever they were together. But he had very rarely offered to do things with her.

The thought flashed suddenly through her mind that perhaps it was an unconscious memory of his neglect that had helped her to say no last evening. She knew very well what it was like not to have the fully committed love of a man she adored—and a man upon whom she was dependent and to whom she owed allegiance and obedience.

"You do not need to imagine it," she said as he brought her hand up to his lips and then held the back of it against his cheek. "You do not need to bear other people's burdens. Only the person concerned can do that. I bore my own burden, and I am still here. I have survived—and rather well, I believe."

He closed his eyes and bowed his head, their clasped hands back on her lap, his other arm still hugging her close to him.

"Why did you run away?" he asked.

"They would not let me see him," she said, "and they were going to bury him outside the churchyard. They did not know what to do with me. I was a burden to them. I did not belong to them, after all—or to anyone else for that matter. They were going to send me away. I preferred to go without waiting. I preferred to have some control over my own fate."

"What makes you believe," he asked her, "that they would have turned you away, that they saw you as a burden?"

"I *heard* Lady Markham say so," she said. "I did not mishear and I did not misunderstand. A burden is simply that—an unwanted load. And that is what she called me. She said I could not stay there."

"And yet," he said, "they searched and searched for you long after you had vanished."

"Is that what Theodore told you?" she asked him.

"Theo was away at school," he said, "as I was. It was Lady Markham herself who told me, and Edith. This morning."

She stiffened and then relaxed against him again, setting her head against his shoulder and closing her eyes.

"Ah," she said. "You did see them, then. Or they saw you. Did you tell them where I live?"

"No," he said. "It was not my secret to divulge—if it *is* a secret."

"I do not wish to see them," she said.

"Were they not kind to you at all, then?" he asked.

"They were very kind," she said. "Perhaps too kind. I made the mistake of believing that I belonged to them. Sometimes when Edith would climb onto her mother's lap, I would climb up there too—and she would never turn me away no matter how strange she must have thought it. Edith was as dear to me as any sister could have been. Sometimes children do not realize by how fragile a thread their security hangs. Perhaps it is as well they do not—most of them grow up before the thread can be broken. But I don't want to talk about this any longer. I wanted simply to enjoy the afternoon."

"I am sorry," he said with a sigh. "I really am sorry."

They lapsed into silence for a while and she

thought how comforting a man's arm could be about her shoulders and his broad shoulder beneath her cheek and his hand clasping hers. She could get used to such comfort, such dependence. How lovely it would feel to be able to transfer all one's burdens onto a man's capable shoulders and curl into the safety of his protection.

And how easy it was to allow one's mind to slip into fiction and to imagine that there was something desirable about giving up one's autonomy, one's very self.

As if there were such a thing as happily-ever-after and no more effort to make in life.

She turned her face against his shoulder and wished life were as simple as a young girl's dreams—a young girl before the age of twelve and the suicide of her father.

His hand left hers and undid the ribbons beneath her chin. She did not lift her face as he drew her bonnet off and set it down on the seat beside her. And then his hand came beneath her chin, cupping it in the hollow between his thumb and forefinger, and lifting her face until their eyes met.

"Susanna," he murmured. "Ah, my sweet, strong Susanna."

She felt anything but strong. Her lips were trembling when his own covered them, warm, parted, wonderfully comforting—and strangely familiar, as if she were somehow coming home. She leaned into him, her one hand spreading over his chest, her other arm twining about his neck to draw him closer. She opened her mouth and felt all the heat and strength of him—all the essence of him—as his tongue came inside.

Passion flared between them, and she moaned at his touch as his hand came beneath her cloak to caress her breasts, to trace the hollow of her waist, the flare of a hip. She kissed him back with a sort of wild abandon, and heat seared them both.

But it was not an entirely mindless embrace. They were at the center of a maze in the middle of a probably deserted park. But it was, nevertheless, possible that they could be interrupted at any moment. And there was more than just that. They had behaved indiscreetly and unwisely at Barclay Court, and they had both suffered as a result.

When she drew back her head, touched her forehead to his, and closed her eyes, he withdrew his hand from inside her cloak and made no attempt to continue the embrace.

"Susanna," he said after a few moments, "I wish you would reconsider—"

But she set two fingers against his lips and lifted her forehead away from his to look into his eyes. They gazed back into her own, darkly violet in the sunlight. He did not attempt to finish what he had begun to say.

"Don't look at me like that," she whispered.

"Like what?" He took her by the wrist and moved her hand away from his mouth.

"With pity and compassion in your eyes." She was suddenly and inexplicably angry as she drew free of him and jumped to her feet. "You are forever wanting to *give*, to *comfort*, to *protect*. Do you never want to *take,* to *demand,* to assert your own wishes? I do not *need* your pity."

And what on *earth* was she talking about? She turned her back on him, took a few steps away to the other side of the clearing at the center of the maze.

His silence was as accusing as words. She knew she had hurt him, but she was powerless now to unsay the words.

"Should I take you again here, then, to slake my desire—but by force this time?" he asked her, his voice horribly quiet—why did he not rage at her? "Should I demand that you marry me so that my honor can be restored? Should I assert myself as a man and a wealthy, titled man at that and take whatever my heart desires from all who stand in my way? Especially women? Is that what you want of me, Susanna? I did not understand. I am sorry—I cannot be such a man."

"Oh, Peter." She turned to look at him. He was still sitting on the seat, his shoulders slightly slumped, his forearms resting on his thighs, his hands dangling between his knees. "I did not mean it that way."

"What *did* you mean, then?" he asked.

She opened her mouth and drew breath and then could not think of anything to say. She did not know quite what she had meant. She had told him last night that he needed to learn to like himself. That had not been quite it either. And she had once told him that he needed a dragon to slay. She was not even sure what she had meant by that.

She wanted him to . . .

To move heaven and earth.

For her. For himself.

She wanted him to *love* her.

How foolish! As if that would make any difference to anything.

"You cannot answer, can you?" he said. "Because you *did* mean what you said. I think perhaps I *do* like myself well enough. It is you who do not."

But he held up a staying hand and smiled crookedly as she opened her mouth and drew breath to speak again.

"Enough!" he said. "I think you must be a very good teacher indeed, Susanna Osbourne. I have never done as much soul-searching as I have since I met you. I used to think I was a pretty cheerful, uncomplicated fellow. Now I feel rather as if I had been taken apart at the seams and stitched together again with some of my stuffing left out."

Despite herself her mouth quirked at the corners and drew up into a smile.

"Then I am definitely not a good teacher," she said. "But you are a good man, Peter. You *are*. It is just that . . ."

He raised his eyebrows.

"I am not only a woman," she said. "I am a *person*. All women are persons. If we are weak and dependent upon men, it is because we have allowed men to mold us into those images. Perhaps it makes men feel good and strong to see us that way. And perhaps most women are happy to be seen thus. Perhaps society works reasonably well because both men and women are happy with the roles our society has given them to play. But I was thrown out on my own early in life. I will never say it was a good thing that happened to me, but I *am* grateful that circumstances have forced me to live outside the mold. I would rather be a complete person than just a woman even if I must be alone as a result."

"You do not need to be alone," he said.

"No." She smiled at him. "You would marry me and support and protect me for the rest of my life. And so we move full circle. I am sorry, Peter. I did not mean to deliver such a pompous speech. I did not even know I believed those things until I heard them come out of my mouth. But I *do* believe them."

"It is as I thought, then," he said, getting to his feet and handing her her bonnet. "You are happier without me. It is a humbling reality."

And she could not now contradict him, could she?

She took her bonnet and busied herself with putting it back on and tying the ribbons beneath her chin.

"Will you do one thing for me?" she asked him.

"What?" he asked her.

She looked into his eyes.

"When you go home to Sidley Park for Christmas," she said, "will you *stay* there? Make it your home and your life?" She was appalled suddenly by her presumption.

"And marry Miss Flynn-Posy too?" His smile was crooked.

"If you decide that you *wish* to marry her, yes," she said. "Will you *talk* to your mother, Peter? *Really* talk?"

"Throw my weight around? Lay down the law?" he said. "Leave misery in my wake?"

"Tell her who you are," she said. "Perhaps she has

been so intent upon loving you all your life that really she does not know you at all. Perhaps—*probably*—she does not know your dreams."

She felt horribly embarrassed when he did not immediately reply. How *dared* she interfere in his life this way? Even when guiding and advising the girls at school about their various problems and about their futures, she was careful never to be as dogmatic as she had just been.

"I am sorry," she said, "I have no right—"

"And will *you* do one last thing for *me?*" he asked her.

Reality smote her like a fist to the stomach. *One last thing.* This time tomorrow he would be long gone. He would be only a memory and not even the purely happy one she had persuaded herself earlier in the afternoon he would be. The last several minutes had destroyed that possibility. She looked at him in inquiry.

"Will you allow me to take you to meet Lady Markham and Edith?" he asked her.

"Now?" she said.

"Why not?" he asked her. "Lawrence Morley, Edith's husband, has taken lodgings on Laura Place, only a stone's throw away. I promised to call there before leaving Bath. And I promised Edith that I would ask you if she may call on you or if you will call on her."

She shook her head.

"Do consider," he said. "I do not know if it is my place to tell you this, but there really were letters, you know—to Lord Markham and to you."

There was a coldness about her head and in her nostrils.

"Letters?" Somehow no sound came out with the word.

"From your father." He took one step closer and possessed himself of both her hands, which he held very tightly. "I have no idea if they were kept, Susanna, or what their contents were. But ought you not at least to see Lady Markham?"

There had been letters—one of them for her.

Her father had written her a letter!

Disclosing *what*? What had the letter to Lord Markham disclosed?

But as quickly as shock had come, panic followed on its heels.

"It would be as well if they have been destroyed," she said, pulling her hands free again and going back to the seat to rescue her gloves. "There is no point in trying to go back after all these years to rake up an old unhappiness that drove a man to his death." She fumbled to pull on the gloves. "It can only cause more unhappiness for the living."

"Have you ever *not* been back there, Susanna?" he asked.

He did not explain his meaning. He did not have to. Of course she had never let go of the past. How could she? Those things had happened and her suffering had been dreadful. The past was a part of her. But she had moved beyond it. She lived a life that was secure and meaningful and happy when compared to the lives of many thousands of other people. Nothing could be served by going back. It was too late.

"William Osbourne wanted to be heard," he said. "He had something to say."

"Then he should have *said* it," she said, whirling about to face him, "to Lord Markham and to me. He said precious little to me in twelve years. He would not even talk about my mother, who was a yawning emptiness in my life. He might have spoken to me instead of killing himself. He might have loved me instead of seeking the comfort of death."

"You loved him," he said softly.

"*Of course* I loved him."

"Then forgive him," he said.

"Why?" She was swiping angrily at the tears that were spilling from her eyes, her back toward him.

"It is what love does," he said.

She laughed—a shaky, pathetic sound.

"All the time," he said. "*All* the time."

If he just knew. If he just *knew*.

"Very well." She spun around to face him. "Let us go, then. Take me to them. Let us ask about the letters—and their contents. But know in advance, Lord Whiteleaf, that it may be a Pandora's box that will be opened, that once it is open it will be impossible to close it again."

"But this does not concern *me*," he said. "I believe it is something you need to do for yourself. The letters may not even still exist, Susanna, and yours may never have been opened before it was destroyed. It is just that I think you ought to meet Lady Markham and Edith again. You need to give them a chance—the chance you believe your father denied you."

She stared at him and then nodded curtly.

"Let us go, then," she said.

"*If* we can find our way out of this maze," he said, his eyes suddenly softening into a smile.

"Now I really, *really* wish we could be lost here forever," she told him, smiling ruefully despite herself.

"Me too," he agreed. "We should have gone and built a cabin on the top of Mount Snowdon when we had a chance, Susanna."

He offered her his arm and she took it.

19

It seemed to Peter as they approached Laura Place, the diamond-shaped street at the bridge end of Great Pulteney Street, that this was the damnedest time to discover that he was not in love with Susanna Osbourne after all.

He *loved* her instead.

And there was a world of difference between the two types of love.

He loved her, yet much of the time she disliked him and even despised him.

If there *was* a God, then that deity must be a joker indeed. At the risk of appearing vain in his own eyes, he would have to say that almost every other young lady he had ever met—and he had met a large number just in the five years since reaching his majority—both liked and admired him and would even be prepared to love him if he set himself to wooing them.

He was going to leave Bath early tomorrow morning, and nothing was going to stop him this time. He could hardly wait to be on his way, in fact. If he had not committed himself to this afternoon call, he would start his journey now, this afternoon.

They had walked all the way from Sydney Gardens in silence.

"This is the house," he said at last after keeping his eyes on the numbers. And he stepped up to the door and rapped the knocker against it.

He would have taken Susanna's arm again, knowing how nervous she must be feeling, how reluctant she was to make this call, but he did not do so. His mother and his sisters had overprotected him, and it seemed that without realizing it he had learned to do the same with other people—especially the woman he loved. She did not want his support or protection. She did not need them either, dash it.

The ladies had just returned from shopping, the manservant who opened the door informed them. He would see if they were receiving visitors. He glanced at the card Peter handed him and raised his eyebrows before turning away.

Two minutes later, they were being ushered into a small drawing room abovestairs, and Edith was introducing a thin, fair-haired, bespectacled young man to Peter as Lawrence Morley, her husband. Then she turned to Susanna, two spots of color high in her cheeks.

"You *are* Susanna," she said. "Oh, of course you are. I could not mistake that hair or those eyes anywhere. You have grown up but really you have not changed at all. I was convinced it *was* you in the Abbey with Peter last evening." She stretched out both her hands. "Oh, just *look* at you. Lawrence, dearest, this is the Susanna Osbourne we were telling you about at breakfast."

Susanna hesitated before placing her hands in Edith's, but then Edith pulled her into a tight hug.

Lady Markham, meanwhile, was standing quietly farther back in the room. She had nodded to Peter, but now her eyes were fixed upon Susanna.

"All these years," she said when Edith stepped back, her eyes shining with unshed tears, "I have feared that you were dead, Susanna."

"No," Susanna said, "I did not die."

"Miss Osbourne, Lord Whitleaf," Mr. Morley said, "do come and have a seat closer to the fire. You must have walked here—I have not heard a carriage in the street."

"We have been strolling in Sydney Gardens," Peter explained as they all sat. "It is a beautiful day."

"For November, yes," Morley agreed, "though it is a little nippy even so, I daresay. You were dressed warmly, I trust, Miss Osbourne? You left your out-door garments downstairs?"

"I did, sir." She smiled. "My cloak and gloves are warm enough for even the coldest day."

"You were wise to wear them today, then," he said. "Edith sees sunshine and wants to step outside even before the servants have ascertained that it is warm enough and that no strong wind is blowing and no dark clouds are looming. I daresay the Abbey was drafty last evening, but she *would* insist upon going to the concert. I was relieved that my mama-in-law went with her to insist that she keep her cloak about her shoulders. Edith is recovering from a recent confinement, as you may know."

"No, I did not," Susanna said, looking at Edith. "How lovely for you."

"We have a son," Edith said with a smile. "He is quite adorable, is he not, dearest? He looks like his papa."

Polite chatter followed while a tea tray was carried in and Lady Markham poured and handed around the cups and saucers and offered them all a slice of fruitcake.

"Susanna," Edith said at last, "do you *live* in Bath? *Where* is your house?"

"I teach and live at Miss Martin's School for Girls on Daniel Street," Susanna said. "I teach writing and penmanship and games among other things."

"Games?" Morley said. "I hope nothing too strenuous, Miss Osbourne. Vigorous exercise is unhealthy for young ladies, I have heard, and I readily believe it. I daresay they would be better employed with a needle or a paintbrush. Vigorous games are excluded from most academies for young ladies, and rightly so."

"You *teach*," Lady Markham said before Susanna could reply—and while Peter was still entertaining amused memories of her rowing and flushed and laughing in the boat races at Barclay Court. "However did that come about, Susanna?"

"I went to London," she explained, "and registered at an employment agency. But I was fortunate enough to be singled out and sent as a charity pupil to Miss Martin's school here. I was a pupil until I was eighteen, and then I was offered a position as junior teacher."

"You went to London," Lady Markham said. "But how did you get there, Susanna? You were a *child*. And we checked all the stagecoach stops for miles in every direction."

"I went into my father's room," Susanna said. "There was some money there in a box on his dressing table, and I took it, as I supposed it was mine. There was a valise too, big enough to hold most of my things but small enough for me to carry. I walked and begged rides for most of the way. There was not enough money to be squandered on transportation."

"It is to be hoped, Miss Osbourne," Morley said, "that you did not sit on hay, as so many travelers do when they do not ride in carriages or on the stagecoach. Hay is often damp even when it feels dry."

"I do not believe I ever did sit on hay, sir," she said.

"Oh, Susanna," Lady Markham said, setting her cup and saucer down on her empty plate, "*why* did you leave as you did, without a word to anyone? Of course, you were dreadfully upset, poor child, but I fully expected that you would turn to us for comfort. We were almost like a family to you—or so I thought."

Peter noticed that Susanna had taken only one bite out of her piece of cake. He noticed too that her cheeks were paler than usual despite all the fresh air she had been out in for the last couple of hours.

"As you just observed, ma'am," she said, "I *was* very upset and I *was* just a child. Who knows why I fled as I did? No one would let me see my father and so I could not quite believe that he really was dead. And then I heard that he was not going to be allowed burial inside the churchyard and I knew that he *was* dead. I—"

"The church must be firm on such matters of principle," Morley said, "regrettable as—"

"Dearest," Edith said, interrupting, "I am very much afraid that Jamie might have awoken and will be wanting one of us even though Nurse is with him."

He jumped to his feet. "I shall go to him immediately," he said, "if you will excuse me, Miss Osbourne, Lord Whitleaf, Mama-in-law. But I am sure you all *will* excuse the natural anxieties of a new father."

"Thank you, Lawrence," Edith said. "You are very good."

Had the circumstances been different, Peter would doubtless have been vastly diverted by the fussy but seemingly good-hearted Morley and by the relationship between him and Edith, who looked as if she might be genuinely fond of him. But Peter was feeling Susanna's distress—and that of his lifelong neighbors too.

"Markham would not let you—or even me—see your papa," Lady Markham said after Morley had closed the door behind him, "because . . . well . . ."

"I understand," Susanna said. "He shot himself in the head. But he was all I had in the world, and I was not allowed to go near him. And then there was to be the indignity of his funeral. I suppose I wanted to put as much distance between all of it and myself as I possibly could."

"You did not even say good-bye to *me*," Edith said. "First there was all the dreadful upset in the house and I was not allowed to leave my room even to go as far as the nursery. And then, when I sent Nurse to fetch you, she could not find you. And then *nobody* could find you. Oh, I *am* sorry." She leaned back in her chair. "Your suffering was obviously many, many times worse than mine. And you were only twelve. You appeared very grown-up to my eleven-year-old eyes, but you were incapable of making any mature decisions. I just wish—ah, never mind. I am *so* happy to see you again and to know that life has worked out well for you. You are actually a *teacher* in a girls' school. I am quite sure you must be a *good* teacher."

Incredibly, the conversation turned to that subject as they debated the advantages and disadvantages of sending girls to school rather than having them educated at home.

They were not going to probe any more deeply into Susanna's reasons for running away, Peter thought, and she was not going to elaborate. And they were not going to mention the letters William Osbourne had left behind—and she was not going to ask.

It seemed strange to him that she did not want to know more about them, that she was not frantic to discover what her father had had to say in the last hour or so of his life, when he had known he was about to end it. In Sydney Gardens, after the first moment when she had looked as if she were about to faint, she had spoken of Pandora's box and appeared quite reluctant to pursue the matter.

In some ways perhaps it was understandable. All these years she had believed that her father died without leaving any clue to his motive or feelings, without saying good-bye to her or making provision for her. Now she knew that he had left something behind. But there was certainly something to be said for the old proverb about letting sleeping dogs lie, especially when eleven years had passed.

The moment for any meaningful truth to be spoken seemed almost to have passed now too. They had all settled, it seemed, into the polite and amiable conversation typical of any afternoon call.

He supposed he ought not to interfere further. He had half bullied Susanna into coming here. He had kept his promise to Edith. All three ladies would perhaps now be satisfied, Lady Markham and Edith in knowing that she was alive and well and happily settled, Susanna in knowing that they had not hated her or abandoned her without an effort to find her. If her running away and Lady Markham's overheard words had not been quite satisfactorily explained, well, perhaps they were all content never to dig deeper.

He ought not to interfere. None of this was any of his business.

He interfered nevertheless.

"I was telling Miss Osbourne a short while ago, ma'am," he said into a momentary lull in the conversation, "about the letters discovered inside a ledger in Mr. Osbourne's desk after his death."

Three pairs of eyes turned upon him in something that looked like reproach. Then Susanna closed hers briefly.

"Yes," Lady Markham said. "There were two, one addressed to Markham and one to Susanna."

"What did he say?" Susanna asked, her voice terribly strained. "Did he explain why he did it?"

"I believe he did," Lady Markham said while Edith set down her plate. "It was addressed to Lord Markham, you must understand, Susanna, not to me. I—*we*—will always remember your father with respect and even affection. He was a good and efficient secretary."

"But you did see the letter?" Susanna asked.

"Yes," Lady Markham admitted, "I believe I did."

"What did it say?" Susanna asked. "Please tell me."

Something struck Peter suddenly and he got to his feet.

"Perhaps," he said, "you would all prefer it if I were not here since this has nothing whatsoever to do with me, has it? Shall I leave the room? May I wait for Miss Osbourne—"

But Lady Markham had raised one staying hand and he sat again.

"No," she said, her voice sounding weary. "There is no need to go. There was something in your father's past, Susanna, something that had remained hidden for years but had finally come to light. Things were becoming ugly for him. He thought shame would be brought down upon you and himself and upon Markham for having employed him and housed him. He thought, I suppose, that he would be dismissed in disgrace and would have no further means of support for himself and a young daughter. He could see no other way out but to do what he did. That is all I remember. It was very tragic, but nothing can be done now to change the unfortunate outcome."

It all seemed a little thin and evasive to Peter. *I believe I did. That is all I remember.* Would not every word of a suicide note be seared on the brain of anyone who had read it—especially when the man had lived and worked and shot himself in one's own home?

"And *my* letter?" Susanna asked softly.

"To my knowledge it was not opened," Lady Markham said.

"Was it destroyed?" Susanna asked.

"I do not know." Lady Markham blinked rapidly. "I cannot imagine Markham burning it, but I do not know."

"Perhaps Theo knows, Mama," Edith suggested. "Oh, surely it is still in existence."

"It is probably as well if it is not," Susanna said. She got to her feet, and Peter rose too. "If my father did anything so very wrong before I was born, it seems to me that he atoned for it with a life of hard work and loyal service to Sir Charles. I do not want to know what it was he did. I do not want to know who . . . Oh, it does not matter. I would rather leave him in peace. I do thank you both for receiving me and for the tea, but I must go now. I have been away from the school for a whole afternoon and must not neglect my duties any longer."

"Susanna," Edith said, jumping up too, "do call on us again. Perhaps we can go walking together or shopping. Perhaps—"

"No," Susanna said. "My teaching duties occupy

me almost all day every day, Edith, and there is the Christmas concert coming up to keep me even busier. I had last evening off and this afternoon. I have used up my quota of free time for quite a while. I . . . You have your husband and son now to occupy your life. We move in different worlds. It would be best to leave it that way."

Edith folded her hands at her waist. She looked hurt.

"I shall write to you," she said. "I daresay you will be able to find a few spare minutes in which to read a letter."

"Thank you." Susanna gave her a tight smile.

"This *has* been a pleasure," Lady Markham said. "You will never know, Susanna, how many times over the years I have lain awake wondering what happened to you, wondering if you were alive or dead and if we could have done anything more at the time to find you. I am delighted that you came. You will see her safely back to Miss Martin's school, Whitleaf?"

"I will, ma'am," he said, bowing.

But it seemed to him as they stepped out onto the street a few minutes later that the visit had not settled a great deal. Perhaps it did not have to, though. Susanna seemed not to want to find out exactly what had happened eleven years ago and why. Perhaps the comfort of knowing that her father *had* written to her was enough. It would not be enough for *him*, but that was not the point, was it?

And at least the visit had given pleasure to Lady Markham and Edith and had perhaps persuaded

Susanna that she had not been the unwanted burden she had thought she was.

"Are you glad you came?" he asked, drawing her arm through his.

She turned her head to look at him briefly.

"Yes," she said. "I would have been afraid to set foot beyond the school doors for fear of running into them. Now I have come face-to-face with them and discovered that they are just people and just as I remember them. Edith is pretty, is she not? I hope she will be happy with Mr. Morley."

"Even though you never could be?" He chuckled.

"But I was not asked to be, was I?" She laughed too.

It was good to hear her laugh again.

And so the end had come. She might have been celebrating her betrothal now. Instead she was about to say good-bye.

By her own choice.

Susanna knew as they walked along Great Pulteney Street in silence and turned onto Sydney Place that memories of her visit to Lady Markham and Edith would return to haunt her for some time to come, along with her decision not to press on with inquiries into the contents of her father's letter to Sir Charles Markham or into the possible continued existence of the letter he had written her.

But she could not think of any of that now.

Her heart was heavy. She felt that with every step she took she trod on it, increasing her pain.

Yet at the beginning of the afternoon she had been

so hopeful that it could all end cheerfully and amicably. The fact that she loved him was of little significance. Given the circumstances of her life, it would have been strange indeed if she had *not* fallen in love with him. She would recover. How could she not? A happy marriage between them would be impossible for all sorts of reasons, and she would rather lose him altogether and forever than have an *unhappy* marriage with him.

But, oh, at the moment it was very hard to think such sensible thoughts. In an hour's time she would think them, perhaps. Tonight she would think them, and next week, and next month. But now . . .

"I shall be making an early start for London in the morning," he said as they turned onto Sutton Street and the school came into sight.

"Yes," she said. "There cannot be much to keep a visitor in Bath, especially at this time of year."

"I have spent a pleasant few days here, though," he said.

"I am glad."

They spoke to each other like cheerful, polite strangers.

"It has been good to see you again," he said.

"Yes."

"Perhaps," he said, "we will meet again sometime."

"Yes, that would be pleasant."

Their footsteps slowed and then stopped altogether before they turned onto Daniel Street.

"Susanna," he said, his hand covering hers on his arm, though he did not turn his head to look down at her. "I want you to know before I leave that I *do* care for you. I know you do not like me half the time or approve of me the other half, but I do care. I think we were friends once. I think in many ways we still are. But when we became more than friends on that one afternoon, it really *was* more. I was not just a lustful man taking advantage of being alone with an innocent woman. I *cared* for you. I know you do not want me or need me. I know you are happy with the life you have. But I think perhaps in some way you have cared too, and I wanted you to know that . . . Well. Was there ever a more muddled monologue, and just at the time when I most wanted to be eloquent and say something memorable?"

"Oh, Peter," she said, clinging to his arm, "I *do* like you. Of course I do. And of course I approve of most of what I see in you. How could I not? You are always so very kind. And I care for you too."

"But not enough to marry me?" he asked her, still not looking at her.

"No." It was easier just to say no than try to explain—it was impossible, anyway, to explain all her reasons. "I do thank you, but no, we would not suit."

"No," he said softly, "I suppose not. I will leave you here, then."

"Yes." Panic grabbed at her stomach, her knees, her throat. She slid her hand from his arm.

He turned then and took both her hands in his, squeezing them so tightly for a moment that she almost winced. He lifted them one at a time and set her gloved palms to his lips.

He raised his eyes to hers—and smiled.

"An already glorious November day has seemed warmer and brighter because of your presence in it," he said, misquoting his very first words to her. "Thank you, Susanna."

And so he drew a smile from her even though her heart was breaking.

"Foolish," she said. "Ah, foolish."

And somehow they both laughed.

"Good-bye, Peter," she said.

And because she could not bear any more, she dashed with ungainly haste around the corner and up to the door of the school, and she lifted the knocker and let it fall with more force than was necessary.

She glanced toward the corner as Mr. Keeble opened the door, but there was no one there. She stepped inside, and the door closed behind her.

And now it seemed to her that there was nothing left to live for. Nothing at all. She was in too much distress to notice the melodrama of the thought.

I want you to know before I leave that I do care for you.

Mary Fisher, one of the middle school boarders, was on her way up the stairs. She turned back when she saw who had come through the door.

"Oh, Miss Osbourne," she cried, all excitement, "we and Mr. Upton have made the changes you wanted to the sketches for the scenery and finished them. They are ever so gorgeous. Do come and see."

"Of course. I can hardly wait. Lead the way, then, Mary," Susanna said, smiling brightly as she pulled loose the ribbons of her bonnet. "Have you been working all afternoon? How splendid of you."

I want you to know before I leave that I do care for you.

. . . before I leave . . .

And now he was gone.

20

Peter went straight from Bath to Sidley Park—to stay.

Will you do one thing for me? And this was it. She might never know he had done as she asked, and how his coming here could benefit her anyway he did not know. But here he was. He loved her, and so he had honored her final request.

He hoped that love would go away again as suddenly as it had come. He did not like the feeling at all. It was a dashed miserable thing, if the truth were known.

His mother was ecstatic to see him. She scarcely stopped talking about Christmas, which would be absolutely perfect now that he was home to enjoy all that she had planned for him. Four of his sisters— Barbara, Doris, Amy, and Belinda—were to come to Sidley Park for Christmas, all except Josephine, in fact, the middle one in age, who lived in Scotland with her husband and his family. And of course the presence of four sisters was going to mean too the presence of their spouses and children—nine of the latter among the four of them. And because it was Christmas, numbers of their in-laws of all ages had been invited too. None of his uncles—he *had* made himself clear to them five years ago, though in the intervening years since he had seen them occasionally in London and learned to be cordial with them.

And of course the Flynn-Posys were coming for Christmas.

Well, he would endure it. He would even enjoy it. He would establish himself as host.

His mother took him into the dining room the day after his arrival and explained to him all that she planned to have done in there for his comfort and delight.

"I'll think about it, Mama," he said. "I may have some ideas of my own."

"But of course, my love," she said, beaming happily at him. "Whatever you want provided it will not ruin the overall effect of what I have planned. How *lovely* it is to have you home again."

He left it at that. It had never been easy to talk to his mother—it had always seemed something akin to dashing one's brains against a rock.

Will you talk to your mother, Peter? Really talk? . . . Tell her who you are. Perhaps she has been so intent upon loving you all your life that really she does not know you at all. Perhaps—probably—she does not know your dreams.

He had never really talked to his mother, or she to him. He had confronted her once, of course—ghastly memory—but they had both been horribly upset at the time, and they had not used the opportunity to open their hearts to each other, to establish a new and equal relationship of adult mother and adult son.

That would change. He would talk to her. He *would* hold firm against her iron will. It just seemed somewhat absurd that the provocation was probably going to be a lavender dining room.

He spent a good deal of the time before Christmas away from the house. He liked to go and sit in the dower house, sometimes for hours on end, lighting a fire in the sitting room and enjoying the peace he found there. He had always loved the house, and it had always been well kept even though it had been inhabited during his lifetime only by the girls' governesses and the tutors he had had before going away to school and sometimes during school holidays. It was a small manor in its own right and was set in the middle of a pretty garden in a secluded corner of the park.

It would, in fact, be the ideal home for his mother . . .

He visited his neighbors again. And he called on Theo.

"I must thank you, by the way," Theo said as they sat in his library sipping brandy, "for taking Susanna Osbourne to call on my mother and Edith in Bath. They both wrote to tell me all about it the very next day. I suppose because I was away at school at the time of Osbourne's death and Susanna's disappearance, I did not realize quite how upsetting it all was for them. My mother has been thinking all these years that she must be dead."

"Are the letters still in existence?" Peter asked.

"Yes, indeed," Theo said, stretching out his booted feet to the blaze in the hearth. "They were at the back of the safe in Osbourne's old office where I never look—it is stuffed with old papers that I must go through one of these days. I had never even read the letter Osbourne wrote my father until I found both letters after my mother wrote. Susanna's is still sealed. I suppose I ought to send it on to her even though my mother seems to think she is not interested in seeing it. Queer, that."

"I think it is more that she is afraid to read it," Peter said.

"Eh?" Theo said, giving a log a shove farther onto the fire with the toe of one boot. "What would she be afraid of? Ghosts? I suppose it might put the wind up someone, though, to see a letter written more than a decade ago in the hand of a dead man."

"I think she is afraid of what she will find there," Peter said. "Sometimes it seems better not to know what one thought forever lost in the past. But I do wonder if the not knowing will fester in her now that she knows about the letter. Does she know it still exists?"

"Not unless my mother has told her," Theo said. "Sometimes I wish I had a secretary of my own. Writing letters is not my favorite occupation. I suppose I must write one, though. I can hardly just bundle up her father's and send it off to her without comment, can I?"

"Is there likely to be something in your father's letter that would not be in hers?" Peter asked. "Remember that hers was written to a twelve-year-old."

Theo raised his eyebrows and considered the question as he gazed into the fire and took two more sips from his glass. Then he looked at Peter.

"I say, Whitleaf," he said, "what the devil is your interest in all this?"

"Just that," Peter said. "Interest."

"You told me you had met Susanna during the summer," Theo said. "And then you were with her in Bath of all places, at a concert in Bath Abbey, and then in Sydney Gardens, and then at Edith's. She isn't your mistress by any chance, is she? Morley won't like it if you took your mistress to call on him and Edith."

But he chose to find the mental picture amusing, and first chuckled and then threw back his head and laughed outright.

"He would probably have a fit of the vapors," he said. "Lord knows what Edith sees in him, but it *was* a love match."

"Susanna is not my mistress," Peter said, without joining in the laughter. "And I would thank you, Theo, for not making that suggestion ever again. I offered her marriage, and she refused me."

"Eh?" Theo frowned. "Why the devil? She is a *schoolteacher,* isn't she? And last time I looked you were a viscount. It would be a brilliant match for her, wouldn't it? And that's a colossal understatement."

Peter did not answer the question.

"I think she needs to know the full truth," he said. "Everything you know and everything your mother knows and everything both letters can tell her. It may be upsetting for her, but I don't think she will be able to put the past fully behind her until she knows all there is to know. He was all she had, Theo, and he deliberately put a bullet through his brain."

"Well, yes," Theo said. "Poor devil. I say, I wonder if she would like to come here for Christmas. I'll wager Edith would be ecstatic, and I think my mother would be pleased too—she is coming home the day after tomorrow, by the way. I'll see what she says. Come to think of it, though, I have a hankering to see Susanna again myself. I used to be rather fond of her. I can remember teaching her to row a boat one summer. She was damned good at it too for all she was just a little bit of a thing with sticks for arms and a shock of red hair. Does she still have the hair?"

"It is auburn," Peter said.

He had *not* been trying to lead Theo in the direction of inviting her to Fincham. He had been thinking more of Theo's going down to Bath, taking Lady Markham with him and both letters so that the two of them could spend some time with her and help her deal with the past.

"You *will* invite her?" he asked.

Theo looked at him and chuckled before getting to his feet to fetch the brandy decanter.

"I will indeed," he said, "and you can decide whether to give Fincham a wide berth over Christmas or haunt it every day. How firmly did she mean no when she said it? And how disappointed were you? They are rhetorical questions, Whitleaf—another fellow's love life is not my concern. But I'll fetch Susanna here if she will come. She may not, of course. It sounds to me as if she is a lady with a mind of her own—

something that showed up when she was twelve years old, I suppose. More brandy?"

He held the decanter suspended over Peter's glass.

"It's dashed good," Peter said, holding his glass up. "Smuggled, I suppose?"

"Is there any other kind?" Theo asked.

She would say no, Peter thought. Of course she would say no.

There was not even any point in wondering how he would behave if she did come. *Would* he stay away from Fincham? Or would he haunt it every day?

But he would never know, would he? She would not come.

Eleanor Thompson did indeed join the staff of Miss Martin's school as geography and mathematics teacher. At first Claudia expected that she would come after Christmas, but she was very eager to start immediately and so moved into the school directly from her hotel and began her duties as soon as Claudia had adjusted the timetable and teaching loads.

She proved an instant favorite with the girls and her fellow teachers alike. She was a strict enough disciplinarian, but she also conducted her classes with humor and good sense. She was too late to do anything spectacular—her own word—for the Christmas concert, like directing a play or a choir or organizing maypole dancing. She would busy herself instead with the less glorious work behind the scenes, she announced the day after her arrival, and she worked during almost every spare moment after that, guiding a group of volunteer girls as they brought alive Mr. Upton's sketches for the various sets, and as often as not wielding a brush herself.

"And to think," she said with a weary sigh late one evening in Claudia's sitting room as she rubbed at a stubborn spot of paint on her right forefinger, "that until Christine married Bewcastle and turned all our lives on their collective head I considered that the perfect life was sitting quietly at home in our cottage with an open book in my hand."

"And do you still think the same thing?" Susanna asked with a twinkle in her eye.

Eleanor laughed. "Just occasionally," she admitted. "Like this morning, for example, when Agnes Ryde uttered a Cockney curse when she could not solve a problem in mathematics and I had to resist the temptation to pretend I did not understand. It does help, I suppose, that Agnes is a favorite of mine, even though I am sure you would tell me, Claudia, that teachers ought not to have favorites. Agnes has *character*."

"Altogether too much of it at times, I am afraid," Claudia said ruefully. "But one cannot help liking the girl."

"She actually told me yesterday," Lila said, "that learning to speak correctly by pretending to be a duchess as I had suggested is *fun*. She even smiled when she said it. And she cocked one haughty eyebrow and presented her hand to me as if she expected me to kiss it."

They all laughed, and Susanna got to her feet to pour them each a second cup of tea.

"Did your letter this morning upset you, Susanna?" Claudia asked after they had all settled again.

At first Susanna had thought it must be from Frances or Anne, but then she had seen that it was addressed in an unfamiliar hand.

"It came from Lady Markham at Fincham Manor," she said. "That is in Hertfordshire, where I grew up," she added for the benefit of Lila and Eleanor.

"And?" Claudia said, her cup suspended halfway to her mouth.

"I have been invited to spend Christmas there," Susanna said. "Edith and Mr. Morley and their son will be going too. My invitation comes directly from Sir Theodore Markham himself. It is exceedingly kind of him and of Lady Markham, who told him, I suppose, of our meeting in Bath a few weeks ago, but I will say no, of course. I would have written back today if I had not been so busy with drama and a set of essays to mark after classes were over."

"Susanna," Lila said, her voice incredulous, "you have a chance to spend the holiday with a baronet and his family at a country home, and you are going to say *no?*"

"But of course," Susanna said, still smiling. "I had a two-week holiday at the end of August. It would be too, too greedy to ask for another now."

"And yet Lila and I will be here over the holiday, as well as Claudia, to look after the girls who will remain," Eleanor said.

"But I have no wish to go," Susanna protested. "I would far rather stay here with all of you."

They talked for a few minutes longer until Eleanor got to her feet and declared cheerfully that she needed her sleep if she was to survive another day as a school-teacher. Lila left with her. Susanna would have followed them after stacking the dishes neatly on the tray if Claudia had not spoken to her.

"Something in that letter upset you more than a simple invitation to spend Christmas would have done," she said. "Do you wish to talk about it, Susanna? But *only* if you wish."

Susanna stared at her for a moment before sighing and sinking back into her chair.

"I cannot go back to Fincham Manor, Claudia," she said. "There are too many unhappy memories associated with it."

"And it is too close to Sidley Park," Claudia said. It was not a question.

"Yes." Susanna looked down at her hands.

They sat in silence for a few moments. Viscount Whitleaf's name had not been spoken between them since the afternoon when Susanna had said good-bye to him. The pain had been too intense to share with even the dearest of friends, and Claudia, as usual, had sensed and respected that fact.

"Is it perhaps *necessary* that you go back?" Claudia asked, breaking the silence. "Now that the past has been raked up again, whether you wished it to be or not, ought you perhaps to put it properly to rest this time?"

Susanna lifted her eyes to gaze into the dying embers of the fire.

"There were letters," she said. "I did not tell you

that after my visit to Laura Place, did I? My father wrote two before he died—one to Sir Charles Markham and one to me. They are both still in a safe at Fincham. Theodore asked Lady Markham to inform me that he will send me mine if I wish, but that he strongly recommends that I go to Fincham to see both letters and to speak with him."

"Oh, Susanna!" Claudia exclaimed. "What a shock it must have been for you—but what a delightful one—to discover that your father wrote to you after all before taking his life. And how exciting to find out today that the letter still exists! Do you not ache to read it? I will send you there tomorrow if you wish so that you will not have to wait one day longer than necessary."

"I do not want to see it," Susanna said.

Claudia stared at her and raised her eyebrows.

"I *know* why he killed himself," Susanna said, "and I cannot bear to read what he thought suitable for a twelve-year-old's eyes. He loved Viscountess Whitleaf, Claudia, but she was cruel to him and broke his heart. Lady Markham told me a few weeks ago that there was something shameful in his past that was about to expose him to disgrace and dismissal and poverty, but I do not believe it. I *know* the truth. Viscountess Whitleaf killed my father as surely as if she had pulled the trigger herself. Or it could be said that his own weakness in being unable to live on with a broken heart was what killed him."

There. She had never said it aloud before. She had tried not even to think it—that one person could wield such emotional power over another, and that the other could not find the strength of character or will to fight back. She had *seen* them together. She had *heard* them. She *knew*. She had always known.

Her father had left her, abandoned her forever, because he had not been able to live without the love of a cruel woman who did not care the snap of two fingers for him—and those had been the viscountess's own words.

It was no wonder Susanna had cringed from the name *Whitleaf* on that country lane near Barclay Court during the summer.

"Oh, Susanna," Claudia said, "Viscountess *Whitleaf* of all people? You poor dear."

"You can see now why I want nothing to do with any of it," Susanna said. "Or with *him*."

Claudia sighed. "Why do we persist in believing that we can control our lives provided we work hard and live decently and mind our own business?" she said. "You really do not deserve any of this now. You did not deserve any of it when you were twelve either. But here you are stuck with it."

"No, I am not," Susanna said. "It is all history. The present is what matters. And I have my life and my friends here in the present and am quite happy, Claudia. I *am*."

"Except," Claudia said, "that the sunshine has gone out of you, Susanna."

They stared at each other.

"Perhaps no one else has even noticed," Claudia continued. "You are as energetic and as cheerful and as busy as ever. You smile and laugh as much as you ever did. But I have known you a long time, and I love you as if you were my younger sister—and *I* know that the sun has stopped shining in your life."

Susanna closed her eyes briefly and then opened them again.

"All I need is time," she said. "I *will* prove that a broken heart can mend, Claudia, and that life is always worth living. I need a little more time, that is all."

It was pointless, she supposed, to deny to Claudia—or herself—that her heart *was* broken. Sometimes she found herself wondering if she would find the strength to refuse that marriage offer if it were made now. It was a good thing there was no danger of any such thing happening. All other considerations aside—and there were many of them—she could never marry the son of Viscountess Whitleaf.

"I am about to offer some unwanted advice," Claudia said, "something schoolteachers excel at, alas. Accept your invitation. Go to Fincham Manor for Christmas. Hear what Sir Theodore Markham has to say. Read your letter—and the other one too if he renews his offer to show it to you. Know the truth in your father's own words—know it from Sir Theodore's point of view. You already believe you know the worst, and so nothing can come as a terrible shock to you. See the place you fled eleven years ago and lay some ghosts to rest. As for Viscount Whitleaf and his mother—see them too if you will and if the opportunity presents itself, or avoid seeing them if you so choose. But deal with it all, Susanna. Deal with it and move on so that the sun can shine in you again."

"I feel," Susanna said, "as if a wound had been ripped open during the summer and then other wounds inflicted on top of it. A few times since then it has seemed that they have filmed over only to be torn open again. They have been healing now, Claudia. They really have. I do not want . . . I cannot bear . . ."

"But your letter this morning exposed the wound again," Claudia pointed out. "For how long will it fester, Susanna, now that you know your father spoke to you before he died—but you refuse to listen? And when will the hurt be renewed yet again if you ignore it now?"

"I could have Theodore send the letter here," Susanna said.

"You could, yes," Claudia agreed. It seemed that she would say more, but she closed her mouth.

"It is late," Susanna said, glancing at the clock on the mantel, "and I am *so* weary. You must be too."

"I am indeed," Claudia said, getting to her feet. "And now I suspect I have doomed you to a sleepless night, Susanna. But I believe you would have had one anyway after receiving that letter. It is strange, is it not, how one event can be the innocent cause of another quite unrelated to it? We were both elated when Anne arrived back from Wales in August just in time for you to go to Barclay Court with Frances and the earl. If she had been even one day later, none of all this would have happened. But then, perhaps it would have found a way to happen anyway. Perhaps it is impossible to avoid our own fate. I *must* be tired. I am talking nonsense."

Susanna left the room after saying good night, and climbed the stairs to her own room. She was in bed a few minutes later, huddled beneath the bedcovers against the chill of the night. But sleep did indeed evade her for a long time.

If *only* Anne had not come home until a day later. If *only* the Duchess of Bewcastle and Viscountess Ravensberg had not planned a wedding breakfast for Anne and Mr. Butler here in Bath. If *only* she had not gone to Bath Abbey for that evening concert and so seen Lady Markham and Edith again. If *only* she had never known that her father had written her a letter.

And if only Claudia had agreed with her decision to write back to Theodore tomorrow refusing his invitation and even declining his offer to send her father's letter.

Why did she not want to read that letter? The question woke her up fully again just when she was starting to feel drowsy.

Did she want to turn her back on her father as he had turned his on her? Was it a type of revenge for the suffering he had caused her? Did she want to hurt him even though he was not alive to feel the pain?

Papa, she thought, turning her face into her pillow.

She had not even thought of him by that name for years and years.

And finally, just before she fell asleep at last, she realized that in truth she had no choice. Having Theodore send the letter here might satisfy an empty craving within her, though she doubted even that. But there were other things to know, places to see, people to talk with.

She had to go back.

She had to hear it all, see it all, read it all.

Perhaps it could all be done without her ever having to set eyes upon Viscount Whitleaf. She had seen him only once during her childhood, after all.

And if she *did* by some chance see him again, well then . . .

But her mind could not cope with that possibility.

One thing at a time.

Tonight it was enough to know that she was going to go back.

Enough to fill her with dread.

And yet, the decision made, she slept.

21

Susanna arrived at Fincham Manor very late in the afternoon three days before Christmas, having traveled post. She had left Bath early on the morning following the Christmas concert and all the other busy activities that came with the end of term. She was tired even before she started the journey. She was exhausted by the time it ended.

The fact that she had dreaded coming did not help, of course.

She had wondered how it would feel to step into the house again after all these years. When she had left it eleven years ago, her father had just killed himself and she had just heard Lady Markham describe her as a burden. She had been running away.

But though it all looked startlingly familiar, it also seemed like a place she must have visited during another lifetime. She felt no great emotional connection with it.

This time, of course, she was staying in a guest chamber in the main part of the house rather than in the pretty little attic room next to her father's. She was a guest of the family.

Edith and Mr. Morley had already arrived for Christmas, and a few other guests were expected. The whole family gave Susanna a warm welcome—Theodore even shook her hand warmly after she had curtsied to him, and then held it in both his own while he assured her that she had grown into a rare beauty. He had grown into a great bear of a man himself, with wild, unruly dark hair and a genial face. She had worshipped him as a child and still instinctively liked him.

"You will want to freshen up and change for dinner, Susanna," he said. "I *may* still call you Susanna?"

"Only if I may still call you Theodore," she said.

He laughed heartily.

By the time dinner was at an end and she had drunk a cup of tea in the drawing room with Lady Markham and Edith while the two gentlemen drank their port in the dining room, Susanna was finding it hard to keep her eyes open.

"Susanna is very weary," Lady Markham said when the gentlemen arrived in the room. "I do think that any business you planned to discuss with her tonight, Theodore, must wait until the morning."

Her letter. It was in this very house—the words her father had written to her just before he died. She had come specifically to read it. And now that she was here she was almost sick with the longing to see it, to hold it, to read it. But not tonight. She needed to be wide awake and strong.

"I was going to suggest the very same thing, Mama,"

Theodore said. "Will that suit you, Susanna? Would you like to retire for the night now?"

"Yes, please," she said, getting to her feet. "Thank you, Theodore. And thank you for inviting me here."

"We will talk tomorrow, then," he said. "And later tomorrow our other guests should be arriving."

Lady Markham walked with Susanna up to her room.

"I am very happy you came," she said. "I have always felt that the story of eleven years ago was never properly ended. I have felt it even more since seeing you in Bath. Now perhaps we can all end the story, Susanna, and remain friends after you return to your school. Good night. Do have a good sleep."

And Susanna did—have a good sleep, that was. She remembered nothing between setting her head on her pillow and waking to the sounds of a maid lighting a fire in the small fireplace in her room. There was a cup of steaming chocolate on the table beside her bed.

What luxury!

But as she dressed a short while later, her teeth chattered, not so much from cold as from sick apprehension of what the morning held in store.

First, though, she had to sit through breakfast and smile and make light conversation and assure Edith— quite truthfully—that she would indeed like to go up to the nursery with her to see Jamie.

"But not yet, Ede," Theodore said, getting to his feet at the end of what had seemed an interminable meal. "Susanna and I have business first. I'll fetch your letter, Susanna, and you may read it wherever you wish—in your room or in the drawing room, which is always empty at this time of day. Or in the library if you prefer."

But suddenly she could not wait even long enough for him to bring it to her. She got to her feet too.

"I will come with you if I may," she said.

"Certainly," he said, and she followed him from the room.

But he hesitated outside a certain room, his hand on the knob, and Susanna instantly knew why. It was the study that had been her father's. It was where he had shot himself.

"I'll go in and get it," he said, smiling kindly at her. "It will just take a minute."

"Please," Susanna said, touching his arm, "may I come in too?"

He heaved an audible sigh and opened the door to allow her to precede him inside.

It was a disturbingly familiar room even though she had not come in here many times as a girl. Her father had used to leave the door ajar most days, however, and she had often stood outside, smelling leather and ink and listening to his deep, pleasant voice if there was someone in there with him. Often it had been Theodore, and she had listened to them talk about horses and racing or about fishing, Theodore's voice eager, her father's indulgent. She had always longed to push the door open and go in to join them. Perhaps her father would not have turned her away. Perhaps he would even have welcomed her and let her climb onto his knee. Perhaps—and this was a novel thought—he had felt as neglected by her as she had by him. Perhaps he had thought that as a girl she *preferred* to spend all her days with Edith.

She was standing at the desk, she realized, running her hand over the leather-edged blotter while Theodore watched her silently. She looked up at him and half smiled.

"It is strange revisiting a portion of one's life one had thought long gone," she said.

"It is cold in here," Theodore said after regarding her for a few moments. "I will find the letter and you can go somewhere warm to read it."

"Thank you," she said. She supposed it *was* cold in here since there was no fire in the hearth and she could hear the wind rattling the windows, beyond which the sky was a leaden gray. But even if she had not been wearing a winter dress and the soft wool shawl Claudia had given her as an early Christmas gift, she did not believe she would really have felt it this morning. "But I want to read the letter here. May I, please, Theodore?"

This was where the letter must have been written, she realized—on this very desk. Just before . . .

Theodore did not argue. He stooped down on his haunches to light the fire, and then he stepped up to the safe and opened it. He turned with a folded, sealed sheet of paper in his hand. Susanna could see that it was somewhat yellowed about the edges.

"I will leave you for a while, then," he said, "and then come back to answer any questions you may have—*if* I can answer them, that is. I was away at school at the time, and I was not told much. But I have read my father's letter, and I have spoken with my mother."

"Thank you," she said, but as he handed her the letter, she realized that in fact there were two. Her hand closed about them, and she shut her eyes until she heard the quiet click of the door as he left.

She seated herself carefully behind the desk and looked down at the papers in her hand.

Her own letter was on top. The words *Miss Susanna Osbourne* were written in the firm, sloping, elegant hand that she recognized instantly as her father's. His hand had not even shaken at the end, she thought as she set the other letter down on the desk, but her own was shaking as she held it. She slid her thumb beneath the seal and broke it before opening out the sheet.

"My dearest Susanna," she read, "you will feel that I have abandoned you, that I did not love you enough to live for you. When you are older, perhaps you will understand that this is not true. My life, if I were to live on, would suddenly change quite drastically, and therefore so would yours. Perhaps I would face that change if I were alone as I faced another when I was much younger. Who knows? But I cannot subject you to it. I have been accused of two dreadful crimes, one of which I committed, one of which I did not. But my innocence in the second case does not matter. It will not be believed in light of the first.

"I am ruined, as perhaps I deserve to be. Your mother has already paid the ultimate price. It is time I did too. And I do it—or so I tell myself, trying to give my life some touch of nobility at the end—so that you may live. You have family, Susanna—mine and your mother's. And either one will be happy enough to take you in once I am gone. They would have taken you at your birth, but I was too selfish to give you up. You were all I had left. I have given instructions to Sir Charles, and you will be united with your family. They will be good to you—they are good people. They will love you. You will have a secure, happy girlhood with them and a bright future. I promise you this though life will probably seem very bleak to you now as you read. I will take my leave of you, then, my dearest child. Believe that I do love you and always have. Papa."

Susanna rubbed the side of her thumb over that final word. *Papa.* Had she really called him that? But of course she had. It was only afterward that she had changed his name to *my father.*

I do it so that you may live.

Must she bear that burden too?

Perhaps I would face that change if I were alone.

There was no mention of Viscountess Whitleaf or of choosing death rather than life without the woman he loved. But would a father admit such a thing to his twelve-year-old child anyway?

He *had* loved the viscountess. She had seen them together one afternoon just before his death. She had been hiding under a hedgerow close to the road that led from Fincham to the village, about to come out because it had become obvious to her that Edith must have tired of the game when she could not find Susanna and had gone home to wait for her to put in an appearance. But then along had come Susanna's father, walking beside

Lady Whitleaf's horse until they both stopped a mere stone's throw away. Susanna had stayed where she was, too embarrassed to be seen crawling out of a hedgerow. She had even been able to see them, though she had hoped they would not see her.

"Do you think I *care*?" Lady Whitleaf had said, her voice filled with scorn as she tossed her head so that the pink feathered plume in her riding hat nodded against her ear. "I do not care the snap of my fingers for you and never have."

It had struck Susanna that she was very beautiful.

"I am sorry," her father had said, possessing himself of her hand and carrying it to his lips. "I truly am sorry."

"You will be very sorry indeed for having set your sights so high," she had said, snatching back her hand. "And for having molested me."

"*Molested?*" He had taken a step back. "I am sorry if you see my actions that way."

"I do." She had looked down on him as if he were a worm beneath her feet. "That I should have deigned to take even a moment's notice of a mere government secretary! I hope your heart *is* broken. It deserves to be. I hope it drives you to your death."

And she had driven her spurs into the horse's side and gone cantering off down the lane.

While Susanna had sat paralyzed in her hiding place, biting her knee through the cotton fabric of her dress, she had watched her father pass a hand wearily over his face before turning and trudging off back in the direction of the house.

Her mind returned to the present and the letter in

her hand. She could hear the fire crackling to life in the fireplace. She could even feel a thread of warmth from its direction.

She had *family*—or had had eleven years ago, on both her mother's and father's side. They would have taken her in—but not her father. What had he done to offend them so?

I have been accused of two dreadful crimes, one of which I committed . . .

Her mother had paid the ultimate price, and now it was his turn.

The ultimate price for what? What dreadful crime had called for the deaths of two people?

Her father had killed himself for her sake. Without her he might have struggled on. He had kept her after her birth even though he might have sent her to live with his family or her mother's. He had been too selfish to give her up.

Susanna lowered her forehead to the desk to rest on the open letter.

So many thoughts and emotions to churn around in one body and mind!

But only one thought came at her with any real clarity—or rather the memory of three words written on the paper beneath her.

. . . my dearest child.

Theodore was going to come back, she thought suddenly, and sat up again. Her father's letter had raised as many questions as it had answered. Perhaps there were some answers . . .

She reached her hand toward the other letter, whose seal, she could see, was already broken. But did she want to know the secrets of the man who had been her father? How could she *not* want to know, though, after reading her own letter? Was it really not as she had thought all these years? Was *one* of the impediments to her marrying Peter—though there were a thousand others—to be removed?

She drew Sir Charles's letter toward her and opened it. Her eyes went straight to the body of the letter, closely written and in just as steady a hand as her own letter.

"You listened kindly to me a few days ago," she read, "when I told you my sordid, long-held secrets before the Viscountess Whitleaf could do it for me. I have never had a high opinion of blackmailers or of those who allow themselves to become their victims. You were even gracious enough to refuse to accept my resignation—at least until we saw how much the lady talked and what the gravity of the resulting scandal would be.

"The situation has become far graver, however. Now that her original threat to come to you with my story has been thwarted, she plans to go to the world with another story of how I have molested and even ravished her. It would be a silly lie, perhaps, if not for two facts that will surely make her story generally believed. One is the truth of the other story she will now undoubtedly share with the world. The other is the mild gossip that arose around the lady and myself in London last year—and the truth of the fact that yes, for a while we *were* lovers. My mistake—one of too many to count in my life—was to try ending our liaison myself instead of waiting until such time as she chose to end it herself.

"It distresses me to have brought so much potential scandal to you and your family and this home. You will not be able to continue to champion me. I am ruined and may even be facing criminal prosecution. I see no way out but to do what will already be done by the time you read this. Perhaps my death will silence the lady and so prevent all scandal except what will be the inevitable result of my suicide.

"But I cannot wait until after I have left Fincham. There is Susanna, you see. She has long been all that is truly precious in my life. Lady Markham and Miss Markham have always been remarkably kind to her, for which I cannot possibly express the full extent of my gratitude. Be kind to her in one more thing, I beg you. Send her to my father with the enclosed letter. He is an honorable and good man. He will give her a home and kindness and even love.

"I thank you, Sir Charles, for allowing me the privilege of serving you . . ."

Susanna did not read the last few sentences. She set the letter down on top of the other one.

She *had* been right, then, though not in the way she had thought. Lady Whitleaf *had* driven him to his death. That little snippet of conversation she had overheard between them had meant something a little different from what she had thought, but the outcome had been the same.

Except that he had died not because he loved the viscountess, but at least partly because he had loved *her*.

She has long been all that is truly precious in my life.

. . . *my dearest child.*

She must have been dilly-dallying a great deal over the letters, she realized, when after a brief knock the door opened and Theodore came back into the room. He had been gone for a whole hour, she saw when she glanced at the clock on the mantel.

"I have brought you a cup of tea," he said, coming to set it down on the desk before going to poke the fire into renewed life.

"Theodore," she said, "what had my father done in his past that was so very bad?"

He straightened up and turned to look at her.

"Are you sure—" he began.

"Yes." She grasped the edges of her shawl with both hands and drew it closer about her shoulders, even though the room was no longer as chilly as it had been. "I need to know."

"My father had told my mother," he said. "Your mother was once married to your father's elder brother, Susanna, but she and your father . . . loved each other. It seems that his brother confronted him about it and there was a fight in which his brother died. The whole thing was explained away as a tragic accident—and I daresay there was truth in the claim—but your father was sent away. Your mother followed him, though, and they married. Marrying one's brother's widow is not expressly forbidden, but it is certainly frowned upon. And this was only a month or so after her bereavement. Both families renounced them."

He was talking of *her parents,* Susanna thought, her hands balling into fists on the desktop as she stared down at her whitened knuckles.

"And one year later she died," Theodore said.

"My father knew her. He told my mother that they were devoted to each other, Susanna. He also said that you looked like her."

Her mother had died having *her*. Susanna bit down hard on her upper lip. She had risked all, even scandal and ostracism, only to die in childbed.

And her father had died by his own hand twelve years later when his past finally caught up to him and a malicious woman was out to destroy him. Susanna could only imagine the enormity of the guilt with which he must have lived all the years she had known him. Yet he had always been quietly courteous, gentle, and affectionate.

She looked like her mother.

"My father confronted Lady Whitleaf after the funeral," Theodore said. "She denied that she had ever intended to act with such malicious intent as described in that letter by your hand. He had been presumptuous and familiar with her, she claimed, and she had been about to make a private complaint about him to my father—that was all. The matter was dropped, but there was a coolness between my parents and her ever after. My parents believed Osbourne's version."

Susanna spread her hands, palm up, and examined them closely.

"The third letter was sent on to your grandfather," Theodore said, "even though you could not be sent with it. I believe he implemented his own search for you, but you were lost beyond a trace until Whitleaf found you this past summer."

"I was not lost," she said quietly as she drank her tea, thankful for the hot liquid, "and he did not find me."

"In a manner of speaking," he said, smiling. "May I take you to my mother and Edith in the morning room?"

"Yes," she said with a sigh. "Theodore, perhaps I should leave tomorrow and return to Bath so that you may have a quiet family Christmas without feeling obliged to entertain me."

"That would break Edith's heart," he said, "and hurt my mother. And I would not be happy about it either. We have other guests coming later today, remember."

"All the more reason for me to leave," she said, frowning.

"Not so." He stood in front of the fire, lifted onto the balls of his feet, and then rocked back on his heels again. "I am expecting Colonel and Mrs. Osbourne and the Reverend Clapton from Gloucestershire—your two grandfathers and your paternal grandmother."

Susanna stared mutely at him.

"My mother suggested it," he said, "as soon as you wrote back to say you would come. I wrote to them the same day and they did not hesitate. They are coming to meet you."

She swallowed and heard a gurgle in her throat. She pushed her cup and saucer aside and curled her fingers into her palms to find them clammy.

"My grandparents?" she half whispered.

"Lord," he said, lifting onto the balls of his feet again, "I don't know if I have done the right thing, Susanna. But I know my father would have done all he could for you, and my mother always loved you almost as if you were her own. I thought it only right to do more or less what your father wanted mine to do—

except that I am bringing your grandparents to you rather than sending you to them."

She was not all alone in the world. She had three grandparents and perhaps other relatives. She had read it in both her father's letters, yet somehow the knowledge had not fully lodged itself in her brain until now.

She had relatives, and they were coming here to Fincham Manor.

Today.

Susanna lurched to her feet, pushing her chair away with the backs of her knees as she did so.

"I have to get out," she said.

"Out?" Theodore's rather bushy eyebrows drew together until they almost met over the bridge of his nose.

"Out of doors," she said, feeling as if she were about to suffocate.

"You don't mean home to Bath?" he said. "You are not going to leave, Susanna? Run away again?"

What *did* she mean? She scarcely knew. Her mind felt as if it were close to bursting with all it had been forced to take in during the past hour or so.

She drew a deep breath and released it slowly.

"I just need to walk outside for a while, Theodore," she said. "I need fresh air. Will you mind? Will it seem terribly rude? I do not mean to run away."

"I'll come with you," he said, still frowning. "Or perhaps Edith or my mother—"

But she held up a hand.

"No," she said. "I would rather be alone. I need to sort out my thoughts."

"Ah," he said. "Take all the time you need, then, Susanna. And then come back and get warm and enjoy Christmas with us. We will do all in our power to see that you do."

"Thank you."

She hurried upstairs to fetch her cloak and bonnet and gloves and don her warm half-boots, vastly relieved when she did not pass anyone on the way to her room. If only she could get back downstairs and outside . . .

But she was not so fortunate this time.

Theodore was standing in the hall as she came downstairs, probably waiting to see her on her way. A newly arrived visitor was talking with him there. For only a fraction of a second did Susanna think that perhaps this was one of the expected houseguests. But then, almost simultaneously, she realized that the visitor, broad-shouldered in his many-caped greatcoat, was a young man and that he was Viscount Whitleaf.

He looked up at the same moment and their eyes met.

She was flooded with such a powerful and unexpected longing that she only just found the strength not to dash down the remaining stairs and hurl herself into his arms.

"Miss Osbourne," he said.

"Lord Whitleaf."

She came slowly downward. She wondered if he had known she was coming to Fincham Manor.

"Susanna is going out for a walk," Theodore said. "I have offered to accompany her, but she needs to be alone. She has just been reading the letter her father wrote her on the last day of his life. Do go without further ado if you wish, Susanna. I'll take Whiteleaf in to see my mother. He has an invitation to extend."

"Later, Theo, if it is all the same to you," the viscount said without taking his eyes off Susanna. "I will go back outside with Miss Osbourne—if she will accept my company."

The thought of his mother—of what his mother had done—flashed through her mind, but he was not his mother. And suddenly she could not bear the thought of going out alone, of leaving him behind.

"Thank you," she said, and turned to leave the house without looking back.

22

"One could say without too much exaggeration," Peter had remarked just last evening to Bertie Lamb, his favorite brother-in-law, Amy's husband, *"that the house is packed to the rafters and bulging at the seams."*

The crowd was made up mostly of relatives and relatives of relatives—and of course the Flynn-Posys, who were *not* related to anyone else there but who obviously had hopes of rectifying that situation at some time in the foreseeable future. Arabella Flynn-Posy was seventeen years old and dark-haired and dark-eyed and remarkably pretty despite a mouth that had a tendency to turn sulky at the slightest provocation. His mother adored her—and *her* mother adored *him.* An imbecile with a pea for a brain would have understood their intentions.

"But your mother is ecstatic," Bertie had said. "So are your sisters. And I am partial to a crowd myself, I must admit. Jolly good show about the ball, old chap—it will brighten things up around here."

His mother was, of course, *not* ecstatic about that

one thing, Peter knew. But he had impulsively decided that he wanted to invite all his neighbors to a grand Christmas celebration at Sidley Park, and he had gone ahead and invited them all to a ball on the evening of Christmas Day without consulting anyone except his cook and his butler and his housekeeper, who would be directly involved in the preparations—and who were now dashing about in transports of delight at the prospect of a Sidley *ball*.

His mother had been the last to be told.

Well, no, not quite the last.

He still had not been to Fincham Manor when he told her. It really would be too bad if the Markhams were unable or unwilling to attend the ball since he would quite readily admit in the privacy of his own mind that the whole thing had been arranged for them. Well, not *them* precisely.

The ball was for Susanna.

Love did *not* die very quickly, he had discovered during the intervening weeks. It did not even *fade* quickly—or at all. And it was a deuced depressing thing if the truth were known. His only hope, he had tried to tell himself since learning that she was indeed to come to Fincham, was to stay away from her and trust they did not inadvertently run into each other over the holiday.

So what had he done to put that very sensible decision into effect? He had arranged his first-ever ball at Sidley for her, that was what. And now he had driven himself over to Fincham to extend the invitation—in person, of course, because he knew she must have arrived by now.

And now here he was a mere few minutes later, hurrying out of the house faster than he had hurried in out of the cold, his invitation having been mentioned to Theo but not—as was right and proper—delivered formally to Lady Markham and to Edith. But that could wait. So could warming his hands and his feet and the rest of his person.

Susanna needed him—or so he told himself.

She had changed in the course of a few weeks. Her face looked pinched and pale, her eyes dark-shadowed in contrast. And it seemed to him that the changes went beyond what the distress of the morning must have brought her.

He caught up to her on the terrace outside and took her firmly by the arm. She was looking about as if she did not quite know in which direction she wanted to walk.

"Come to the stables," he said. "With any luck my curricle will still not be unhitched. Let me take you for a drive."

"Yes," she said without looking at him. "Oh, yes, please."

This was not quite how he had visualized the morning, he thought as they walked in silence to the stable block and into the cobbled yard, where indeed his horses were still hitched to his curricle. But she had already read her letter—had *just* read it, apparently.

He helped her up to the high seat and took his place beside her. He took the ribbons from the groom's hands and gave the horses the signal to start. He could not help remembering the last time she had ridden beside him thus when they had gone to Miss

Honeydew's cottage together. He glanced down into her face, shaded by the brim of her bonnet, but she was staring ahead.

As soon as they were on the driveway he took his horses to a faster pace. He had the distinct feeling that she needed to leave Fincham behind, at least for a while.

She looked up at him, her cheeks already slightly rosy from the cold, and laughed quite unexpectedly.

He urged his horses to an even faster pace.

"Anyone for a race to Brighton and back?" he asked.

This time when she laughed there was a somewhat reckless gleam in her eyes, and he kept up the pace for several minutes, concentrating upon what he was doing. He had not exactly sprung his horses, but he had also never traveled at this speed with a lady passenger beside him.

"Oh, Peter," she cried, "this is *wonderful!*"

He knew that her exuberance was very close to hysteria. But there was nothing he could do for her except this—to *be* with her, to give her the illusion of escape, however brief.

But eventually he slowed down. They had the wind behind them, but even so it was a cold winter's day, and speed did not do anything to keep one warm in an open conveyance. Besides which, these lanes had not exactly been designed for reckless driving.

"Tell me about your Christmas concert," he said.

"Oh, it went very well," she told him. "It always does, of course, but every year we fear the worst. There were no disasters and only a few very minor crises, none of which were obvious to the audience, I daresay. Not that the audiences at such events are ever very critical. They come fully intending to be pleased. It was a large audience—I was *so* pleased for the girls."

She proceeded to tell him about the play she had directed, the choirs, the solos, the dancing, the Nativity tableau Miss Thompson had organized at the last moment, and the end-of-term prizes presented by Miss Martin.

"Miss Thompson has joined the staff, then?" he asked.

"She never did leave Bath," she said. "I do believe she is enjoying herself, and we all enjoy having her— especially Claudia. They must be very near each other in age, and they have struck up a close friendship."

She turned her head toward him after another minute or two.

"You came home to Sidley, then?" she said.

"I did," he told her. "You asked me to, if you will remember, and I came directly from Bath. I have been here ever since."

She gazed at him in silence while he looked ahead along the road.

"I have even quarreled with my steward," he told her.

"Oh, dear," she said.

He grinned. "It was not exactly a quarrel," he said. "I made a suggestion and he rejected it without even hearing me out—very gently and tactfully as if I were still a half-wit nine-year-old. I looked him in the eye and told him I did not enjoy being interrupted, and I thought his lower jaw was going to scrape on the floor. He listened after that with both ears and both eyes, made one small suggestion, which was very sensible, and we came to an agreement. It may be my imagination, but it has seemed to me in the week or so since it happened that he now looks upon me with something bordering on respect."

"Oh, Peter." She laughed. "How splendid of you. I wish I had been there to see you pokering up and telling him that you did not *enjoy* being interrupted."

"If he had been very observant, though," he said, "he might have noticed that my knees were knocking together."

She laughed again.

"Where are we going?" she asked.

He had *thought* he was just driving aimlessly about the lanes in the vicinity of Fincham, but now that she had asked he realized that he was headed in a very definite direction—toward Sidley Park, in fact, though he knew in the same moment that it was not the house that was his destination.

"I don't think," he said, "you are quite ready to go back to Fincham yet, are you?"

"No," she said.

"But you *do* need to get in out of the cold," he said. "I'll take you to the dower house at Sidley. It's empty but well kept. We will light a fire in the sitting room and warm up. And you can tell me about your letter—or not, as you wish. You can sit there for as long as you need to—either alone or in my company."

"You are very kind," she said.

But there was no more light chatter or laughter.

They had served their purpose—she was now calm whereas it had been clear that she was in high distress when he first saw her.

There was no more conversation at all, in fact, as he drove them the rest of the distance, turning onto the long driveway to Sidley, turning off it again almost immediately to take a narrower, wooded trail to the dower house.

He helped her down, unhitched the horses before leading them into the stable stalls and laying out some feed for them, and then took Susanna into the house.

"It is very prettily situated," she said.

"Yes," he agreed, taking her by the elbow and leading her to the sitting room. "I have always loved it almost more than the main house. I have always felt at home here."

The sitting room was also the library. There were several tall bookcases filled with books, many of them his boyhood favorites. The large sofa and chairs were of soft, ancient leather, probably in no way elegant in the eyes of the fashion sticklers, but marvelously comfortable.

He went down on one knee by the fireplace without first removing his greatcoat, and lit the fire that was already laid there.

"Come and warm your hands," he said.

"I like this room," she said as they stood side by side, almost shoulder to shoulder, holding out their hands to the thin flames that would soon crackle into full life. "It is cozy. I could be happy here."

"Could you?" He turned his head and found himself in the middle of one of those moments of heightened awareness. He was sure she was blushing even though her cheeks were already rosy from the cold.

She lowered her glance and removed her bonnet. She undid the fastenings of her cloak too, though she left it around her shoulders as she sat in the chair to one side of the fire. He threw off his greatcoat and took the chair at the other side.

This, he supposed suddenly, was not at all proper.

But to the devil with propriety.

"I am glad you chose to read the letter," he said, "and I am glad you chose to do it here. Was it very hard to read?"

She touched her middle fingers to her temples and made circles there for a while as she looked down at her lap.

"I had not realized," she said, "what a . . . *living* thing handwriting is. It was his handwriting, and it was as familiar as his face. I felt as if I were looking at him a few minutes before his death."

He said nothing.

"He loved me," she said, looking up into his face and lowering her hands.

"Of course he did."

"He thought his death would be the best thing for *me*," she said. "He was facing disgrace and perhaps worse, and he chose death for *my* sake. Can you imagine anything more foolish than that?"

He watched tears well into her eyes. She blinked them away.

"How could his death benefit *me*?" She drew a deep breath and released it slowly. "He made provision for me, and told me I would be *happy*."

"Provision?" he said.

"Oh, Peter," she said, "they are coming to Fincham today—my two grandfathers and my grandmother, all the way from Gloucestershire. But they are *strangers*. Whatever am I to do?"

He thought of her as a twelve-year-old in London, trying to find employment and of the same child being sent to school in Bath as a charity girl, all alone in the world. How very different her life would have been if she had waited.

He would never have met her—except on that one barely remembered occasion when they were children.

"I would not plan on *doing* anything if I were you," he said. "Meet them and allow the relationship to develop from there. They are your blood kin."

"I am so frightened," she said. "And what a very foolish thing to say." She sat farther back in her chair.

"It might be worth remembering," he said, "that as they draw nearer to Fincham today, they are probably very frightened too."

"I had not thought of that," she said. "Do you suppose it is true?"

"If they are prepared to make such a long journey in the dead of winter just to meet you," he said, "I would say it is undoubtedly true."

"Oh," she said, and she closed her eyes.

He let her rest while he poked the fire in order to disperse the flames more evenly. A shower of sparks crackled up the chimney.

"They sent him away," she said without opening her eyes, "after he had fallen in love with his brother's wife and then killed his brother in a fight. But she followed him and they married."

"Your mother?" he asked, seating himself again.

"Yes," she said. "I think it must have been a great and very painful love. One filled with guilt. I wonder if they ever knew a moment of happiness."

Probably not. The William Osbourne he remembered had certainly not been an unfeeling brute of a man.

"He wrote," she said, "that my mother paid the ultimate price when she died giving birth to me and that now it was his turn."

"But why then?" he asked. "Why did he wait twelve years?"

He thought she would not answer him, and he certainly would not press. This was her story. He had no right to hear it unless she chose to tell him. But she did answer after a while.

"His secret was out," she said. "He had recently told Sir Charles himself since someone was trying to blackmail him by threatening to expose him. But then sh—. But then that *person* decided to ruin him anyway by telling untrue stories that surely would have been believed when his past was disclosed too."

It sounded, Peter thought, like something a woman might do—a scorned woman. And Susanna had been about to say *she* before she used the more neutral *person* instead. Poor Osbourne. Perhaps he had tried to find comfort in another woman's arms, and it had cost him his life.

He was facing disgrace and perhaps worse, she had said earlier. Worse than disgrace?

Had *rape* been the threatened charge, then?

"It has just struck me," she said, "that my one grandfather and grandmother lost two sons within twelve years of each other, and that my other grandfather lost a daughter. And that the circumstances must have been particularly painful for all of them."

"And then," he said, "they lost you when you disappeared."

"Theodore told me," she said, "that they searched for me but could not find me."

She spread both hands over her face.

He knew after a few moments that she was not weeping but that it was costing her an enormous effort to control her tears. He got up out of his chair, crossed to her, and without really thinking of what he did, scooped her up into his arms, leaving her cloak behind, and sat on the sofa with her on his lap. He cradled her head against his shoulder and held it there when she buried her face against him, her hands still covering it, and wept.

He knew that she was weeping out eleven years' worth of grief—for her mother and father, for her grandparents, perhaps for her dead uncle. And for herself. He held her and let her cry as long as she needed to. At last he offered her a handkerchief, and she took it and dried her eyes and blew her nose before putting it away in a pocket of her own.

"I am sorry," she said, resting the side of her head against his shoulder again. "Did you even know I was at Fincham?"

"I did," he said. "Why do you think I went there this morning?"

"Theodore said something about an invitation for his mother," she said.

"An invitation for you all," he said, "but especially for you. There is to be a ball at Sidley on Christmas evening. We have a houseful of guests and I have invited everyone from the neighborhood too. It will be the first grand event that I have hosted at Sidley. You must come."

"Oh, no, Peter," she said, sitting up and looking down at him with troubled eyes. "I cannot possibly do that."

"You can," he said. "It is *for* you. I thought you would be proud of me. It is a very little dragon I have slain, but I have done it anyway. It was my idea, and I have done all of the planning and all of the inviting. Don't refuse to come. Please don't."

He would not want to attend himself if she did not—and that would lead to a mildly absurd situation.

"As host," he said, "I will have to dance all evening. I will have to waltz with someone else if you are not there."

"Oh, Peter," she said, cupping one of her palms about his cheek.

"Tell me you don't want me waltzing with anyone but you," he said.

"Peter—"

"Please tell me."

She bowed her head and closed her eyes.

"I cannot *bear* the thought of you waltzing with anyone but me," she half whispered.

"Susanna—"

She opened her eyes and looked into his, her own still somewhat reddened from the weeping.

"I really cannot bear it," she said, but he was no longer sure she was talking just about the waltz.

He spread his hand over the soft curls at the back of her head and drew it down toward his until her arms came about his neck and he kissed her.

And he knew at that moment that love would never die, that it would never fade away altogether. The time might come when he would meet and marry someone else. He might even be reasonably happy. But there would always be a deep, precious place in his heart that belonged to his first real love. To Susanna.

But he was not going to think meekly about that someone else and that reasonably happy life he might live. He was not giving up what he really wanted without a fight. He might never have been much of a knight during his twenty-six years, he might never have been in the habit of searching out dragons to fight and quell—indeed, he had run from them five years ago. But he would find one and fight it to the death if Susanna were the prize.

Or perhaps even if she were not.

Her face was a little above his, cupped in his hands, her auburn curls spilling over his fingers, her eyes very green.

"Let me take you upstairs," he found himself saying. "There is no fire up there, but the bedcovers are warm. Let me make love to you."

He felt as though he had walked out to the end of a plank, a helpless prisoner on a pirate ship. He felt more vulnerable than he had ever felt in his life before.

If she said no, every dream he had ever dreamed would be shattered. For he was not asking her just to bed with him. He was asking for her love. He was offering his own.

He was offering everything he had, everything he was.

Did she know that? Did she understand?

He watched her swallow.

"Yes," she said.

23

She should, of course, have said no. This time she knew exactly what she had agreed to—future pain, the danger of consequences. And she knew too that afterward, sometime before she returned to Bath, he would offer her marriage again—and that she would refuse again. She even knew that his feelings for her were deeper than just liking. She knew that her refusal would hurt him.

She did not care about any of it.

Sometimes love was to be grasped in any form and in any manner it was offered. And sometimes love must be given in the same way. After a morning of emotional turmoil, she wanted, more than anything else in this world, to give love, to pour it out recklessly and unstintingly.

"Yes," she said again, and got to her feet.

He set a guard in front of the fire and took her by the hand. They left the room and went up the wide staircase together without speaking and turned to their right, past several closed doors, until he opened one that led into a front-facing room, obviously the main bedchamber, which was fully furnished, just as the downstairs was. The bed was made up.

"Susanna," he said, turning to her, taking both her hands in his and holding them against the lapels of his coat, "are you sure?"

She was. She had never been more sure of anything in her life. She wanted to give, and she wanted to receive, and it struck her suddenly that both were equally important components of love. She loved him and would give him her body. She would allow him to give to her in exchange.

"I am," she said. "Make love with me, Peter."

"*With* you." He smiled as he leaned his head closer and touched his lips lightly to hers. "Yes, I like it."

She let him unclothe her, first her dress, then her stockings, then her undergarments. She thought at first that she would be embarrassed. But how could she be when his eyes worshiped her and his hands too as he stripped the clothes away? And there was something undeniably erotic about the cold room and his warm hands. Her arms were covered with goose bumps, partly from the cold, partly from the anticipation of what was to come.

He kissed her again, more deeply this time, his tongue coming into her mouth, his hands on either side of her waist and then spreading over her buttocks to bring her fully against him—naked body to fully clothed body.

Desire sizzled through her.

"You are so beautiful, Susanna," he said against her lips. "So very beautiful."

Her fingers fumbled at his neckcloth until she discovered the way to remove it. She pushed his coat off his shoulders and down his arms until it fell to the floor. She undid the buttons of his waistcoat and sent it to follow his coat. She pulled his shirt free of his breeches, and he raised his arms so that she could lift it off over his head.

While he watched her through narrowed eyes, she set her palms flat against his chest and moved them up over the light dusting of hair to his shoulders, down his arms, back to his shoulders, and down to the waistband of his breeches. He was neither large nor brawny—he was slender and beautiful. But his chest and shoulders and upper arms were firmly muscled. She spread her hands over his chest again and set her face between them, kissing him.

He was warmer than either her hands or her lips. He smelled wonderfully of his usual cologne.

She felt the throbbing of sexual desire low in her womb and down between her thighs. She felt her breasts tauten, her nipples harden. She shivered.

He chuckled softly as he kissed the top of her head.

"I'll do the rest," he said. "Besides, you are freezing to death."

He turned and drew back the bedcovers and watched as she lay down, his eyes moving over her.

Ah, how could she possibly feel embarrassed beneath such a hot gaze? But she *had* been too embarrassed to remove his breeches. How silly! She smiled at him, and he covered her to the chin with the heavy covers before pulling off his boots and his stockings and then his other lower garments. He did not turn away as he did so. He watched her watching him, saw her realize that he was ready for her.

"Is it warm under there?" he asked with a grin.

"It will be," she said.

"It certainly will," he agreed as she slid over on the bed and he lay down beside her. "And very soon too."

She wondered suddenly what it would be like to be married to him, to share a bed thus every night, to share bodies with frequent regularity, to . . .

Ah, never mind. She had today.

He lifted himself onto one elbow and looked down at her, his face inches from her own, his eyes smiling into hers.

"I would like to be the Hercules of long endurance," he said, "and keep us both panting in anticipation for the next hour or so. But I doubt it is possible. Will you mind?"

"No." She smiled back. "I want to feel you inside me." Her cheeks grew hot at the boldness of her words.

And yet it was a shock—a wonderful shock—when he rolled on top of her, slipped his hands beneath her as his legs spread hers wide, and came deep inside her with one smooth, firm thrust. Smooth, she realized, because she had been very ready for him too. And painless this time.

She drew a deep breath and released it slowly as she slid her feet up the bed so that she could tilt herself to allow him deeper access. Ah, yes, she was as ready for him as he was for her, but please, please, let it not all be over too soon.

She tightened inner muscles about him and found

the resulting sensation wondrously pleasurable. He was long and hard.

He drew his hands free and lifted some of his weight onto his forearms and looked down into her face.

"There is nowhere in the world I would rather be," he said before kissing her. "Let's love each other."

And that was what they did after he had turned his head away to rest on the pillow beside her and lowered some of his weight back onto her. He withdrew and entered again and withdrew and entered and set up a slow, firm rhythm of love. And this time, because she knew what happened and knew too that she could make love as well as submit to being made love to, she moved to the same rhythm, rotating her hips, pulsing with her inner muscles.

It lasted a long, wonderful time as their breath became labored and their bodies slick with sweat, as her passage became wetter and a rhythmic sucking sound accompanied their movements.

It might just be possible to swoon with pleasure, Susanna thought—until pleasure began to be overlaid with something else. At first it was a needling ache where he worked in her, and then something that bordered almost on pain as it spread downward to her legs, upward through her womb to her breasts and into her throat and behind her eyes.

And then it *was* pain—a strange, unbearable pain that did not quite hurt but . . .

But there were no words.

She heard herself moan.

The rhythm changed then. It became faster and

deeper, and his hands were beneath her again, holding her steady so that there was no escape. Her own rhythm vanished as she strained toward him, every muscle taut.

And then something blossomed deep within and opened almost like the multiple petals of a rose, pushing back the tension in rippling waves as they bloomed until she surrendered to relaxation with a soft exclamation of surprise.

"Ah," she said.

The aftermath of tension set her to trembling all over then as she sank into the blessed fulfillment of sexual desire. Not that she used quite those words in her mind. She had not known that there *was* such a thing.

He had stopped moving too, she realized. But he was still hard and firm and deep inside her, and his body was still tense. He had stopped so that she could savor her own pleasure.

She felt weak with a glorious exhaustion, but she wrapped her arms about him, twined her legs about his, and turned her head to kiss the side of his face.

He took his pleasure swiftly and lustily, and it surprised a languorous Susanna to discover that even in satiety more pleasure was possible. She felt the warm gush of his release and lifted one hand to rest over the damp hair at the back of his head.

"Susanna," he murmured against her ear.

"Peter."

They both slept, without uncoupling.

• • •

Somehow while he had slept, Peter discovered, he had moved to Susanna's side. She was cradled in his arms, her head in the hollow between his neck and his shoulder. She was still sleeping.

It was a thought that had woken him—a memory actually.

A memory of being in William Osbourne's office at Fincham with Theo when they were both boys, learning script writing. And of his mother hurrying into the room without knocking, looking startled, and then scolding him for not being in Theo's room, where she had supposed he would be.

He had assumed at the time that she had been looking for him.

Now, for some odd reason when so many years had passed, he thought that if that had been the case, the look on her face would surely have been relief, or perhaps annoyance. Not *surprise*. And why had she not knocked? It was true that the office belonged to a mere secretary, but even so, he was a gentleman. And his office was in a private home that was not his mother's.

And why the devil was he wondering about such unimportant matters now? Why had such a trivial memory woken him up? Just because Osbourne was fresh in his mind?

He yawned, burrowed his nose in Susanna's hair, kissed her head lightly—and drew back his head rather sharply.

The devil!

It was surely not his mother . . .

It could not have been!

Good Lord, Osbourne, though a gentleman, had been only Markham's secretary, and his mother was the highest of high sticklers. She would never have . . .

Yes, she could have.

Osbourne had been a handsome devil. Not that Peter had ever noticed that when he was a boy, but looking back he could see that, yes, the man had enjoyed more than his fair share of good looks.

His mother must have been lonely—he *knew* she had been lonely. She had told him so later—six years later. Five years ago.

So must Osbourne have been lonely.

Of course, anything that *might* have happened between them could have been initiated on Osbourne's side. His mother might not have given him any encouragement at all. Perhaps the charges that had led him to kill himself had been true.

But his mother had been hurrying into that study, and no one had been coercing her. It even seemed to Peter now that there had been a look of eagerness on her face before surprise had replaced it, though there was no way of verifying that impression.

But dash it all—what a devil of a coil!

He just hoped his imagination had become overactive and was playing wild and nasty tricks on him.

But it was not with his imagination that he had seen his mother with Grantham—with Bertha's *father*—five years ago. He had walked into her unlocked dressing room at Sidley after the slightest of knocks, on some unremembered mission, and . . . Well, and there they had been, the two of them. They had not even stopped first to lock the door.

Blood hammered through his temples. What if that had not been an isolated incident in his mother's life—as she had sworn to him it was?

What if his mother had driven Osbourne to his death?

And here he was holding Osbourne's daughter in his arms. He had just made love to her. He was determined to marry her if she would have him.

She was awake. She had opened her eyes and tipped back her head and was looking at him sleepily, her cheeks slightly flushed.

Lord, but he loved her. The realization—and the force of his feelings—shook him.

If she had known about this all along, even before reading her letter—*if* his thoughts had led him down the right path, that was—was it why . . .

Lord bless him, *of course* it was why. And what was it he had said to her—his very first words to her?

Miss Osbourne, an already glorious summer day suddenly seems even warmer and brighter.

He could almost hear himself say those exact words.

What a consummate ass!

At the same moment she had been recognizing his name and recoiling from him.

"Mmm," she said now and kissed his chin and then his mouth when he lowered his head.

She was not recoiling from him now, though. Perhaps his guesses were way wide of the mark.

"Mmm to you too," he said, rubbing his nose across hers.

"Ought we to go back yet?" she asked him with a sigh. "We must have been gone for an age."

He had been going to propose marriage to her again after they were finished with the sex. He had decided that downstairs as soon as she had said yes. He would love her silly and then, before she could recover her wits and harden her heart, he would slip the question into their waking conversation. And then during the Christmas ball he would make the grand announcement.

She would not marry him in a million years if his mother had been her father's lover and had then tried blackmailing him and driven him to despair and death.

Not to mention how his mother would react if he presented William Osbourne's daughter to her as his prospective bride.

Somehow—perhaps because he did not want to believe it—he knew that his guess was correct.

"They know you are with me," he said. "They probably know too that we left in the curricle. They will assume that I have brought you over to Sidley and that you have stayed for luncheon and an afternoon visit."

"Why is it," she asked, snuggling closer, "that I so often imagine myself running away and running free? I ran away once and it now seems that I must have done the wrong thing. Except that running away took me to Bath, and I have been happy there. Why do I want to run from happiness?"

"Because it is not everything you want or need or dream of?" he suggested. "I would run away with you to the end of the world now if I thought that doing so would bring us to that mythical state of happily-ever-after. I think I was actually serious during the summer, Susanna, when I suggested we go off walking in Wales together. Indeed, I *know* I was. But I would not ask you to do anything like that again."

"Oh," she said softly.

"Because there is no such state," he said. "There *is* no happily-ever-after to run to. We have to *work* for happiness. I am going to do things the right way from now on. I decided that as soon as I left Bath. Don't ask me what I am going to do or how I am going to do it. I don't know. But at the end of all this I am going to have slain a dragon or two, and I am going to *like* myself. Then perhaps I'll have more to offer the world—and you—than simple gallantry."

She gazed at him and her eyes filled with tears, though she smiled too.

"I am not sorry I ran away that first time," she said. "I like what happened to my life. And if I had not run, I would not have met you again, would I? But I won't run again. I'll go back to Fincham and meet my grandparents, though for some reason it will be one of the hardest things I have ever done. And then after Christmas I will go home to Bath and continue striving to be the best teacher I can possibly be."

"You are not sorry we met again during the summer, then?" he asked her.

"No."

"Neither am I," he said.

"But I must get back to Fincham," she said. "Soon."

She raised herself on one elbow and leaned over him to kiss the side of his face and trail kisses along his jawline. Then she kissed his mouth. Her free hand pressed against his shoulder until he turned to lie on his back.

By Jove, he thought, his interest piqued, she was going to make love to him.

By the time they had reached the bedchamber earlier, he had been so bursting with desire for her—and she for him, he had judged—that he had proceeded without delay to the main feast. She, it seemed, was more disciplined.

She was also as skilled as any courtesan—though no, perhaps that was not quite so. Perhaps it was just that he was very ready to be aroused by her. But however it was, she had overcome the modesty that had caused her to hesitate to remove his breeches earlier. Her hands roamed all over him, stroking, caressing, pausing, rubbing, teasing in all the right places, and her mouth and her tongue and her teeth followed suit.

He lay still for a while, his hands flat on the mattress on either side of him, enjoying the sheer perfection of her touch, marveling at her boldness, at her instinctive knowledge of how best to arouse him without driving him too early to madness. But when she suckled one of his nipples, biting it lightly with her teeth, laving it with her tongue, his hands came up to sink into her soft auburn curls, and he groaned and then laughed softly.

"Mercy, woman," he said.

She lifted her head and smiled down into his face, her cheeks flushed, her eyes heavy with desire.

"But I have no wish to show mercy," she said, her voice low and throaty as she brought her lips to his and teased them with the tip of her tongue.

This was beginning to be agonizing.

And then she brought herself right over him, straddling him with her legs, her knees on either side of his hips, her hands supporting herself on either side of his head.

He skimmed his hands down the lovely curve of her back to spread over her firmly rounded buttocks. She had lovely breasts, not overlarge but firm and nicely shaped. He felt the hardened nipples brush against his chest as she lowered her mouth to his again. With the lower part of her body she rubbed lightly over his erection.

Agony had passed its beginning, but this was *her* lovemaking—he would proceed at her pace.

"Witch," he murmured.

She raised herself then onto her knees, holding herself above him and biting on her lower lip as she took him in one hand, set him against her opening, and brought herself down on him.

Ah!

She was hot and wet, and her inner muscles clenched about him as she drew him deep.

He set his hands lightly on her hips and drew a slow breath. There was a certain type of agony that was also exquisite, and this was it. He would not spoil it with urgency. He smiled slowly up at her.

"To repeat myself," he said, "there is nowhere I would rather be."

She set her hands on either side of his waist,

hugged his hips more tightly with her knees, lifted herself almost away from him, brought herself down again, and repeated the motion over and over again. She closed her eyes and lowered her chin to her chest.

Good Lord, he thought, before sensation engulfed him, she was riding him. He let her ride for a while, awash in pleasure and desire, and then his hands pressed more firmly on her hips, and he rode with her for a few minutes until they both broke rhythm, she to press downward, he to thrust upward, both to shatter into fulfillment at the same moment.

It was beyond extraordinary.

It was beyond bliss.

And it was not sex, he thought as she came downward to lie on top of him and he covered them both with the bedcovers. Not *just* sex.

It was love.

He had never before seen much connection between the two.

He held her for several minutes, not sleeping, knowing that she did not sleep either, knowing that she was telling herself that this was the end.

It was not the end. If someone cared to bring on a whole regiment of dragons, all of them armed to the fangs with fire and brimstone and other assorted deadly weapons, he would take on the lot of them bare-handed.

This was *not the end*.

This was the end, Susanna thought, her shoulder pressed to Peter's, drawing some warmth from him as the curricle turned onto the driveway leading to Fincham Manor. Oh, she would quite possibly see him again after today. It was even probable that she would have to go to the ball at Sidley that he had mentioned earlier, though she would not even *think* about that yet.

But really today was the end. The end of an affair of the heart that could have no future. *Now* was the end.

It was also the beginning of something else. She wondered if her grandparents had arrived yet.

Her *grandparents*.

She still felt partly numbed at the unfamiliar thought.

Today she was going to meet three people who were closely connected to her by blood after believing for eleven years that she was all alone in the world.

But they were strangers.

Would they even like her?

Would they hold it against her that she was the product of a marriage that ought never to have been?

But they were coming here, were they not?

Would *she* like *them*?

How would she even greet them?

"It looks," Peter said, "as if the visitors have arrived."

And sure enough, there was a large old carriage standing outside the stable block. Her heart sank.

"Afraid?" he asked, turning his head to look down at her.

"Very." She drew her cloak more tightly about her.

"Is it not strange," he said, "how life can plod along placidly for years and then, for no clear reason, can be suddenly filled with one turmoil after another? And it has happened for us both in differing ways—and began for both of us at the same moment, when we arrived together at the fork in a narrow lane in the quiet Somerset countryside one summer afternoon. Such a seemingly innocent encounter! And here we are as a result of it all, and you are facing an ordeal that has nothing really to do with me. May I come in with you?"

"Please do," she said as he drew the curricle to a halt before the doors into the house and jumped down to assist her.

She thought as she entered the house a few moments later that perhaps she ought to have said no. Perhaps her grandparents would recognize the name *Whitleaf* as she had during the summer. But it was too late now. Besides, she could not bear to say good-bye to him and then have to go upstairs to the drawing room alone.

The newly arrived visitors were there and expecting her, the butler informed her as he took her cloak and bonnet from her and she fluffed up her curls and brushed her hands over her dress. He turned to lead the way.

She did not take Peter's arm. If she did, she might cling. This was something she must do herself, even if she *had* chosen to have him accompany her for moral support.

Lady Markham, Edith, Mr. Morley, Theodore— they were all in the drawing room, Susanna saw as soon as she had crossed the threshold. So were three strangers, all of whom got to their feet at sight of her. Theodore came striding toward her.

"Susanna," he said, taking her hand in both of his and squeezing it before letting it go, "you must come and meet Colonel and Mrs. Osbourne and the Reverend Clapton, your grandparents."

The lady was slender almost to the point of thinness, with white, carefully coiffed hair, a lined face, and a sweet mouth. The colonel was broad-chested and tall and very upright in bearing. He was bald and had a thick white mustache, which drooped past the corners of his mouth almost to his chin. He looked very distinguished. He looked like an older version of Susanna's father. The clergyman was shorter and thinner. He had fine gray hair and eyeglasses and supported himself with a cane.

Her *grandparents,* Susanna thought, gazing one at a time at the three strangers.

She dipped into a curtsy.

And then the lady came hurrying toward her, both hands outstretched, and Susanna set her own in them.

"Susanna," the lady said. "Oh, my dear, I believe I would have known you anywhere. You look just like your mother, though surely you have something of the look of my son too. Oh, my dearest, dearest girl. I *knew* you were not dead. All these years I have said it, and now I know that I was right."

Her chin wobbled and her eyes filled with tears.

"Please do not cry, ma'am," Susanna said, hearing a gurgle in her own throat. "Please do not."

"Grandmama," the lady said. "Call me Grandmama. Please do."

"Grandmama," Susanna said.

And then of course, there was no way of stopping the tears of either of them from flowing—and somehow they had their arms about each other, Susanna and this stranger who was not a stranger at all but Papa's mother.

Peter was clearing his throat, though not in an attention-seeking way. So was the Reverend Clapton, who was leaning on his cane with both hands. Lady Markham and Edith were smiling with happiness. Mr. Morley looked as if he were in raptures. Theodore was beaming genially.

The colonel withdrew a large white handkerchief from a pocket of his coat, blessing his soul rather fiercely as he did so, held the handkerchief to his nose, and blew into it loudly enough to wake the dead.

24

"*This is very pleasant, Peter,*" *his mother said,* sinking into the best chair, which he had drawn near the fire in the library. "Just the two of us together for a cozy chat. It does not happen often enough."

He seated himself across from her. He had asked her to join him in the library after almost everyone else had retired for the night and only a few of the younger people were still amusing themselves in the music room.

"You are warm enough, Mama?" he asked her.

"I am," she said. "My love, it was very naughty of you to leave the house this morning to deliver one of your invitations and not return until late in the afternoon. However, you *were* very attentive to Miss Flynn-Posy this evening. She is a sweet girl, is she not?"

"Very," he agreed. "And doubtless she will make some man a wonderful wife someday soon. But she will not be mine."

She looked a little surprised at such a categorical statement. But she smiled as she relaxed back against the cushions.

"You may well change your mind during the coming days," she said.

"I will not change my mind," he told her. "I have already chosen the woman I wish to marry."

He watched her eyes light up with interest.

"Peter?" She clasped her hands to her bosom and sat up straighter.

"I am just not sure she will have me," he said.

"Oh, but of course she will have you, whoever she is," she cried. "You know you are one of the greatest matrimonial prizes—"

He held up a hand.

"Mama," he said, "she is Susanna Osbourne."

"Who?" She sat back again, all the animation draining from her face.

"William Osbourne's daughter," he said. "I love her, and I mean to have her if she will have me. I met her during the summer—she was staying with the Countess of Edgecombe not far from Hareford House. I saw her again in Bath when I went there with Lauren and Kit to attend Sydnam Butler's wedding breakfast. And I have been with her today. She is at Fincham Manor for Christmas. Her grandparents have come there to meet her. I have invited them all to the ball here on Christmas night."

She licked her lips. Her hands, he noticed, were gripping the arms of the chair.

"I suppose she set her cap at you," she said. "If she has you believing she will not have you, Peter, that is just her cunning, believe me. You cannot seriously—"

"She wanted to have nothing to do with me during the summer," he said, "after she had heard my name."

Her lips moved, but she did not speak.

"Mama," he asked, and it was an enormously difficult question to ask, "what was your relationship with Mr. Osbourne?"

"My?—" She bristled suddenly. "You are surely being impertinent, Peter. I am your mother, I would have you remember, even if you *are* now grown up."

"You were lovers," he said.

"How dare you!" Her eyes widened.

"Just as you and Grantham were," he said. "Except that then you told me it was the only time it had happened since my father died and that it had happened because you were lonely and could not help yourself. And yet it had been going on for a long time, and on the occasion when I saw the two of you together, you were here, in *my* home, with both Bertha and her mother as my guests under the same roof."

"Peter!" She looked ashen.

She had admitted only that one lapse to him at the time. He had learned differently from other people, but he had never confronted her with his knowledge. She had been quite broken up, and he had been distraught. Good God, she was his *mother*.

"Lady Grantham doubtless knew about the affair," he said, "but all her lady's education had taught her to turn a blind eye. Heaven knows what suffering and what humiliation she bore in silence. Bertha certainly knew even before I was fool enough to blurt out to her what I had just discovered. But she had been trained by her mother and had accepted her father's infidelity long before I told her about it."

Worse, Bertha had gazed at him uncomprehendingly as he spoke and had then asked him if all men were not like her father. When he had assured her that *he* was not, that *he* would be faithful to her until death, she had actually recoiled from him and told him what a child he was—though he was two years her senior. She had no intention, she had told him, of tying herself to him for life once she had performed the duty of presenting him with a son, perhaps two. He surely could not be so naïve as to ask it of her.

"And my uncles knew," he said, "and were only chagrined that you had neglected to lock your door."

They had told him in no uncertain terms that it was time he accepted some of the realities of life. And yet *they* were the ones who had sheltered and educated him all through his boyhood. He was a naïve child, they had told him—the same words Bertha had used—and had better keep his mouth shut about what he had seen and get ready to announce his engagement the following day, as planned. It was time he grew up.

Instead he had summoned every member of the house party to the drawing room within the hour and announced that there was to be no engagement and that they would all kindly leave Sidley before noon the next day. He had told his uncles that they were absolved of all future obligations toward him since he was now an adult and was no longer in need of either their guardianship or their advice.

His mother he had left to her tears—and to Sidley. He had bolted only one day after his guests.

He had not excused her. He had not even believed her lie—he had accepted that her affair with Grantham was of long standing. But he had believed that she had loved Grantham. Now he wondered if that had been so, or if it had mattered anyway. Grantham had been a *married man*—and the two of them had been prepared to arrange a marriage between their offspring.

She was clinging tightly to the arms of her chair now, gazing at him with wide-eyed indignation.

"But it is not about Grantham that I wish to speak," he said. "It is about Mr. Osbourne. You *did* have an affair with him, did you not? But something happened to end the liaison. My guess is that *he* ended it. Had he told you about his past before then? Or did you find it out some other way? However it was, you threatened to go to Sir Charles with your knowledge."

He had no proof of any of this, it struck him suddenly. It would be terrible indeed if he were wrong and had made such accusations against his own mother. And yet he longed to be proved wrong.

"Peter," she said, "if *this* is what that woman has been telling you, I will do all in my power to free you from her evil clutches. You have always been—"

"Susanna did *not* tell me," he said. "She told me about the contents of the letter her father had written her and the one he had written Sir Charles, but she did not name his blackmailer."

"William wrote a letter to *her*?" his mother asked.

He stared bleakly at her.

"Just before he shot himself," he said. "He felt that suicide was the only protection he could offer her. If he had lived, she would have been exposed to all the ugly consequences he would have faced from the charge of rape."

She recoiled.

"How can you use that word in your own mother's hearing?" she asked him. But then she sank back in her chair again, looking suddenly smaller and older. "I said only that he had harassed and molested me, not that . . . And it was true. I told Sir Charles so after William's death. I would never have . . . Peter, you must believe me."

He felt his shoulders slump. He *had* been hoping, despite everything, that perhaps he had been wrong, that perhaps it had been someone else. But he had remembered during the ride back to Sidley from Fincham that it was about the time of Osbourne's death that the coolness had developed in the relations between his mother and the Markhams.

"I did not know he would *kill* himself," she said. "How could I have known that? How could he punish me so?"

"But you would have taken away his reputation, his character, his freedom, Mama," he said. "Whatever he had done in the past he had surely lived down. He had a *child* to support."

"I condescended," she said, her voice jerky and rather breathless. "I *condescended* to his level. And then, when I went to London on one occasion because *he* was there, he let me know that he was not pleased. And then he started avoiding me even at Fincham and finally told me it was all over between us. The presumption, Peter. The humiliation! You must understand. I loved your papa, but my life was very empty without him. I was willing to allow that man . . ."

Ah, just the explanation she had given five years ago when he had confronted her.

"You drove him to his death," he said quietly. He felt physically sick.

"He was foolish!" she cried. "He must have *known* that I was just upset with him, that I would not really have ruined him."

"And yet," he said, "after he had been to Sir Charles and confessed about his past, you were very ready with new threats."

"I would not have—" she began.

"Wouldn't you?" he asked her. "He obviously thought you would. He staked his life on it."

She spread her hands over her face, and he sat staring at her, appalled at what he had learned today, at what he had guessed, at what she had now confirmed. And at the knowledge that she had twice been prepared to wreak havoc with other people's lives because of her sexual needs and her loneliness.

He hated to think of his own mother in such a way.

Was this one of the dragons he must fight? If so, the price was high indeed. Nothing would ever be the same. But the same as what? He had brushed much beneath the metaphoric carpet five years ago. He would do so no longer.

"You do not know how I have suffered, Peter," she said, tearful now—as she had been the last time. "If he did it for revenge, he certainly had the final word. Do you think I have not felt like a murderer all these years? But it is unfair. I did not mean him any harm. I was fond of him. I have always been your mother, and I know it is hard to see your own mother as a woman.

But I *am* a woman, and I was lonely. We were both widowed. He had loved his wife as I loved your father. He even told me at the end that he could not continue with me because his heart had broken at her death and he could not forget her. But for a time we were almost happy. We were not hurting anyone."

He almost felt sorry for her. She had done something monstrous, but she was surely not a monster. And the worst thing about her monstrosity must always have been that she could not atone—Osbourne was dead. *Would* she have brought false accusations against him if he had lived? There was no way of knowing, and he did not *want* to know. But she had done irreparable harm anyway.

He was very tempted to get up, to take her hands in his and draw her to her feet and into his arms, to comfort and reassure her, to send her off to bed. But he had done that the last time, after Grantham. If she needed forgiveness, it was her own she must seek, not his.

Besides, there was one more thing he needed to say, and it was best to say everything now tonight and hope that tomorrow they could both start piecing their lives back together.

She spoke before he could, though.

"Peter," she said, "you *cannot* marry his daughter. You must see that. It would be an impossible, horrible situation."

He drew a slow breath.

"And yet it would have been perfectly fine for me to marry Bertha?" he asked her.

She did not reply.

With the commonsense part of his mind he agreed with her, though. The past would always be there between him and Susanna, the knowledge that his mother and her father had been lovers, that she had caused his death. It would be far better to allow Susanna to return to Bath, to go to London himself after Christmas and set his mind to choosing a suitable bride during the Season. Eventually they would forget each other, and when they *did* remember, they would both be glad they had not taken a chance on happiness.

But he had renounced simple common sense since leaving Bath behind him a few weeks ago. He was reaching for happiness, or if happiness proved impossible, then at least for self-respect. He would no longer avoid the darker corners of his life.

It was altogether possible—even probable—that Susanna would not have him after all, but he would not lose her just because he had chosen to tiptoe his way past his dragons. Even after she was gone he would have to live with himself. And finally he was determined to like the person who lived inside his body.

Not that he particularly liked himself at the moment.

"The only question to be settled on the issue of Miss Osbourne, Mama," he said, "is whether *she* will marry me under the circumstances. She has already refused me once."

She looked sharply at him with a curious mixture of indignation and hope on her face.

"Mama," he said after drawing a deep breath, "I want Sidley to become *my* home."

She stared at him.

"It *is* yours, Peter," she said. "If you do not spend more time here, it is your own fault. You know how often I have urged you to come."

"Because it has always been more yours than mine," he said.

"Sidley has been yours since you were an infant," she said. "I have always kept the household running smoothly for you. I have always kept it beautiful for you. Lately I have begun some refurbishings, all for your sake."

"But I have never been consulted about anything," he said.

"Because you are never *here*," she cried.

It was true enough. She did have a point there.

"I ought to have taken over both the house and the estate when I reached my majority," he said, "but I did not for reasons we need not rehash yet again. I have my own ideas on how both should be run, and now I am ready to implement them. I want to make friends of my neighbors. I want them *here* for frequent entertainments. I want them to feel welcome, to feel at home here. I want to *live* here most of the time."

"Peter," she said, looking more herself again, "this is wonderful! I shall—"

"I want it for *myself*, Mama," he said, "and for my wife and children if I marry."

She smiled uncertainly at him.

"Perhaps," he said, "you would like to redecorate and refurnish the dower house and move there when it is ready."

"The *dower* house?" Her eyes widened in indignation.

"I have always loved it," he said. "You could surely be contented there."

"It is where the *governesses* and *tutors* always lived," she cried.

"Then we will look around for a suitable house for you in London," he suggested. "There will be company there for you most of the year, and plenty of entertainments, and all the shops. And you will always be welcome here as a visitor."

She leaned back in her chair and stared at him— and there was a moment at which he was aware that her chin tilted slightly upward.

"I have always lived here in order to keep it for you," she said. "You are my only son. I took on the responsibility when your father died, and I have not relinquished it since. I have given my life for you."

It was, he realized, a moment when some rebuilding was possible.

"And I will be eternally grateful," he said. "I had a marvelously secure childhood. I was never in any doubt that I was loved. And I am glad I did not marry too young. I have had the chance to live out my early manhood and find out who I am and what I want of my life, secure in the knowledge that you and my home were always here for me. But now I have arrived at that point of self-discovery, Mama, and I can set you free to enjoy *your* life in any way you choose. I know you have been lonely here."

It was not entirely the truth that he spoke, of course, but there *was* truth in it nevertheless. And despite everything, he would always love her and always be grateful that she had loved him during his childhood.

"I think," she said, "I would *like* to live in London."

Perhaps she did not speak the entire truth either. And yet it struck him that she probably *would* be happier there. And there was a certain relief in finding that she had rejected the idea of moving to the dower house.

"We will see to it after Christmas," he said. "But I have kept you up very late, Mama. You must go to bed now. Tomorrow will be busy, I daresay."

"Yes."

But she did not immediately get to her feet.

"Peter," she said, "I could never love another man as I loved your father. William Osbourne, George Grantham—they meant nothing to me, though I was fond of them both. I certainly did not mean to do anyone any harm."

"I know you did not."

He knew no such thing, alas, but it was not his place to pour recriminations on her head. He got to his feet and offered her his hand. When she was standing before him, small, fragile, still lovely, he kissed her forehead and then her cheek.

"Good night, Mama," he said.

"Good night, Peter."

She left the room without another word, her back straight, her step light and firm.

He looked toward the brandy decanter but rejected the idea of pouring himself a glass. If he started drinking tonight, he knew he would not stop until he was thoroughly foxed.

Several times during the course of Christmas Eve Susanna thought about Claudia and Eleanor and Lila and the girls who would be at the school for Christmas. They were there *right now,* she thought. She tried to ground herself in the reality of that thought, but it was hard to believe in it. It was hard to believe anything that was happening around her either.

It was as if she had stepped into some strange dream.

Life had been so routine, so predictable, so *dull,* until the end of the summer. And yet there had been a certain contentment, even happiness, about the dullness.

Yesterday seemed unreal. Could she really have gone willingly to the dower house at Sidley Park with Viscount Whitleaf? Had she really gone to bed and made love with him there? *Twice?* The second time entirely initiated by her?

And today, were these strangers with whom she was spending almost all her time really turning so quickly into familiar, even dear, relatives? Was it possible to feel a close familial connection to people of whose very existence she had been hardly aware until yesterday morning?

But her grandfather Osbourne looked so very much as her father would have looked, if he had lived so long, that she would hardly have been able to drag her eyes away from him had her grandmother not had Papa's eyes—and if she had not insisted upon holding Susanna's hand much of the time and patting it and gazing at her in fascinated wonder. And her Grandfather Clapton really did have her own eyes, though their color had faded closer to gray than green, and she could imagine, looking at his thin gray hair, that it really had been auburn at one time. He had a way of nodding and smiling quietly, leaving most of the talking to the other two, that drew her eyes and tugged at her heart.

Grandmother and Grandfather Osbourne had no surviving children, and she was their only grandchild. Their lives must have been filled with the most terrible sadness. They had had two sons.

By running away, she thought, she had robbed them of knowing her from the age of twelve until now. But then, they were the ones who had banished her father. Not that she would judge them for that. He had interfered with their elder son's marriage and then caused his death in a fight. She longed to know details of that fight. Had the death been entirely accidental? Had her father's brother fallen and hit his head on a stone, for example? But she would not ask.

Her grandfather Clapton had three surviving daughters and eight grandchildren apart from Susanna. Her aunts and cousins, he told her, smiling his quiet smile. The eldest was married to his successor in the village church—and *their* son was a curate in a church not far away.

She had aunts and uncles and cousins.

"How different my life would have been if I had

not left Fincham in such a hurry all those years ago," she said.

"And ours too, dearest," her grandmother said, patting her hand.

"But would you go back now and change your life if you could?" Grandfather Clapton asked gently. "I believe our lives unfold in perfect but mysterious ways, understood clearly only by our Lord."

"That is something you *would* say, Ambrose," Grandfather Osbourne said irritably. "I have not seen much perfection in the lives of my own family, only endless mystery. And if the Almighty is responsible, I will have a quarrel to pick with him on Judgment Day."

"I cannot know if I would change the course of my life or not," Susanna said, smiling at all of them and understanding already that her grandfathers did not always see eye-to-eye upon every issue. "I *wish* I had known you all sooner, and I do look back upon the couple of weeks I spent in London with some horror. But I spent six happy years at Miss Martin's school, and I have loved my teaching job there during the past five years. I am proud of what I have made of my life."

Her grandmother patted her hand.

"Teaching is all very well," Grandfather Osbourne said, "for a lady with no family or for a lady whose family has only slender means. I am not an enormously wealthy man, Susanna, but I am certainly not poor either, and you are all we have. It is time you came home with us. It is time we found you a good husband to look after you when we are gone."

Her grandmother smoothed a hand over hers, and

Susanna could feel her bent arthritic fingers against the back of her hand.

"I think, Clarence," she said, "Susanna may have already found him for herself. Viscount Whitleaf is a very handsome and charming young man, and it seemed to me yesterday that he thinks the world of our granddaughter. He has invited us all to attend the ball at Sidley Park tomorrow evening, but I had the feeling that it is Susanna with whom he wants to dance more than anyone else."

"I daresay it would not be me, Sadie," Grandfather Osbourne said with a bark of laughter. "But a *viscount*. That is aiming high, though not impossibly high. We have a perfectly respectable lineage. And so does Ambrose."

"And you *were* a colonel," Grandmother Osbourne reminded him.

"Hmm," her grandfather said. "I shall have to find out what that young man's intentions are."

Susanna pulled her hand away from her grandmother's in order to clap both hands to her cheeks.

"Oh, Grandfather," she said, "please do not say anything to him."

She was blushing, she realized. She was also laughing. Her grandfather had known her for less than twenty-four hours, and already he was trying to take charge of her life.

Could it *possibly* be less than twenty-four hours? She already *loved* them, all three of them. How absurd!

How indescribably wonderful!

She had just realized something, though. They

must not know about Viscountess Whitleaf's part in the death of her father. They had not reacted in any way to his name.

They were not alone together all day, the four of them. Lady Markham, Theodore, Edith, and Mr. Morley were all tactful enough to remain in the background most of the time, but they all came together at mealtimes, and after luncheon Susanna and her grandmother went up to the nursery at Edith's invitation to see Jamie since this was apparently the most wakeful, alert, and cheerful part of his day.

"And of course," Edith said, "I want you to see him at his very best."

They stayed up there talking for longer than an hour after admiring the baby and handing him from one to the other and coaxing smiles from him. Susanna's grandmother held him in the crook of one arm while they sat and talked, and cooed down at him when he demanded attention.

It was during that hour and a bit, Susanna discovered later, that Viscount Whitleaf had called with two of his brothers-in-law and young Mr. Flynn-Posy.

She also discovered that during the visit her two grandfathers had gone off to the library with Viscount Whitleaf while the others had visited in the drawing room. Neither of them volunteered any further information—about who had initiated the private meeting or what the topic of conversation had been. And Susanna did not ask lest her grandparents think that she really was interested in him.

He was gone by the time she came downstairs.

But she would see him at the ball, she thought,

with a heart that tried to sink and soar at the same time, leaving her feeling horribly confused and not a little upset.

She *must not* begin thinking that an impossibility might after all be possible.

It was Peter who had asked to speak privately with the two elderly gentlemen who were staying at Fincham. While he was disappointed to learn on his arrival that Susanna was up in the nursery with Edith, he was also glad to find his plan easier to implement than he had expected it to be. He had merely asked Theo if he might use the library for a few minutes in order to have a word or two with Colonel Osbourne and the Reverend Clapton, and Theo had agreed—with a smirk.

Peter had come to the point after a few preliminary conversational niceties. Or, to be more accurate, it was the colonel, frowning ferociously and harrumphing through his large mustache, who brought him to the point.

"I understand, Whitleaf," he said, "that you had my granddaughter out in a *curricle* yesterday afternoon, without even so much as a groom up behind."

Peter felt very much as if a shotgun had been pressed to his spine.

The other old gentleman gazed genially at him—with perhaps a thread of steel behind the mild eyes.

"I did," he confessed—no point in lying and pretending to have had *six* eagle-eyed grooms all clinging to the back of his curricle to play chaperone. "I hope, sirs, to ask your granddaughter during tomorrow night's ball to honor me with her hand in marriage. I would like the blessing of both of you before I do so."

It had occurred to him last night that this was perhaps something he ought to do. Less laudably, it had also occurred to him that she might look more kindly upon his suit if he had their blessing.

A third thing that had occurred to him, of course, was that they might be very familiar indeed with the name of *Whitleaf*, and that he might be dooming his hopes to a horrible dashing if he approached them thus.

The Reverend Clapton beamed at him from his chair by the fire.

The colonel frowned fiercely at him from his stance by the desk.

"Why?" he barked. "Why do you wish to marry our granddaughter?"

"I have conceived a deep affection for her, sir," Peter said.

"Even though she was a dowerless nobody when you did it?" the colonel asked him, and Peter felt sorry for all the soldiers who had served under this man—theirs must not have been a comfortable life.

"Yes, sir," he said.

"Then you are a fool, Whitleaf," the old man said.

Peter raised his eyebrows.

"If loving Miss Osbourne for herself makes me a fool, sir," he said, "then I can only plead guilty."

"Which you must confess, Clarence," the clergyman said in a mild voice, "is an excellent answer. I would be inclined to give my blessing without further ado."

"Hmm," the colonel said, and it suddenly occurred

to Peter that the man was enjoying himself. "Well, she isn't a dowerless nobody, Whitleaf. She is a not inconsiderable heiress. What do you have to say to that?"

"That it is very pleasant for Miss Osbourne, sir," Peter said, "but that it has no effect whatsoever on my feelings for her."

"And what do *you* have to offer her, young man, apart from your affections, which may come cheap for all I know?" the colonel asked.

And Peter understood that they had entered the marriage negotiation phase of the conversation. His suit, he guessed, had been granted.

So he had won the approval of two elderly gentlemen.

That, he supposed, though, was going to be the easy part.

25

No one could remember the time when the last grand entertainment had been held at Sidley. For days the neighborhood had been buzzing with the news that there was finally to be a ball there, and on Christmas Day of all days. It seemed like a special gift from the young viscount.

He had always been liked and admired from afar. It had always been said that he was warmer, more human, than the viscountess, his mother. And now they were convinced of it. He had delivered the invitations personally and had begged everyone to come, to join his family and friends in a great celebration of the season—as if *they* were the ones doing *him* a favor.

No one would have missed the ball for any consideration whatsoever. Anticipation of the moment when they might decently leave for Sidley overshadowed all other observances of Christmas, even the morning church service and the dinnertime goose.

It was much the same at Sidley itself, though there was an afternoon party for the children in the drawing room hosted by the viscount and attended by many of their parents while most other adults rested in their rooms in preparation for the evening's revels.

The house was lavishly decorated with holly and pine boughs and ribbons and bells and a Yule log in the drawing room. There was also a large and intricately woven kissing bough there—the creation of three of the viscount's sisters—suspended from the center of the ceiling and the focus of much interested attention and stifled giggles after its appearance there late on Christmas Eve.

The house was filled too with enticing Christmas smells, even late in the day, long after the goose and the plum pudding had been cleared away from the dining room table. The smell of mince pies was the most dominant, but there was too the spicy aroma of the wassail, which was to fill the huge bowl in the refreshment room as soon as the ball began.

Peter enjoyed the day even though he had rarely spent a busier one. He was genuinely fond of all his sisters and brothers-in-law and nieces and nephews, and he found all the other guests congenial company. He was particularly delighted by the romance that appeared to be developing between one of Barbara's young brothers-in-law and Miss Flynn-Posy. Whether the lady's mother was equally delighted was unclear, but that was not his concern.

His own mother proved remarkably resilient. She showed no traces of the upset she had suffered two evenings ago. She spoke of the ball to everyone with an enthusiasm that suggested it had always had her full approval. She had even begun to speak out during the past two days about setting up a home for herself in London before the spring Season began so that she might enjoy more social life.

"It is high time," she told Lady Flynn-Posy and Barbara and Belinda. "Peter is quite old enough now to fend for himself."

Peter enjoyed the day, but it was the evening for which he waited with mingled eagerness and anxiety.

The eagerness was for the fact that this felt like his coming-of-age party. Tonight he would finally be the master of Sidley Park, entertaining his guests and neighbors as he planned to do for the rest of his life—regardless of the outcome of his other plan for the evening. It was the uncertainty of that outcome that caused his anxiety, of course. He was not at all certain that Susanna would have him even if he and her three grandparents all went down on their knees before her and begged.

Susanna Osbourne had a sometimes-annoying tendency to think for herself and decide for herself.

Not that he would have her any other way, of course.

But his newfound confidence in himself and determination to live his own life and take on the duties and responsibilities of his position would not be dependent upon Susanna's answer. They would not be worth a great deal if they were.

He *did* have her to thank. He would possibly have drifted on in much the same way as ever if he had not met her. But he was not dependent upon her—just as she was not on him. It was an exhilarating thought, but it did nothing to soothe his growing anxiety as he dressed for the ball.

The fact that he was titled and wealthy meant nothing to her—a humbling thought. If he was to win her, he must do it as himself—and for the first time in five years he felt that there was some self worth offering. But his name went along with that self. He was *Whitleaf,* and there, he knew, was the stumbling block.

"That will do," he told his valet, who had already discarded three perfectly decently tied neckcloths as unworthy of his artistry before tying this fourth.

His valet—another individual who had a mind of his own, dash it all—tipped his head to one side and considered his handiwork with frowning concentration.

"It will, m' lord," he agreed. "It only needs the diamond pin—just so—just . . . *there*. Perfection, m' lord."

It was still a little early, but Peter went downstairs anyway and wandered into the ballroom, which looked festive with all the decorations and smelled of greenery. Candles burned in the chandeliers overhead and in wall sconces. Two great fires burned in the fireplaces at either end of the room. They failed to warm the large, high-ceilinged room quite adequately, but they did take the chill off the air. And once the ballroom was filled with people, and once those people began to engage in the exertions of a few country dances, there would be more than enough warmth in the room.

The orchestra had arrived. Their instruments were laid out on the small dais in one corner of the ballroom. They were probably belowstairs, feasting on goose and stuffing.

A few servants were busy in the refreshment room beyond the ballroom. Peter wandered through there to chat with them. His only real concern about the ball had been his realization that the extra work would be a burden on the resident servants and would necessitate the hiring of more. But he had discovered when he asked that the prospect of serving at a grand ball at Sidley excited them all—even before they knew that he was doubling all their wages for both today and tomorrow. And tomorrow he would also present them all with a Christmas bonus that was more generous than usual.

And then he could hear that some other people—relatives and guests from the house—had arrived in the ballroom and he went back in there to speak with them. Soon now the first of the outside guests would arrive. He would greet them all at the ballroom door with his mother and Barbara and Clarence.

It was, he realized fifteen minutes later as he shook hands with Mr. Mummert and bowed to Mrs. and Miss Mummert, complimenting them both on their appearance and thanking them all for coming, the first time he had stood in a receiving line. It was the first time he had been the host of such an event.

It would not be the last, by Jove.

The party from Fincham was almost the last to arrive. Lady Markham came along the line with Theo, and Peter greeted them heartily. His mother and Lady Markham, he noticed, nodded civilly to each other. Edith and Morley followed and then Colonel and

Mrs. Osbourne. Susanna came last with her maternal grandfather.

Peter discovered that his heart was thudding so hard in his chest that he could actually *hear* it.

She was wearing the same green gown she had worn to the assembly in Somerset and to the concert in Bath Abbey. Her hair was brushed into soft curls, some of which were held in place by a little pearl tiara, which matched her pearl necklace. The pearls looked glossy and new and were, he would be willing to wager, a Christmas gift from one or more of her grandparents. Perhaps the delicate ivory fan she carried in one gloved hand was from the other.

Her cheeks were flushed but her eyes were downcast. She was not smiling. She would rather be anywhere else on earth than where she actually was, Peter guessed. Perhaps she would never forgive him for this. Perhaps she would always remember it as one of the worst evenings she had ever spent.

"It is good to see you again, sir," he said, bowing to the Reverend Clapton, who beamed genially back at him. "And you too, Miss Osbourne."

She raised her eyes briefly to his.

"Thank you, my lord," she said.

There was no one coming along directly after them. He spoke up before he should, perhaps, miss the opportunity.

"Will you honor me by dancing the second set with me?" he asked. "And the first waltz?"

He would dance the last one with her too—he hoped.

Her grandfather beamed even more jovially.

She hesitated for only a fraction of a moment.

"Thank you," she said. "That will be pleasant."

He would have asked for the opening set, but he would not embarrass her by singling her out so notably before all his family and neighbors. He would open the ball with Barbara.

The Reverend Clapton was bowing to his mother and smiling as he exchanged civilities with her. Peter was more than ever convinced that the name *Whitleaf* meant nothing to the gentleman—or to the Osbournes.

But Susanna's eyes were downcast again as she curtsied, and he could feel his mother stiffen.

"Miss Osbourne," she said, "how delightful that you are staying at Fincham at just this time. Do enjoy the ball."

"Thank you, ma'am," Susanna said without looking up at her.

It must have been an excruciating moment for each of them, Peter thought. Was he quite, quite mad to believe that he could ever marry Susanna and live happily-ever-after with her? But no, he had already decided that he did not believe in happily-ever-after. And he had already decided too that he would fight for happiness.

The moment was past, and both ladies were still in the ballroom, and both were smiling.

"Peter." Barbara linked an arm through his. "It is surely time to start the dancing. I am quite unwilling to delay any longer since I am to dance the *opening set* with my handsome brother. I will be the envy of every other lady in the room."

He laughed as he led her onto the floor, to the head

of the set that soon formed for the first country dance. Suddenly he felt lighthearted and filled with hope. It was Christmas, after all, the time of year most devoted to hope and new dreams and love.

"I am amazed to see Susanna Osbourne here," Barbara said. "Do you remember her? Her father was that unfortunate secretary of Sir Charles's who took his own life. We were always discouraged from having anything to do with her because her father was basically a servant, though Edith played with her all the time. And yet I always believed there was something of a friendship between Mama and Mr. Osbourne."

"I met her only once as a child," Peter said. "But I met her again this past summer at John Raycroft's and again during the autumn at the wedding breakfast in Bath I attended with Lauren and Kit."

"Did you?" she said with interest.

And then she glanced at Susanna, who was being led onto the floor by Theo, and looked back at him more sharply.

"Oh, *did* you!" she said.

Susanna reflected in some wonder on the fact that until the end of August she had never attended a single ball or assembly, whereas now she had been to two, *and* she had waltzed in the Upper Assembly Rooms in Bath.

And tonight she even had her grandmother as her chaperone and one grandfather to smile kindly at each of her prospective partners and another to frown suspiciously at them.

Although half the guests were clearly members of the *ton* and might have intimidated her a few months ago, all of them were just as clearly prepared to enjoy themselves. And the other half of the guests were what she thought of as ordinary people. They reminded her of Frances's neighbors whom she liked so well.

The ballroom, heavily laden with Christmas greenery and decorations, was breathtaking. Even without the decorations it would be a lovely room, she guessed. It was amazing that she had lived so close to Sidley for twelve years without once even so much as seeing the house.

She would have been enjoying herself enormously, she thought at the end of the fourth set as the very young and eager Mr. Flynn-Posy led her back to her grandmother's side, if only . . .

Ah, her life had been blighted with if-onlys since the summer.

She would forget them for tonight. She would simply enjoy herself. She had already danced four sets in a row—one of them, a set of vigorous country dances, with Peter. The next set was to be a waltz.

She would not even think of it as the last waltz.

"You dance so prettily, Susanna," her grandmother said, taking her by the hand and drawing her down to sit beside her. "And you *are* so pretty. How proud I am of you, and how happy to have lived to see this day."

And then Peter was there again, bowing and smiling and charming her grandmother, and finally turning to *her* and holding out one hand.

"This is my waltz, I believe, Miss Osbourne," he said.

And then once more they were waltzing. Except that this time, though she smiled into his eyes and smelled his cologne and felt the exhilaration of every step they took, she did not lose herself in the dance. This time she was aware of his home about them and his family and neighbors. She was aware of her own family and almost wept at the novelty of the thought. She was aware of her friends—and the Markhams and Morleys *were* her friends and always had been. She did not know what Lady Markham had meant in that long-ago snippet of conversation she had overheard outside the nursery, and she had not asked, but she knew now that Lady Markham had always cared for her and would have somehow continued to do so. It really *must* have been a burden to be left so suddenly with an orphan child and not to know what to do with her.

And she was aware of Christmas, that season of love and family and peace and generosity.

It was all, she thought, simply magical.

"A penny for them," Peter said as they twirled about a corner, and she remembered that he had said that to her once before, after their walk to the waterfall. She had been feeling melancholy then.

"You *do* belong here," she said. "I am so glad I have seen you here in your own proper milieu. I think your dream is within your grasp."

He smiled as he twirled her again—and somehow they ended up outside the ballroom doors, and he was taking her by the hand and striding purposefully off with her in the direction of the hallway. Except that they did not go all the way there, but stopped outside a closed door, which he opened, and then proceeded inside before he closed the door firmly behind them.

It was a library, she could see, a beautiful, cozy room dimly lit by a fire burning in the hearth and a single branch of candles on the mantel.

"Peter?" she said. "The waltz? My grandparents . . ."

". . . know that I am bringing you here," he said. "At least, your grandfathers do, and I suppose your grandmother does too. She smiled *very* sweetly at me in the receiving line."

He released her hand and strode over to the fire and busied himself with poking it into fresh life.

Susanna went a little closer herself and sat on the edge of a chair.

Her grandparents *knew*?

But they did *not* know . . .

He straightened up and stood gazing into the fire, his back to her. She waited for him to speak. And she ached with love for him. And with a knowledge of his kindness, his tenderness, his passion, his very essence.

"My mother drove your father to his death," he said.

Ah, so he knew? But surely he had not known two days ago.

"He killed *himself*," she said. "He might have made a different choice."

"She has lived with remorse ever since," he said, "a fact that does not, of course, excuse what she did. I love her, Susanna. I always have, and I always will. Love, I have discovered, does not judge. It just *is*."

"My mother and my father did dreadful things," she said. "Among other things they broke the hearts of my grandparents. They caused the death of my uncle. But I have always loved them both though I never knew my mother."

"What I mean," he said, resting one hand on the high mantel and dipping his head forward, "is that I will never renounce her, Susanna. I will always visit her, and she will always be welcome here, though it will not be her home for much longer. We will be finding somewhere for her to live in London. If I were ever asked to choose between her and you, I would not do it. I would refuse. One cannot choose between love and love. One can choose only by judging one choice better, more worthy, than the other."

She swallowed.

"Peter," she said, "you do not have to make a choice. I am going back to school in a few days' time. My grandparents want me to go and live with them, but I have said no. I will gladly spend holidays with them. I will write to them constantly, but I will not live with them. Or with you."

His head dipped even farther forward, and there was a lengthy silence between them while she listened to the waltz music coming from the ballroom. Then he straightened up and turned to look at her.

"Tell me you do not love me," he said.

She shook her head slowly.

"*Tell* me."

"Love does not have anything to do with anything," she said.

"I beg to disagree," he said. "Love has everything

to do with everything. Tell me you do not love me and I will take you back to the ballroom and we will not see each other again after this evening. Tell me, Susanna. But tell me the truth."

She had never seen him so serious. His face looked drawn and pale in the candlelight. His eyes were intense on hers.

"Peter," she said, looking sharply down at her hands, "it would be distasteful, even sordid, when your mother and my father . . ."

". . . were lovers," he said. "Did it seem sordid at Barclay Court? Did it seem sordid at the dower house two days ago? It *is* an ugly fact, and it *should* make any connection between you and me somewhat distasteful. But we cannot do anything to change the past. It is as it is. Are we willing to give up the present and the future because of it? Life is not perfect, Susanna. We can only live the reality of what is. It would not be possible without love. I know it is something of a cliché to say that love makes all things possible, but I believe it does. It is not a magic wand that can be waved over life to make it all sweet and lovely and trouble-free, but it *can* give the energy to fight the odds and win."

She raised her eyes to his.

"And love is something we have in abundance," he said. "Tell me if I am wrong."

She said nothing.

"Not just a sweet, sentimental, romantic kind of love," he said, "though there is that too. You have the gritty kind of love, Susanna, which would sacrifice your own happiness if necessary and carry on with life without bitterness. And I have learned a great deal about it in the last little while. I love my family and my home. And I love you."

"Peter," she said, but she shook her head and could say no more. She bit her lower lip.

"Are you going to destroy our love," he said, "just because I am wealthy and titled and you are a school-teacher—though you are something of an heiress too, I was informed yesterday. And just because I am *Whitleaf*? Just because I will always honor my mother? Just because she and your father once sought comfort for their loneliness with each other?"

She closed her eyes.

"Or are you going to marry me?" he asked her. "Are you going to make three elderly people in the ballroom very happy by allowing me to make an announcement tonight?"

"Oh, Peter!" She looked up sharply. "That is *grossly* unfair."

He stared grimly back at her. And then he smiled. And then grinned.

"It is rather, is it not?" he said. "But *will* you? Make them happy, that is?"

She had simply *despised* all those girls in Somerset who had melted beneath his every smile—until, that was, she had realized that it was his sheer likability they had responded to. But even so . . .

Was she to become one of them?

"What does your mother have to say about this?" she asked him. "Have you told her?"

"I have," he said. "My mother has been possessive, a little domineering, even selfish, in her dealings with me during my lifetime, Susanna, but there is no doubt in my mind that she loves both my sisters and me totally. She will love my wife rather than lose me. I cannot promise you an easy relationship with her, but I believe I can assure you that it will not be impossible—unless it is to you."

She gazed at him. Was this really possible after all, then? Or was she listening with her heart rather than with her common sense?

Was it with one's heart that one *ought* to listen?

And then he took away all her power to listen with anything *but* her heart. He closed the distance between them, possessed himself of her gloved hand in both his own, and went down on one knee before her.

"Another horrible cliché," he said with a grin. But the grin faded almost immediately. "Susanna, will you please, please marry me? If you cannot truthfully tell me that you do not love me, will you tell me instead that you will marry me?"

And the only protest she could think of making was an utter absurdity.

"Peter," she said, leaning a little closer to him, "I am a *teacher*. I have obligations to my girls and to Claudia Martin. I cannot simply walk out in the middle of a school year."

"When does it finish?" he asked her.

"July," she said.

"Then we will marry in August," he said. "The month we met. That particular dragon, you see, was not even worthy of the name. A mere worm. Any others?"

"Oh," she said helplessly, "there must be *dozens*."

"Then you had better name them quickly," he said,

"or it will be too late. I am going to kiss you very thoroughly and then bear you off in triumph to the ballroom. Supper follows the waltz—the perfect time for announcements. I arranged it that way."

"You are very confident, then, Lord Whitleaf," she said.

"I am not," he said. "Heaven help me, I am not, Susanna. Put me out of my misery. Tell me that you love me—or do not. Tell me you will marry me—or will not. Please, my love. I am *not* confident."

She supposed the dozen reasons for saying no would rush at her long before the night was out. She supposed equally well that she would vanquish them one at a time by the simple expedient of remembering how he looked at this precise moment—anxious, his eyes full of uncertainty and love, down on one knee. And by remembering how *she* felt at this moment—overwhelmed by love.

She drew her hand free of his, cupped his face with both hands, and leaned forward to kiss him softly on the lips.

"I do," she said softly, "and I will."

"I *knew*," he said, "that I should have done this in the drawing room rather than in here. There is a kissing bough there. I suppose, though, I will manage well enough without one."

And suddenly he was on his feet, bringing her to hers at the same time and drawing her into an embrace that proved his supposition quite correct.

And the strange thing was, Susanna thought—when she could think at all—that it was not in any way a lascivious kiss that they shared, lengthy as it was. It was one of joy, of hope, of commitment, of love.

Ah, yes, those dozen reasons were not going to stand even a moment's chance of being allowed a hearing.

"My love," he said against her lips. "My *love*."

"Peter," she said.

And they kissed again before he placed her hand very formally on his arm and led her back in the direction of the ballroom.

The music had stopped.

Everyone was already at supper.

Her betrothal was about to be announced. Her *betrothal*.

26

The wedding of Susanna Osbourne to Viscount Whiteleaf was solemnized at the church near Alvesley Park in Wiltshire on a perfect day in August.

Alvesley had been chosen from among a number of contending places—for a number of reasons. Although Susanna's grandparents had been eager to host the event in Gloucestershire, even they admitted that their homes and the village inn could not possibly accommodate all the distinguished guests who would be invited and that the assembly rooms above the inn would be a shabby location for the wedding breakfast even if they had been large enough.

Sidley was a serious contender, but how could Susanna's fellow teachers travel so far when there were charity girls to look after? And the viscount would not hear of marrying his lady *without* her friends in attendance.

For a while only Bath seemed a viable option—and one that was perfectly acceptable to both the bride and the groom—until Lauren, Viscountess Ravensberg, and the Duchess of Bewcastle again took it upon themselves to organize wedding celebrations. Though actually it was Eleanor Thompson who set the plans in motion when she informed her sister in her weekly letter of the predicament concerning the charity girls and commented upon the vast size of Lindsey Hall.

No one ever knew—or asked—how the duchess persuaded the very toplofty Duke of Bewcastle to take in twelve schoolgirls for a whole week surrounding the wedding of one of their teachers, but she did, and his grace was even seen to smile upon her during the wedding itself, a rare enough public display of affection.

Alvesley it was, then, and guests came from every corner of England, it seemed, and even from Scotland and Wales—the viscount's sister and her husband from the former, Mr. and Mrs. Sydnam Butler with David and their four-month-old daughter from the latter. The viscountess came from London, where she had enjoyed a gratifyingly successful Season, having drawn the admiring attentions of two distinguished widowers. She came despite the fact that she had not seen Lauren, her niece, since the latter was a baby. The viscount's sisters and their families came, as did some of his friends, most notably Theo Markham and John Raycroft with his new bride.

Susanna's grandparents came with two of her aunts and their husbands, whom she had met during a visit at Easter. And all her closest friends were there— Claudia Martin, Anne Butler with Mr. Butler, and the Countess of Edgecombe with her husband, newly returned from a singing engagement in Paris. Eleanor Thompson was there and Lila Walton and Cecile

Pierre, the French and music teacher, and even Mr. Huckerby had made the journey from Bath. And of course, the twelve charity pupils attended the wedding too, supervised by Miss Thompson and Miss Walton, though they were so thoroughly awed by the occasion and the company that no supervision was really necessary. Even Agnes Ryde was mute and wide-eyed.

It was a wedding worth waiting for, as the bride and groom agreed after the event. But, ah, the wait had been tedious in the extreme.

On three separate occasions between Christmas and August the viscount had traveled to Bath. On two of those occasions he had stayed for a week, on the third for ten days. And yet he had found his sojourns there almost more frustrating than the long spells when he was *not* there, since Susanna flatly refused to neglect any of her duties—or would certainly have done so if he had ever asked. During those weeks he had come to understand that a teacher's work was more a way of life than a job. There was almost literally no spare time, even for a languishing fiancé.

Apart from the dreariness and frustrations of the wait, though, they had been happy months for Peter, who felt that all his dreams had suddenly come true and would come to full fruition once he had a wife by his side at Sidley—not that a wife had been part of the original dream. Once she *was* there, he doubted that he would ever want to step beyond the bounds of Sidley and its neighborhood—his home, his circle of contentment and happiness.

Susanna *did* have regrets about the life she would leave behind on her marriage. The school had been home and haven to her as a girl. It was where her be-wildered, badly bruised heart had healed. It had been home and workplace during her young adulthood. She loved teaching, she loved the girls, she loved her fellow teachers, especially Claudia, who had been both sister and mother as well as friend to her for many years.

But all women must leave behind their homes and their families when they married. And in her case it was, she believed with growing conviction as the months passed, a worthy exchange. She could never have been truly happy as an unmarried woman, with no man, no children, no home of her very own. Not *truly* happy. And she loved Peter far more deeply than she could have imagined loving any man. Perhaps it was because she liked him and admired him as much as she loved him.

And there was no school near Sidley, she had dis-covered. It was a lack she meant to rectify, and though Peter had merely laughed when she had mentioned it during one of his visits to Bath, it had been an affec-tionate, indulgent laugh, and there had been love and admiration in his eyes.

She had dreaded the end of school in July, telling herself with each passing event that it was the *last* in which she would be involved. At the same time, she had thought the end of term would *never* come.

She was to have a *wedding* in August.

She was to marry *Peter*.

She was to spend the rest of her life with him, for as long as they both lived.

But August came, as it inevitably does each year.

And with it came the wedding day, a perfect blue-skied sunshiny day.

Peter was sitting at the front of the church, John Raycroft beside him, aware that the pews behind them were filling with guests, though he did not turn his head to look.

He felt, in fact, as though it would be impossible to turn his head if he tried. Surely for once in an otherwise exemplary career, his valet had knotted his neckcloth very much too tightly, though the man had almost wept over its perfection after standing back to examine his handiwork an hour or so ago.

He ought not to have come so early, he thought, as his stomach started to feel like a churning cauldron.

What if she simply did not come?

What if someone spoke up during that dreaded silence after the vicar had asked if anyone knew of any impediment to the marriage?

What if his tongue tied itself in knots?

What if he dropped the ring?

What if Raycroft had forgotten to bring it?

"Do you have the ring?" he whispered out of the side of his mouth.

"I do," Raycroft whispered back with smirking complacency—though he had been just as much of a wreck two months ago when Peter had been *his* best man. "Just as I did when you asked five minutes ago."

What if she said *I don't* instead of *I do*? Or was that *I won't* and *I will*? He could not for the life of him remember what the correct wording was. He must listen *very* carefully to the vicar when the time came.

What if? . . .

Oh, Lord.

And then there was a distinct swell in the hushed murmurings from the pews behind, and he guessed that Susanna must have arrived with Colonel Osbourne. And then he was sure of it as he looked up at the vicar and the Reverend Clapton, who was celebrating the nuptial service with him, and saw that the latter was beaming with grandfatherly pride as his eyes focused on someone at the back of the church.

Peter stood and turned as the organ began to play.

And there she was.

Finally the phrase made perfect sense to him.

She was dressed from head to toe in delicate ivory, her gown fine lace over satin, her bonnet covered with lace, one layer of which covered her face. She looked small, almost fragile, beside her large grandfather with his erect military bearing. She also looked incredibly lovely. And no bonnet or layer of lace could obscure those bright golden-red curls.

As she came closer, he could see her face and her eyes. They were looking back into his own, huge with anxiety and perhaps wonder and—oh, yes, and definitely with love.

Ah, Susanna.

Even now he could not quite believe that they had overcome the odds to reach this moment.

He realized that he had been gazing back, an identical look on his own face. But no one was going to speak during that moment of silence, and no one was going to drop the ring, and Raycroft *did* have it with him. His tongue would remain unknotted, and she would say *I do* or *I will,* whichever it was.

All was well.

He smiled slowly at her and felt such a welling of happiness that it almost threatened to overwhelm him.

He smiled, and suddenly the sunshine shone as brightly inside the church as it did outside.

But he looked so much like the man who had dazzled and terrified her on the lane from Barclay Court almost exactly a year ago that she marveled how a stranger could become the very beat of her heart in so short a time. And this time it did not matter that he was Viscount *Whitleaf.* It was a name, a title, that she would share in a few minutes' time.

He was dressed elegantly in black and cream and white.

There surely could be no more handsome man in the world.

Her inexplicable terror vanished.

She had wept in her grandmother's arms early in the morning but had been unable to explain even to herself why she did so. Grandmama had said it was because she was in love, that if she were marrying for any other reason, she would do so with steely calm. She had blown her nose and laughed.

But the terror had remained, and it had been very difficult to stay dry-eyed when Anne and Frances came to her dressing room to hug her, and very nearly impossible when Claudia had arrived and held her close for surely a whole minute before releasing her.

"Susanna," she had said, "I found it difficult to let Frances and Anne go—they were and are dear friends. But you are more than a friend. You came to me as a bewildered, sullen, unhappy girl, and I loved you from the first moment, well before your true nature shone through. I *would not* let you go to any man who was unworthy of you or to anyone you did not love with all your heart. Though what I would do to stop you I do not know."

She had laughed and stepped back and dried her eyes.

"Ah," she had said, "why did I neglect to notice that all three of you were young, lovely women? If I *had* noticed, I would not have befriended any of you in a million years. I would have remained aloof."

She had laughed again and looked fondly at each of them in turn.

And now, Susanna discovered as soon as Peter smiled, she was not terrified at all. Why should she be? This was her wedding day, and here they were at church together. And there was something more than the smile itself to dazzle her.

There was the look in his eyes.

It warmed her from the roots of her hair to the tips of her toes.

"Dearly beloved," the vicar began.

And indeed it was a brief moment of time after the long wait. But a glorious moment nonetheless. Peter spoke his responses, she spoke hers, the shiny gold ring slid onto her finger—ah, but she could not list all the moments. It was all one jumble of happiness.

And then the vicar—no, Grandpapa Clapton—was pronouncing them man and wife and leading them off to the vestry to sign the register. And Peter was lifting her veil up over the brim of her bonnet and—quite scandalously—kissing her briefly right on the lips. With the vicar and Mr. Raycroft and both her grandfathers looking on.

The organ was beginning a loud, joyful anthem as they came out of the vestry and proceeded along the nave, past the pews occupied by their relatives and friends. It seemed to Susanna that she had never smiled so much in her life—and yet she bestowed a special smile on her girls, seated side by side in two pews, all neatly clothed in their Sunday best, all on their very best behavior.

She had once been one of them.

A gaily decorated open barouche awaited them outside the church gates. A crowd of villagers had gathered to enjoy the show. But they did not hurry toward the gates. The congregation spilled out behind them, and they were caught up in hugs and handshakes and smiling greetings. They were also showered with rose petals, mostly by the girls.

They were flushed and laughing by the time they had climbed into the barouche and someone had closed the door and given the coachman the signal to drive off toward Alvesley for the wedding breakfast.

Susanna sat across one corner of the seat, Peter across the other corner, their hands clasped on the seat between them, their fingers laced as they waved to the crowd in the churchyard and out on the road.

And then, apart from the stiff-backed coachman, they were alone together.

Susanna looked at Peter. He was smiling back at her.

"Come here," he said softly.

"Why?" She smiled too.

"Because I say so," he said, "and you are my wife."

His eyes danced with merriment.

"Indeed?" she said, and stayed where she was.

He sighed out loud and moved across the seat toward her.

"There goes my dream of a docile wife and a happily-ever-after," he said, setting his arms about her and drawing her very firmly against him so that her hands were splayed against his chest. "I suppose you are going to make me fight dragons for the rest of my life?"

"Every day," she assured him.

His eyes laughed into hers, and hers laughed back.

"May I kiss you, then, Lady Whitleaf?" he asked.

"I thought," she said, "you would never ask."

But her laughter was cut off when his mouth covered hers.

And joy became more joyful.

How could an absolute be improved upon?

It was *definitely* not a problem to be pondered today.

Susanna wrapped one arm about her new husband's neck and kissed him with all the ardor in her soul.

They could still hear the church bells pealing in the village behind them.

About the Author

MARY BALOGH is the *New York Times* bestselling author of the acclaimed Slightly novels: *Slightly Married, Slightly Wicked, Slightly Scandalous, Slightly Tempted, Slightly Sinful,* and *Slightly Dangerous,* as well as the romances *No Man's Mistress, More than a Mistress,* and *One Night for Love.* She is also the author of *Simply Love* and *Simply Unforgettable,* the first two books in her dazzling quartet of novels set at Miss Martin's School for Girls. *Simply Perfect,* the fourth book in the quartet, will be available in April 2008 from Delacorte Press. A former teacher herself, Balogh grew up in Wales and now lives in Canada.

Read on for a sneak peek
at the next enchanting novel
in Mary Balogh's series
featuring the teachers at
Miss Martin's School for Girls.

Simply Perfect

CLAUDIA MARTIN'S STORY

Coming in spring 2008

From Delacorte Press

MARY BALOGH

SIMPLY PERFECT

Simply Perfect
on sale spring 2008

Claudia Martin had already had a hard day at school.
First Mademoiselle Pierre, one of the nonresident
teachers, had sent a messenger just before breakfast with
the news that she was indisposed with a migraine
headache and would be unable to come to school, and
Claudia, as both owner and headmistress, had been
obliged to conduct most of the French and music classes
in addition to her own subjects. French was no great
problem; music was more of a challenge. Worse, the ac-
count books, which she had intended to bring up to date
during her spare classes today, remained undone, with
days fast running out in which to get accomplished all
the myriad tasks that needed doing.

Then just before the noonday meal, when classes
were over for the morning and discipline was at its slack-
est, Paula Hern had decided that she objected to the way
Molly Wiggins *looked* at her and voiced her displeasure
publicly and eloquently. And since Paula's father was a
successful businessman and as rich as Croesus and she
put on airs accordingly while Molly was the youngest—
and most timid—of the charity girls and did not even

know who her father was, then *of course* Agnes Ryde had felt obliged to jump into the fray in vigorous defense of the downtrodden, her Cockney accent returning with ear-jarring clarity. Claudia had been forced to deal with the matter and extract more-or-less sincere apologies from all sides and mete out suitable punishments to all except the more-or-less innocent Molly.

Then, an hour later, just when Miss Walton had been about to step outdoors with the junior class en route to Bath Abbey, where she had intended to give an informal lesson in art and architecture, the heavens had opened in a downpour to end downpours and there had been all the fuss of finding the girls somewhere else to go within the school and something else to do. Not that that had been Claudia's problem, but she *had* been made annoyingly aware of the girls' loud disappointment beyond her classroom door as she struggled to teach French irregular verbs. She had finally gone out there to inform them that if they had any complaint about the untimely arrival of the rain, then they must take it up privately with God during their evening prayers, but in the meantime they would be *silent* until Miss Walton had closed a classroom door behind them.

Then, just after classes were finished for the afternoon and the girls had gone upstairs to comb their hair and wash their hands for tea, something had gone wrong with the doorknob on one of the dormitories and eight of the girls, trapped inside until Mr. Keeble, the elderly school porter, had creaked his way up there to release them before mending the knob, had screeched and giggled and rattled the door. Miss Thompson had dealt with the crisis by reading them a lecture on patience and decorum, though circumstances had forced her to speak in a voice that could be heard from within—and there-fore through much of the rest of the school too, includ-ing Claudia's office.

It had *not* been the best of days, as Claudia had just been remarking—without contradiction—to Eleanor Thompson and Lila Walton over tea in her private sit-ting room a short while after the prisoners had been freed. She could do with far fewer such days.

And yet now!

Now, to cap everything off and make an already try-ing day more so, there was a marquess awaiting her pleasure in the visitors' parlor downstairs.

A *marquess,* for the love of all that was wonderful!

That was what the silver-edged visiting card she held be-tween two fingers said—the *Marquess of Attingsborough.* The porter had just delivered it into her hands, looking sour and disapproving as he did so—a not unusual expression for him, especially when any male who was not a teacher invaded his domain.

"A *marquess,*" she said, looking up from the card to frown at her fellow teachers. "Whatever can he want? Did he say, Mr. Keeble?"

"He did not say and I did not ask, miss," the porter replied. "But if you was to ask me, he is up to no good. He *smiled* at me."

"Ha! A cardinal sin indeed," Claudia said dryly while Eleanor laughed.

"Perhaps," Lila suggested, "he has a daughter he wishes to place at the school."

"A *marquess?*" Claudia raised her eyebrows and Lila looked suitably quelled.

"Perhaps, Claudia," Eleanor said, a twinkle in her eye, "he has *two* daughters."

Claudia snorted and then sighed, took one more sip of her tea, and got reluctantly to her feet.

"I suppose I had better go and see what he wants," she said. "It will be more productive than sitting here guessing. But of all things to happen today of all days. A *marquess*."

Eleanor laughed again. "Poor man," she said. "I pity him."

Claudia had never had much use for the aristocracy—idle, arrogant, coldhearted, nasty lot—though the marriage of two of her teachers and closest friends to titled gentlemen had forced her to admit during the past few years that perhaps *some* of them might be agreeable and even worthy individuals. But it did not amuse her to have one of their number, a stranger, intrude into her own world without a by-your-leave, especially at the end of a difficult day.

She did not believe for a single moment that this marquess wished to place any daughter of his at her school.

She preceded Mr. Keeble down the stairs since she did not wish to move at his slow pace. She ought, she supposed, to have gone into her bedchamber first to see that she was looking respectable, which she was quite possibly not doing after a hard day at school. She usually made sure that she presented a neat appearance to visitors. But she scorned to make such an effort for a *marquess* and risk appearing obsequious in her own eyes.

By the time she opened the door into the visitors' parlor, she was bristling with a quite unjustified indignation. How dared he come here to disturb her on her own property, whatever his business might be.

She looked down at the visiting card still in her hand.

"The Marquess of Attingsborough?" she said in a

voice not unlike the one she had used on Paula Hern earlier in the day—the one that said she was not going to be at all impressed by any pretension of grandeur.

"At your service, ma'am. Miss Martin, I presume?" He was standing across the room, close to the window. He bowed elegantly.

Claudia's indignation soared. One steady glance at him was not sufficient upon which to make any informed judgment of his character, of course, but *really*, if the man had any imperfection of form or feature or taste in apparel, it was by no means apparent. He was tall and broad of shoulder and chest and slim of waist and hips. His legs were long and well shaped. His hair was dark and thick and shining, his face handsome, his eyes and mouth good-humored. He was dressed with impeccable elegance but without a trace of ostentation. His Hessian boots alone were probably worth a fortune, and Claudia guessed that if she were to stand directly over them and look down, she would see her own face reflected in them—and probably her flat, untidy hair and limp dress collar as well.

She clasped her hands at her waist lest she test her theory by touching the collar points. She held his card pinched between one thumb and forefinger.

"What may I do for you, sir?" she asked, deliberately avoiding calling him *my lord*—a ridiculous affectation, in her opinion.

He smiled at her, and if perfection could be improved upon, it had just happened—he had good teeth. Claudia steeled herself to resist the charm she was sure he possessed in aces.

"I come as a messenger, ma'am," he said, "from Lady Whitleaf."

He reached into an inner pocket of his coat and withdrew a sealed paper.

"From Susanna?" Claudia took one step farther into the room.

Susanna Osbourne had been a teacher at the school until her marriage last year to Viscount Whitleaf. Claudia had always rejoiced at Susanna's good fortune in making both an eligible marriage and a love match and yet she still mourned her own loss of a dear friend and colleague *and* a good teacher. She had lost three such friends—all in the same cause—over the course of four years. Sometimes it was hard not to be selfishly depressed by it all.

"When she knew I was coming to Bath to spend a few days with my mother and my father, who is taking the waters," the marquess said, "she asked me to call here and pay my respects to you. And she gave me this letter, perhaps to convince you that I am no impostor."

His eyes smiled again as he came across the room and placed the letter in her hand. And as if at least his eyes could not have been mud-colored or something equally nondescript, she could see that they were a clear blue, almost like a summer sky.

Susanna had asked him to come and pay his respects? *Why?*

"Whitleaf is the cousin of a cousin of mine," the marquess explained. "Or an *almost* cousin of mine, anyway. It is complicated, as family relationships often are. Lauren Butler, Viscountess Ravensberg, is a cousin by virtue of the fact that her mother married my aunt's brother-in-law. We have been close since childhood. And Whitleaf is Lauren's first cousin. And so in a sense both he and his lady have a strong familial claim on me."

If he was a marquess, Claudia thought with sudden suspicion, and his father was still alive, *what did that make his father?* But he was here at Susanna's behest and it behooved her to be a little better than just icily polite.

"Thank you," she said, "for coming in person to deliver the letter. I am much obliged to you, sir. May I offer you a cup of tea?" She willed him to say no.

"I will not put you to that trouble, ma'am," he said, smiling again. "I understand you are to leave for London in two days' time?"

Ah. Susanna must have told him that. Mr. Hatchard, her man of business in London, had found employment for two of her senior girls, both charity pupils, but he had been unusually evasive about the identity of the prospective employers, even when she had asked quite specifically in her last letter to him. The paying girls at the school had families to look after their interests, of course. Claudia had appointed herself family to the rest and never released any girl who had no employment to which to go or any about whose expected employment she felt any strong misgiving.

At Eleanor's suggestion, Claudia was going to go to London with Flora Bains and Edna Wood so that she could find out exactly where they were to be placed as governesses and to withdraw her consent if she was not satisfied. There were still a few weeks of the school year left, but Eleanor had assured her that she was perfectly willing and able to take charge of affairs during Claudia's absence, which would surely be no longer than a week or ten days. Claudia had agreed to go, partly because there was another matter too upon which she wished to speak with Mr. Hatchard in person.

"I am," she told the marquess.

"Whitleaf intended to send a carriage for your convenience," the marquess told her, "but I was able to inform him that it would be quite unnecessary to put himself to the trouble."

"Of course it would," Claudia agreed. "I have already hired a carriage."

"I will see about *un*hiring it for you, if I may be permitted, ma'am," he said. "I plan to return to town on the same day and will be pleased to offer you the comfort of my own carriage and my protection for the journey."

Oh, goodness, heaven forbid!

"That will be quite unnecessary, sir," she said firmly. "I have already made the arrangements."

"Hired carriages are notorious for their lack of springs and all other comforts," he said. "I beg you will reconsider."

"Perhaps you do not fully understand, sir," she said. "I am to be accompanied by two schoolgirls on the journey."

"Yes," he said, "so Lady Whitleaf informed me. Do they prattle? Or, worse, do they giggle? Very young ladies have an atrocious tendency to do both."

"My girls are taught how to behave appropriately in company, Lord Attingsborough," she said stiffly. Too late she saw the twinkle in his eyes and understood that he had been joking.

"I do not doubt it, ma'am," he said, "and feel quite confident in trusting your word. Allow me, if you will, to escort all three of you ladies to Lady Whitleaf's door. She will be vastly impressed with my gallantry and will be bound to spread the word among my family and friends."

Now he was talking utter nonsense. But how could she decently refuse? She desperately searched around in her head for some irrefutable argument that would dissuade him. Nothing came to mind, however, that did not seem ungracious, even downright rude. But she would rather travel a thousand miles in a springless carriage than to London in his company.

Why?

Was she overawed by his title and magnificence? She bristled at the very idea.

At his...*maleness,* then? She was uncomfortably aware that he possessed that in abundance.

But how ridiculous that would be. He was simply a gentleman offering a courtesy to an aging spinster, who happened to be a friend of his almost-cousin's cousin's wife—goodness, it *was* a tenuous connection. But she held a letter from Susanna in her hand. Susanna obviously trusted him.

An *aging spinster?* When it came to any consideration of age, she thought, there was probably not much difference between the two of them. Now *there* was a thought. Here was this man, obviously at the very pinnacle of his masculine appeal in his middle thirties, and then there was she.

He was looking at her with raised eyebrows and smiling eyes.

"Oh, very well," she said briskly. "But you may live to regret your offer."

His smile broadened and it seemed to an indignant Claudia that there was no end to this man's appeal. As she had suspected, he had charm oozing from every pore and was therefore *not* to be trusted one inch farther than she could see him. She would keep a *very* careful eye upon her two girls during the journey to London.

"I do hope not, ma'am," he said. "Shall we make an early start?"

"It is what I intended," she told him. She added grudgingly, "Thank you, Lord Attingsborough. You are most kind."

"It will be my pleasure, Miss Martin." He bowed deeply again. "May I ask a small favor in return? May I be given a tour of the school? I must confess that the idea of an institution that actually provides an *education* to girls fascinates me. Lady Whitleaf has spoken with enthusiasm about your establishment. She taught here, I understand."

Claudia drew a slow, deep breath through flared nostrils. Whatever reason could this man have for touring a girls' school except idle curiosity—or worse? Her instinct was to say a very firm no. But she had just accepted a favor from him, and it was admittedly a large one—she did not doubt that his carriage would be far more comfortable than the one she had hired or that they would be treated with greater respect at every toll gate they passed and at every inn where they stopped for a change of horses. And he was a friend of Susanna's.

But really!

She had not thought her day could possibly get any worse. She had been wrong.

"Certainly. I will show you around myself," she said curtly, turning to the door. She would have opened it herself, but he reached around her, engulfing her for a startled moment in the scent of some enticing and doubtless indecently expensive male cologne, opened the door, and indicated with a smile that she should precede him into the hall.

At least, she thought, classes were over for the day and all the girls would be safely in the dining hall, having tea.

She was wrong about that, of course, she remembered as soon as she opened the door into the art room. The final assembly of the school year was not far off and all sorts of preparations and rehearsals were in progress, as they had been every day for the past week or so.

A few of the girls were working with Mr. Upton on the stage backdrop. They all turned to see who had come in and then proceeded to gawk at the grand visitor. Claudia was obliged to introduce the two men. They shook hands, and the marquess strolled closer to inspect the artwork and ask a few intelligent questions. Mr. Upton beamed at him when he left the room with her a few minutes later, and all the girls gazed worshipfully after him.

And then in the music room they came upon the madrigal choir, which was practicing in the absence of Mademoiselle Pierre under the supervision of Miss Wilding. They hit an ear-shattering discord at full volume just as Claudia opened the door, and then they dissolved into self-conscious giggles while Miss Wilding blushed and looked dismayed.

Claudia, raising her eyebrows, introduced the teacher to the marquess and explained that the regular choirmistress was indisposed today. Though even as she spoke she was annoyed with herself for feeling that any explanation was necessary.

"Madrigal singing," he said, smiling at the girls, "can be the most satisfying but the most frustrating thing, can it not? There is perhaps one other person out of the group singing the same part as oneself and six or eight others all bellowing out something quite different. If one's lone ally falters one is lost without hope of recovery. I never mastered the art when I was at school, I must confess. During my very first practice someone suggested to me that I try out for the cricket team— which just happened to practice at the same time."

The girls laughed, and all of them visibly relaxed.

"I will wager," he said, "that there is something in your repertoire that you can sing to perfection. May I be honored to hear it?" He turned his smile upon Miss Wilding.

" 'The Cuckoo,' miss," Sylvia Hetheridge suggested to a murmur of approval from the rest of the group.

And they sang in five parts without once faltering or hitting a sour note, a glorious shower of "cuckoos" echoing about the room every time they reached the chorus of the song.

When they were finished, they all turned as one to the Marquess of Attingsborough, just as if he were visiting royalty, and he applauded and smiled.

"Bravo!" he said. "Your skill overwhelms me, not to mention the loveliness of your voices. I am more than ever convinced that I was wise to stick to cricket."

The girls were all laughing and gazing worshipfully after him when he left with Claudia.

Mr. Huckerby was in the dancing hall, putting a group of girls through their paces in a particularly intricate dance that they would perform during the assembly. The marquess shook his hand and smiled at the girls and admired their performance and charmed them until they were all smiling and—of course—*gazing worshipfully at him*.

He asked intelligent and perceptive questions of

Claudia as she showed him some of the empty class-rooms and the library. He was in no hurry as he looked about each room and read the titles on the spines of many of the books.

"There was a pianoforte in the music room," he said as they made their way to the sewing room, "and other instruments too. I noticed a violin and a flute in particular. Do you offer individual music lessons here, Miss Martin?"

"Indeed we do," she said. "We offer everything necessary to make accomplished young ladies of our pupils, as well as persons with a sound academic education."

He looked around the sewing room from just inside the door but did not walk farther into it.

"And do you teach other skills here in addition to sewing and embroidery?" he asked. "Knitting, perhaps? Tatting? Crochet?"

"All three," she said as he closed the door and she led the way to the assembly hall. It had been a ballroom once when the building was a private home.

"It is a pleasingly designed room," he said, standing in the middle of the gleaming wood floor and turning all about before looking up at the high, coved ceiling. "Indeed, I like the whole school, Miss Martin. There are windows and light everywhere and a pleasant atmosphere. Thank you for giving me a guided tour."

He turned his most charming smile on her, and Claudia, still holding both his visiting card and Susanna's letter, clasped her free hand about her wrist and looked back with deliberate severity.

"I am delighted you approve," she said.

His smile was arrested for a moment until he chuckled softly.

"I do beg your pardon," he said. "I have taken enough of your time."

He indicated the door with one arm, and Claudia led the way back to the entrance hall, feeling—and resenting the feeling—that she had somehow been unmannerly, for those last words she had spoken had been meant ironically and he had known it.

But before they reached the hall they were forced to pause for a few moments while the junior class filed out of the dining hall in good order, on their way from tea to study hall, where they would catch up on any work not completed during the day or else read or write letters or stitch at some needlework.

They all turned their heads to gaze at the grand visitor, and the Marquess of Attingsborough smiled genially back at them, setting them all to giggling and preening as they hurried along.

All of which went to prove, Claudia thought, that even eleven- and twelve-year-olds could not resist the charms of a handsome man. It boded ill—or *continued* to bode ill—for the future of the female half of the human race.

Mr. Keeble, frowning ferociously, bless his heart, was holding the marquess's hat and cane and was standing close to the front door as if to dare the visitor to try prolonging his visit further.

"I will see you early two mornings from now, then, Miss Martin?" the marquess said, taking his hat and cane and turning to her as Mr. Keeble opened the door and stood to one side, ready to close it behind him at the earliest opportunity.

"We will be ready," she said, inclining her head to him.